Peter William Clayden

# Samuel Sharpe

Egyptologist and Translator of the Bible

Peter William Clayden

**Samuel Sharpe**
*Egyptologist and Translator of the Bible*

ISBN/EAN: 9783337110307

Printed in Europe, USA, Canada, Australia, Japan

Cover: Foto ©Raphael Reischuk / pixelio.de

More available books at **www.hansebooks.com**

Bing

# SAMUEL SHARPE

*EGYPTOLOGIST AND TRANSLATOR OF*
*THE BIBLE*

BY

## P. W. CLAYDEN

LONDON
KEGAN PAUL, TRENCH & CO., 1 PATERNOSTER SQUARE
1883

LONDON:
PRINTED BY WOODFALL AND KINDER,
MILFORD LANE, STRAND, W.C.

5354

25/9/90 &

# CONTENTS.

—◆—

# LIFE OF SAMUEL SHARPE.

## CHAPTER I.

### PARENTAGE.

In the year 1805 an overwhelming domestic calamity occurred to a happy middle-class family, living in what was then the West-end of London. The father was a man of much refinement and culture, the friend of Flaxman and Porson, of Opie, Shee, and Stothard; the mother, who was his second wife, was the sister of Samuel Rogers the poet. The children were young, excepting a daughter of the first marriage, who was twenty-three. At the beginning of the year they consisted of four boys and a girl, the eldest of whom was only nine years old, and the youngest two years. The father's business was that of a brewer in King Street, Golden Square; the family lived at 10, Nottingham Place, Marylebone. In the spring of this fatal year business difficulties pressed heavily on the head of the family, and domestic trouble came to complicate them. Fever, which was the scourge and terror of households in the time of our grandfathers, made its appearance in the house. The little girl, then five years old, and a boy of three were successively attacked, and in the absence

of the elder half-sister from home the whole stress
of devoted and exclusive attendance upon them fell
on their mother. She would not spoil her step-
daughter's holiday by telling her of their illness, and
the anxiety proved too much for her. While they
were yet ill another boy was born, she herself took
the fever and died—probably by misadventure in the
wrong administration of medicine—when the child
was little more than a fortnight old. The loss of
his wife weighed heavily on the father's spirits, and
five months later, when his bankers, who were his
children's uncles, had been obliged to tell him that
he was ruined, he was found dead in his brewery,
leaving one younger daughter and five sons to the
care of their elder sister, who was the sole surviving
issue of the earlier marriage.

Of the family thus suddenly bereaved Samuel
Sharpe was the second son. He had been born in
the house in King Street, Golden Square, on the
8th of March, 1799. His elder brother, Sutton
Sharpe, was born in 1797; his sister Mary, who
came next to him, in 1801; his brother Henry
in 1802; William in 1804; and Daniel in 1806.
Their father, Sutton Sharpe, had married his
first wife, Catharine Purchas, in 1779; and the
surviving offspring of this marriage, Catharine
Sharpe, was born in 1782. He became a widower
in 1791; and in 1795 married Maria Rogers, a
younger sister of Samuel Rogers. This second
married life lasted but nine years and a half.
Gloomy as was its end, it had been singularly
happy. His young wife had speedily gained the
complete confidence and affection of her step-

daughter, and not even business anxieties could cast a shadow over the home which she brightened by her sunny temper, and ornamented by her dignity and grace. Her husband was given to fits of melancholy, which she charmed away. He was fond of society, in which she was also fitted to shine. He possessed cultivated literary and artistic tastes, to which she admirably ministered, and which she fully shared. He inherited ample means, which his generosity to his brother involved beyond rescue; and it was probably her fortune which kept him from earlier ruin. In her efforts on behalf of her husband and family her step-daughter Catharine gave her constant support. Catharine was thirteen years old at her father's second marriage, to which she had looked forward with aversion. Writing nearly thirty years later, Catharine speaks of her dislike to the domestic change and the opposition it roused in her girlish mind. The dislike and opposition were soon charmed away. Catharine says of her stepmother:—" She was mildness itself. She made me her companion and friend. In spite of all my determination to the contrary, I could not help loving her; though, in the quiet uniform life I then led, I could not help regretting the more active and amusing one I had quitted. We spent six months at Hampstead, and then took a house in Nottingham Place, where many happy years were spent, ending only with that deep affliction which altered the whole prospect of my future days."

The two women, thus brought together, were well worthy of each other. They were the first and second mothers of this family of children. The deep affliction which altered the whole prospect of Catharine's future days was prevented by her devotion and courage from marring the fortunes of her half-brothers and sister. The training she gave them, and to which she sacrificed her personal prospects and wishes, fitted them all to play worthy and successful parts in life. Each of the brothers attained in after years a considerable measure of distinction and success ; and it was their uniform testimony that they owed it, in very great degree, to their elder half-sister—whom they addressed and spoke of familiarly as "sister"—who had been left in charge of them at their father's death, when she had herself just entered on her twenty-fourth year.

In the case of a family thus left there might be more than usual difficulty in tracing the origin of any of the mental and moral characteristics by which they were afterwards known. The subject of this memoir has, however, left behind him a record, addressed to his children and dictated to one of his daughters in 1854, which, though not an autobiography in the strict sense of the term, is a full sketch of his family and personal history. In continuing it fifteen years later in his own handwriting, he warns his daughters "not to be persuaded by anybody after my death that these, or any other particulars about my life, can be of public interest." This, however, is rather a matter for the public to decide. The modesty of the caution is a characteristic feature, which makes it the more important that his life should be written. It is a life which in its untiring industry, its unostentatious benevolence, its devotion to truth, and its

ardent love of learning, coupled as these noble
characteristics were with a singular and too unusual
absence of all desire for public recognition, or for
any other reward than his own satisfied sense of
duty, was one of the happiest examples of the
qualities which have made the middle class the
strength and sweetness of English society.   His
own view was, that his mother's family had handed
down to her descendants "the larger half of our
traditional opinions and tastes "; but it will be seen
that the contribution on the father's side was by no
means inferior to it.   The following is his account of
his father :—

Sutton Sharpe, of No. 10, Nottingham Place, Marylebone, was the son of Joseph Sharpe, of Bridge Street,
Blackfriars; and of Ann, his wife, daughter of William
Telford, of Isleworth.   He was born on the 20th of
September, 1756.   His father and the family before him
had carried on the trade of needle-makers in Blackfriars
for several generations.   Joseph Sharpe, born in 1727–8,
was the son of Sutton Sharpe and Ruth Stokes.   This
Sutton Sharpe, born in 1699, was the son of Robert
Sharpe and Elizabeth Barnes.   Robert Sharpe was born in
1669.   But this Sutton was apprenticed as needle-maker
in 1713, not to his father Robert, but to another Sutton,
probably his uncle.   This latter Sutton Sharpe we find
mentioned in Chamberlain's "Notitia" for 1723, as one
of the Commissioners of the Lieutenancy for the City of
London at the beginning of George the First's reign.

But to return to my own father.   In the year 1779 Sutton
Sharpe was married at Croydon to Catharine Purchas, by
whom he had one daughter, Catharine, born in 1782.   His
wife died nine years afterwards.   In September, 1795, he
was married a second time, to Maria, daughter of Thomas

Rogers, of Newington Green and of Freeman's Court, Cornhill, banker. Her brother Samuel gave her away. My sister Catharine was then thirteen years old. They took a house at 10, Nottingham Place, Marylebone, and went into it as soon as it was ready to receive them.

Sutton Sharpe had been brought up to his father's trade as a needle-maker. On his father's death he carried on the business, first in partnership with his mother, and afterwards alone; when his mother retired to live at Croydon. But the high price of food and wages in London was driving all such manufactories to a distance. Needles could not longer be made profitably in the centre of an increasing capital, and he gave up the family trade and became a brewer in King Street, Golden Square. This business he carried on, though with very moderate success, till the time of his death.

There seem to have been other reasons for this change of trade. In the journal written by his eldest daughter Catharine, and dated New Ormond Street in the year 1823, to which reference has already been made, she says under the date of 1793 :—

My father now gave up his business and joined his brother in King Street, Golden Square, with the idea of attending to a considerable sum which he had lent him to embark in that concern, and to restrain, if possible, his expensive habits. I went to school, but my father chiefly instructed me at home. I adored my uncle, and was the constant companion of all his pursuits, which were so various as to afford me constant improvement and delight. He was a great mechanic, and I head-workman, or rather " scrub," keeping everything in order, and arranging all the contents of his study and workshop. He taught me to ride and drive, and initiated me early into all the knowledge of the stable. He was a rough master, but he taught me well, and banished everything like fear from my mind, so that I early became a bold and experienced horse-woman ; and many were the delightful excursions for which I was indebted to his kindness. He had a young family, but they were all too little to be anything but playthings.

The uncle who had thus influenced her character, and through her the group of children afterwards left to her care, died, after a long illness, in 1797, leaving a large family quite unprovided for. Her father's property also suffered seriously. The widow and children lived with their grandmother, Sutton Sharpe's mother, at Croydon, till her death, in 1798.

Samuel Sharpe further says of his father :—

From his childhood he (Sutton Sharpe) had always been fond of reading and of works of art. He drew very well with chalk. While attending to business he entered himself as a pupil in the Royal Academy, and drew there from the life—a privilege which was then open to all. There he gained the friendship of Flaxman, Opie, Shee, and Stothard, and continued intimate with them till his death. He was also acquainted with Holloway, the engraver, and was one of those friends by whose advice Holloway undertook his great work, the cartoons of Raphael. He was acquainted with Bewick, so well known for his wood-cuts, and that artist gave him a copy of his celebrated Chillingham Bull, on a sheet of vellum. His own tastes led him chiefly to draw from the antique statues and Greek vases. He encouraged my mother and sister in the same congenial employments. . . . . I hope the love of Art may long continue hereditary in our family. My uncle's collection of pictures and antiquities is well known to everybody, and after looking at them I have often been pleased to remember a remark made to him by Mr. Boddington, which used to be repeated to me by Mr. Maltby—"You know, Rogers, we all owe these tastes to Sutton Sharpe."*

* Rogers himself made the same admission of indebtedness ; speaking to William Sharpe in 1842 he said, " William, all I know of art I learned from your father."

By his first marriage my father had become acquainted with William Maltby, afterwards the Librarian of the London Institution, and with Richard Sharp, the author of "Letters and Essays," but better known as Conversation Sharp. By his second marriage he became the brother-in-law of Samuel Rogers, the poet, and his love of learning made him intimate with many other men of letters besides the artists before mentioned, who were often at his house at No. 10, Nottingham Place. Among these were William Morgan, the mathematician, Coombe, the author of "Dr. Syntax," Mrs. Opie, the artist's second wife, and Matthew Raper, a Vice-President of the Antiquarian Society, who dedicated to him a Greek . Vocabulary, and Home Tooke, the author of the "Diversions of Purley," towards whose democratic principles he had a strong leaning. Richard Porson, the eminent Greek scholar, was often there, and gave him copies of his first two plays of Euripides, the "Medea," and "Hecuba." In the latter he wrote, in his beautiful writing, "*Optimae Spei Puero Sutton Sharpe. In Graecis literis proficienti et profecturo Editor.*" At this time he had but slight knowledge of the Greek language, and though Porson called him "Puer," he was already forty-five years old. He was well acquainted with Italian, which he thought not studied so much as it deserved to be.

In politics my father was an earnest reformer, and my earliest recollection of such matters is my wearing in my cap when seven years old a blue cockade, Sir Francis Burdett's colours at the Middlesex election. I remember also my father taking me to the Croydon Assizes to show me the Judge sitting on the Bench. As we were entering the Town Hall the constable at the door stopped a man in a working dress from entering, saying that there was not room for him; whereupon my father turned away, much to my disappointment, and would not enter at that time, to mark his disapproval of the different treatment that was shown to a good and a bad coat by a man in authority. My father wore powder and his hair tied in a queue; but his brother Joseph had followed the example of Charles James Fox, and marked his politics by cutting off his tail and wearing a black head of hair.

It will be seen from this account of their father and his family that the band of brothers must have inherited from him a good many of the intellectual characteristics which distinguished them all. Sutton Sharpe and his younger brother Joseph were both men who took a lively interest in public affairs, and lived and moved in the full current and movement of their time.

The name of Sutton seems to have been hereditary in the Sharpe family, though there is nothing to show whence it was derived. There have probably been Sutton Sharpes ever since the Commonwealth, and the name is now borne, in the branch of the family with which we have to do, by Henry's youngest son. Robert Sharpe, the great-grandfather of the Sutton who was the father of Samuel, was born in London three years after the Great Fire, and died in 1718. His son Sutton, his second son and fifth child, was apprenticed in the last year of Queen Anne's reign to an older Sutton Sharpe—probably Robert's brother—who was then a person of much consideration in the City of London. The Sutton thus apprenticed was married in 1726, and seems to have been as strongly resolved that his own name should be perpetuated as Gibbon's parents were that there should be an Edward Gibbon. He called his second son Sutton ; and after the child's death, in babyhood, called the third, who was

born later, by the same name. This child died, and
a fourth was born and christened Sutton. The
fourth died in babyhood, and a fifth was called
Sutton and died. The sixth and last boy was given
the same name and survived. But it was the eldest
brother Joseph, who had been born eleven years
before, who perpetuated the name in the family.
He called his eldest son by the name that five of
his own younger brothers had borne, and this Sutton
was Samuel's father. He was brought up to his
father's business, but he inherited literary and artistic
tastes, which his sons afterwards found to be more
consistent than he could make them with business success. An exquisitely finished pencil portrait
of him by his friend Flaxman—now in the possession
of Mrs. William Sharpe—shows him to have had a
broad forehead, full cheeks, and square chin, with a
well-chiselled nose, a mouth that bespoke refinement
rather than determination, and eyes with an expression of thoughtful melancholy. It is a noble face,
and immediately strikes every one who sees it as
the portrait of a person of distinction. There is a
full length sketch in red chalk of his first wife by
Sutton Sharpe himself, which shows Flaxman's influence on his taste, and indicates the possession by her
of much of that decision and energy which distinguished her daughter Catharine. Perhaps the most
graceful of all the sketches which Flaxman did for
his friend was one in which the attitude of the
" Portrait of the Author " in Southey's " Doctor "
was anticipated. Miss Sarah Rogers and her
younger sister Maria, Sutton Sharpe's second wife,
were sitting together, with Miss Rogers's hand in

those of Mrs. Sharpe, when something passing in
the street caused them both to turn their heads
away, Miss Rogers starting forward in an attitude
of curiosity. Struck with the graceful group thus
made, Flaxman cried out to them not to move, and
sketched them on the spot—the backs of both heads
turned to him. The sketch recalls his illustrations
of the "Iliad" and "Odyssey." A characteristic
portrait of Catharine Sharpe, bearing the date of
1802, is another of the relics of Flaxman's friendship. That was the year when Sutton Sharpe had
met the sculptor and his wife in Paris. Peace had
been proclaimed, and there was a great rush of
English artists and people of taste to that city to
see the statues and pictures—the spoils of Europe—
in the Louvre. Sutton Sharpe found friends everywhere in the city, where he lodged with Samuel
Boddington, partner in business of "Conversation"
Sharp. His letters to his wife, who had been taken
to Paris by Mr. and Mrs. Towgood on their wedding-
tour ten years before, are full of pleasant accounts
of his intercourse with Benjamin West, with Fuseli,
who was then at the height of his fame, with Far-
rington, who was Fuseli's companion in this journey,
with Mr. and Mrs. Opie, and with other eminent
persons ; among them Helen Maria Williams, the
translator of Humboldt. Twenty years later Samuel
Sharpe called upon Miss Williams in Paris to carry
a volume from Mr. Rogers. She spoke to him of
his father's visit, and said that when she received
his card she thought it was the very agreeable
Mr. Sharpe who had been introduced to her by
Mr. Boddington in 1802.

On the mother's side there was, perhaps, a more distinct transmission of moral qualities. We have already seen that Samuel Sharpe considered that the larger half of their traditional opinions and tastes came from the strongly Nonconformist strain derived from what may properly be regarded as a Puritan ancestry. He traces his mother's family in what he considered to be "the line through which our opinions have chiefly come down to us." This line leads up through the grandmother, Mary Radford, daughter of Daniel Radford and his wife Mary Harris (granddaughter of Dr. Coxe), to Eleanor Henry, who had married Samuel Radford of Chester, and of whom Daniel Radford was the eldest son. Eleanor Henry, who died in 1696, was the sister of the Reverend Matthew Henry, the Commentator on the Bible, and was third daughter and fifth child of the Reverend Philip Henry, one of the most eminent of the clergy who were ejected on the English Black Bartholomew in 1662. Samuel says of this branch of the family tree :—

The Reverend Philip Henry, incumbent of Worthenbury, in the county of Flint, was the son of a page in the service of Charles I. He was born in the palace of Whitehall; he had been the playfellow of the Prince of Wales and the Duke of York; and his principles of loyalty were strengthened by seeing the King beheaded on the scaffold. But his pious and serious mother brought him up as a hearer and admirer of the Presbyterian Divines, who during the Protectorate filled the parish churches and cathedrals. From Westminster School he went to Oxford, and in due time was appointed to the living of Worthenbury, and ordained a clergyman of the Church of England, by Presbyterian ordination. On the return of Charles II., when Episcopacy was again established, and the Book of Common Prayer ordered to be read in the churches, Philip Henry was one of the two thousand clergymen who, for conscience sake, gave up their incomes and left their homes. When the day of trial came they left those spheres of usefulness which had hitherto been their pride and pleasure, and withdrew into obscurity, and many of them into painful want, rather than comply with those requirements of the Act of Uniformity which they felt hurtful to their consciences. The struggles of mind that they then endured, and the legal persecutions they suffered from that time till the landing of William III., taught them the use and the worth of private judgment in religion, and strengthened their dislike of creeds. These feelings and opinions were, of course, religiously taught to their children, and even now mark the characters of their descendants in the seventh and eighth generations.

Philip Henry's only son was the Reverend Matthew Henry, an eminent Dissenting Minister, first of Chester, and afterwards of Hackney; and author of an Exposition of the Bible, which is still highly valued for its devotional earnestness. He was one of the original trustees of Dr. Williams's Public Library.* Philip Henry had also four daughters, of whom Eleanor, the third, was born in 1667, and married Samuel Radford of Chester in 1688-9. She inherited the serious, religious disposition of her father, as appears from the short memoir of her written by her brother Matthew, and she died in 1697, aged thirty.

Samuel and Eleanor Radford left one son and three daughters, who, on the death of their father and mother, were brought up by their uncle Matthew. Daniel Radford, the son, removed to London, and became a warehouseman in Cheapside, and a director of the Union Insurance Office in Cornhill. He married Mary, the daughter of Samuel Harris of Newington Green, and there

* Now in Grafton Street, Gower Street.

he and his wife lived, in the house nearest to London on the west side of the Green. Their only child, Mary, was born in the year 1735; and in the year 1738, her mother, Mary, died. Daniel Radford continued to live at Newington Green with his little daughter, and invited into the house, as her companion, Mary Mitchell, a daughter of his sister Mary. In the year 1760 Mary Radford married Thomas Rogers, my grandfather. They lived with her father and her cousin on the Green; and when Daniel Radford died Mary Mitchell continued to live with Thomas and Mary Rogers, and when they died she continued to live with their children.

The little village of Newington Green had not been unknown in the annals of Presbyterian Dissent. Here several of the ejected ministers took up their abode, and some of them maintained themselves by teaching; and their schools turned out some scores of Nonconformist ministers, as well as many other good scholars. Among others, Charles Morton, who had been rector of Blissland, in Cornwall, kept a school here, till he removed for safety and liberty to New England. Under him the celebrated Daniel Defoe, the author of " Robinson Crusoe," was educated for the ministry, though he never entered on that office. " I was first," he said, " set apart for, and then set apart from the honour of that sacred employ." In this retired spot the silenced Nonconformists sometimes met together for public worship. In 1708 the little society ventured to build a meeting-house on the north side of the Green, and of this congregation Samuel Harris was a member. Daniel Radford was afterwards treasurer to the congregation till the year 1767.

The opinions of the congregation underwent several changes, which were common to the whole of the English Presbyterians. They proclaimed the right of private judgment, and rejected the use of creeds. The purpose for which the meeting-house was built, as declared in the

Trust Deed, was simply for the use of Protestant Dissenters, and the worship of Almighty God. Hence the English Presbyterians, being free to change, became unorthodox more quickly than they owned it, or perhaps were aware of it. They never held the Athanasian opinions, and were early charged with being Socinians.

It was, however, not quite so early that the congregation at Newington Green became unorthodox; but in the year 1758, while Daniel Radford was treasurer, they chose as their minister Mr. Richard Price, afterwards better known as Dr. Price, who had already declared his Arian opinions.

Into this Dissenting community Thomas Rogers, as we have seen, married in 1760. He took up his abode with his young wife in her father's house—the house before mentioned. Here they had four sons and three daughters born to them, besides those who died in infancy. Daniel Radford died in 1767, and left by will one hundred pounds towards increasing the minister's salary in the meeting-house on the Green.

Thomas Rogers was the only son of Thomas Rogers, of the Hill, near Stourbridge, who was a glass manufacturer in that neighbourhood, and of Martha, a daughter of Richard Knight, of Downton. He was thus a cousin of Richard Payne Knight, the antiquary, who left his collection to the British Museum, and of Thomas Andrew Knight, who wrote on Horticulture. At the same time I may as well mention that his wife Mary Radford was descended through her mother from Dr. Coxe, Physician to Queen Mary, and they were thus related to his grandson, William Coxe, the author of "Russian Discoveries."*

· Thomas Rogers the younger, now of Newington Green, was at first in partnership with his father-in-law, as a ware-

* Better known as the author of the "History of the House of Austria." He was Archdeacon of Wilts and Rector of Bemerton.

houseman in Cheapside, but in the year 1760 he established a banking-house in London, under the firm of Welch, Rogers and Olding. It was situated at first in Cornhill, but afterwards at the bottom of Freeman's Court. These houses are now pulled down, but they both stood in the area in front of the Exchange Buildings. At Newington Green Thomas Rogers and his wife lived in rather strict attention to their religious duties. They attended at the little chapel where the Reverend Dr. Towers preached on Sunday morning and Dr. Price in the afternoon. They met regularly for family worship, when Mr. Rogers read the Bible and prayers to his children ; and it was when Samuel was about eleven years old that one night after closing the Bible he explained to them that Boston, in America, was in rebellion because the English Parliament had attempted to tax them without their consent, and solemnly exhorted them always to wish success to the Americans because they had justice on their side.

As was natural for a Dissenter, Thomas Rogers was always a staunch Whig in politics. He voted for Mr. Byng, father or son, at every Middlesex election, except when displeased with the Coalition Ministry. In 1780 he was elected member of Parliament for Coventry, but his return was petitioned against, and as his politics were well known as unfavourable to the Ministry his election was declared void by a vote of the whole House. When the Dissenters established a college at Hackney, where their sons could receive a liberal education without being required, as at Oxford and Cambridge, to subscribe to any articles of religion, Thomas Rogers was one of its most zealous supporters, and was chosen chairman of the Committee of Management. He was one of the trustees of Dr. Williams's Library. In 1792 he became a member of the Society of the Friends of the People, associated for the purpose of obtaining a Parliamentary Reform, and he signed the memorable declaration on that subject in company with the great names of C. Grey, J. Mackintosh,

P. Francis, W. H. Lambton, G. Tierney, S. Whitbread, R. B. Sheridan, T. Erskine, W. Smith, and others. This was the year which ended in the imprisonment and trial of Louis XVI., when friends of liberty were branded by Pitt and Burke as friends of anarchy; the year after Dr. Priestley's house at Birmingham had been burnt down by the mob.

In the year 1776 Thomas Rogers lost his wife, and the care of his house and children then fell to her cousin, Mary Mitchell. He himself died in the year 1793, and the following lines were written by his son Samuel on the occasion of his last illness :—

> There in that bed so closely curtained round,
>     Worn to a shade and wan with slow decay,
> A father sleeps ! Oh, hushed be every sound !
>     Soft may we breathe the midnight hours away !
> He stirs—yet still he sleeps. May heavenly dreams
>     Long o'er his smooth and settled pillow rise,
> Nor fly, till morning thro' the shutter streams,
>     And on the hearth the glimmering rushlight dies.*

Customs are so far changed that it may be interesting to mention that according to the fashion of the day Thomas Rogers wore a three-cornered cocked hat. His hair was dressed with powder and tied behind in a queue. His coat on dress occasions was of a light colour. The cuffs were very inconveniently large, and on one occasion he carried off a guinea unawares from the banking-house, and found it in his cuff when he reached home. There were no stage-coaches at Newington Green, so he usually went to town in his own carriage. Umbrellas for rainy weather were almost unknown, but the house at Newington Green possessed one, which was made of oiled cloth, and stood in the hall, and was held by the man-servant with two hands over the heads of the ladies as they stepped from the door to the carriage.

* Poems, p. 187. "Written in a Sick Chamber, 1793."

C

Of my uncles, Daniel, the eldest, was sent to Cambridge. He was of delightful guileless simplicity, without a thought that was hidden from you, and was liked by all his acquaintance. His father meant him for the Bar, and had great hopes of his being a distinguished man. But he did not like the law ; he preferred classics. He married his cousin, Martha Bowles, and went to live in the country—much to his father's disappointment. He dwelt first at Lincoln, where he was intimate with Dr. Paley ; but he afterwards removed to Wassal Grove, near Hagley, where he had a farm. There I visited him and spent my time most delightfully, sometimes rambling in Hagley Park with his daughters, sometimes walking over the farm with him, and then returning to his study, where he would pull down book after book to follow a reference or trace a thought with an enthusiasm and richness of memory that was most encouraging to anybody fond of knowledge. He had at that time been studying Persian. He was a magistrate for Worcestershire, and died in 1829. He is highly spoken of by Sir Edgerton Brydges in his Autobiography, and Charles Lamb, who had met him occasionally at the houses of his brothers, Henry and Samuel, wrote the following sonnet upon his death :—

> Rogers, of all the men that I have known
> But slightly, who have died, your brother's loss
> Touched me most sensibly ;  There came across
> My mind an image of the cordial tone
> Of your fraternal meetings, where a guest
> I more than once have sate ; and grieve to think,
> That of that threefold cord one precious link
> By Death's rude hand is severed from the rest.
> Of our old Gentry he appeared a stem ;
> A magistrate who, while the evil-doer
> He kept in terror, could respect the poor,
> And not for every trifle harass them—
> As some divine and laic, too oft do.
> This man's a private loss and public too.

Thomas and Samuel, the two next sons, were brought up for business. After leaving Mr. Pickburn's school at Hackney they read for some time under Mr. Burgh, who had written " On the Dignity of Human Nature." They were then taken as clerks, and afterwards as partners, into their father's banking-house in Freeman's Court. Thomas died within a year or two of that event, in his father's life-time, and his brother's feelings towards him are described in some beautiful lines in the " Pleasures of Memory "—

> Oh thou ! with whom my heart was wont to share
> From Reason's dawn each pleasure and each care,
> With whom, alas ! I fondly hoped to know
> The humble walks of happiness below ;
> If thy blest nature now unites above,
> An angel's pity with a brother's love,
> Still o'er my life preserve thy mild control,
> Correct my views, and elevate my soul ;
> Grant me thy peace and purity of mind,
> Devout yet cheerful, active yet resigned ;
> Grant me like thee whose art knew no disguise
> Whose blameless wishes never aimed to rise,
> To meet the changes Time and Chance present
> With modest dignity and calm content.
> When thy last breath ere Nature sank to rest,
> Thy meek submission to thy God expressed ;
> When thy last look ere thought and feeling fled,
> A mingled gleam of hope and triumph shed :
> What to thy soul its glad assurance gave,
> Its hope in death, its triumph o'er the grave ?
> The sweet Remembrance of unblemished youth,
> The still inspiring voice of Innocence and Truth !
> —" Pleasures of Memory." Second Part, pp. 43, 44.

Samuel, the poet, had wished to be sent to the Man-chester Presbyterian College, but while his father lived he was kept in strict attention to the banking business. This was of course broken in upon by occasional journeys, besides the annual visit to The Hill, near Stourbridge. He spent one winter in Devonshire, as he had been threatened with an attack upon the lungs. He made a journey to Paris before the outbreak of the French Revolution ; and he paid a visit to Edinburgh, where he made the acquaintance of Dr. Robertson and Mr. Adam Smith, and where he met Mrs. Piozzi, to whom his poems had before introduced him. On the death of his father, in 1793, he was more at liberty to follow his own tastes.

He inherited an ample property and a prosperous business, and into this he soon introduced his younger brother Henry to manage it for him. He had already published his " Ode to Superstition " and " Pleasures of Memory," and his society was eagerly courted by persons of rank and talent. He first took chambers at Paper Buildings, in the Temple, but afterwards he built a house for himself in St. James's Place, which he gradually enriched with his valuable collection of pictures, vases, and other works of art. His literary friends had been Dr. Price, Dr. Priestley, Mrs. Barbauld, Mr. Horne Tooke, but now Charles James Fox, Grattan, and Erskine became his frequent guests, and for fifty years his house has been one of the chief centres of attraction with men of letters and men of taste.

Henry Rogers, my youngest uncle, was educated under Priestley and Belsham at the New College, Hackney, of which his father was one of the principal founders. As soon as he was of age he joined the banking house in Freeman's Court. . . . . He was the patron of all his nephews and nieces, to whom they at all times looked for help and advice. To me and my brothers and sisters he was like a second father, and though he was the youngest of our uncles, his constant wish to be of use to us, and to have us near him, made us all look up to him as the head of the family. In 1824 he retired out of business, and thereby made room for my admission into the firm.

Martha, my eldest aunt, married Mr. John Towgood, who was also a Dissenter, a grandson of the Reverend Micaiah Towgood. He was a member of the firm of

Langston, Towgood and Company, and in 1811, being the only survivor that wished to continue in business, he united his bank to that of his brothers-in-law, under the firm of Rogers, Towgood and Company.

Maria, my mother, was, I have always heard, the favourite of the family, from her goodness of heart and winning manners. She was sent with one or both of her sisters to a boarding-school at Stoke Newington, kept by Mrs. Crisp. And it was on meeting his sister with a troop of the girls of this school in their walks that Samuel Rogers wrote the following lines. He never thought them good enough to print among his poems, but they are interesting as being among the hasty works of a writer who for the most part finished everything with great care.

To a Party of Young Ladies who were Sitting on a Bench in Queen Elizabeth's Walk at Eight o'Clock last Thursday Night.

> Evening had flushed the clear blue sky,
>    The birds had sung themselves to sleep,
> When I presumed, I don't know why,
>    In old Queen Bess's walk to peep.
>
> And there was she ; Her belles and beaux
>    In ruffs and high-crowned hats were there !
> But soon, as you may well suppose,
>    The vision melted into air.
>
> When hark ! Soft voices, thro' the shade,
>    Announced a little fairy train.
> And once, methought, sweet music played,
>    I wished to see, but wished in vain.
>
> For something whispered in my ear,
>    " Away, away ! At this still hour,
> Queen Mab, with all her court is here,
>    And he who looks will feel her power."

I shut my eyelids at the sound,
And found, what every youth will find,
That he who treads on sacred ground
Is sure to leave his wits behind.

*Saturday, May 14th, 1785.*

My mother died in April, 1806, leaving six children, of
whom the youngest was only a fortnight old, and my
father died in September of the same year. The following
lines, from my uncle's poem of " Human Life," mention my
mother's death:—

Such grief was ours—it seems but yesterday—
When in thy prime, wishing so much to stay,
'Twas thine, Maria, thine without a sigh,
At midnight in a Sister's arms to die !
Oh thou wert lovely—lovely was thy frame,
And pure thy spirit as from Heaven it came !
And, when recalled to join the blest above
Thou diedst a victim to exceeding love,
Nursing the young to health.　In happier hours,
When idle Fancy wove luxuriant flowers,
Once in thy mirth thou bad'st me write on thee ;
And now I write—what thou shalt never see.*

\* " Human Life," p. 82.

# CHAPTER II.

## CHILDHOOD AND SCHOOL-TIME.

THE elder half-sister, to whose care the orphan family were left, and of whose training by her father and uncle an account has already been given, was happily possessed of great vigour and decision. She was only nine years old when her own mother died, and now at the age of twenty-three she found herself called to discharge a mother's duties towards her father's second family. Her own grief for the loss of her second mother ("the first sorrow I had known," she says, "for I was too young to feel the loss of my own mother,") was too great to allow her to do much to alleviate her father's sorrow. "The only consolation that presented itself," she continues, "was the promise of becoming a mother to her children, and so far as in me lay to repay the debt of gratitude I owed her." The five summer months during which Sutton Sharpe survived his wife were the gloomiest period in the family history. He refused to be comforted, and his daughter looked back in after years with much needless self-reproach upon her failure "to afford him the consolation he required." His death was accelerated by pecuniary difficulties, and he was found to have left his family in such a position that it was needful to give up the

home in Nottingham Place. There was for a time
the prospect that the children would be scattered.
His whole property had been involved in the brew-
house into which he had been drawn by his brother,
and the business had not succeeded. He died without a will, and it became the duty of his daughter
Catharine to administer the estate, which she did
with the assistance of Mr. John Towgood, who had
married Martha Rogers, and of Mr. Henry Rogers,
the unmarried youngest brother. When the business
was wound up it was found that there would not be
enough to pay the business debts, so that the furni-
ture and library in Nottingham Place had to be sold.
After this sacrifice, which she felt most bitterly,
though she made out the catalogue of the library
with her own hands, nothing remained to the family
from the wreck of their father's property; but
their mother's small fortune had been settled on
them, and they consequently had enough to live on.
Looking back on this period of anxiety and difficulty seventeen years afterwards, Catharine writes in
her journal the following graphic account of her inward
struggles and outward difficulties. A more interesting picture of a strong and earnest mind, girding
itself up to a great and self-sacrificing task, has
rarely been given :—

We spent some time at Walthamstow, where the Towgoods
then lived, who most kindly gave us room till our future plans
could be finally settled. From the moment I regained sufficient composure for reflection I felt there was only one course
to pursue, to secure either my own self-approbation or the
welfare of those who then alone occupied my thoughts. This
was to take the whole superintendence of their education upon
myself. If they were separated amongst their various rela-

tions their individual advantages might perhaps be greater than my limited means could procure, but the great bond of family union would be broken, the early affection which most strongly unites the members of a large family would have no existence in a divided state, selfish feelings and gratifications would take the place of those which should connect them through life and teach them to labour for the good of others. These were the motives which, at the time, influenced me in the decision. It depends on them to declare whether such decision was a right one. For myself I can only say I have been perfectly satisfied with the result; and placed again in the same circumstances I should most assuredly act the same part.

We took a house in Paradise Row, Stoke Newington, as being there in the midst of our most intimate friends. Here I had leisure to examine my own mind, and many thoughts it cost me. I must not only educate these children, but I must educate myself if I would hereafter become their guide and counsellor. I must render myself worthy of being consulted. These and many such thoughts occupied my mind, and many are the nights I have nearly passed in pacing the apartment, for, till the duties of the day were past, I never suffered their encroachment, as they rendered me incapable of exertion. Perhaps the greatest difficulty I had to contend with was the want of some friend whose thoughts and feelings were in unison with mine, and on whose judgment I might rely. That friend was separated from me by many thousand miles.* Her letters tended more to strengthen my good resolutions than all my other friends.

Such was the spirit in which this courageous woman accepted the responsibility which the early death of her father and stepmother imposed upon her. English family histories are happily full of such unnoticed and unintrusive devotion to family interests and domestic duties. Catharine Sharpe's life from this time forward was one of uncomplain-

* This was Mrs. Ashburner, formerly Miss Morgan, who had removed with her husband and young family to India.

ing self-sacrifice. She gave up everything for these children. She put aside her prospects in life and devoted her youth, her talents and her accomplishments, to the task of educating them and keeping them together. She was forty-one years old when the journal was written, and the greater part of her noble task was done. For seventeen years she had been doing the part of mother and father to her father's children, and had been rewarded by the complete success of her efforts to keep a home for them and to preserve in them the sense of family life. Her marked individuality had impressed itself on the household. Every one of them regarded her with the deepest gratitude and affection ; and each was ready to give her training the credit of much of the success they afterwards attained.

The next entry in her journal is under the date of 1807 :—

Sam and Sutton went to Mr. Cogan's school, the four others remained with me. The next fourteen years were passed in our house in Paradise Row, certainly the most active and laborious years of my life.

In 1809 :—

This year Mary and Henry accompanied me to Wassal, and there my mind experienced the first real enjoyment after a period of intense suffering. This visit, besides the gratification it afforded me, was of inestimable advantage. Under Mr. Rogers's kind instruction I improved materially my knowledge of Latin, and was enabled thereby to keep the boys in my hands much longer than I otherwise should have done. Years now passed on in one uniform routine. My days were employed in the education of the children, my evenings in my own improvement. I recollect no particular event that needs record. Miss Andrews assisted me with the children.

Samuel writes respecting this period of his life :—

On the death of my father we six younger children fell to the care of our elder sister, Catharine, who most dis-interestedly took charge of our education. She was be-friended in her task by my unmarried uncles and aunt, Samuel Rogers, Sarah Rogers, and Henry Rogers, but more particularly by my uncle Henry. Sutton and I were sent on a visit to my uncle Daniel Rogers, to be out of the way, while my sister, leaving Nottingham Place, moved into a smaller house, and with my uncle's family at Wassal Grove, near Hagley, we spent six months most happily, too young to understand the loss that had befallen us. On our return we found my sister in lodgings in Church Street, Stoke Newington, from which she shortly removed to a house in Paradise Row, in the same village. This was within a short walk of my uncle Henry and aunt Sarah, who with Mrs. Mitchell were living at No. 10, Highbury Terrace. From Stoke Newington Sutton and I were sent to Mr. Cogan's school at Higham Hill, Waltham-stow.

I was eight years and three months old when sent to school at Midsummer, 1807. There I stayed seven years and a half, returning home to Stoke Newington three times a year for the holidays. At school I made fair pro-gress in Latin and Greek. I learned a little French and Mathematics, and during the play hours I read many of the best English histories and other standard works, which were always within our reach in the school library. During the holidays I learnt drawing and Italian from my sister.

This spending his play hours in reading was characteristic of Samuel Sharpe's boyhood. He differed from his brothers by a somewhat unnatural gravity. Though he was the second and Sutton the

elder, Catharine writes quite instinctively, " Sam and
Sutton." He became her chief counsellor as he
grew up. He was fonder of books than of amusements. As a young man he went into society much
less than his brothers, and in his riper years it was
with difficulty that he could be torn away from his
library, his manuscripts, and his favourite studies,
even for a summer holiday. In this characteristic he
resembled his old teacher Mr. Cogan, who for thirty-
six years was never absent from his school duties a
single day in pursuit of pleasure. Mr. Cogan's
reputation as a schoolmaster was universal in the
first quarter of the present century. The house at
Higham Hill, Walthamstow, was always full, and an
unusual number of his pupils gained distinction or
success in after life. Dr. Parr, in a letter to Archbishop Magee, speaks of him as " an accurate Greek
scholar, and a diligent and discriminating reader of
the best critical works which have been lately
published at Berlin, Leyden, Göttingen, Leipsic and
Paris, and at home by Porson, Blomfield, Gaisford
and Elmsley." He was said to have read more
Greek than any living man. His method was to
ground his pupils in the grammar of the classical
languages, and he probably estimated their ability
and measured his esteem for them by their success
in Latin and Greek composition. Speaking to the
late Rev. J. J. Tayler of Mr. Disraeli (afterwards
Lord Beaconsfield), who had been one of his pupils,
he once said :—" I don't like him. I never could get
him to understand the subjunctive." Mr. Cogan
died in 1855, at the age of ninety-three. His father,
who was a medical practitioner at Rothwell, in

Northamptonshire, had been born in the year 1698, so that these two lives of father and son covered nearly a hundred and fifty seven years of English history, including the whole reigns of Anne, the four Georges, and William the Fourth, and linking together those of William the Third and Queen Victoria.

The schooling-time was short; for in accordance with the usual custom in those days, Samuel Sharpe was taken from his lessons and sent to business when he was approaching sixteen. He writes in 1854 :—

When wanting two months of being sixteen years old, at Christmas, 1814, I left school just as I was beginning to feel my lessons a pleasure, and therefore without rejoicing, though without regret; and I was taken by my uncles into their banking-house as a clerk. At the desk in Clement's Lane, Lombard Street, I have remained for forty years, with various feelings and various fortunes. I have grown up, I have married, seen my children born and friends die around me, changed my dwelling, but always in business hours remained at 29, Clement's Lane, Lombard Street. While a clerk at Clement's Lane I walked backwards and forwards from Paradise Row, and I continued my school studies both before breakfast in the morning and on my return home in the evening. My reading at this time was as much the effect of quiet habit as from a love of knowledge. I enjoyed the pleasure of feeling my progress, but I sat at my books because I had neither pocket-money nor high spirits to lead me into more foolish amusements.

It was at this time, when I was about sixteen years old, that my uncle Henry gave me a ticket of admission to the London Institution, then in the Old Jewry, now in Moorfields. Here I used occasionally to spend an hour or two between business and going home, and great was the advantage I received from being able to use the books of reference there placed by Mr. Porson and Mr. Maltby, and to choose for myself out of 30,000 volumes. Many years afterwards I bought a share in the Institution, and I have been a reader there for forty years. It was not till about the year 1837 that I first visited the reading-room in the British Museum.

Stoke Newington at that time was a very advantageous place of residence for us. Mrs. Barbauld often drank tea with my sister, and as often I went to her house to fetch my sister home after an evening spent there. At Dr. Aikin's house I was more intimate, as he had for a short time a grandson living with him, who was my fellow-student, or rather teacher, in botany and chemistry. There I was at liberty to go on a Sunday evening as an uninvited guest, and listen to the literary conversation of Dr. Aikin and Miss Aikin and their friends. Mr. Maltby, the Librarian of the London Institution, spent one summer in lodgings within two doors of us. We were frequent visitors at Mr. Morgan's at Stamford Hill, who kindly gave me advice on Mathematics, and once most good-naturedly lit the furnace for me in his laboratory on a Good Friday, because that was the only day on which I had a holiday, and I went to see him decompose potash into its metal base. At my uncle Henry's in Highbury Terrace we were always welcome, and there, as I got old enough to know the value of good society, I sometimes found Stothard and Westall, and Sir Thomas Lawrence, and Ottley, and Charles Lamb, and Thomas Moore, and " Russian " Tooke and Mr. Tuffin, with other friends who were even better in conversation though less known. Once or twice a year we visited my uncle Sam in St. James's Place, where we felt ourselves less intimate, but had the advantage of seeing his choice collection of pictures, and where I occasionally met Campbell, Wiffen, Foscolo, Turner, Luttrell, Jekyl and other men of letters, besides those whom we saw at Highbury.

Amongst the inhabitants of Stoke Newington was an intelligent old lady, Mrs. Decastro, a Portuguese Jewess, who used to say that her father and mother were the last persons who were burned alive for being Jews. She was then about seventy years old, and they were burned when she was two years old, in the Island of Goa, the Portuguese colony in the East Indies. The Portuguese law against the Jews was enforced in the colonies long after it had been allowed to fall into disuse at home.

It was in this quiet period of nine years, filled with diligent attention to business during banking hours, and with improving and delightful study in the morning and evening, that the foundations of his success both as a scholar and a man of business were laid. His punctuality and exactitude struck everybody who knew him. It was said that he never left home a minute too early or too late, and a story lingered in Stoke Newington that the keeper of the turnpike gate at the end of Paradise Row set his clock for several years by the young clerk as he passed through the gate on his way to the city. He was extremely cautious in business, and conscientious in every relation he sustained. His father's misfortunes, which had deeply impressed him as he gradually heard from friends of their serious extent and consequences, produced in him an almost extreme objection to any approach to extravagance. The father had been too fond of society—the son despised it too much. His sister complained that he

would never dress in the evening, and that he wore
at her parties in New Ormond Street the clothes in
which he had come from business.  He disliked mere
visiting all his life, but always sought the society of
men whose character or attainments made them
worth knowing.  In such society he was always
welcome.  His lively interest in all literary and
scientific subjects, his wide and diligent reading, and
his inherited love of art, opened the doors of artists
and scientific men and men of letters, which remained closed to many better dressed but less intelligent persons.

While Samuel was thus going backwards and
forwards between Clement's Lane and Stoke Newington, gaining the confidence of his relatives in
the banking-house and becoming a mainstay of his
motherly half sister at home, the other members of the
family were also pushing into life.  His elder brother
Sutton, who had been regarded as one of the most
promising boys in Mr. Cogan's school, was articled
in 1815 to the eminent firm of Messrs. Graham,
Kinderley and Domville, of Lincoln's Inn.  He had
been a diligent student at school, where he had
gained an extensive acquaintance with English
literature, to which he had added, in his holidays,
a good knowledge of chemistry.  During the five
years in which he was articled he showed the same
diligence in the study of law.  Mr. Kelly, afterwards
Sir Fitzroy Kelly, was a clerk in the same office and
taught Sutton Sharpe, who was one year his junior, the
Italian language.  Sutton was a good French scholar
and translated for an English publisher " De Pradt on
the Colonies.".  On the expiration of his clerkship he

determined not to practise as a solicitor, but to go to
the Bar.  For this purpose he entered himself in the
Middle Temple and took chambers in King's Bench
Walk.  He became the pupil, first of Mr. Richmond,
the conveyancer, and afterwards of Mr. Spence, who
was in large practice as an equity draughtsman.  He
was called to the Bar on the 21st June, 1822.  The
sister, Mary, who was two years younger than
Samuel, was in feeble health, and had never left
home.  She received her education from Miss Andrews, the governess, and her sister Catharine.  The
cultivated tastes of her brothers filled their home
with a literary atmosphere; and Mary's delicate
health made it quieter perhaps and more restful, but
none the less happy.  Henry, too, was far from
strong, and for this reason was never sent to Mr.
Cogan's school, as his elder brothers had been, but
was taught first by his sister and the governess, and
in 1812, at the age of ten, went to the day school
kept by Mr. Bransby at Stoke Newington.  But he
was as diligent as all the rest ; and laid the foundation of a solid education in a school time of five
years.  While at school he formed a warm friendship
with William Drusina, a schoolfellow from Hamburg,
and acquired from him the elements of German.
On leaving Mr. Bransby's in 1817, Henry went on a
visit to his friend's mother in Hamburg.  It was a
long voyage in those days ; and he was three weeks
at sea.  His sister had a plan for sending him to
school in Hamburg, and he was eventually placed in
the family of Mr. and Mrs. Knoop, who had a son of
his own age.  Here he stayed five years, during which
he made himself as familiar with German as with his

D

native language, besides acquiring French, Spanish and Portuguese. Mrs. Knoop became a second mother to him and spoke of him as her English son. Henry himself became so much attached to Hamburg that he seriously thought of settling there ; and went into a merchant's office. In his few visits to England he looked back to Hamburg as his real home ; and to the end of his life retained many of his friendships there and paid the city a holiday visit every three or four years. His sister, however, succeeded in persuading him not to settle abroad, and he returned to England in the same year in which his brother Sutton was called to the Bar. He went into the office of Mr. Van Zeller, a Portuguese merchant, and lived with his brothers and sisters in New Ormond Street.

The two younger brothers, William who had been born in 1804, and Daniel who was born in 1806, seem to have been kept under home teaching till the year 1816. Their sister writes in her diary in that year: "William and Dan went to Mr. Bransby's school ; Henry went to Hamburg ; Miss Andrews left us." William was afterwards sent to a boarding-school at Cheam. It was his sister's desire that he should be an architect. He seemed born to be an artist, and very early showed a correctness of eye and hand, and a power of calculation and arrangement, which together seemed to justify his sister's choice. His own desire was in harmony with her wish ; but it was not to be gratified. His artistic talent was only to be the pleasant recreation of a hardworking life, and his power of calculation and arrangement was to be used in giving invaluable advice and aid to those who asked it from him. As Sutton had resolved to take the higher branch of the legal profession, William, at sixteen years of age, was put in his place in Sir William Domville's office, where he remained till he was twenty-one.

Daniel, the youngest, was naturally the last at school. He had two years at Mr. Bransby's, and then, at twelve, was sent to Mr. Cogan's, where Benjamin Disraeli was one of his schoolfellows, and where, like his two elder brothers, he got thoroughly grounded in the classics. He left Mr. Cogan's at sixteen and returned to the new home, to which the family had removed in the year before, in New Ormond Street.

It was while Daniel was still at school, but after the other four were all settled at business, that the removal from Paradise Row had been resolved on. Their sister's plan had been to keep them together as much as possible, to make them appreciate the comfort of home, and to preserve in them the sense of family life. For this purpose the country—for in those days Stoke Newington was so regarded—had suited them admirably in their boyhood; but it suited them no longer. Catharine herself gives a full account of her reasons for making the change :

The period was now approaching that seemed to require a change in our way of life. Hitherto a residence in the country had been most desirable for the family. Sutton being in chambers, Sam was the only one settled, and he could return of an evening to tea. But now William was to be articled in the same office as his brother, their hours would not allow of his returning at night to Newington. The last fourteen years had passed in their education as children ; they were now to take their stations in the world as men. The most ardent wish of my heart had ever been, when this period did arrive, to be enabled

still to keep the family together, and afford these young men a
home such as they would prefer, from inclination, to any more
independent way of life. But should I have the power of making
it so? All rested on myself (for I could with pride assert that
they were, every one of them, such as any parent might glory
in), and however right I might be in theory I might fail in
practice. We took a house in New Ormond Street. In the
autumn Henry returned to us from Hamburg, finally to settle
in this country.

Samuel gives his own account of this period of his
life :—

In 1821 I removed with my sister to No. 12, New Ormond Street. At that time Sutton was a barrister in the
Temple, Henry had returned home from a clerkship in
Hamburg, William was in an attorney's office, and Dan
was at school. Here I continued with the same quiet and
studious habits. Our removal into London took me a little
more into society, but not much. I became a Fellow of
the Geological Society by the introduction of Dr. Bostock,
and intimate with Joseph Woods, the architect and botan-
ist, and Bicheno the naturalist, who both lived in Furni-
val's Inn. With them I used sometimes to meet several
men of Science, such as Colby and Drummond, of the
Trigonometrical Survey, Horsfield, Bell, Yarrell, and other
members of the Linnæan Society. But certainly my most
valuable friend at this time was Joseph Janson. My acquaintance began with him at Stoke Newington while my
cousin Sarah, afterwards my dear wife, was a governess in
his brother's family at Stamford Hill. He was a most
judicious, sensible man ; a deep thinker, and clear in
conversation and a great reader. When I was nineteen
years old, he was eight-and-twenty ; and it certainly was
one of the events of my life when he invited me to join
him in a tour through the Netherlands and Holland to
some of the picturesque parts of the Rhine. The difference in our ages made the invitation most flattering, and

the journey most instructive, and he kindly accommodated himself to what was necessary on my part, that we should travel at small expense.   I have known many men of greater learning, I have received from others greater advantages in the way of introduction to men of letters, but I have never had any friend whose conversation was to me so improving.   Our journey occupied exactly four weeks. During my clerkship in Clement's Lane I was allowed such a holiday about once in three years.   I spent the first most agreeably with my uncle Dan at Wassal Grove, turning over with him the books in his valuable library, and rambling in Hagley Park with my cousins.   This journey with Joseph Janson was my second holiday.   My third was again with Mr. Janson and his cousins, Mr. and Mrs. Barton, to Paris, where I had the pleasure of seeing Humboldt, and passing an evening with Helen Maria Williams.   My fourth holiday I spent with my brother Dan in a ramble through North Wales.

The year 1822 was memorable in the family history as that in which the youngest of the boys left school and went into business.   Catharine writes as follows under the date 1822 :   "Dan joined Henry in Mr. Van Zeller's office."   She was now forty years old.   The best part of her life had been devoted to this group of orphan children, and she now had the satisfaction of seeing them all more or less settled in life.   After the line just quoted she writes in her journal—it is the last entry but one in what remains of her diary :

Thus they were all now established in their respective branches, all present anxiety about them at an end ; and here I feel my efforts cease.   I have done all in my power for their advantage, the rest must depend upon themselves.

They must now make their own way in the world. I have laboured to make them active, independent, industrious, and I feel confident I have not laboured in vain, and that if I live I shall see them upright and conscientious members of society.

# CHAPTER III.

## BUSINESS AND FAMILY LIFE.

THE removal of the family to New Ormond Street was very soon followed by an important change in the fortunes of the subject of this biography. We have already seen how his admirable business qualities gained the complete confidence of his relatives in the banking-house, and how in the beginning of 1824, when he had been nine years serving as a clerk, he was admitted as a partner. Catharine records it in a supplementary entry in her diary, the last words the diary contains :—

This year (1824) was ushered in by a most joyful and un-expected event. Sam was taken into the firm at Clement's Lane. Mr. Henry Rogers, who, at my father's death promised to be a father to the children and a brother to myself, has invariably kept his word to us all. He now withdrew from the concern, appointing Sam in his place. Independently of the great advantage in a pecuniary point of view, his choice was most gratifying, as proving his high confidence in Sam's character, who, henceforward, is to assist the others in their progress through life, now that he is himself established.

Samuel speaks of this improvement in his position as giving him a moderate income, but making no change in his habits of life. He continued to live during the next three years and a half with his

brothers and sisters in New Ormond Street. It was
a happy and prosperous household ; the brothers full
of intellectual eagerness and enthusiasm, the sisters,
in their very different modes, entering into all their
pursuits, and enjoying their lively talk. During
this residence in New Ormond Street many friendships were formed. One of these was with Mr.
Edwin Wilkins Field, who was the same age as
William Sharpe. Mr. Field was the eldest son
of the Rev. William Field, Unitarian minister of
Warwick, the friend and biographer of Dr. Parr.
His grandfather, who was the founder of the London
Annuity Society, had married Anne, the great-
granddaughter of Henry Cromwell, son of the
Protector. Mr. Field was articled in 1821 to Messrs.
Taylor and Roscoe, Solicitors, of King's Bench Walk,
Temple. William Sharpe had been articled in the
previous year ; and the two clerks, having many
feelings and opinions in common, became intimate
friends. In 1826 they began business together as
solicitors in Bread Street, Cheapside. Mr. Field
became engaged to his partner's sister, Mary Sharpe,
and they were married in 1830. Mary's health had
always been a source of anxiety to her family, and
it did not permanently improve after her marriage.
Soon after the birth of her only child, she died
suddenly, during a visit to Leamington, in the second
year of her married life. This was the first break in
the family since the double bereavement in 1806.
Writing in 1840 Samuel says :—" Last time I was at
Warwick it was to be present at the funeral of my
sister Mary, and this time I was pleased to see the
slab which her husband has put up to her memory in

Mr. Field's chapel." Mary possessed much of the brightness and sweetness which were the great charm of her mother. Her son, who was named after the family of his grandmother, is Mr. Rogers Field, the eminent sanitary engineer.

The closest intimacy of the Sharpe family was with Mr. and Mrs. Kinder and their sons and daughters. Mr. Kinder was a merchant, trading with the United States, whom the Orders in Council had nearly ruined, as they did so many others, and who had removed to London. Mrs. Kinder, his second wife, was the daughter of Dr. Enfield, the compiler of "Enfield's Speaker," and author of the "History of Philosophy." Mr. Kinder and his eldest daughter were living at Stoke Newington in 1806; and Catharine Sharpe had removed thither from Nottingham Place in order to be near them. She had taken the next house, and a communication was opened between the two dwellings. The Kinders had removed to Cheapside before the Sharpe family came into New Ormond Street; and this latter change restored the former intimacy. One of Samuel Sharpe's most cherished recollections in his later years was that of spending an evening with Dr. Channing, at their house in Cheapside, in 1822. Dr. Channing was then but little known in England, and he visited this country as an invalid in search of health and quiet. The connection of the Kinders with the United States brought many American Unitarians to their home. Among the other friends of those days were many men who became distinguished in later years—Charles Crompton, afterwards Mr. Justice Crompton; Charles Fellows, who was knighted for his valuable researches in Lycia; James Carter, afterwards Sir James Carter, who was for many years Chief Justice of St. John's; Mr. Thomas Field Gibson, one of the Commissioners for the Exhibition of 1851; Mr. Henry Roscoe, son and biographer of the eminent historian; Mr. Yate Lee, and Mr. Reginald Parker (afterwards partner of William Sharpe). With their uncle Samuel Rogers there was intercourse both of business and of family connection and friendship, and more especially with his brother Henry Rogers, who was justly regarded by the family as a second father, and who had given Samuel Sharpe a junior partnership in the bank. Mr. Henry Rogers is still remembered by friends and neighbours at Highbury as the light and charm of the circle he moved in. He was the kind of man Emerson may have had in view, when in his essay on Character he wrote, "I revere the man who *is* riches; so that I cannot think of him as alone, or poor, or exiled, or unhappy, or a client, but as perpetual patron, benefactor and beatified man." Among the circle of friends at Highbury was the family of Mr. James Bischoff. Mrs. Bischoff was the sister of Mr. Stansfeld of Halifax, whose son, the Right Honourable James Stansfeld, has long worthily represented that town in Parliament. Mr. Bischoff's third daughter married the Rev. Thomas Madge, the eminent and revered successor of the Rev. Theophilus Lindsey and the Rev. Thomas Belsham in the pulpit of the Unitarian Chapel in Essex Street. Mrs. Madge and her younger sister still live in the home of their childhood in Highbury Terrace. Their friendship with Mr. Henry Rogers and his nephews and nieces, especially with their neighbours Samuel and William Sharpe, continued unbroken to the end ; and is now perpetuated in the present generation of the Sharpe family.

The young men, thus brought together by business relations and by personal and family friendships, formed a very energetic and strenuous group. There are glimpses in letters and journals of gay evening parties, and of boating excursions on the river. The Thames of sixty years ago differed less from that of the days of Queen Elizabeth than from the river which the present generation of Londoners see from the Embankment. Mr. Edwin Field writes in his diary, about the year 1824 : " Swam from Waterloo to Blackfriars Bridge, and could have gone twice as far with the greatest ease." Some of the Sharpes kept a boat at the bottom of Arundel Street, Strand, and it was no uncommon event for them to take their elder sister and their friends for pleasant excursions on the then undefiled stream. Samuel Sharpe was not often with his brothers in these excursions. He was more disposed to spend any leisure which business and study left him in visits to Stamford Hill. One of his principal friendships was with Mr. Joseph Janson, brother of Mr. Halsey Janson, of Stamford Hill, in whose house lived his cousin, Sarah Sharpe. She was a daughter of his father's younger brother, Joseph, the King Street brewer, who had exerted so much influence on the mind of Catharine Sharpe in her girlhood, and whose early death in 1797, at the age of thirty-one, left a great gap in his niece's life.

Joseph Sharpe had a family of eight children, three
of whom died in childhood, and a fourth at the age
of twenty-one. Samuel Sharpe knew only four of
them: Sutton, who became a lieutenant in the navy,
and died in 1823 at the same age as his father,
thirty-one; Joseph, who entered the service of the
East India Company and died in India, leaving one
son; Charlotte, who lived unmarried, survived her
brothers and sisters by thirty years, and died at
Cherbourg in 1881, at the age of ninety; and
Sarah, who became his wife. His cousins and their
mother had lived with their grandmother Sharpe
at Croydon till her death. They had no elder
relative to take care of them when their mother
died, and when Sarah, who was the youngest, left
school, Catharine Sharpe placed her as governess in
the family of Mr. Halsey Janson of Stamford Hill.
She lived there twelve years, and during the latter
part of the time her cousin Samuel was a frequent
visitor at the house, from which, in 1827, he took
her away as his wife. She was three years older
than he, having been born in 1796. The engagement
had not been a long one. There are a couple of
letters from her written in February and September
1820, thanking him for presents, but plainly showing
that she was not then actually engaged to him.

On their marriage they took a house in Canonbury
Place, No. 4, where they lived the quiet domestic
life which both of them preferred, keeping very little
company. She was a cultivated woman, and made
her studious husband just the kind of home which
suited his inclinations and habits. Their attachment
to one another was very great, and they were not

anxious for society. Samuel Sharpe had always
objected to his sister's open evenings in New
Ormond Street. He complained that only people
whom nobody wanted to see ever found time to go
to such parties. He had an intense dislike of the
show and emulation which are among the great evils
of modern society. He had determined from the
first to live very far within his means ; and this determination met with the full sympathy of his wife.
He used to say that one of the most generous things
which can be done towards one's friends is to live
less expensively than they; that those who do anything
for show, will always find some one who must outdo
them, and that it is a benefit to such to leave to them
the satisfaction of their ambition, and to go one's own
way and live by one's own rule. All his life he had
the courage of these opinions. From the first setting
up of his household in Canonbury Place to the
remote day when he went to his own room in his
house in Highbury Place to lie down and die, there
was in his home nothing superfluous, nothing to
parade, or even to indicate wealth. It was the fit
home of a man of learning and taste, with traces
of his love of Egyptian lore. In this quiet life the
years flowed on, with very few important changes to
mark their progress. He himself, writing in 1854,
sums up in half a dozen sentences the domestic
events of four-and-twenty years :—

On our marriage we took a house in Canonbury Place,
No. 4, and lived quietly, with very little visiting. There
five of our children were born, beside one that died within
a few weeks of its birth. They were all for the most part
educated at home by their mother, and it is unnecessary for

me to describe her good qualities to them, as they all remember her and cherish her memory. In 1840 we removed to a larger house, No. 32, Highbury Place. There my youngest child was born; and there, in June, 1851, my dear wife died. My six children have most dutifully and affectionately done their best to lessen the blank of widowhood to me; and they make me yet more grateful to their mother's memory, by letting me see what I owe to her forming their minds so carefully.

It is, perhaps, right to follow to some extent the example thus set, and to pass over with but brief notice the purely domestic history of these years. But the quietest and most uneventful life can only be appreciated and understood when it is seen, like a jewel, in its setting. A man's qualities are not the result of his environment, any more than those of the steel blade are due to the workman who shaped it; but his exhibition and expression of them are moulded by the circumstances in which he is placed. We have already seen what were the early influences which determined much of Samuel Sharpe's conduct. The family group in New Ormond Street were, from the first, deeply interested in all the public events of their time. The young men, all of whom, except Daniel the youngest, were Liberals, had qualified themselves as voters for the county of Middlesex and for the City of London, that they might throw their influence on the Liberal side. In the exciting political struggles of those times it was the duty of every Liberal to get and to use as much voting power as the law allowed him. Samuel Sharpe acted on this principle. He took up his freedom in the Haberdashers' Company for the sake of the City vote it

gave him. He also held a qualification as a free-
holder for Middlesex. The country was then
under the blight of a long Tory ascendancy. Mr.
Fox had died in the same month as Sutton
Sharpe, September 1806. In 1807 the Ministry
of All the Talents had been dissolved after a
short thirteen months of office, and a Tory reign
of twenty years' duration had set in. One of the
earliest recollections of these young men in their
boyhood was the assassination of Mr. Perceval, the
Prime Minister, in the lobby of the House of Commons, in 1812. He was succeeded by Lord Liverpool, and during the fourteen years that followed, it
must have seemed to the people at large as though
Lord Liverpool at the Treasury, Lord Eldon in the
Chancellorship, Lord Castlereagh at the Foreign
Office, and Lord Sidmouth as Home Secretary, had
become the permanent rulers of England. They had
the credit of bringing the great war to a successful
close, and the nation's gratitude for Peace, together
with the reaction against the doctrines of the French
Revolution, enabled them to resist with success all
suggestions for Reform. The old King died and the
Regent came to the throne ; but Lord Liverpool's
reign was not broken.

The relations between the ruling classes and the
people of this country had been illustrated in 1819
by the dispersion of the great meeting for Reform
in Manchester, by a combined charge of cavalry and
yeomanry, who rode down upon the unarmed multi-
tude, killing eleven, and wounding several hundreds.
They were further exhibited on the popular side by the
irresistible burst of applause which, three years later,

broke from the assembled crowd when the coffin of
Lord Londonderry was carried into the Abbey.  The
fierce political hatred which such events reveal made
the Reform movement of those days a difficult and
dangerous task, compared with which all later
political agitation has been mere play.  It was sup-
pressed civil war.  The Reformers of those days
risked their personal liberty in the effort "to make
the bounds of freedom wider yet."  If a man called
attention to an abuse, he was probably accused of
libel or sedition and sent to prison.  If he tried to
do a little good to his neighbours, he was sure to
bring on himself suspicion and discomfort.  The
Parliamentary leaders, Lord Grey and Lord John
Russell, had everything against them in the two
Houses of Parliament ; but they were supported by
the growing intelligence and enlightenment of the
times ; and commanded the personal allegiance of
the most vigorous minds of the younger generation.
They were the leaders of a great host; the captains
of an army which grew in numbers and in zeal every
year.  They could have done nothing without the
constant and hearty support of unnamed men, who
risked much and gained nothing—whom no history
records, no monuments celebrate, and no titles have
adorned.  The struggle for liberty, enlightenment,
and social progress in England, as in the United
States, has been a soldier's battle.  It has been the
case of Cromwell's Ironsides over again.  All over
England, Wales and Scotland, there have been small
groups of religious people, with an Independent, or
Baptist, or Quaker meeting-house, a Unitarian or
Presbyterian chapel as their centre, on whom the

burden of nearly every political and social conflict has fallen. It was to such men the Whig leaders looked for support; it was from them that politicians like Lord Russell, who did not sympathize with their nonconformity, caught their enthusiasm for bettering the world. These were the men who started Sunday-schools and day-schools, and woke up both Parliament and the Church to their duty to the great masses of the people. They were fired by "the enthusiasm of humanity," and the Whig leaders found, as Mr. Gladstone has found, that to be at their head is to lead an invincible host.

Like all men who had been Reformers before Reform, Samuel Sharpe looked back with enthusiastic admiration to the heroic age of Liberalism. He could compare the present with the past. He had lived in the old intolerant era of the Georges, and in the new Liberal England of the present reign. He felt that he had had a share in the decisive struggle by which the greatest bloodless revolution in history had been brought about. To his latest days he spoke with enthusiasm of Lord Grey's leadership, of the devotion with which he had inspired his followers, of the quiet persistency with which he upheld the popular cause in adverse times, and of the long delayed triumph which came at last. No veteran fighting his battles over again and thrice slaying the slain could dwell upon the past with deeper feeling. His voice often trembled as he spoke. Not that his Liberal sympathies were limited to the past. They followed every Liberal movement of the time, and no young politician welcomed with more gladness the great national awakening which in the spring of

E

1880 swept the Beaconsfield-Salisbury administration
into Milton's limbo and called Mr. Gladstone back to
power. He naturally felt that the controversies of
later years had less significance than the decisive
conflicts of his earlier days. Then everything
was at stake, and it may well have seemed to
those who took part in the struggle that almost
everything was won. It was in the first year of
his married life that the Test and Corporation
Acts were repealed; and in the very next year
the Duke of Wellington was compelled to con-
cede Catholic Emancipation. Everything else followed: the Reform Bill in 1832; the abolition of
slavery in the West Indies in 1834; the reform of
the Corporations in 1835; the Dissenters' Marriage
Act in 1836. A period of fierce agitation, coming
very near at times to actual civil war, led to seven
years of continuous and beneficent change, which
realized much for which the best friends of liberty
had longed and worked, and which transformed the
English world.

In these struggles Samuel Sharpe took an active
though not prominent part. He had struck a blow
at the Test and Corporation Acts in a magazine
article which, under the title of "Who paid for the
London Mansion House?" had reminded the world
that the building was erected with money wrung from
Dissenters by fines. He wished that this ingenious
extortion should be remembered, and his statement
of its method was republished in 1872. It is to the
effect that the Mansion House was built in the years
from 1739 to 1753; and a fund of £18,000 which
had been accumulated by the fines of Dissenters was

voted by the Corporation towards its cost. These fines had been levied under an Act of the Restoration era, by which every person who accepted an office under the Corporation without taking the Communion according to the rites of the Established Church was subject to a fine of £500. An earlier Act requires every man who is elected as Sheriff to pay a fine of £400 to the Corporation if he declines to serve. In the reign of George the Second it occurred to a shrewd lawyer that these two Acts could be worked together to the great disadvantage of Dissenters · and the great advantage of the City purse. Accordingly a Dissenter was elected Sheriff. As he could not conscientiously take the Sacrament he chose the alternative of declining to serve, and paid his fine of £400. Another Dissenter was immediately elected, and took the same course. The election of Dissenters was repeated till forty-five had paid the fine for refusal to serve. The Dissenters were then roused to resistance, and the forty-sixth refused either to serve or to pay. An action was brought against him for the recovery of the fine, but the Judge held that the Act which disqualified a Dissenter relieved him of the duty. The City appealed to the House of Lords, but the decision of the Court below was upheld. The City, however, refused to disgorge the money it had already illegally wrung from the forty-five men it had fined ; and the sum, £18,000, was voted to the building fund of the Mansion House, which, says Samuel Sharpe, "consequently remains as a monument of the unjust manner in which Dissenters were treated in the last century."

He suffered, as all Dissenters did before 1836, from another of the evils which the Established Church so long inflicted on the country. In the early years of his married life the parochial registers were the only legal evidence of birth, and the parish church was the only place in which a marriage could be legally solemnised. He and his brothers and sisters had all been christened at Marylebone Church; and his marriage to his cousin Sarah, which took place from Mr. Janson's house at Stamford Hill in 1827, had necessarily been performed by the parish clergyman in the parish church. But he and his wife had definitely taken the position of Nonconformists, and he probably held in those days, the opinion which he advocated all the rest of his life, that the ceremony of baptism belonged only to the missionary days of Christianity, and had no significance in Christian countries. Apart from this objection, the baptismal ceremony of the Church of England, which is appropriate and beautiful to those who hold its doctrines, involves an implied pledge to bring up the children as members of that Church. To give this pledge without the intention of keeping it was as impossible as any other act of insincerity to Samuel Sharpe and his wife. Their children, therefore, were not baptized at church, and not registered by the parish, as the parish officers registered baptisms only and not births. The Dissenters, however, had set up a registration of their own. In the older chapels of the English Presbyterians, nearly all of which became Unitarian in their theology, baptismal registers were regularly kept; for other Dissenters a complete and organized registration of births was carried on at

Dr. Williams's Library. A friend of the mother was usually present at the birth of the child; and her signature was added to that of the parents in the notice which was sent to the Library. In this way a very complete system of registering births had been established among Dissenters for generations before the Registration Act of 1836. The births of Samuel Sharpe's first four children were registered in this mode. These non-parochial registers were formally legalized and collected at Somerset House under the new Act. So much easier in England is political reform than that which touches ecclesiastical exclusiveness, that the passing of the Registration Act, which for the first time put all citizens on an equality in the legal recognition and official record of the births of their children, was one of the latest results of the Reform Act; coming later than the abolition of slavery and the reform of the Corporations.

It was in some degree on account of these relics of the evil days of enforced ecclesiastical uniformity that Samuel Sharpe was driven by a sense of public duty to separate himself from the Established Church. He tells us how he became not only a political Nonconformist, but a theological Nonconformist too—

It was soon after removing to New Ormond Street that I first subscribed to a Unitarian place of worship. Not that I then particularly examined the subject to form my opinions, but that I examined my feelings and made up my mind that having a general disapproval of the creeds and articles of the Church, it was right to profess that disapproval. In taking this very important step, I was helped to an impartial decision by the circumstance that I had friends and relations belonging to both sects. My father's family were not Dissenters, and my mother, though before her marriage she had attended upon Dr. Price, Dr. Towers, and others at Newington-green meeting-house, yet after her marriage she always accompanied my father to Marylebone Church. We children had all been baptized by the parish clergyman, and as soon as we were old enough always went to Church regularly. But after the death of our father and mother, we were thrown very much among our mother's relations, and therefore from the age of eight I had been in the unusual position of being taught to go to Church, and to adopt the Church opinions, while, with the exception of my brothers and sisters, I was wholly surrounded by Unitarians. When controversies arose at school, I always took the orthodox side. I read books upon the subject; I afterwards read the Greek Testament critically, and more particularly Griesbach's text, a copy of which had been given me by Mr. Joseph Janson. I thus gradually formed my opinions, and it was upon consideration of the odium and legal disabilities that yet remained attached to a denial of the Trinity, that I made up my mind that it was a duty to bear my share of the burden.

The Unitarian Chapel to which he thus attached himself was the new one which had then just been erected in South Place, Finsbury, for the late Rev. W. J. Fox. Mr. Fox had come to London in 1817 as the successor to the Rev. William Vidler, at the old chapel in Parliament Court, Artillery Row. He was a forcible and eloquent speaker, with an exquisite voice, a perfect delivery, and that kindling power which is the true mark of the orator and the preacher. His sermons speedily attracted a great congregation, which overflowed the small building in Parliament Court, and rendered needful the erection of a more capacious chapel. At South Place the congregation found room for expansion, and expanded accordingly. Those who listened to Mr. Fox in those best days of his ministry, never forgot its elevating influence on their thoughts and lives. Those who remain still speak with gratitude of the stimulus to thought, the inward refreshment, the encouragement to every noble deed and lofty hope, which his sermons communicated to them week by week. When they had once felt the charm they could not miss an opportunity of yielding to it again. They were drawn to the preacher by the irresistible attraction of his eloquence and insight. He taught them as one that had authority, and not as the commonplace expounders of texts. He spoke as one who could communicate to others what he saw, and felt and handled of the word of life. Perhaps no greater benefit can come to young people of quick intelligence than to fall under the spell of such a preacher. It changes, for them, the whole aspect of the world. The influence may pass away, but it may also endure, and when it endures it produces an elevated tone of thought and character which keeps life pure and worthy. Mr. Fox's preaching had such a lasting influence on many of the young people who come within the scope of this biography. Fifty years afterwards some of them still speak of it with enthusiasm ; and look back on it as the most marked and most valuable religious influence which has ever been exerted on their lives.

It was, however, at a later period that Samuel Sharpe's great services to the Unitarian church took place. In these earlier days his main interest turned in other directions. He and most of the young men who formed his group of friends had attached them-

selves to Mr. Fox's congregation, and some of them
were in those days admirers of Mr. Fox rather than
members of the Unitarian body. They afterwards
became liberal supporters of Unitarian Christianity,
and lived lives which did honour to its principles ;
but the zeal which Samuel Sharpe exhibited in
after years for the Unitarian view of Christianity
was at this period of his life spread over many
social, political, and scientific pursuits. The
movement for the establishment of public ele-
mentary schools which had originated with Dr.
Bell, and took popular shape under Mr. Joseph
Lancaster,—antagonists as these two men thought
themselves—commanded the warm interest and support of Samuel and some of his brothers. A Lan-
castrian school, afterwards called a British School,
was established in Harp Alley, Farringdon Street,
and in this school Samuel, Henry and Daniel Sharpe
taught classes for many years, on their way to the
City in the morning. In this school Mr. Edwin Field
formed a drawing class, and turned away once a week
from the busy work of a rising lawyer to teach poor
children the accomplishment in which he found
delightful recreation. Daniel Sharpe differed from
his brothers in the possession of a genius for natural
science. In 1827 he joined the Geological Society,
of which he afterwards became President. Samuel
was elected a Fellow of that society probably about
the same time. His interest, however, was in antiquarian and mathematical investigation rather than
geological inquiry, and hence we find him contributing to the *Philosophical Magazine* in July,
1828, an article " On the Figure of the Cells of

the Honeycomb." In the August number in the same year is an article, illustrated by a drawing, " On the Vitrified Fort of Dunnochgoil, in the Isle of Bute." In the same Magazine for August, 1831, is a paper "On the Theory of Differences," in which four propositions are carefully worked out. At the same time he was laying the foundation of his Egyptian knowledge, and pursuing the studies which, in much later years, enabled him to revise the authorised English version of the Old and New Testaments.

There would be nothing remarkable in all this intellectual activity if it had characterised a life of studious leisure. But Samuel Sharpe, like his contemporary Mr. Grote, was all the time an active member of a banking firm. With wide differences of temperament and opinion, there was a curious parallelism between the two men. They had each gone to business at sixteen, had both thrown themselves into the agitation for political reform, and had each spent the leisure which young men usually give to enjoyment in study and self-improvement. But Samuel Sharpe had less opportunity, though not less capacity, for entering on public life. For many years he was obliged to pay very close attention to business. He had become a partner in 1824 ; and the terrible monetary crisis in 1825, when business houses were falling and banks stopping payment all over the country, must have caused him the keenest anxiety. In a very few years the chief responsibility for the bank in Clement's Lane rested upon him ; and he had a full sense of its magnitude. Happily he took to business not only the characteristic caution which

the times greatly needed, but the zest and activity
and thoroughness which belonged to him in all he
did. His time was thus divided between business
and home ; and the energy which even the management of a bank did not exhaust was thrown into his
favourite studies. Yet, with all this work, no home
duty was neglected. He did not shut himself up
with his books and papers. He had no study, but
worked in the room in which his wife sat and his
children might come to play. On the days when he
was at home to dinner he carved with a child upon
his knee. The father's studies and writings were no
burden in the family. They did not turn home into
a workshop ; they were not allowed even to make it
any the less home. Much as he loved his books,
his hieroglyphics, his manuscripts and his proofs,
they did not alienate him from his family, who seemed
to share his studies and to love them almost as much
as he loved them himself. He was by no means
without that love of fame which Milton calls the last
infirmity of noble minds ; but he had been called to
a life of business work, and he made himself con-
tented in it. He was willing even to forego all
thought of public life and to satisfy an unquenchable
love of knowledge and an irrepressible mental activity
by the favourite studies which occupied his holidays
and filled his evening leisure.

Family life at this period was not without its anxieties. The children were delicate, and his own strength
was sometimes overtaxed. Letters from his wife,
written during visits to the seaside, exhibit much
concern for his health. She urges him to go more
to his brother Henry's at Hampstead, or to run down

to Margate by the steamer on Friday, and back on Monday, to get a whiff of the sea breeze to revive his spirits. In business he was cautious and anxious, though few shadows of pecuniary care seem to have fallen on his home. To such a man the enthusiasm with which he took up his various intellectual pursuits made them the best form of recreation. In the City, he was the banker and man of business; at home, he was the politician, the philanthropist and the student. For many years he and his brothers, Henry and Daniel, dined together at their office in the City; and the hour was given to pleasant social intercourse. The interval in business was a rest from business—filled with political and literary and scientific talk. The freshness of mind thus kept was a marked characteristic of all three. They all had that reserve of energy which is the characteristic of successful men. There was zest in everything—in teaching poor children in Harp Alley school in the early morning, in the routine of bank or counting-house all day, in the politics or literature, or geological science, or Egyptian antiquities, or philanthropic efforts on behalf of the young working men of their neighbourhood, which occupied the evening. To such men alternation of activity was a kind of rest—change of work was better than play.

## CHAPTER IV.

### EGYPTIAN STUDIES.

IT was during these earlier years, while his young family was growing up around him, and while he was still in business, that Samuel Sharpe's chief works on Egyptian History and Antiquities were published. His interest in the subject is easily accounted for. The study had, for all Europe in those days, the charm of novelty ; it had for him the fascination of a series of enigmas, of which every patient student might hope to puzzle out the answers. This was the kind of intellectual exercise in which Samuel Sharpe delighted. His brother Daniel found similar interest in careful attempts to interpret the Lycian Inscriptions, and in similar study of the larger problem set by Nature herself in the strata which geological science was just beginning to read. In later years Samuel Sharpe made a careful and ingenious attempt to read the Sinaitic Inscriptions, and his fondness for inquiries of this kind was so great, that if an advertisement in cypher came under his notice, he would sit down and work at it till he had found the key and read it off. The hieroglyphics offered a similar problem. For many ages they had presented an insoluble enigma to the world. Various guesses at their meaning had been made, but they were mere

guesses, and all were wrong. Even Champollion
was misled in his earlier investigations by the false
assumption which had made his predecessors stumble
on the threshold of their investigations, that the
hieroglyphic signs were ideographic ; that is to say,
that each figure or combination of figures stood for
an idea rather than for a sound. The discovery of
the Rosetta stone, with its threefold inscription, first
in hieroglyphics, then in the demotic or enchorial
character, and lastly, in Greek, seemed to offer a clue
to the interpretation of the mysterious signs. But
even this clue could not be followed till the traditional
mode of regarding the hieroglyphics had been
abandoned. Champollion himself made nothing of
it till a Somersetshire Quaker, who had studied at
Edinburgh and Göttingen, and afterwards graduated
at Cambridge, brought to the question the habits
and methods of modern science. Dr. Thomas
Young, whose much ridiculed discovery of the inter-
ference of rays of light with each other, has been
admitted, since his death, to have established the
undulatory theory, applied himself to the problems
which the Rosetta stone presented, and found the
way to solve them. Here was an inscription the
meaning of which was known, but it was in unknown
characters and an unknown language. It might be
assumed that each character stood for the same
thing wherever it occurred, and the first task was to
fix the meaning of each sign or group of signs. Dr.
Young was able to do this. He distributed the
hieroglyphics of the inscription into sentences corre-
sponding with those in the Greek, and then distinguished many of the single signs. He found that

kings' names were written within an enclosing line
forming an oval, or ring; that names of private
persons were followed by the sitting figure of a man
or woman; and, that the hieroglyphic signs were
used as sounds or letters to spell out the word or
name. He thus deciphered the name Ptolemy in
the Rosetta stone, and that of Berenice on another
monument. By this means five letters of the hieroglyphic alphabet were fixed. With the key thus
found, Champollion took up the task. Dr. Young
died in 1829 while he was at work on the Egyptian
Vocabulary; but he left the clue he had successfully
grasped in the hands of many eager followers.
Champollion had the advantage of a bilingual
inscription found on an obelisk at Philae, and,
applying Young's discovery to it, he spelled out the
name of Cleopatra in the hieroglyphic characters.
Other names were slowly added, and at length a
whole alphabet was formed. As words other than
names were spelt out, it was soon seen that the
Egyptian language, though not the extinct Coptic
of the translation of the New Testament used by
the Egyptian Christians, was probably an earlier
form of the same dialect. Champollion threw suspicion on his own discoveries by inventing Coptic
words, or assuming that the words he read were those
of lost forms of the Coptic; but the general results
of his method are now universally accepted by
Egyptian scholars. The revelation of the meaning of
the hieroglyphics of Egypt is one of the most striking triumphs which inductive science has ever won.
It belongs entirely to the present century, and Young
and Champollion divide its honours between them.

They were both dead when Samuel Sharpe turned
his attention to the subject. But the effect of their
discoveries on the public mind was still fresh. They
had lifted the corner of a veil which had been closely
drawn for more than three thousand years. The
glimpses of Egypt in the Bible history, and in the
classical writers, had kept alive a general interest in
that mysterious land ; and the promise which seemed
now to be given, that its history was to be read and
its secrets brought to light, kindled the imaginations
of students. A new world seemed to be opening to
them. Every step in the progress of discovery gave
them new glimpses into the ever widening past—
fresh extensions of human history backwards into
the dawn of time. The great corridors of the
Egyptian temples led men back beyond what they
had thought to be the beginnings of civilization, to
times not only before the Flood, but before the
period at which Archbishop Usher's accepted chronology had fixed the Creation itself. It was supposed by many that the learning of the Egyptians
was all inscribed upon their monuments, that it had
been lost when the key to the hieroglyphics was
hidden, and would be revealed to the generation
that should unlock them. Samuel Sharpe did not
share these exaggerated anticipations. He said,
with truth, that nothing more than praise of the dead,
or expressions of religious hope, or words of regret
and tenderness, is to be looked for in the inscriptions
found in tombs. In temples little else than religious maxims is to be expected, and on votive
monuments nothing is usually placed but fulsome
catalogues of a great man's deeds. The papyri on

which, probably, the actual literature, the science, and
the philosophy of the ancient Egyptians were really
written, have perished.   Such treatises were not
likely to be enclosed in the mummy-cases which
have preserved such of these relics as have come
down to our times.   But though exaggerated expectations have been disappointed, it is still true that
great results have been attained.   The history of
Egypt has been spelled out ; and great and unex-
pected light has been thrown on the early history of
civilization, and on the origin of some theological
conceptions which have exerted great influence on
the world.

Dr. Young's account of his discoveries was the
starting point of Samuel Sharpe's investigations.
Mr. John Gardner Wilkinson, whose later work on the
" Manners and Customs of the Ancient Egyptians"
gained for him the honour of Knighthood, had already
published his "Materia Hieroglyphica," dating his
preface from the Pyramids ; another book, with a
dedication dated from Thebes, and a " Topographical
Survey" of Thebes.   When he had mastered these
and all the chief works on the subject, including
Champollion's, had studied Coptic, and had begun
to form a hieroglyphical vocabulary for himself,
Sharpe turned back to the rudiments of Egyptian
knowledge in the classical and Hebrew writings.   As
the basis of a careful historical investigation, he compiled his first book, "The Early History of Egypt
from the Old Testament, Herodotus, Manetho, and
the Hieroglyphical Inscriptions."   Before he ventured to publish this volume, he naturally consulted
his uncle, Samuel Rogers.   Rogers was full of encour-

agement. To his nephew's modest under-estimate of himself, he replied in the vein for which he was celebrated : " Why! surely you can do it if Wilkinson can ; his only thought is where to buy his kid gloves !" Like many of Rogers's sayings, this expression hit off the foible of an able and estimable man. Wilkinson's best friends would have recognized it with a smile. Mr. Bonomi, writing some years later, made similar fun of the same weakness. " We have got Wilkinson down here with an immense variety of waistcoats, some of them very distinguished ones too." Wilkinson, however, had done much to advance knowledge. In writing his works he had an advantage over Sharpe which Rogers overlooked. He had spent twelve years in Egypt, and had himself brought over and given to the nation many of the relics which Sharpe had been studying in the British Museum. It was, of course, quite possible that though the work of discovery must be carried on upon the spot, the task of careful comparison and laborious induction could best be undertaken by a quiet student, exercising his patient ingenuity upon the material in the quiet of home. This was Samuel Sharpe's contribution to the slowly accumulating knowledge of the Egyptian antiquities. Patient labour in transcription of the hieroglyphics, and ingenious use of knowledge already gained in adding to it by a process of induction, were his chief services to this branch of learning.

The problem he set himself to work out is thus stated in the Introduction to his Vocabulary : —" Granted a sentence in which most of the words are already known, required the meaning of others." He adds that the problem is not always capable of being set in this form, and that when it is so set, it admits only of a solution more or less exact. His method was to reject all hypotheses, and, following Dr. Young, to bring the common-sense of a man of business, and the knowledge and experience of a man of the world, to bear on a sub-ject in which traditional methods had led to no results. The inquiry entered on in this independent spirit led him to independent conclusions. Both in his Egyptological and his Biblical studies the results he arrived at were in many points opposed to those which had gained general acceptance. But in each of these fields of investigation his great advantage was that he was free from common prepossessions; that he had no foregone conclusions to support, and that there was no temptation to him to "make his judgment blind." He had the patience and the unresting energy which could follow up a slight clue as far as it would lead; and would feel its way along a blind path, making sure of every step before the next was taken. This slow and sure method has neither the interest nor the romance of the bold exercise of the divining faculty, which leaps to con-clusions without troubling to form the premises; but what it loses in attractiveness it gains in permanence and value.

He speaks of these Egyptian studies as having been his "amusement during many years," and describes how he was led to them :—

While living at Canonbury I belonged to a book-club, which met once a month to order books and circulate

them among the members. We bought Dr. Young's
" Account of Discoveries in Hieroglyphical Literature,"
and shortly afterwards Wilkinson's " Materia Hieroglyphica,"
which was then new, and with these books I was much
interested. I had been latterly working after the hours of
business at " Woodhouse's Astronomy " and making observations with one of Troughton's Circles, as well as reading
La Place's " Mécanique Céleste." I was not displeased
with my progress in mathematics, and felt my labour fully
rewarded by being able to enter on the threshold of that
great mathematician's discoveries. But in the case of
Egyptian Hieroglyphics I soon found myself in a different
position. After studying Dr. Young's discoveries and
then Mr. Wilkinson's in his " Hieroglyphical Extracts," I
verified and corrected their alphabets and vocabularies by
the help of the inscriptions in the " Materia Hieroglyphica."
I procured the folio volume of plates of hieroglyphics,
published by Dr. Young for the Egyptian Society; read
Champollion's " Précis du Système Hieroglyphique," and
Salt's " Essay on Hieroglyphics," and had the pleasure of
fancying that I knew as much as or more than my teachers,
and that I could push the knowledge of hieroglyphics
beyond the state in which the published writings of the
discoverers had left it. I studied the Coptic language in
the translation of the Bible by the help of Mr. Tattam's
" Lexicon Ægypticae Latinum," and began to form a
hieroglyphical alphabet and vocabulary for myself.

The study of the language seemed to assume a knowledge of the history of the country. I therefore turned
aside for a moment to see what historians had written on
the subject, and this was of sadly little use. They had all
followed Herodotus and Diodorus, and neglected Manetho
as useless. But the reading of the hieroglyphical names of
the kings had proved that Manetho's lists contained the
true skeleton of Theban and Egyptian history. Mr. Isaac
Cory had lately published in a very convenient form the

fragments of Manetho, together with those of Eratosthenes and other Eastern writers, and Mr. Wilkinson, at the end of his "Thebes and Egypt," had given a more correct list of the hieroglyphical names of the Egyptian kings than he had before published in his "Materia Hieroglyphica." With the help of these works I wrote my "Early History of Egypt from the Old Testament, Herodotus, Manetho, and the Hieroglyphical Inscriptions," which I published in 1836. This was my first attempt at authorship, beyond one or two papers in the *Philosophical Magazine.* The work was hastily and badly put together, without the least pretence of neatness of style. It contained the raw materials for a history, but they were not put into shape. The only part of any worth was the view of Egyptian chronology thrown into the form of a table to explain which of Manetho's dynasties reigned in succession, and which ruled over part only of the country and reigned at the same time with others. In this table I ventured to propose a much shorter view of Egyptian chronology than had been adopted by any other inquirers, and many years afterwards I applied the same mode of reasoning to the Hebrew chronology in the Book of Judges, which I thus made shorter than it is usually considered to be.

The book which its author thus unfavourably criticises is a thin quarto of 172 pages with half a dozen plates. This style was adopted on the representation of Mr. Moxon, the publisher, that a quarto of large type and ample margin was the only shape in which a scholar could put his work before the public. It was the usual form of publication in 1836. The book is more comprehensive than its title indicates. Its object, as expressed in the preface, was "to collect out of the writings of the ancients every particular relating to the History of

Egypt before the conquest of that country by the Persians." The extracts from each historian are given separately, and their value is discussed, but no attempt is made to weave them into a connected narrative. These materials for history are followed by a series of essays on the Egyptian Year, on the Physical Character of the Egyptians, on their Mythology ; on the Coptic, Ethiopic and Enchorial Languages, on the Hieroglyphics and Hieratic writing, and on the dates of the Trojan War and the Jewish Exodus. The plates contain a chart of the early history of Egypt on the plan of Dr. Priestley's chart ; a Map of Egypt, a copy of the Stone discovered at Abydos by Mr. W. J. Bankes, containing the names of Kings ; a plate of the names of the Kings of Thebes ; a collection of hieroglyphics, with explanations enabling the student to read the preceding names ; and a copy of part of the astronomical sculpture from the Memnonium, with the enchorial alphabet and some enchorial writing. This volume was part of the basis on which his future History was built. Its chief value to its author was in giving him an introduction to Egyptian students ; who at once perceived that a very fresh and original mind had come into the field of Egyptian inquiry. With the pride of a young writer, he naturally took an early copy to Rogers, who had encouraged him to publish it. Rogers's congratulation was — " Now you will have the honour of lending money to poor authors." Sharpe's account of its reception is in the somewhat depreciatory spirit in which all his references to his own works are written. " My book deserved, and gained, but little notice. In Germany it was blamed by Ideler in a Latin quarto ; but it introduced me to Mr. Cullamore, Mr. Isaac Cory and Mr. Bonomi, and to Dr. Lepsius on his first visit to England, and before he had gained his after celebrity."

The publication of this volume led on to another work. He had completed the review of the history of Egypt in the classical writers and returned to the study of the hieroglyphics. Mr. John Williams, afterwards Secretary of the Astronomical Society, with whom he had become acquainted, had made a collection of the inscriptions in the British Museum. These he borrowed in order to increase his vocabulary, but found it needful to recopy them on a reduced scale. After some inquiries he found,—

That it gave me no more trouble to lithograph and publish a hundred copies for the use of other students than to make one copy for my own use. Accordingly in the Spring of 1837 I completed a volume of " Egyptian Inscriptions from the British Museum and other Sources." This contained sixty folio plates, rudely but carefully drawn, and was the largest body of hieroglyphical writing that had yet been published, as it contained more matter than Dr. Young's handsomer work, the " Hieroglyphics " of the Egyptian Society.

This large and laborious work indicated to other students the serious and business-like spirit in which their new ally had entered the field of Egyptian study. It was again, however, the author himself who got the chief benefit of his labour and outlay. It enabled him to accumulate the material for his next publication. While copying the inscriptions, which he did with his own hand and with much trouble and great sacrifice of time, he was carefully studying their contents and adding to his knowledge of the hieroglyphics. Every new plate added several fresh words to those he already knew, and thus amply repaid his toil. He was consequently enabled in the autumn of 1837 to publish his third work, a thin quarto of the same size and appearance as the first, entitled "Rudiments of a Vocabulary of Egyptian Hieroglyphics." It contained a thousand and fifty groups of characters, or words, and an Introduction, with an Essay on the Grammar. In the case of every word, one or more references were given to published inscriptions as proofs of the meaning assigned to it. His independence of judgment had already led to divergence from other authorities, of which he says:—

To show my opinion of the rashness with which conclusions had been formed by Champollion and some of his followers, I placed in the title-page the following quotation from Bacon's "Novum Organum":—"There are, or may be, two ways of seeking and finding truth; the one, from observation and particulars jumps to universal axioms, and from the truth of these finds out the intermediate axioms, and this is the way in use. The other, from observation and particulars, raises axioms by a continued and gradual ascent till at last it arrives at universal axioms, and this is the true way, but it has not yet been tried." I distrusted Champollion's results too much even to quote them, but I did not feel bold enough to write against those from whom I differed. As for their pedantic and misleading practice of writing in Coptic letters words of their own creation, I simply remarked that all words which I printed in the Coptic character might be found in Mr. Tattam's "Lexicon." This practice of inventing

Coptic words Dr. Lepsius afterwards gave up on my persuasion.

This Vocabulary of Hieroglyphics, like his two former books, was addressed to scholars and students rather than to the public. There was nothing popular in its form, style, subject or treatment. It resulted in the further establishment of a recognised position for its author among Egyptian scholars. The influence he was able to exert on Dr. Lepsius is an illustration of the recognition his labours gained for him among the small group of men who understood the matters with which he dealt. It is usually among his own craft that an artist or a man of letters first makes his reputation. It is they who tell the outer world what he is and at what value it must estimate his work. The world is not always guided by the opinion of experts ; and sometimes a man of genius is first recognised outside the profession he adorns. But as a rule a reputation, like charity, begins, as it were, at home. Mr. Sharpe's reputation among Egyptian scholars was that of an independent student and thinker. Many of his conclusions differed from those of other students and writers. They respected his accuracy and admired his courage and independence, but did not follow him to his results. " I am a heretic in everything," he used to say, "even among Unitarians." But many of his boldest emendations in the translation of the New Testament have been practically adopted in the Revised Version, and both in Hebrew History and in the interpretation of the Egyptian monuments he now occupies a middle and probably

safe position between extreme scepticism and un-
reasoning trust.

His next work, "Egypt under the Ptolemies," was
an immense advance in point of form and execution
upon the first three.   It was published in the same
quarto shape, with large type and ample margin,
but instead of a series of essays, as the first quarto
had been, this was a continuous narrative.   In an
Introduction he briefly sketches the early history in
an essay which practically epitomises the contents
of his first work, "The Early History of Egypt;"
and then writes the History of Egypt from the
accession of Ptolemy Soter to the death of Cleopatra.   He says :—

I had intended to stop when Egypt ceased to be
governed by native sovereigns, when it became a Greek
kingdom under Alexander's successors.   But I found that
the ancient architecture and language and civilization by
no means stopped when the newer civilization was introduced, and that by not carrying on my inquiries into
modern times I had overlooked much which threw light
upon antiquity.   I therefore wrote the "History of Egypt
under the Ptolemies," making use in the first instance of
the references in Gillies' "History of Alexander's Successors," in the ancient Universal History, and in Brucker's
"History of Philosophy," adding thereto whatever an
industrious search enabled me to discover in the Greek
and Latin authors.   By this time I had gained some
experience in writing and enlarged my views of authorship.
I wished to be an historian rather than an antiquary ; I
ventured upon moral reflections, and thought of wording
my sentences so that they might be listened to with
pleasure when read aloud.   I read every part of it as it
was written to my dear wife and children.   This wholesome

practice I never afterwards omitted, and I always made use of their good taste and judgment to warn me against the use of hard words, as well as to tell me whether my sentences could be readily understood, and whether they conveyed the meaning that I wished them to bear. I published my " Egypt under the Ptolemies " in the autumn of 1838.

The sale of these Egyptian publications was by no means encouraging. Though they were always spoken of with respect when mentioned either by my friends or the critics, yet they received very little notice. They taught me, however, that I could write what was safe from blame and ridicule even if it received no praise. I knew that sooner or later they would get read by those engaged in the same studies, if not by the public, and in the meantime I turned aside to another task.

This other task was the revision of the English translation of the New Testament in accordance with Griesbach's text. He appears to have turned to this work, if not in the temporary discouragement the above sentences indicate, at least in the resolve to pause till those engaged in the same studies had read his books. He had not long to wait for this recognition, though it was not surprising that his books were not widely read or that the sale was small. The three volumes were addressed rather to students than to the reading public ; moreover, they were quartos, and the day of the quarto was already gone. He had, however, become known more widely than he imagined. The industry, the careful regard for accuracy, and the complete independence of thought he had exhibited, gradually gained the respect of students, and through them of the outside world. There is a glimpse of him in the year in which his "Egypt under the Ptolemies" was published in Mr. Henry Crabb Robinson's Diary. Crabb Robinson writes :*—"At Peter Martineau's I had a very agreeable chat with Samuel Sharpe. One must respect a banker who can devote himself after banking hours to the study of Egyptian hieroglyphics, although he is capable of saying that 'every one of Bacon's Essays shows him to be a knave.' Had he said that the Essays show him to be merely a man of intellect, in which neither love, admiration nor other passion is visible, I could not have disputed his assertion." Crabb Robinson was not an Egyptian student, and his expression of respect for Sharpe's devotion to the subject shows the impression he had already made on men of general information and culture. The sweeping criticism of Bacon was, as Crabb Robinson himself found when he knew Samuel Sharpe better, a strong expression of his extreme detestation of everything which he thought to be even tinged with insincerity or dishonesty. Crabb Robinson seems to have felt that the fling at Sharpe was altogether undeserved, for seventeen years later he added to this entry :— "Remark, written in 1855. He is now one of the friends in whose company I have the greatest pleasure, though I still think him a man in whom the critical faculty prevails too much. I once expressed my opinion of him to himself in a way I am pleased with : 'Sharpe,' I said, 'if every one in the world were like you, nothing would be done ; if no one were like you, nothing would be *well* done !'"

* "Diary, Reminiscences and Correspondence of Henry Crabb Robinson," edited by Dr. Sadler, vol. iii. p. 146.

As a parallelism has already been shown in one or two matters between Mr. Sharpe and Mr. Grote, this criticism of the former may be compared with an entry made in Mr. Cobden's journal in 1837, respecting the latter:—"He is a mild and philosophical man," writes Cobden of Grote, "possessing the highest order of moral and intellectual endowments, but wanting something which, for need of a better phrase, I shall call *devil*. He is too abstract in his tone of reasoning, and does not aim to convince others by any proof excepting that of ratiocination."* This last expression exactly describes Samuel Sharpe ; though he had a little of the something which Cobden thought to be wanting in Grote. It came out, however, in his vivacious conversation, in such expressions as that which offended Crabb Robinson, and did not sufficiently appear in his earlier writings.

* Morley's " Life of Cobden," vol. i. p. 137.

# CHAPTER V.

## SOCIAL, DOMESTIC, AND RELIGIOUS RELATIONS.

IT was fortunate for the progress of free Biblical study in England that this pause in Samuel Sharpe's Egyptian studies took place. He could not wait in idleness till his writings were appreciated. " I was born to work," he would say, as he sat down to some new task ; and in work he found his recreation all his life. There are surely but few men who would have chosen such an undertaking as retranslating the New Testament to fill up an interlude in the laborious investigation of the Egyptian hieroglyphics. The choice was characteristic of Samuel Sharpe. The work seemed waiting to be done, and he came forward to do it. In common with all Unitarians and nearly all scholars, he lamented the obvious defects both of the Authorized Version and of the Received Text, of which it was a translation ; and it seemed to him almost a matter of course, that as he now had leisure he should make a better version himself. The precedents were not encouraging. Mr. Belsham's " Improved Version " had been received by the ignorant as an attempt to re-write the New Testament in an unorthodox sense, and scholars who had more zeal for orthodoxy than care for truth or charity, lent their sanction to this misrepresentation.

Among Unitarians, however, it met with the respect
due to the work of a scholar. In a few passages it
was perhaps open to the charge that it was tinged
with Mr. Belsham's opinions: but the Authorized
Version, with equal or greater bias, gives the orthodoxy of king James and his translators the benefit
in every doubtful passage.

Griesbach's edition of the Greek text did much to
raise a desire among scholars for a better representation in the English language of what the Evangelists and Apostles really wrote ; and so widely was
this desire spread among Nonconformists, that a few
years after Mr. Sharpe's "New Testament Translated from Griesbach's Text" appeared, a volume
giving the Authorized Version with more than twenty
thousand emendations, was widely circulated among
orthodox ministers and Sunday school teachers.
The compilation had been made by Dr. Conquest, a
London physician, who had diligently and carefully
collected the improved readings of various scholars,
and who based on his want of knowledge of the
original texts a claim of impartiality. The book was
an *omnium gatherum*, with no claim to scholarly
accuracy ; but it did a useful work in removing much
ignorance. The popular wish for an amended version
to which Dr. Conquest appealed, and which he did
much to confirm, had not been manifested, and had
scarcely begun to be felt when Samuel Sharpe turned
to the translation of Griesbach's text. He therefore
had the honour of doing something towards creating
the interest to which his work appealed, and which,
nearly forty years later, was to ensure the very general
acceptance and the extensive use of the Revised

Version of 1881.  He gives his reasons for undertaking it—

I had long been an admirer of Griesbach's labours on
the New Testament, and I determined to publish a new
version corrected according to his text.  I was dissatisfied
with Wakefield's translation as too loose and free, and with
the Improved Version* as partial to the translator's
own opinions.  Moreover, it was clear that the scholars of
Oxford and Cambridge, who were best qualified for the
task by their learning, never meant to undertake it.  Accordingly, I spent my leisure of the year 1839 in completing a translation of the New Testament, and I published
it in the spring of 1840.  I was not without some fears as
to how it would be received.  I should have been chiefly
pained by the charge of rashness and presumption.  I
should also have been very sorry to have been blamed for
any sectarian bias.  But the translation escaped both of
these charges.  It was reviewed both by the orthodox and
the unorthodox, who freely pointed out its faults, but cast
no blame on the translator for venturing on the task.  One
of the orthodox reviewers said that as this volume was not
meant to be read in churches, I might as well have corrected all the faults in the Authorized Version ; while one
of the unorthodox reviewers, judging from the first chapter
of the Epistle to the Hebrews, declared that its translator,
who was unknown to him, was not a Unitarian.

Shortly before I published my New Testament, Mr.
Edgar Taylor, my brother William's partner, died ; and I
then learned that he also had been busy upon the same
employment.  He had finished more than three-quarters

---

* Mr. Belsham's.  It was published anonymously by a
" Society for Promoting Christian Knowledge and the Practice
of Virtue, by the distribution of Books."  Its full title was,
" The New Testament in an Improved Version, upon the basis
of Archbishop Newcome's New Translation ; with a Corrected
Text and Notes Critical and Explanatory."

of his translation and had printed as far as he had written. He had left a wish that his book should be finished by a layman, and Dr. Hutton advised his widow to ask me to complete it. But I declined the task, and gave as a reason that I was publishing a translation of my own. She then engaged the Rev. William Hincks to complete her late husband's translation, and the two were published about the same time. Mr. Taylor's translation was more approved of by the Unitarian ministers than mine, and therefore at the time by the Unitarians. The aim of the two was not quite the same. Mine was meant to be more literal, to show peculiarities and difficulties rather than to conceal them, and to express what would be understood by the early disciples rather than by modern readers. His was less harsh in its change of words, though we both kept to the Authorized Version as far as we thought the sense allowed. These two translations quite threw into the background among Unitarian readers Mr. Belsham's "Improved Version."

My translation of the New Testament was certainly a rather hasty publication; but I determined that the next edition of it should be better. I compared it with Mr. Taylor's. I re-examined all the texts criticised by the reviewers. I listened to the remarks of my friends among the Unitarian Ministers, and I continued to turn over such works on Biblical criticism as came in my way. My best critic was certainly Mr. Thomas Glashan, a surgeon, who then lived in the neighbourhood of Aberdeen. He was wholly unknown to me, and wrote me a letter modestly expressing his doubts about six texts, in which he thought I was mistaken. I was really startled by the soundness and accuracy of his judgment. He had mentioned the six chief faults in the book; faults certainly greater than any that had been pointed out by the reviewers. In answer I thanked him warmly for his advice, and begged that he would favour me with any further remarks. I profited much by a series of letters from him on Biblical Criticism, which extended over some years.

The work thus begun was never afterwards dropped. The first edition of " The New Testament Translated from Griesbach's Text " was published in the spring of 1840; but it was no sooner issued than he began further revisions. This was his custom with all his books ; they were read and re-read, and at every reading corrections and additions were made. Each book was prepared for the issue of a second edition whenever the publisher asked for it. The result of the publication of the New Testament was that henceforth he had two studies instead of one. He returned to the study of hieroglyphics as soon as this work was through the press, but from this time forward Egypt occupied only a share, and, after a while, a decreasing share of his attention, which for some years was divided between the antiquities of the Nile valley and Biblical history and criticism. The world soon knew him as the historian of Egypt; in his old age he thought of himself chiefly as the translator of the Bible. He says :—

I returned to the hieroglyphical inscriptions, chiefly with a view to the enlargement of my vocabulary. I began by tracing part of the sarcophagus of Oimenepthah I. in Sir John Soane's Museum, which is one of the most beautiful and valuable of the Egyptian monuments. I also borrowed one or two sculptured objects from friends. Some of these plates, when published, reached the hands of Mr. A. C. Harris, a wealthy merchant of Alexandria, who, generously and unasked, sent me over as a present a tin box containing a large collection of paper casts from tablets belonging to Signor D'Athanasi. With the help of these I published, in December, 1840, a second volume of Egyptian Inscriptions, containing sixty more lithographed plates. Every plate, as I drew it on the transfer paper, added a few more words to my vocabulary, which was now growing to twice the size of my published volume.

The tracing of these hieroglyphical inscriptions occupied him for seven months, and was a laborious though, on the whole, an agreeable task. He had efficient help from his daughters, and especially from his eldest daughter. Many of the plates are hers and bear her name. He records in his diary on the 17th of November, 1840, that he had on that day finished the last plate, and says that he might miss the work if he had not the Vocabulary waiting for him. "I am glad that it is done," he writes, "and feel myself too old, and my time too valuable ever again to begin a work of mere manual labour." He was less than fifty-two years old when this entry was made, and there were thirty years of hard work before him. The volume was a most useful one, and is still valuable to Egyptian students. He says of it with truth :—

I can look back on it with some pride. The French and Tuscan Governments have published large and beautiful volumes of plates of Egyptian antiquities, Wilkinson and Burton, the travellers, have also published plates of hiero-glypics ; the Egyptian Society, under Dr. Young, published a volume of hieroglyphics. All these have beauty and value far above mine, but mine is by far the largest collection of hiero-glyphical inscriptions ever yet published ; and as, in a trading point of view, the money and labour are wholly wasted it is not likely soon to be passed.

The trading point of view was not his, and he was

as far as possible from thinking that the money and labour were wasted. Such books could never be produced for profit. They are for the few, and it is fortunate for that few that men can be found to expend money and labour upon them. They were produced in this instance out of pure love of knowledge, and the satisfaction of promoting a cherished and delightful study was its own abundant reward.

There is another entry about the same volume on the 8th of December, 1840 :—

I to-day received from the printer the last number of my Egyptian Inscriptions. I had pleasure in drawing them and pleasure in finishing my task. I print 102 copies, give away fifteen to my friends, the public libraries seize five, to which, however, they are quite welcome, and the rest are for sale, but I put my expectations too low to be much disappointed. My publications are wholly an expense. But I have my satisfaction in it. It is not more expensive than keeping a saddle-horse.

This last remark indicates the relation which at this period of his life his literary work bore to his other activities. It was his recreation. What other men would have spent on keeping a saddle-horse or in costly journeys in the autumn holiday, or in other forms of pleasure, he expended in the advancement of learning. Farther on it will be seen how large a part of his income in later years was devoted in a different form, but in the same spirit, to this noble purpose.

The Diary in which the above entries were made begins at the end of September, 1840, and ends in 1848, with occasional entries thirty years later. It gives many glimpses of his home, of his friends, of various calls on his literary industry, and of the feelings with which he regarded his work. Here are glimpses of two well-known men. On October 7, 1840, he writes :—

Charles Fellows called on me last week with his observations in Asia Minor for fixing the latitude and longitude of several cities which he has been the first person to visit. I have spent six or eight hours already in reducing them, and at last have the pain of telling him that they are not exact enough for the longitude. He has been very successful and has brought home some beautiful drawings and inscriptions. I strongly urged him to publish in his journal a list of all his coins, stating in what places they were found. Alfred Stothard [the son of the painter] called on the same evening with his medal of Dr. Lee. It is a good likeness and I bought it of him, out of regard for himself and the doctor.

A few days later he says :—

I called on Charles Fellows, who is getting his journal ready for the press. He is anxious to prove his Lycian inscriptions and sculptures older than the conquest of that country by the Greeks, B.C. 560. But the sculptures, though joined with Lycian inscriptions and mythology, are of Greek art, not very old, the Lycian characters are mostly borrowed from the Greek, and this evidence from style of art is conclusive against everything. His monuments must have been made about B.C. 500.

The evidence is perhaps not quite conclusive, since Greek civilization was gradually making its way in Asia Minor, before the Macedonian conquest. These Lycian Inscriptions, with others copied by the Rev. E. T. Daniell, Mr. Edward Forbes, and Lieutenant Spratt were afterwards the subject of careful investigation by Daniel Sharpe, who communicated the results of his acute inquiries to the Philological Society in some very striking papers, which were

published in its Proceedings. Mr. Fellows's "Journal
of a Second Tour in Asia Minor" was published,
"with an Appendix on the Ancient Lycian Language
by Mr. D. Sharpe." Two of the inscriptions were
bi-lingual, in Greek and Lycian, and the clue thus
given enabled him to determine the Lycian alphabet
and to read the inscriptions on the Lycian coins. In
an entry in his diary Samuel Sharpe expresses his
satisfaction that his brother Daniel was busying himself with these inscriptions, and adds, " I think it a
better subject than his Geology. A man should
understand something of the sciences as well as of
letters, but when he chooses one for his more particular path, I would recommend some branch of
literature. The study of antiquities, though not the
highest branch, embraces enough of language and
history to make it a pursuit highly liberalizing to
the mind." Geology was, nevertheless, the study in
which Daniel Sharpe afterwards gained distinction.

In his second visit to Lycia, Sir Charles Fellows
took out with him a young artist to act as draughtsman. This was Mr. George Scharf, who was then
beginning to be known, and whose careful drawings
of sculptures and inscriptions added much to the
value of the volume on Lycia, which he further
adorned with his exquisite illustrations. Mr. Scharf
soon became known as an art critic and the illus-
trator of many valuable works. He was director of
the Gallery of Old Masters at the Manchester
Exhibition in 1857; and is now Curator of the
National Portrait Gallery at South Kensington. In
his early days Mr. Scharf was an occasional visitor
at Highbury Place.

In this year, 1840, there is an account in the Diary of the spending of the summer holiday. These holidays were always short, usually three weeks late in the summer, or in the early autumn. Before his marriage he had visited Scotland, Wales, and the Rhine, and had been twice to Paris, but after his marriage he never again went abroad. The three weeks' holiday in 1840 was spent at Leamington, " in the neighbourhood," he says, "of our friends, the Fields." The Fields were busy, for it was September, and their autumn work had begun. The Rev. William Field, of Leam, whose son, Edwin, had married Mary Sharpe, was then preaching two sermons every Sunday at Warwick, and another at Kenilworth, where, out of pure zeal for doing good, he was keeping the little spark of an old Liberal congregation alive and glowing. He was seventy-four, but his natural force was not much abated. We get a glimpse of him in the Diary as giving an hour's lesson in geography or history every morning to a class in the girls' school, kept by his wife and two daughters, superintending the preparation of one son for matriculation in the University of London, and helping another in his undergraduate studies. The family of the Fields had from the old days at Stoke Newington exerted a strong influence for good upon the family of the Sharpes. Mrs. Field was worthy of her husband. She was a woman of great energy and capacity, and the fine characteristics of the father and mother came out again in their children. The great Hall of the Royal Courts of Justice contains a marble statue, erected by subscription as a permanent memorial of their eldest son, the brother-in-

law of Samuel Sharpe. In presiding over the influential meeting of eminent lawyers and artists at
which this memorial was resolved upon, Lord
Selborne said that no man had more to do in
bringing the scheme for the erection of the new
Courts of Justice to a successful issue than Mr. Edwin
Field. " In everything that was done," said Lord
Selborne, " he was the most active and useful man
of all, perhaps, who were engaged in doing it."

Mr. Edwin Field was not at Leam when the
Sharpes were at Leamington during this holiday.
·The Fields introduced them to the Misses Lawrence
—four ladies who had some time since retired from
the school to which Mrs. Field and her daughters
succeeded. Mrs. Tagart, wife of the Rev. Edward
Tagart, who had been one of their pupils, had just
copied out for Miss Lawrence the family tree of the
Rev. Philip Henry, of whose ancestral relation to the
Sharpes, through the Rogerses, an account has
already been given. Samuel Sharpe assisted Miss
Sara Lawrence in turning the genealogical tree into
a volume, tracing as far as possible all the descendants
of the ejected minister. Miss Lawrence carried out
the inquiry, with his help, with great patience and
minuteness, and after four years was able to issue a
volume, which is, perhaps, one of the most striking
records of family growth ever put together. It contains two hundred and ten surnames, many of them
belonging to the most influential and respected of
middle-class families ; and curiously shows one mode
in which the moral influence of the ejected clergy has
spread itself through the healthiest portion of English society. Sharpe writes about his share in the

work that he hoped he "should lead the persons therein mentioned to aim after what is good. It could hardly feed vanity to tell them they were descended from a clergyman who was turned out of his living ; but it might perhaps remind them of the true dignity of moral independence." There is nothing on which a family has more reason to congratulate itself than on a Puritan ancestry. It is, in almost equal degrees, a guarantee of physical energy, of intellectual vigour and of moral health.

The Fields, as has been already said, got their Puritan vigour through their descent from the Lord Protector of the Commonwealth. Their grandmother was the great granddaughter of Henry Cromwell, the son of the Protector, who died before his illustrious father. The Miss Lawrences, like the Sharpes, were descended from the Henrys. Mr. Sharpe and his wife had great satisfaction in making the acquaintance of this branch of the family. Of his general doings during this Leamington holiday he writes :—" My employments were taking short walks with my dear wife and children, and helping her with the lessons. For myself I only drew two plates for my Egyptian Inscriptions. We made no pilgrimage to the birthplace of Shakespeare, nor went to Dr. Parr's vicarage of Hatton, nor examined the battle field of Edge Hill." His short periods of country recreation were all of this character. They were opportunities of spending all the day with his family, father and mother entering into the amusements of the children, and enjoying their play. They were essentially family holidays.

The family at this time consisted of five children,

three daughters and two sons, Emily twelve, Matilda ten, and Mary seven years old, Frederick nearly six, and Albert not quite two years. There are glimpses in the Diary of the home relations between this busy father and his children. He records their birthdays as they come round, and tells of the little presents they make to each other. When he enters the sending to the printers of the last proof of " Egypt under the Romans," he adds, " I date my preface on Albert's birthday." On the 12th of November, 1840, he writes, " Frederick's birthday. He is six years old, each of his sisters has a present for him, Emily's was given him by letter from Hastings. Mamma's was a wheelbarrow." Emily's visit to Hastings to be with her Aunt Catharine is duly recorded, with a wish that she may benefit " by being in such good hands, and away from our control for a short time." There is a congratulatory note on her return five weeks later. The next day is her birthday. She is twelve years old, and her father and mother have agreed " that punishments ought now to cease, we should treat her as much as possible as an equal, if there is disobedience she will no doubt be brought round by kind words when the time is a little gone by." A Sunday school had then just been established by his influence and advice at Newington Green, and in the next year the two eldest girls, one under thirteen, the other under eleven, were to attend as teachers. " My two girls," he writes on the 26th September, 1841, "attended to teach at the Sunday school. Emily never misses. Matilda hardly goes without being urged. But I have discovered what will make her more regular ;

it is the pleasure of rewarding her pupils with a cake." On his birthday, the 8th of March, he records the little presents given him by the children, and the pleasant incidents that accompany the gifts. These small domestic details are sufficient glimpses of the interior of the home. They show that the man of many pursuits was by no means withdrawn by his studies from sympathy with his children.

On returning from the visit to Leamington he found on his table the proof-sheet of the *Christian Teacher*, which had been sent to him by Mr. Kinder, containing a review—probably the first—of his New Testament. "We are all so well pleased with ourselves," he writes, "that at the first reading I was troubled with the criticisms, but on an after-reading I made up my mind that it was a favourable review, and that I ought to be well pleased with its praises." On a later day he says, "The late Mr. Edgar Taylor's translation of Griesbach is now published under the superintendence of the Rev. Mr. Hincks. I have no wish to hear that mine is the best of the two, and should, of course, be pained to have it thought the worst ; but the critics will compare them, and we are put in rivalry against our will."

The names of other friends who visited him, or whom he visited at this period, appear in the Diary. One of the entries illustrates the kind of work which was being done at the Harp Alley School.

1840. October 16th. John Sinnot breakfasted with us this morning. He came to take leave and to return my pocket-sextant, which, however, I told him to keep while it was useful. When I first knew him he was an orphan at the Harp Alley Charity School. He had already been to sea as a boy without

wages, before the mast, and on coming into Portsmouth, the captain, who was pleased with him, gave him a shilling. It was the
first he had ever had, and on landing he bought a spelling-
book with it. His elder brother had told him he would never
get on without learning. After being a year or two at school,
my sister got him a clerk's place to keep a barrister's chambers,
but he would go to sea again. Whenever he was on shore for
a week, he took lessons in navigation. I first taught him to
take a lunar observation; that was the height of his ambition
in the way of learning. He soon got made a mate, and could
always teach any captain he was under. And this poor orphan,
by his own good conduct, determined application, and right-
minded ambition is now, at the age of about six-and-twenty,
captain of a vessel trading between New Brunswick and Liverpool, of 700 tons burden. Next to himself, he is indebted to
my sister. [Catharine.]

Other entries record his visits to the house of his
uncle, Samuel Rogers. Rogers was now in his
seventy-seventh year, and showed some signs of
failing memory. His Tuesday breakfast-parties were
still continued, though his house in St. James's Place
was no longer filled, as it had been in years gone by,
with all the chief men in art, literature, and politics.
The crowd had passed, but distinguished visitors
from all parts of the world still called to see
the great wit and man of taste, and chosen friends
gathered round his table. Sharpe's visits to his
uncle had been more frequent since he had become
known as a writer and a scholar, and for a long
time he was one of the company at the Tuesday
breakfasts. Rogers had fixed on Tuesday to suit
his nephew's convenience, and the nephew pleased
his uncle by quoting the Preacher against his literary
and social breakfasts—honouring them with magnificent blame—"Woe to thee, O Land, when thy

princes eat in the morning." He met at these breakfasts Hallam, Milman, Empson, then editor of the
*Edinburgh Review,* Luttrel—of whom Rogers' said
that none of the talkers he met in London society
could slide in a brilliant thing with such readiness
as he—R. Monckton Milnes, now Lord Houghton,
Kinglake, author of Eöthen, Mrs. Austin, the translator of Ranke's " History of the Popes," and her
daughter, afterwards Lady Duff Gordon, Lord Glenelg, Crabb Robinson, Gleig, Sir J. Gardner Wilkinson,
Panizzi, and many others. Crabb Robinson was the
greatest talker of the group. When he was late,
Rogers would call merrily to his guests, " If you
have anything to say, say it now, for Crabb Robinson
is coming." In the conversation at these Tuesday
breakfasts, where, in addition to one or two members of his family—often one or two of his young
nieces—there were about half-a-dozen well-selected
guests, there must have been ample material for
interesting recollections. At this period, and for
years to come, Rogers was still himself. Moore, in
his Diary, wrote of him, during a visit to Lord Lans-
downe at Bowood in December, 1841—" Rogers
stayed more than a week. Still fresh in all his faculties, and improved wonderfully in the only point
where he was deficient—temper. He now gives the
natural sweetness of his disposition fair play." It is
this latter characteristic on which his nephew in his
few memoranda of his visits chiefly dwells. These
are the entries :—

November 8, 1840. I dined at my uncle Sam's.
Besides the family there was Mr. Maltby and Mr. Uwins,
the painter. The latter agreed with me in thinking that

A. Stothard had made the skull too small in his medal of Dr. Lee.

November 29.   I breakfasted in St. James's Place. My uncle quoted a remark of Henderson's that " Akenside stalked along like one of his own Alexandrines set on end." He was a tall, stiff man.   Also, somebody's remark that " Memory is a great trust, and it is not everybody who can be trusted with it."   But I lost my morning.   R. M. Milnes was there.   He is a poet, and has ability ; but it is hidden in his wish to be a fine gentleman.   He is young, and may perhaps outgrow it.   My uncle gave me, "in solemn trust," as he said, a MS. in his own handwriting, a form of family prayer which, when a young man, he used to read every evening in his father's family.   It was written by Dr. Price.

December 1.   Dined at St. James's Place to look over old papers and other family records.   My uncle and aunt were a good deal affected.   On looking at the Births and Deaths in his father's family Bible, he said that any merit in his style arose from his reading the Bible and keeping to its Saxon idiom.   Speaking of children's marriages he quoted Mrs. Barbauld, as saying that the world would be better if the old meddled less in the affairs of the young. He thought Macaulay unfair in his review of Bacon's character for not giving the whole of Dryden's tribute to his virtue as well as his greatness.   Somebody had asked him the week before for his autograph, and had very much pleased him by the choice of the lines, which he wished copied out.   " The choice hit him between wind and water."   It was the note to " Italy " on Petrarch's Arqua in praise of the habit of looking for beauties and over-looking faults.   He used to say that nobody could give pain in an anonymous review without being the worse man for having done it.   Speaking of Wordsworth's poetry in terms of but moderate praise, he said that, " at any rate, Wordsworth never wrote to give pain nor against the cause of goodness," which he thought the greatest of all faults in a writer; and he agreed with me that Sterne was a great instance of how the greatest talents go unrewarded by fame if they offend against virtue. He said he never, when he could help it, missed seeing the sunset, and regretted that by being in bed we lost the sunrise. He often felt inclined to stop the people in the streets to show them a glorious sky. Looking at such wonders of Nature he thought should be cultivated as a habit.

¯ December 4. My uncle Sam called in Clement's Lane. He quoted my father as saying that a man who was clever at getting rich was generally good for little else, and mentioned Mr. Harman's saying to him, " I am sorry R. Sharp [Conversation Sharp] died so rich." He had left £200,000—"a very pretty capital," he remarked, " to begin the next world with." On Boycott's saying he did not wish to live long, my uncle replied that if every day he contrived to make somebody happier or better, he would not wish to limit his days.

February 22, 1842. I breakfasted with my uncle Sam, and we walked to look at Milton's house, No. 19, York Street, Queen Square, Westminster. Jeremy Bentham, whose garden backed upon it, had put up a stone against the back to preserve the memory of it. He brought me home in his carriage with a present of Matthew Henry's Bible, which had been Daniel Radford's copy.

The aunt whom he speaks of meeting at his uncle's house was Sarah Rogers, who was a little younger than his uncle and a little older than his mother. Like her brother, she gathered together at her home in Hanover Terrace, Regent's Park, persons who were eminent in art and literature. At this period her nephew and his wife met at her dinner-parties, among other eminent persons, Tom Moore, Turner, the painter, Dr. Burgon, now Dean of Chichester, Dr. Skey, and Mr. Gruner, then a well-known engraver, who designed the decorations of the Queen's palaces, was entrusted by the Queen with Prince Albert's plans for the Mausoleum at Frogmore, and was afterwards Director of the Museum at Dresden. There are no records in the Diary of these visits ; and it is unfortunate that those above quoted are all that the Diary contains respecting his visits to his uncle during the years from 1840 to 1844. Others occur in later years, and will come in at their appropriate place.

There are occasional references to other friends. Mr. William Rayner Wood calls after passing his Matriculation Examination at the new University of London ; and Samuel Sharpe urges that a junior school should be established in connection with Manchester New College, which, at that time, there was some intention of doing. Henry Crabb Robinson comes to tea and talks of the ill-treatment of Thomas Clarkson by the sons of Wilberforce. Next morning Robinson takes his host to University College, and gives him a copy of the Charter, "which I must study," writes Mr. Sharpe, "now that I am a proprietor." University College little knew that the greatest benefactor to its school had that morning been entertained, like Abraham's angels in the legend, unawares. Another day a call on Dr. Lee is recorded. It was a visit of thanks "for his complimentary mention of me in his address to the Numismatic Society." Dr. Rénouard was there— a man of great learning, who "knows what everybody has written about, and what is doing in each

subject, but his unceasing talk is unbearable." Dr.
Lee is very appropriately described as a man
"whose good nature is seen in everything he does,
though it is not always accompanied with judgment."
On the 11th December, 1840, "spent the evening at
Mr. Warren's. Dr. Hutton was the only person
present who agreed with me in blaming the war
in Syria and China. Lord Palmerston's success
makes everybody overlook his faults. Mr. Madge
was very warlike." Sharpe had been opposed to this
war all through. A month earlier he had entered in
his Diary some warm praises of Louis Philippe for
his speech, telling the Chambers he was doing all he
could to preserve peace, and asking for their help in
his endeavours. "His single word, if he had been
guided by Thiers, would have deluged Europe with
blood, and stopped the march of civilization for half
a century." A paper for the Numismatic Society, on
the return of the Phœnix, or end of the cycle, on the
coins of Antoninus, is recorded as an effort "to keep
up my character as one of the contributors." A
fortnight later "a good paper on Charles the Second's
coins," is recorded, with the addition that "Dr. Lee
kindly lent Dan the Zendavesta for his Lycian
inquiries," and that "S. Stothard is engraving a medal
of Ackerman." But a month later the entry occurs,
"I wasted an evening at the Numismatic Society.
The antiquarians are such a small minority that
foreign subjects are introduced."

These entries by no means exhaust the record of
his activities. There were discussions at the Islington Institution, in which he took part for the sake of
the younger men, and remembering how valuable such

meetings had been to him in earlier days. At one of these meetings the mythology of the ancients was under discussion, and he reminded the audience that the old gods were made in different ways, sometimes by the deification of conquerors and lawgivers, sometimes by personifying attributes. He says of this speech, that "the orthodoxy of some was rather shocked, perhaps with reason, for the deifying of Jesus and the personifying of God's Spirit are much the same." In another entry he records, that "Hennell, and some other followers of Strauss, who do not believe in the miracles, have opened a chapel," and expresses his satisfaction that "they keep the name of Christians, for then they will cling to the practical doctrines." He adds, "I quite agree with Locke in thinking that the miracles are the difficulty rather than the proof of Christianity. We all find the proof in the Divine truth of the morality, which we recognize by our own moral sense." Here is a further glimpse of his religious views :—

*October* 20, 1840.—I met the "Theological party" of the Unitarian Ministers, at the house of the Rev. Thomas Cromwell. The subject of discussion was "How far may our Lord have been influenced by the mistaken opinions of his age." All agreed that he was so in the case of the demoniacs, some added, in attributing disease to sin, and some added, in the belief in a devil. But these two cases may be rather in his phraseology than in his opinions. Some added, in the prophecies which he thought pointed to himself; but here he is not so bold as the writers of the New Testament. I thought, in the use of the ceremony of Baptism. It was an instructive evening; Dr. Hutton, Mardon, Kenrick, and two or three others.

*October* 28.—Mr. Madge preached at Newington Green, at the opening of the chapel after the repairs. "Unitarianism," he remarked, "is the form of worship which Jesus himself taught and practised." This the orthodox would almost acknowledge, but would say that Trinitarianism is taught by the writers of the New Testament ; which is itself the word of God. We think Jesus a higher authority than the writers of the New Testament ; they think not. Madge's sermon was first rate.

*November* 25.—Mr. John Travers called and told me of the Rev. Thomas Wood's resigning his pulpit at the Brixton Unitarian Chapel. He had preached a sermon against the miracles, or at least that they were rather difficulties in our way than evidences of the truth of Christianity, which rests on the evident truth of its precepts. This is what Locke said, that its morality makes us believe the miracles, not the miracles the morality. On this some of his congregation said that he was not preaching Christianity as they approved, and he resigned. But the majority have begged him to withdraw his resignation. Our Presbyterian forefathers built their meeting houses for the worship of God, without a creed ; I am sorry to find their Unitarian descendants departing from that good practice. Brixton Chapel is for Unitarianism in the sense of Priestley and Belsham ; it is so declared in the title deeds. So when the minister was called upon to defend himself, he had to do so by quoting Priestley, not the New Testament.

The departure from the good old practice of the Presbyterian forefathers, which he thus laments, did not go far. Indeed, the whole position of their Unitarian descendants differs from that which this Brixton case indicated. The system of putting doctrinal statements in trust deeds has been left to the theological Mrs. Partingtons, who invented these parchment barriers against the tide of theological change ; and even the apparent test which is involved in affixing to places of worship the doctrinal name of Unitarian, is met with constant protest. In this matter the change has been so great, that Samuel Sharpe, who in 1840, was in advance of his contem-

poraries, was in 1880 sometimes spoken of as behind
them.  It was they that had changed.  His strong
common sense could not consent to regard the mere
statement of an obvious fact as a doctrinal limitation,
and he, therefore, insisted that Unitarian chapels
which, in the later years of his life received his
liberal contributions, should be called by their proper
name of Unitarian.  He was by no means blind to
the objections which are urged against this course.
The great principle embodied in and represented by
the group of Free Churches of which the Unitarian
body consists, is that of leaving the institutions
themselves open to the possibility of theological
change.  The individuals who compose them are
Unitarians, and are glad to confess their discipleship to the only form of Christian belief which
seems to them to be worth the attention of educated
men in this scientific age.  Their objection to call
their places of worship by the name they are themselves proud to bear, is due to a noble desire to
leave their successors free, and not to pledge preacher
or congregation to any form of doctrine whatever.
Samuel Sharpe, however, spoke of the avoidance of
the Unitarian name as an act of cowardice.  He
contended that in a place where the worship is
Christian but not Trinitarian, it is only honest and
right to let all the world know the fact.  The world
will never understand why places of Unitarian worship should not be called by the Unitarian name.
The great majority are so called ; and will continue
to be. Mr. Sharpe's definition of the words Unitarian
and Unitarianism was, that Unitarianism is the non-
Trinitarian form of Christianity, and that a Unitarian

is, historically and actually, a Christian who rejects the Trinity.  He was warmly attached to the Christian name, and though to the end of his life he retained his objection to Baptism and the Communion Service, he was an earnest disciple of apostolic Christianity; a careful student and zealous defender of the Old and New Testament ; and held in generous scorn the pretensions of those who, while still calling themselves Unitarians, disavow the discipleship to Christ and Christianity which the word implies.

# CHAPTER VI.

## HISTORICAL AND POLITICAL WRITINGS.

THE pause in the Egyptian studies was not long. The "New Testament translated from Griesbach's Text" was published in the spring of 1840; the second volume of the Egyptian Inscriptions at the end of the same year, and early in 1842 the author was again in the field with a "History of Egypt under the Romans." During the whole of these two years he had been gathering the materials for this further contribution to Egyptian History. As his search for references to more ancient historical events in the authors who wrote during the reigns of the Ptolemies, had led him to write the history of Egypt under those sovereigns, so, in reading later writers for facts about the Ptolemaic period he got the materials for a history of Egypt after the Roman Conquest. This work, he tells us, differs from the other two. He speaks of it as "the history of a province rather than of a kingdom ; the history of opinions and controversies rather than of political events." It brought him into direct contact with the Alexandrian speculations, out of which such dogmas as that of the Trinity arose. He had to describe the rise and progress of Christianity, and

he could not avoid showing how the pure stream
which flowed from Judea over the waste places of
the Roman Empire was afterwards mingled with
the turbid flood of Greek and Egyptian controversy.
The service thus done to the new Reformation
which traditional Christianity is beginning to under-
go has hardly yet been appreciated at its full value.
It is not necessarily a refutation of a dogma to
show its speculative origin ; but the doctrine of the
Trinity, and the group of false theories of which it
is the key, are not recommended for their reasonable-
ness, but are accepted by those who hold them from
some vague belief that they came from Jesus and
his apostles.   To point out their real source in
Egyptian superstition is consequently to overthrow
them utterly.   In this service to freedom and to
Christianity Samuel Sharpe has rendered important help.   He speaks of it modestly :—

I carefully pointed out the corruptions which were
introduced into Christianity from the old Egyptian superstitions, and I pointed out what I thought the errors in
orthodox opinions the more exactly to make it clear that
when I spoke with blame I meant to blame these corruptions of Christianity and not Christianity itself. As I
aimed at imitating the laborious accuracy of Gibbon, I
was most careful to avoid his habit of attacking indirectly
what he did not choose to attack openly.

Gibbon had not learned to discriminate between
Christianity as it was taught at Jerusalem and
Christianity as it appears in the authoritative and
official presentations of it which clerical organizations continue to keep before the world.   Mr

Sharpe had already made this discrimination. He took nothing from authority, but went to the original sources and made inquiry for himself. Even the Bible was to him, not an infallible oracle, but the record in a religious literature of the noblest and purest line of the unfolding revelation of God the Father and Man the Son. The only creed which he thought it before all things necessary to hold was that of charity.

Any man who starts from the assumption that any opinion is damnable, or any form of sound words is to be accepted on pain of everlasting punishment, is thereby disqualified for the study of science or the investigation of history. He is not free to follow whithersoever the facts may lead. The flaming sword of theological terror stops the way along which a fearless induction might carry him. He will be tempted to "make his judgment blind"; to pass lightly over facts which are opposed to his preconceived opinion ; and to exaggerate the importance of those which may be made to lend it support. Forty years ago all historians and scientific writers were expected to do this. Mr. Bohn's popular edition of Gibbon was edited by "An English Churchman," who replied to Gibbon himself in orthodox notes inserted at the foot of his page. The historian of Egypt has to travel over part of the ground which Gibbon trod. If he is an honest man his works may need similar annotation before orthodox believers will consider them "safe." He can scarcely avoid showing how much that passes for Christianity is a survival of Egyptian superstitions. The author of the "History of Egypt under the Romans" pointed out this clear connection, which stares at the student of Egyptology from every part of the field. With a deep reverence for the Christianity of the Gospels he was the better able to point out the first steps by which it had begun its degeneration into the Christianity of the Creeds. He could thus do what Gibbon was unable to do ; he could distinguish between the faith of the first century and that of the third and fourth, and was preserved from Gibbon's mistake of confounding the aberrations of the Church with the teachings of its Master.

The " History of Egypt under the Romans " was published in a more popular form than his previous works. It was a thin octavo with the authorities quoted in notes in the margin. After a short historical introduction, it begins with the entry of Augustus into Alexandria in the year 29 B.C., and ends with the Arab conquest of Egypt and the burning of the Library of Alexandria in 640 A.D. The author's habit of carefully emending his writings as soon as they were issued was curiously exhibited to the readers of the first edition of this work, by the printing at the end of the volume of some pages of additions which the reader is to drop in at their appropriate places in the first half of the work. The whole of this work, amended and in great part re-written, was afterwards incorporated in the " History of Egypt."

In speaking in his autobiographical sketch of the writing of this book he says :—

While writing this, my third history, I continued my attention to style. I read aloud again and again parts of our best English writers to learn their methods of forming their sentences. I wished that my writings, like theirs, should be fitted for the ear, not only for the eye. But I never ventured upon poetic flights, or figures of speech ; I only hoped to correct the dry stiffness of my own style, and to express my meaning in the manner most simple and most easy to be understood.

This account of the careful formation of his style is the more interesting because it shows his own clear perception of its chief defects. It is as transparent as a running stream, but it catches no colour from the sky. The *Edinburgh Review* expressed a wish that the gods had made him more poetical. This was probably the unrealized feeling of his readers, and the absence of the poetic flights and figures, on which he says he never ventured, unquestionably limited the popularity of his writings. But it is a defect which is intimately related to his chief worth as a historian and a critic. Nothing is more misleading in history than the glow which a lively imagination sheds over the narrative. The amusing story is one thing ; the trustworthy account may be quite another. Everybody reads a brilliant and imaginative historian, but nobody implicitly trusts him. There may be as wonderful an atmosphere in his picture of the past as in Turner's landscapes, but the imaginative reproduction of historical scenes and characters is necessarily coloured by the glowing medium through which they are seen. Absence of colour does not necessarily make a narrative more accurate ; but the deliberate choice of neutral tints takes away a temptation to exceed the limits of actual knowledge.

Sharpe's Egyptian Histories are plain, unvarnished narratives of facts and inferences. They tell all that was known at the time ; and no more. Like his other writings, they take an independent and original view of the subjects with which they deal. The reader who looks for information feels that he is in contact with a mind which never sees things in their merely conventional aspects, but applies a shrewd common sense to everything which comes before it. Sharpe approaches the study of Egyptian antiquities without any preconceived view ; without prepossessions of any kind. He is consequently not afraid to go whither the facts lead, and neither cuts short his inferences nor stretches them on the rack to make them fit some bed in which they must lie. If he is wrong it is by error of judgment, not by the warping influence of preconception or prejudice.

For two or three years after the publication of the " History of Egypt under the Romans " the literary activity of its author was scattered over various fields. He was becoming known both as an Egyptian scholar and a student of the Bible, and appeals were made to him for literary help. He had the honour of lending money to poor authors, in accordance with his uncle's anticipation ; he had also the satisfaction of writing articles for many publications which could not pay their writers. As a rule, voluntary service of this kind is inefficient service. The literary workman is as well worthy of his hire as any other labourer, and publications which cannot afford to pay their contributors never succeed, and rarely deserve success. Samuel Sharpe, however, was one of the very few men who never needed and never took any remuneration for their writings. In these days when statesmen are handsomely paid for articles in the magazines, and work done by accomplished writers is often published over the signature of men who merely lend it the sanction of their well-known names—taking the fame and leaving to the unknown writer the remuneration—unpaid literary work is going out of fashion. The payment is still sometimes spoken of as an honorarium, but the expression is almost the only remaining relic of the old feeling that a literary man must know no other motive than the love of knowledge or of fame. In this respect Sharpe belonged to the older school. In the early days of his literary activity he had no income that he did not earn—but he earned it in business and never by his pen. Everything he wrote represented a hearty interest in the subject, and his interests covered a large field. They were literary, social, political, and theological.

His family always knew of everything that had employed his pen. " All that he was busy upon, all that he had at heart," says his eldest daughter, " came out in his conversation, which was very full when he was not actually reading or writing. During the first twenty-five years of my remembrance of him his general talk was of politics, of which he conversed earnestly and even hard. During the last twenty-five years it was the politics of the Unitarian body. Of conversation upon his own studies and pursuits, that respecting science was almost before my time ; in the earlier part of the period covered by my recollections it was on Antiquities, later on it was on Biblical subjects ; but these topics were intermingled with classics and literature according to the tastes of the persons he was talking with."

In 1842 he was still in the period of predominant interest in politics. In that year the *Inquirer* newspaper was established with the object of giving the Unitarians a weekly organ which should fitly represent their scholarship, and express their Liberal views on theological and political questions. Its founder was Mr. Edward Hill, who engaged the Rev. William Hincks as editor, with a sub-editor, a writer on the money-market, and a dramatic critic. Hearing of the proposed journal, Samuel Sharpe wrote to Mr. Hincks, offering to send an occasional article on City topics. Mr. Hincks gladly accepted the proffered help, and a kind of double money article appeared in the first number, the second half of which was by Mr. Sharpe. As the money articles which now occupy so important a place in every daily paper owe their present form to a suggestion made by him to the editor of the *Morning Chronicle*, it is worth noting that this was his first article of the kind, and almost his last. It gives an interesting glimpse of the first charge of the revived income-tax. The July dividends had just been paid, and the warrants had been issued with the new levy deducted. There had been no such tax for a quarter of a century. Mr. Pitt's war income-tax of 1799 had been repealed in 1816 and Sir Robert Peel restored it in 1842 as a temporary expedient to enable him to make a beginning in his great readjustments of taxation. It was sevenpence in the pound, but in the *Inquirer* article it is noted that it was not taken off dividends under fifty shillings. The temporary expedient of 1842 has become a permanent instrument of direct taxation; and "its unmitigated injustice," of which Samuel Sharpe spoke in the third number of the *Inquirer*, remains almost unchanged. It is still levied to the same extent on earned and precarious incomes as on those which are independent of the labour of their recipients.

The *Inquirer* soon changed hands. Mr. Hill became tired of the expense before it had reached its fifth number, but Mr. Hincks did not wish it to drop, and succeeded in inducing Mr. Richard Taylor to buy it. Mr. Taylor changed its politics, making it, as Samuel Sharpe says in a history of the paper which he has written on a fly-leaf of the first volume, "decidedly Radical." "On this," he writes, " I ceased my contributions, writing nothing for Nos. 8, 9, 10, and 11." But Mr. Taylor had not been proprietor more than a fortnight when he found the weekly loss more than he was willing to bear, with only a distant prospect of profit. He determined to give it up, and the editor thereupon appealed for help in his own columns, announcing that the sale had already reached 600 copies. The appeal was responded to. A considerable number of subscriptions flowed in, which kept the paper going. Mr. Taylor continued to be the proprietor, but as Mr. Hincks had thus kept it from ruin its exclusive direction was left to him, and as it once more represented his more moderate views Sharpe renewed his connection with it, and wrote every week. After a short time Mr. Hincks paid Mr. Taylor the seventy pounds he was out of pocket by the concern, and put the printing into the hands of Mr. Richard Kinder, afterwards partner in the historical firm of Woodfall, who undertook to print it for the receipts. Mr. Hincks was proprietor, and found his remuneration for his editorial labour in the subscriptions. This arrangement was announced in the twenty-fifth number. The sale was then under 750 copies, but was increasing six or twelve each week. Mr. Hincks, however, was obliged to continue begging for it, and as it was felt to be valuable enough to deserve support, subscriptions were always forthcoming in sufficient amount to enable him to continue it. In July, 1843, when the paper was a year old, the sale had become about 900 a week.

The subsequent history of a paper which has always represented the wide liberality and the love of learning which are a characteristic of the Unitarian denomination, may be here stated on the authority of Mr. Sharpe's memorandum. Mr. Kinder became proprietor of the paper when Mr. Hincks eventually gave it up, and a subscription was raised to enable him to engage Mr. Lalor as editor, while Mr. J. R. Robinson undertook the sub-editing. Mr. Lalor was an accomplished journalist. He had been for many years editor of the *Morning Chronicle* in days when that paper held the leading position in English journalism. He had retired from this influential post on account of ill-health, and even the renewed work on this weekly newspaper proved too much for him, though he received great assistance from Mr. William Richmond, now in New Zealand, and many others. On Mr. Lalor retiring from the editorship Mr. Kinder was compelled for some time to carry

on the paper without an editor, which he did with
the assistance of Mr. Edwin Field, Mr. Macnamara
(one of the Railway Commissioners), Mr. Samuel
Sharpe, Mr. (now Sir) Edmund Hornby, and others.
He then placed the editing in the hands of Mr.
Richard Hutton (now editor and proprietor of the
*Spectator*) and the late Mr. Sandford. When they
resigned the Rev. T. L. Marshall was engaged
as editor by Mr. Kinder, the paper being then
sufficiently established to pay the editor a salary.
In 1863 Mr. Kinder sold it to Mr. Marshall,
Mr. J. R. Robinson and Mr. Whitfield, and Mr.
Robinson at once applied to it the business energy
and practical sagacity which have since given him
the foremost position among the managers of the
London daily papers. As manager of the *Daily
News* Mr. Robinson's admirable discrimination, his
large knowledge of men, and his thorough understanding of the events of the time, have given that
journal the leading position as an organ of foreign
and domestic intelligence. His connection with the
*Inquirer* led to the remodelling of the paper, to the
great increase of its usefulness as a weekly reflex
not only of the Unitarian body but of the whole
movement of theological opinion. In 1864 Mr.
Robinson parted with his share to Mr. Marshall,
and in 1876 Mr. Whitfield retired and Mr. Richard
Bartram became associated with Mr. Marshall both
in its proprietorship and management.

Though Samuel Sharpe was willing to give much
assistance to the *Inquirer* in its early days, a dislike of newspaper work caused him to discontinue
such writing for many years. His own account of

his feeling on the subject is that " though writing for a periodical publication is always attractive, as what you write is sure to be read, it is a bad employment. The writer can hardly take pains or persuade himself to do his best when he knows that what he is writing will be read with carelessness, and never looked at after the first week." This view of periodical writing has often been taken, but there is another side to the question. Anonymous journalism would be almost impossible if it were true that the thought of careless readers made writers careless. Extemporaneous writing is like extemporaneous speech. A man instinctively does his best, with his subject rather than his audience in mind. He writes best, as he speaks best, when his mind is in a glow, and quick pressure or rapid movement brings the glow he needs. Many of Mr. Sharpe's own friends thought that some of the best and liveliest things he ever wrote were among the articles he threw off week after week when in the latest years of his life he contributed to the columns of a new denominational journal.

The articles he contributed to the *Inquirer* during these two years recall many of the political controversies and social difficulties of the times, and throw an interesting light upon the political opinions of the writer. The first article is on the Government Grant for Education. The Whig Ministry had begun the grant a few years before, and it amounted to about £30,000 a year. The Ministry of Sir Robert Peel proposed to continue it, and to increase it by a grant to Hullah's music classes. The *Inquirer* article says :—

This is well as far as it goes, but it is not all that the friends of education expect ; moreover, it is beginning at the wrong end. The first thing should be to remove the present discouragements to education. . . . To begin at the beginning. Why is not the tax taken off books? or, rather, while Oxford and Cambridge print their Greek and Latin classics for the rich on untaxed paper, why is every spelling-book and reading-book for the poor to pay the paper duty? . . . . Why is not every building employed for teaching relieved from Queen's taxes and parish rates? This could give rise to no possible abuse. We do not mean only public colleges and Mechanics' Institutions ; every private schoolmaster while earning his livelihood, every village schoolmistress, is as much an instrument for educating the nation as any University, and their books and schoolrooms should be untaxed,—not for their sakes, but for the good of their scholars. Every schoolroom in the kingdom should be free from taxes ; every book, at least every school-book, should be on untaxed paper—at any rate before money is given to singing classes. Why, the very music books which Hullah's pupils hold in their hands have paid a tax. Sir Robert Peel remarked the other day that drawbacks were very objectionable. Then why not take the paper duty off the books, and the taxes off the buildings used for education, instead of giving a sum of money for its support ?

The same number of the paper contains a short article on the war in Afghanistan, speaking of it as—

One of the most unwise and unjust wars that have been lately undertaken. The Afghans are an independent tribe of mountaineers, bravely defending themselves from a wanton invasion ; and we are attacking those whom we ought to make our allies, a hardy race of men who might become our best bulwark on that side of our eastern possessions, and who would guard those mountain passes which from their distance it would be impossible for us to guard.

The repeal of the taxes on knowledge was a long way off when the above words were written, and the removal of rates on schoolhouses further still—but

I

both have been done ; while in the latest Afghan war, and in the protest against it, the writer lived to see history repeat itself, both in the war and in the disasters to which it led. Happily, he could also rejoice in the spectacle of the more enlightened conscience of the nation rising up against the unscrupulous Minister who had plunged into a wicked aggression to round off a frontier.

He was, of course, a Free Trader in 1842 ; and in an article on the approach of the Parliamentary recess he expresses the hope that Sir Robert Peel, as soon as he had got rid of his corn-growing Parliament, would "relieve his own mind and his suffering countrymen by an Order in Council admitting the bonded corn." The article concludes with the expression of a hope which was abundantly justified a few years later. Its argument was that Sir R. Peel had changed before, and might change again.

First on the Catholic question ; Sir Robert Peel repealed the Catholic disabilities after having been for years the member for Oxford University and the champion of Protestantism. Secondly, at the beginning of this Session, after having allowed his friends up to the last minute to promise that there should be no change he came down upon them with an improvement certainly in the Corn Laws, and with the admission of foreign cattle. After these two instances of his readiness to prefer good sense to the selfish prejudices of his party we are not without hopes that when Parliament meets in February next Sir Robert Peel may be for the third time greeted with the praises of the Opposition as *splendide mendax*.

A letter on "The Morality of the Ballot" shows him to have been at this time, as he always remained, an opponent of secret voting, on the old grounds that an honest man never wants to do anything in the dark, and that a vote being a trust, those on whose behalf it is exercised have a right to see in what way the trust is discharged. There was force in this argument, so long as the suffrage was limited to the ten-pound householders ; but now that the franchise is exercised in boroughs, and is soon to be exercised in counties, by every man who has a permanent habitation and the responsibilities which accompany it, it is no longer possible to regard it in that light. It is a right in the exercise of which every man has a fair claim to such protection as circumstances may render necessary and as the community can give. So far as it is possible to gather from the scanty indications given in the *Inquirer* articles, it was almost solely on this question of the Ballot that Mr. R. Taylor had made its politics too Radical for his contributor at Highbury.

It is difficult for those who live in these days of Free Trade and Liberal legislation to appreciate the crisis through which the nation passed during Sir Robert Peel's Conservative administration of 1841. The papers of the day are full of accounts of distress and disturbance in the manufacturing districts. Parliament was prorogued in 1842 in the midst of a discussion raised by Mr. Tom Duncombe, in the course of which Mr. Hume said it was necessary to place cannon in the middle of Manchester to keep the public peace. Mr. Cobden entreated the Government not to send the Cheshire Yeomanry into that city, but to rely on soldiers of the line, Mr. Ward said that the destitution in Sheffield was so great that the slightest spark would cause an explosion, and Sir Robert Peel, admitting the severity of the distress, charged the disturbances on persons who studiously went about inflaming the public mind. The *Manchester Guardian* of the same week—the second week in August—was full of accounts of serious rioting at Oldham, at Ashton, and at Manchester itself. At Stalybridge a banner was carried about with the inscription, "They that perish by the sword are better off than they that perish with hunger." At Rochdale the dragoons had to be sent for. In Salford the Riot Act was read, and the mayor called all the well-disposed inhabitants to assist in the suppression of "the present riotous and disgraceful proceedings." From South Staffordshire the news of the same week was even more alarming. A letter from Stourbridge says:—"There is not one pit at work. Throughout this whole division of the county nothing is to be seen for miles but idle works, groups of men, women and children begging, and encamped in fields cooking whatever provision they can procure." At Dudley the colliers were all out, and having exhausted the charity of the town, went about in large bodies levying contributions in all the other places in the district. The Scotch miners were all out on a strike, which was described in the newspapers as "the most alarming turn-out which has ever taken place in the mining districts of Scotland." In Aberdeenshire a public warning against agitators was sent out by the sheriff and the municipal authorities announcing their resolve to "repress incitements to popular disturbance."

This is the story of a single week. For a few weeks matters went from bad to worse ; but a fine autumn and a good harvest eventually brought some relief. Then, as in later days, a complaint arose that the tariffs of other countries are against our trade. In a short City article in the *Inquirer* of the 22nd of October our author writes :—"The news from Manchester is very discouraging. Prices of manufactured goods have again fallen, and the prospect for the coming winter is gloomy in the extreme. The *Leeds Mercury* reminds us that within these two years six European kingdoms and the United States have published hostile tariffs, raising the duties on our goods, and in some cases prohibiting them. They are, unfortunately, copying us in our exclusive system." A month later he writes :—"It is easy to foresee that in the coming Session of Parliament the great struggle will be to lower the taxes on food. . . . We must hope that the national distress, which has now reached the agricultural districts, will at last open the land-lords' eyes. Their rents are dependent on our trading activity. Land in England, like land in the back woods of America, would not be worth five dollars an acre if it were not for its neighbour-hood to a crowded manufacturing population ; and yet our landlords have the folly to be jealous of trade."

The landlords have now pretty fully learned the lesson, and their jealousy of trade has almost passed away. Even the farmers now refuse to be turned from necessary reforms in rural administration, and in the laws which regulate the land, by the paltry bribe of a five-shilling duty on corn, which irrespon-sible politicians like Mr. James Lowther pretend to offer them ; while the proposal to restore the duties on manufactured articles has fallen into the hands of Sir Edward Sullivan and Mr. MacIver, whose chief disciples are the sugar-boiling operatives of Bristol and the East-end of London. But in the beginning of 1843 even the repeal of the Corn Laws was some distance off, and only sanguine politicians thought such a revolution in our fiscal policy to be within distant reach. Writing in the *Inquirer* on the 14th of January Samuel Sharpe says :—

It is clear that the measures of the past Session have given us poverty and an income-tax ; and the double inconvenience may perhaps recall the House of Commons, if not too much committed by party pledges, towards the dictates of good sense. At any rate, the former proposals of Lord John Russell to raise an income in that most agreeable of all ways, by allowing the importation of foreign corn and sugar, will stand a chance of being listened to more favourably. Indeed it is not impossible that Sir Robert Peel may feel driven by the distress of the nation to propose them as his own measures. These two proposals to let in foreign corn and foreign sugar would ease the sufferings of the poor, would increase trade, and would replenish the Exchequer ; but then they would widen the breach between the Minister and the mortgaged landlords. On mentioning the mortgaged landlords it is perhaps worth while to say a few words on mortgages. They are in reality at the bottom of the whole Corn-Law difficulty. If corn were admitted at a low duty, and the nation was made more prosperous by the change, the landlords would share in the general advantage. Even if their rents in some cases should fall, they would be more than compensated by the cheapness of every article which they wished to purchase with those rents. But consider the positions of the mortgaged landlord and the mortgagee. To the mortgagee the fall in prices is all gain ; he loses no part of that gain by a fall in rents. But the landlord, if mortgaged, loses just what the mortgagee gains. When the landlord's rents fall, he is only in part relieved by a fall in the prices of the articles which he consumes. One of his great payments remains the same, namely, the interest on the mortgage. And unfortunately as a nation we are governed by mortgaged landlords.

Nobody in those days anticipated that the leaps and bounds by which the national prosperity would advance under complete Free Trade would cause the most remarkable growth of rent which has ever taken place in England ; or that a general fall in rents would be only from this immensely increased amount, and would be delayed for five-and-thirty years. A very large share of the increased wealth which Free Trade and Liberal legislation have brought, has gone, as what Mr. Mill calls "unearned increment" in the value of their property, into the pockets of the landlords. The fall in rents has perhaps come at last, but it is not likely to go so far as to reduce them to anything like what they were in the last days of Protection. The difficulty, clearly stated in the article quoted above, has, however, made itself felt much as the writer anticipated. For mortgages, we must now read settlements. The greater part of the land is overburdened with heavy payments which the landlord is obliged to make to various members of his father's family. These have all been calculated on the exaggerated rental which the soil has paid during the generation since the Corn Laws were repealed. As the rent is now finding its natural level, the whole fall comes out of the margin which constitutes the real income of the life-owner of the property. He may have inherited twenty thousand a year from the rent of farms. Of this he pays perhaps twelve thousand under various settlements, so that his real income is

eight. A fall of twenty-five per cent. in the total
rental leaves him but fifteen thousand out of which
to pay the twelve ; and cuts his own margin down
to three. There are many landlords whose position
is even worse than this, while many more have
profited so greatly by the growth of towns, trans-
forming farms into market gardens, and agricultural
land into building sites, that they can easily afford to
make great reductions in merely agricultural rents.
How the agricultural interest is to maintain itself,
under the very artificial conditions imposed on the
holding and cultivation of the soil, is one of the
unsolved problems of the immediate future.

It is now beginning to be seen that it is the land
question which is really at the bottom of Irish discontent. In the gloomy times from 1842 to 1847
this connection was not fully understood. A nearer
and more obvious injustice, in the shape of the Irish
Established Church, attracted more attention on both
sides of the Irish Sea. In the *Inquirer* articles Mr.
Sharpe showed much political sagacity, in comments
on the whole Irish question which forty years ago
were far in advance of the times. On May 27, 1843,
he writes :—

Three-quarters of the Irish are now demanding a repeal of
the Union with an earnestness and a threatening attitude
which must make their rulers listen to them. Whether or no
the repeal of the Union would heal the evils that the Irish
complain of, we English, perhaps, are not the most impartial
judges, but one thing is quite certain, that the cry for the
remedy proves the existence of the wound, and that if the
repeal of the Union is not the true remedy, it behoves the
Government to say what is. It is the duty of the House of
Commons to set on foot a searching inquiry into the causes

of the Irish discontent. In what points do we wrong them, in what do we insult them?

The answer he gives is that the Established Church is one main cause of the irritation, and must be removed. In another article, which is worth quoting in full, the Egyptian scholar draws a curious and suggestive parallel between this difficulty of his own times and one which belonged to ancient history. It is entitled " A Lesson from History."

Few cases can be more completely parallel than those of Ireland and ancient Egypt when under the government of Constantinople. The more educated Greeks of Alexandria were the Orange party, and their Arian opinions were the Protestantism of the country. They claimed ascendancy as their birthright, and they insulted the " wild " Egyptians by calling them "aliens in blood, aliens in language, and aliens in religion." They supported their ascendancy by the help of troops from Constantinople ; and by a law not unlike the present Irish Arms Bill, they forcibly entered the dwelling of every Egyptian every third year to search for arms. The Bishop Athanasius was the O'Connell of Egypt, who, with a political skill and judgment quite equal to that of the modern Agitator, raised the Egyptians in " passive resistance." Then, as now, the soldiers were many of them of the religion of the oppressed party, and none could be depended upon but the two legions, into which, like our regiments of Guards, they allowed none of these aliens to be admitted. To lessen this difficulty, they set us the example of changing the militia of the two halves of the kingdom ; they moved the Egyptian troops into Thrace, and carried Thracians and Pannonians into Egypt. Their courts of justice were made dependent, and appeals were allowed, at a great expense, from Alexandria to the higher prefect in Constantinople, as from Dublin to the House of Lords. The Egyptians, in their agitation, received addresses from their "sympathizers" of the same religion in Rome, as the Irish from America. Theodosius I., like the Whig Ministry, put an end to the political quarrel at a stroke by putting the natives into offices of trust and

power; but his successors soon lighted up the flames of discontent again by restoring the ascendancy to the minority in
the capital. In short, the Egyptians, like the native Irish,
were the less educated and the more superstitious in religion;
and the Alexandrians, like the Protestants of Dublin, were the
more bigoted in politics. Let us hope that the parallel will
hold no further. From the constant turmoil of this state of
half rebellion, the wealth and prosperity of the country rapidly
lessened. The ascendancy party were lessened in numbers by
emigration from a country in which rents and taxes were no
longer paid. All the religious conversions were from the more
enlightened to the less enlightened religion. The Egyptians
turned a longing eye towards their co-religionists, the Arabs,
as the Irish have sometimes done towards their Gallic
neighbours; and by the Arabic invasion the repeal of the
Union was at last brought about. Let us hope that it may
be avoided in Ireland by the use of a little common sense, by
means which are at once so obvious, and would be so certainly
successful.

This historic parallel still applies. The policy of
"putting the natives into offices of trust and power"
has never yet been carried far enough. An English
peer must still rule in Dublin Castle, and a representative of some English, Scotch, or Welsh con-
stituency be chosen as his Chief Secretary. Irish
legal appointments go to Irish lawyers; and the
political appointments must go to Irish politicians.

The glimpses of the ecclesiastical politics of the
time in these *Inquirer* articles are full of interest.
There were signs of disruption in the Established
Churches both north and south of the Tweed. In
Scotland the disruption took place; in England it
has been avoided. The Evangelicals thought the
Puseyites, as the Romanising party was then called,
ought to go out of the Church; the Puseyites, and
most of the Dissenters, thought the Evangelicals

should secede. The crisis, as it then looked to an intelligent and clear-sighted observer, who belonged to neither party, is thus described in an article on the 9th of May, 1843 :—

The Liberal Dissenters, like ourselves, who have no other wish than that, in the war of opinions, truth should have fair play, can look at the present divisions in the Church with impartial eyes. As long as the Puseyites are in the minority, much as we disapprove of their half-Popish opinions, we cannot feel their existence an evil, though we should think their attainment of power a most serious misfortune. We look upon all endowed creeds and articles of religion as embankments to stop the spread of knowledge, as a declaration on the part of the subscribers that the world can never get any wiser, as pillars of Hercules to fix the *ne plus ultra* beyond which the human mind is not to advance in its search after truth. But during the last century the clergy for the most part held opinions much less erroneous than their creeds, and being only bound by "the elastic bonds of an oath," were usually much more liberal than the Articles. Hence the number of Evangelical clergymen who have entered the Church. But now the Puseyites are recalling the Church to the strict letter of the Articles, and if they persist they seem likely to shake their own foundations by the *reductio ad absurdum*. For example, we suppose few Churchmen consider that the mere baptism, or sprinkling by the priest, will avail without the help of Christian conduct in after life. But the Puseyites, boldly standing upon the Articles, declare that the point at issue between themselves and their Evangelical brethren is that the Evangelicals say that men are to be regenerated by faith, and they, the Puseyites, that they are to be regenerated by baptism. And the Bishop of London, in his charge, declares that the Puseyites are right, that it is the doctrine of the Articles that regeneration is by baptism. We may call this a *reductio ad absurdum ;* but not so the Evangelical clergy. They complain that the Bishop is subjecting them to a heavy persecution. He is as bad as the *Inquirer* in reminding them of their ordination vows in this and on some other points ; and in telling them in the House of Lords that those who do not believe

the Articles should quit the Church. Again, it has been cus-
tomary for the Protestants to declare that the Bible is the sole
foundation for their religion. But the Puseyites, like the
Papists, profess that they are guided by the voice of the
Church, by tradition as declared by the ecclesiastical authorities, and here, as before, they are fully borne out by the
twentieth Article, which declares that the Church has authority
in matters of faith. We think the cause of truth must gain by
this controversy, and as for the Bishop of London, we can certainly not blame him for reminding the clergy of the sacred
nature of an oath.

This is a fair account of the controversy as it
stood in 1843. Forty years have changed the position of the original combatants, and brought new
parties on the scene. The Oxford Movement, the
story of which Mr. Mozley says has yet to be told,
had not developed its full results till long after
Newman, with splendid and admirable consistency,
sacrificed a position of unparalleled influence and
went his way to Rome. Why, at this period, the
movement should have taken Pusey's name has
never been clearly made out. Mr. Mozley, in his
interesting " Reminiscences," says with perfect truth,
that " if there ever could be any question as to the
master spirit of this movement, which now would be
a very speculative question indeed, it lies between
John Henry Newman and Richard Hurrell Froude."*
The lead fell into Pusey's hands when the true
leaders left the Church ; but his name was attached
to the movement while Hurrell Froude and Newman were still its active spirits. He joined them
about 1833 or 1834, and, says Cardinal Newman
in his " Apologia," " he at once gave to us a

* " Reminiscences, chiefly of Oriel College and the Oxford
Movement," vol. i. p. 225.

position and a name.  Without him we should have
had no chance, especially at the early date of 1834,
of making any serious resistance to the Liberal
aggression.  But Dr. Pusey was a Professor and
Canon of Christ Church ; he had vast influence in
consequence of his deep religious seriousness, the
munificence of his charities, his Professorship, his
family connections, and his easy relations with
University authorities."  As a University movement Puseyism has passed away, and the religious
Liberalism against which it was a protest is once
more in the ascendant at Oxford.  As a popular
movement it has become Ritualism ; at its very best,
a marriage of religious awakening to artistic revival ;
at its worst, " a thing of shreds and patches," a mix-
ture of man-millinery and music ; the attempt of
feeble clerical minds to magnify their office.  To
Newman and Froude it was Romanism in reality ;
to the majority of ritualistic curates in these days,
it is—as Lord Beaconsfield called it—" the Mass in
masquerade."

The movement in Scotland was in a very different
direction to a far different result.  It was High
Church in another sense.  It had for its object the
liberation of spiritual organizations from the inter-
ference of secular authority.  Its leader was a much
greater man than Dr. Pusey, or, indeed, than any of
the chiefs of the Oxford movement, excepting Cardinal Newman.  Dr. Chalmers was a man of heroic
nature.  He could not only make a great sacrifice
himself, but could inspire others to make it.  He
had been brought to London to lecture at the
Hanover Square Rooms in favour of Church

Establishments.    He held the principle of State
Churchism, even when he was compelled by obedience to conscience to protest against its inevitable
results.    The agitation of which he was the head
was at first misunderstood in England.    The State
Church party looked on it as equivalent to rebellion ; the Dissenters regarded it, as they now rightly
regard that of the English Church Union, as an
attempt to get the freedom and independence of
Nonconformity without forfeiting the advantages of
Establishment.    This view was perfectly just as far
as it went, but it did not go far enough.    It applied
an English standard to Scotch earnestness.    When
social advantages are in one scale and spiritual
freedom in the other, it is not often on this side of
the Tweed that the spiritual side weighs down the
beam.    It is not doing so in the case of the extreme ritualists.    Our Greens and Mackonochies
will travesty martyrdom, but will not take up the
burden of their freedom.    The men whom Chalmers
led were more in earnest.    If they could not have
within the Established Church the liberty they
believed they ought to claim, they valued it enough
to go outside the Church on its behalf.    Their act of
secession changed the whole aspect of their movement in the eyes of the world.    In an *Inquirer*
article on the 27th May, 1843, Mr. Sharpe expresses the view then taken by English Liberals, and
shows his usual sagacity in anticipating results from
their action which Dr. Chalmers neither expected
nor desired, but which are following at the end of
forty years :—

Since the passing of the English Act of Uniformity in

Charles II.'s reign, when the founders of our Presbyterian congregations earned their undying names by resigning their livings for conscience-sake, our country has not witnessed so grand a moral sight as is now passing in Scotland. Four hundred beneficed clergymen have there resigned their livings and quitted their parsonage-houses and churches, because after long and anxious deliberation they have thought it wrong, under present circumstances, to hold them . . . . Dr. Chalmers, on taking the Chair as Moderator of the Free Assembly of the Church of Scotland, declared their attachment to an Establishment, and that they were no friends of the voluntary system. Be this, however, as it may, we here have more than one-third of the Established Church of Scotland throwing up its share of the emoluments for the sake of freedom of action ; they have become Dissenters, and as such they will act and feel for the future. They will be found a strong addition to the friends of civil and religious liberty, though they are in part driven to take this solemn step by the defeat of their claims of spiritual power. Their successors will not have the same love for Establishments which Dr. Chalmers no doubt truly feels. They, of course, now feel that their secession will make no change in their religious opinions ; so thought our Presbyterian forefathers in leaving the Church of England . . . . In conclusion, while Dr. Chalmers and his followers were receiving the emoluments of the State, and struggling for a freedom and a power wholly inconsistent with such emoluments, we thought them in the wrong ; but now that they have made their choice —and such a noble choice—they have at once put themselves right ; we no longer criticise their conscience or its scruples, but grant them our full respect for having obeyed its dictates.

These extracts sufficiently exhibit the views of their writer on the political, social, and ecclesiastical questions of his time. He made many other contributions to the *Inquirer* on theological subjects, and on questions of scholarship, as well as reviews of books. The various topics thus treated exhibited the wide range over which his knowledge and

his intellectual sympathy extended.    Other work of
the same years may be summed up in his own
words :—

> Another periodical publication which I sometimes wrote
> for was the Rev. Mr. Aspland's *Christian Reformer,* a
> monthly Unitarian magazine.    To this I used to send
> papers on Biblical Criticism.    These were signed with my
> name.    They were usually explanatory of single texts.
> But I was never satisfied with writing for periodical publi-
> cations ; and, after a time, I changed my plan.    Instead
> of writing upon texts, I began a series of papers on the
> several books of the Bible ; and though I sent many of
> them to Mr. Aspland to be published in his magazine, I
> always wrote them with the full intention of collecting them
> together and publishing them in a volume by themselves.

These notes attracted much attention at the time
among the readers of Mr. Aspland's magazine.    The
signature of S. S. became a familiar and very welcome one, and so remained for many years in that
and other Unitarian publications ; though some of his
friends were reminded by it of the letters which the
fanatic Huntingdon, S. S., or Sinner Saved, appended
to his name and inscribed on the panel of his
carriage door.    The intention of collecting and
publishing these criticisms was carried out in 1854
by the publication of a volume entitled " Historic
Notes on the Old and New Testament," of which a
second edition was issued in 1858.

# CHAPTER VII.

## THE FIVE BROTHERS AND THEIR ELDER SISTER.

TIIE five young men who had set out in life during the second and third decades of the century were all well-established at the beginning of the fifth. There are but few family histories in which five brothers attain so high a level of prosperity; and there are still fewer in which all retain so much interest in public matters and keep up with such success and distinction their intellectual pursuits. The references to his brothers in Samuel Sharpe's Diary are not numerous, and there is a melancholy contrast in two which are only separated from each other by an interval of less than fifteen months. He writes on the 14th of December, 1841, "My brother Sutton, since the opening of the two new Vice-Chancellors' Courts, is quite one of the leaders of the Chancery Bar. Lord Lyndhurst has very honourably begged him to join in the Commission to propose the necessary reforms in Chancery. Sutton's abilities are unquestionably great, and he now has the reward of twenty years' industry. All my brothers are nearly equally prosperous."

The reward of twenty years' industry was never to

K

be fully reaped.   On the 21st of February, 1843, his brother writes :—"I left Sutton's chambers last night doubtful whether I should find him alive in the morning.   He had for several weeks been slowly but steadily recovering from a partial paralysis, when a second stroke came on, which Dr. Bright says he cannot survive.   He feels no pain, but medicine can do no more.   During these weeks we have been always with him, and yesterday he thanked me for my visit ; to-day he is unconscious of it. His faculties and his feelings are gone, his mind destroyed, perhaps by the over-exercise of its own powers in his profession.   He had been twenty months Q.C."   He died at midnight on the 22nd of February, 1843, at his chambers in New Square, in the 46th year of his age, and was buried in the Cloisters of Lincoln's Inn, of which he was one of the benchers.   His funeral was attended by his brothers, some near relatives, and a small group of professional friends, among whom were the Master of the Rolls (Lord Langdale), Vice-Chancellor Knight Bruce and Vice-Chancellor Wigram.   They lamented not only the brilliant companion and friend, but the early close of a career which was full of the highest promise.

Sutton Sharpe had been called to the bar in June, 1822.*   He devoted himself to Equity practice, and at once began to attend the Chancery Court of the County Palatine of Lancaster, of which Sir Giffin Wilson was then Vice-Chancellor.   Business rapidly crowded upon him, and in the course of a few years he attained a leading rank among Counsel

* Chap. II. page 33.

behind the Bar. He first gained distinction in the celebrated case of the British Iron Company (Small *versus* Attwood), in which he was one of the counsel for the Company. The *Legal Observer*, in its Memoir of him, says that " To the manner in which he distinguished himself in this suit his rapid rise, is, in a measure, to be attributed." His pleadings are described as " models in their legal acuteness, in their most logical arrangement, and in their lucid phraseology." As in other professions so at the bar, the foundation of a great reputation is first laid among the members of the profession itself. Sutton Sharpe had established his professional fame. He was regarded as the most promising man of his day, and the very highest honours of the profession were already thought to be within his reach. He had given evidence before a Committee of the Lords as to the new judges in Chancery; and before a Committee of the Commons on the removal of the Law Courts from Westminster Hall. The appointment referred to in his brother's Diary arose out of the Act by which the Lord Chancellor was empowered to make improvements in his Court. It was a high proof of the professional confidence felt in Sutton Sharpe that he was at once named by Lord Lyndhurst as a member of the small Commission appointed to prepare the new rules and regulations, his colleagues being the Master of the Rolls, Vice-Chancellor Wigram, and Mr. Pemberton Leigh. He was made a Queen's Counsel by Lord Cottenham, in 1841, and attached himself to the Court of Vice-Chancellor Wigram. Here he at once took the lead, and retained it till he was attacked with what proved to be his fatal

illness at the close of the Michaelmas Term in
1842.

He had always been known as a Liberal, and
as a prominent advocate of law reform. He had
been invited to enter political life, but had made an
early resolution, to which he steadfastly adhered, to
refuse all overtures from constituencies till he had
obtained a distinct lead at the Bar. This coveted
position he had reached, and had already begun
to consider where he should plant his feet on the
first step in the political ladder by which the highest
peaks are scaled. He had the personal qualities, and
as a nephew of Mr. Rogers he had many of the
social advantages, which come strongly to the aid of
a legitimate ambition. The *Morning Chronicle* in
an obituary notice said of him, that "No man was
a more general favourite in society," and that "such
was the amenity of his manners that even in the
times when politics ran highest in the country, as
during the period of the Reform Bill, we do not
believe his stout assertion of his principles ever lost
him a friend." The *Examiner*, in those days the
leading weekly journal, not only spoke of him as
"one of the most valuable men of our time," but
added :—"His career was one of uninterrupted
success, and the most brilliant professional prospects
were before him, but prosperity never in the slightest
degree spoiled him ; and he never forgot an old
friend nor failed to return a hundred-fold an old
kindness." This is high praise ; but other testimonies confirm it. The *Law Magazine*, in an article
on "Recent Reforms in Chancery," made the following tribute to his personal and professional worth :—

We here close our observations on the labours of the Chancery Commission [the Master of the Rolls, V.-C. Wigram, Mr. Pemberton Leigh and Mr. Sutton Sharpe]. There is however another subject to which if we did not advert we should not be doing justice to the feelings of many of our readers, certainly not to our own : we mean the death of Mr. Sutton Sharpe, one of the members of the Commission. When a lawyer has made his way into the lead of one of the branches of the Court of Chancery, he has become a person of some public importance. The transaction of the business of the Court is very much affected by the nature of his abilities; and if he is a person of high feeling and masculine character, his influence is of great avail in regulating the tone and temper of the Court. Such was the position of Mr. Sutton Sharpe at the time of his death. He was the undisputed leader of V.-C. Wigram's Court. His knowledge of his profession in pleading, practice, and principle was very extensive. He had acquired a power of making his statements with clearness and simplicity, and of conducting his arguments with ingenuity and precision. Besides these merits he was a man in whom a long course of uninterrupted success produced neither vanity nor affectation. He never made a parade of his learning, nor endeavoured to crush an adversary by the superior weight of his abilities. Above all he had an integrity and uprightness of mind which made him clear and straightforward in the transaction of business, and utterly averse to any step, however advantageous at the moment, which was in the slightest degree tinctured with unfairness. In consultation he was always ready to discuss, with lawyers far inferior to himself, every branch of his case; in Court he had a manner so mild and a tone so free from offence as to command the goodwill of every one that heard him. His strong understanding and ready judgment guided him to the proper course under all circumstances, and enabled him to give the most useful advice to other men, whatever might be the difficulties under which he was consulted.

But it was not merely as a good English lawyer that Mr. Sharpe was fitted to take a lead in his profession. He had a competent knowledge of foreign law as well as an extensive acquaintance with foreign advocates. There is no doubt that if his life had been spared he would have turned this knowledge of jurisprudence to public benefit. Indeed it is hard to conjecture the full extent of the loss which the public have sustained; for no one can have observed his progress during the last two years of his life without perceiving that he always rose with the occasion, and that the higher his position, the greater the responsibility resting upon him, the more difficult the task to be performed,—the greater was his display of ability. It is clear that his career closed before the powers of his mind were fully developed. His private friends will deplore the loss of one to whom they were affectionately attached; we shall recollect his laborious and successful career, his intellectual and moral qualities, and grieve over the death of an eminent advocate who exercised an influence for honorable and useful ends, and was capable of filling with great public advantage the highest posts of his profession.

An appreciative notice also appeared in the *Journal des Débats,* expressive of the profound regret felt among the literary men and lawyers of the French capital at his loss. It was his custom to spend two months of every vacation in Paris, and he used to say that he had more friends in that city than in London. His knowledge of French History and Literature was probably as extensive as that of any man of his time; and he left behind him a library containing all the best books in the French language. His collection of works on English History and English Law was equally complete; and the Taxing Masters in Chancery subscribed to purchase his Law Library for the use of their office. He had preserved copies of all his opinions, as well as a careful digest of Equity cases, which, being well-bound and indexed, have been found useful by many of his successors though they have never been published. The immense activity

which all these various interests entailed needed a
constitution of iron. In those days men had not
learned the scientific treatment of themselves which
is now generally adopted. A long cessation of work
at the beginning of 1842 would probably have
saved Sutton Sharpe's life. He was out of health
before the vacation, and during his usual holiday in
Paris suffered from a severe attack of diarrhœa,
which greatly lowered his strength. But he returned
to work for the Michaelmas term, and with difficulty
got through it. He then took only a week's rest;
and in the sittings in chambers after term he
became worse. Still the warning was not understood. He went to Brighton for Christmas, but
came back to work as soon as the short holidays
were over, and was speedily laid aside by an attack
of paralysis. He rallied from this stroke, but a
second followed from which he could not recover.

No life has hitherto been written of this brilliant
member of a clever family. His memory is cherished
among the best traditions of the profession which he
adorned ; but so many have fallen, as he did, on the
very threshold of the great career which it offers to
a chosen few, that the world does little more than
cast a passing glance on the ruined expectations
and blighted hopes which so premature a death
involves. Had Sutton Sharpe, like some of his contemporaries, lived through the forty-one years which
passed between the giving of his evidence in favour
of the removal of the Courts of Law from Westminster, and the opening of the new Courts in the
Strand, he must have had a large part in the great
and beneficent reforms which that removal sym-

bolises.   His friends in the profession expected great things from him.   It is by their estimate of his powers, and their sense of the loss his early removal inflicted on the profession and the country, that his intellectual rank must now be fixed.   A few years more and all the world would have recognized him. But the few years were not given him.   Yet no complaint escaped from him in his illness.   He must have felt that he had learned, in Milton's words, "to scorn delights and live laborious days," and that "the fair guerdon" was denied to him.   A few cordially appreciative memorial articles in English and French newspapers, expressions of admiration and deep regret in the publications which represented the legal profession, a general sense all through the members of the bar that a most promising career had closed before its just expectations could be realised, are all that represents his fame.   The *Legal Observer* summed up the services expected from him by saying, "As a man qualified to do great, bold, and wide things in Law Reform, and yet things safe because bold and wide, we believe there are few men now living in this land, by a long interval, to compare with him.   His mind was in itself admirably constituted for such a task, and his early position in a solicitor's office had given him, as we believe, a most essential and very peculiar advantage.   In this point of view we mourn over his death as a serious public loss; a loss which, as far as we can see, is not likely soon to be replaced."

The desire expressed in the obituary notices of Sutton Sharpe that his Life should be written, and that his Digest of Equity Cases, and selections from the carefully preserved copies of his Opinions, should be published, was never realized. His life is an unfinished story, which breaks suddenly off just at the point at which it becomes most interesting to ordinary readers. It had but little incident. It had been spent in the diligent exercise of an arduous profession ; it was little known except to the members of that profession and a large group of attached personal friends ; and it had not yet touched that larger and noisier world of politics, in which most lawyers complete their success and extend and consolidate their fame. To his family the loss was not only that of the eldest brother, but of its most brilliant member. Mr. Rogers and Miss Rogers had indulged the very highest expectations respecting him. Their esteem for him, it may be said their pride in him, was very great. They had followed his professional career with a most affectionate and constant interest. But it was on his sister, Catharine Sharpe, that the loss fell the most heavily. She was now past sixty. For twenty years she had been rejoicing in the steady work and the growing success of the five brothers to whom she had given up her youth. They had all looked up to her, sought her counsel, taken her advice, and enjoyed her hearty sympathy in their domestic relationships, and now the eldest had been struck down on the very threshold of brilliant personal and professional success.

In a letter to Mrs. Samuel Sharpe written within a fortnight of Sutton's death, Catharine Sharpe says that she has once more gone to Brighton, and is beginning to turn her thoughts to her own plans and movements. " I shall be better able," she says, " to decide upon any permanent place of residence and mode of life after entirely detaching myself from present circumstances, when I can bring fresh feelings and ideas to bear upon the subject, and for that purpose I should go abroad." She then makes an earnest appeal to be allowed to take the eldest daughter Emily away with her for the summer. The request was granted after considerable hesitation and some further correspondence, and on August 25th her father writes in his Diary : " Emily has now been two months at Boulogne with my sister ; and all the accounts of her and from her give us full satisfaction." During this journey Catharine Sharpe was herself seriously ill, and it was fortunate that her brother Henry with his wife and four children were spending a long summer holiday at Boulogne, and were able to attend to her in their own lodgings. On leaving Boulogne she joined a family of old and attached friends who were then staying at St. Omer. These friends were Mr. and Mrs. Mallet, and one of their two sons and their two daughters. With her niece Emily and Miss S. Mallet, she visited Bruges, Ghent, Antwerp and some other cities, rejoining the Mallets at Brussels. After remaining a few weeks in that city she returned home with her niece. Two years later she revisited Paris.

During this journey Miss Sharpe corresponded regularly with her cousin and sister-in-law Mrs. Samuel Sharpe, and some of her letters have been preserved. They are written on the large old-fashioned letter paper, in a clear small flowing hand, and are admirably expressed. They are good

examples of English letter-writing in the days which
immediately preceded the establishment of Penny
Postage, and consequently before letter writing
became one of the lost arts. Two of them contain glimpses of France under the Constitutional
Monarchy, and of private friends, which give them
permanent value. The first is from Paris in 1845.

PASSAGE DE LA MADELEINE, NO. 4.
August 14th.

MY DEAR SARAH,

I hope Emily received a little letter I wrote to her soon
after my arrival here, giving her some account of her young
friends. As it was inclosed in another I never feel the same
security of its arrival at its place of destination as if intrusted
to the post. This time I must address myself to you and tell
you how I am going on in this delightful city which seems to
have the peculiar faculty of invigorating people, to judge by
Miss Mallet and myself. We are both greatly improved in
health and strength since our arrival, and able to do a great
deal more without fatigue. We all go on most comfortably
together. I have changed my apartment much for the better,
having now a nice cheerful little room to the front with a view
of the Place, and the back front of the beautiful Madeleine,
built after the model of the Parthenon. Being on the entresol,
I have very little way to go into the street but a long way
upstairs as the Mallets are au quatrième. I breakfast and have
my mornings to myself, when we dine and spend the evenings
together. They have nice airy rooms being so high and
having no houses opposite, however there seem symptoms of
building on the space in front which will shut out all view from
the house, which will be a sad detriment. Being anxious to
renew all my previous impressions of Paris, I have by degrees
been seeing all the objects of interest and curiosity, and Mr.
Charles Paravey has placed at my disposal his medal as
Conseiller d'Etat, at sight of which as if by magic every door
flies open. In short, nothing can exceed the kindness I have
received from them and all their friends here. I never was
made so much of in my life. Paris is wonderfully improved

since I was here last, half the city must have been pulled down to make room for wide streets, foot pavements, splendid shops, excelling ours in size, and this great improvement in the city in light and cleanliness from gas and sewers, must act upon the character of the inhabitants and give them higher feelings of order and propriety. The cleanliness of Paris now approaches to London, while it vastly exceeds it in magnificence. They are laying down most beautiful stone pavement, as smooth as wood, but have not yet arrived at the luxury of sweeping a crossing, which one should think they soon must do as people learn to walk more now they have a trottoir to walk upon.

I do not think the Mallets have the least idea of leaving Paris, but expect to spend the winter here. Gustavus is so much improved in health and strength since they were here, they do not wish to remove him from his present medical treatment till they consider him quite cured. He is grown tall and stout since Emily and I saw him. . . . In the course of the next month I hope to pay my Havre friends a visit, and mean to take her [Miss S. Mallet] with me and hope to get to some of those curious Norman towns, Caen, Bayeux, &c. At Rouen we shall stop on our way. The railroad takes us so far and then there is a steamer on to Havre.

A fortnight back Paris was very gay with the fêtes of July, and we took the opportunity of the Grandes Eaux playing at Versailles in consequence, to visit that magnificent place now dedicated "à toutes les Gloires de la France"—six miles of bad pictures displaying all the events of the Great Nation with the trifling omission of the French revolution, not the slightest reference to which appears. You have Napoleon's battles during the time, and then his entrance into Paris, and his coronation. The water works certainly are magnificent, but a tremendous storm at the time they were playing, was rather more water over-head than was agreeable. We slept there a couple of nights, so had time to see everything quietly.

I shall be very glad of a little news from home again, last time I had four letters by the same post which I should rather had been more equally divided. However, one was from Lucy's own pen with a very satisfactory report of herself. . . . I wish I could hear better accounts of Dan, who does not seem gaining ground. I hope this will find you all well at Highbury, if Charlotte is with you give my love to her, she will quite enter into my admiration of Paris. I have seen Charlotte Life several times. I find her most respectably established here. "Madame Life, Professeur de Langue et Littérature Anglaise," keeping a day school and giving lessons at three francs an hour, her time fully occupied. I am to dine with her some day, and she is to have the honour of cooking my dinner, in the meantime, remembering my former tastes, she has sent me two large plum pies à l'Anglais and was most delighted to see me.

I have been often to the Louvre, where there is so much to see, it is inexhaustible. Since I was here there are many new galleries open; the Spanish, the Egyptian and Etruscan, the gallery of the most exquisite drawings of the Old Masters. I find the only way is to take a bit at a time, and even then it is a most fatiguing thing, the distance between them is so great and they oblige you to come all the way back over their slippery floors instead of letting you out at the other end.

I must now say farewell, my dear Sarah, give my kindest love to Sam and the young ones and believe me

Your affectionate Sister,

C. SHARPE.

Charlotte Life, who is mentioned above, had been a servant of Miss Sharpe's in earlier days. She was a person of great vivacity and intelligence, and had been so much interested in the political and literary talk of the brothers and sisters at the dinner table, that she had sometimes forgotten to hand the dishes or remove the plates. Miss Sharpe's next letter was written during the journey in Normandy of which the above letter speaks.

CAEN,
October 1st.

MY DEAR SARAH,

I must write and thank both you and Emily for your letters which were very welcome to me, as all news from home always is, and this time it was particularly agreeable as giving so favourable an account of Sam, who I trust is too good a philosopher to be influenced by any of the minor crosses and disappointments of life, and therefore if his usual spirits are returned, quite depend upon their lasting. I must also congratulate you all upon having got William and Lucy for neighbours. I always had a presentiment that house would be theirs, and before my return, I expect to find them quite settled in it. When that will be, I cannot exactly say, but certainly mean to find myself amongst you all again before the year is out. . . .

It is now a month since Sophy and I left Paris ; during which time we have seen a great deal, and enjoyed a great deal of pleasure. She is a most delightful travelling companion, her mind so alive to all that is striking, beautiful and interesting. We stayed ten days at Havre amongst all our kind friends who received us with open arms, and by their unceasing attentions made our visit so happy the only painful part was to leave them. We crossed over to Trouville, a beautiful little bathing place where the Worsleys were staying, and spent a few days there, little expecting to see it again ; but we returned there again in our way here in consequence of Mrs. Worsley being in great trouble, occasioned by one of her maids hanging herself, and she alone with the children. So we went over to her, and waited Mr. Worsley's arrival, which little delay has set us back in our proceedings ; for myself it matters not ; but Sophy is too important a person at home to be long spared, and I promised to bring her back in a month.

From Trouville we went back to Lisieux, a most exquisite little town, beautifully situated, and picturesque beyond description from its primitive and antiquated buildings. Modern improvement has not yet begun its work there, except with its Cathedral, which they are plaistering all over; making every part of the exterior of mouldering stone, grey and worn with the lapse of centuries, as white and smooth as a stuccoed house ; filling up all the delicate tracery, and finely marked capitals of the 15th century, and making solid blocks of them. The irretrievable mischief that renovation and restoration are now making in all these beautiful churches is really beyond belief. Those may consider themselves happy who have seen them first. To the next generation they will be lost. There is quite a mania for restoring churches at present; go where you will it is the same. These fine old towers everywhere covered with scaffolding, and that generally foretells the destruction of all the interest it possesses. From Lisieux we came on to Caen where I am now writing. As a place it disappoints me, though I hardly know what I expected. It is situated in a flat uninteresting country which does not appear to advantage after Lisieux, but is full of interesting objects of antiquity. Its Norman churches were built by the Conqueror. The old Castle with a splendid view of the town and the various grotesque costumes of the Norman peasants are exceedingly striking to travellers. We were fortunate in being here at the time of the fair, where we saw to perfection the various dresses of the peasants with caps not to be credited if not seen. They are a remarkably fine handsome people and the young women in their smart gay costume are quite worthy of admiration.

One day we went over to Bayeux which possesses two great objects of interest—the famous Tapestry and a Cathedral curious from containing so many different periods of architecture. The crypt below is supposed to be the earliest known Cathedral with columns quite perfect, and frescoes of the 5th century, and from that period its various parts exhibit specimens of all the later styles of architecture. We were fortunate in finding a most intelligent man, an Italian brought from Italy to restore the wood carvings and who explained the whole to us *con amore*. He had been three years unemployed after being sent for because he refused to paint the curious old carved pulpit, but he has gained his point, and saved the pulpit. From this place we go on to Evreux, and thence to Rouen where we shall stay a few days, and in about another week shall be back again in Paris; having laid in an ample store of fresh ideas, and new objects for thought, which is always desirable as long as faculties are granted us to improve, for every new idea is a new source of happiness to us.

Anne Mallet is coming to spend the winter with Mrs. Vowler, Sophy could not be spared from her duties at home, as she entirely teaches Gustavus. I suppose Anne will set off as soon

as any opportunity offers, and if none, then she will wait for
me. I do not know how she will like the change from the
life of variety and amusement she is leading at Paris. . . .
Tell Emily, Sophy has been very busy sketching all the
beautiful churches we have seen. She sends her kind love
to you all. Pray give mine to Sam and the young ones and
believe me, dear Sarah,

Your affectionate Sister,<br>C. SHARPE.

I have had no news of Charlotte for a long time, is she
returned to France?

The Charlotte Sharpe here spoken of was the elder
sister of Mrs. Samuel Sharpe. She was a person of
great originality and force of character. She eventually took up her abode in Cherbourg, where she
lived for forty-nine years, visiting England every few
years so long as she was able to travel, and dying in
1881 at the great age of ninety.

On Catharine Sharpe's return from these continental journeys she settled for the short residue of
her life in the midst of her London friends. Their
estimate of her is well expressed in a letter from
Dr. Boot, an eminent American, to Mr. Sydney
Brooks, in introducing Mr. William Sharpe, in 1840.
Dr. Boott says:—" His sister is one of my wife's
most cherished friends—a lady of rare and striking
qualities of heart and mind—one who, in the noise-
less tenor of her way, has brought down the blessings
of Heaven on an Orphan Brotherhood, left early to
her sisterly protection, and she is now reaping the
fruits of a life of devoted charity in the happiness
and the love of her foster-children, and the respect
of a large and amiable circle of friends." In this
deserved affection and respect her days were passed.

Her interest in the families of her brothers and their wives continued to the end. She died after a painful illness in 1853, and her eldest surviving brother proposed to describe her on her tombstone as, " The daughter of Sutton Sharpe and almost mother of his younger children." No epitaph could be more appropriate to her and it has lately been inscribed on her grave in Abney Park Cemetery.

At the time of these journeys she was feeling that the work of her life was done. The domestic settlement of each of her three married brothers had given her great cause for satisfaction. They had none of them married early. Samuel, as has been seen, was twenty-eight, Henry had waited till he was thirty-two, and William till he was thirty-seven. Henry, who was the second to settle in a home of his own, had lived with his sister and brothers in New Ormond Street till his marriage. He had gone into business with his brother Daniel in 1829, and the firm of H. and D. Sharpe, established first at Pinners Hall, Broad Street, then at Broad Street Buildings and afterwards at 108 Fenchurch Street, quickly became one of the leading houses in the Portuguese trade. In 1834 he had married Miss Eliza Kinder, second daughter of his sister's intimate friends Mr. and Mrs. Kinder of Stoke Newington and Cheapside.* The marriage gave Miss Sharpe the liveliest satisfaction. It was the closer union of two families who had now been, for the space of nearly a generation, bound together in a very close friendship. It was a happy marriage in every respect. They settled in Broad Street

* Chap. III. p. 41.

L

Buildings, where their first three children were born. But the centrifugal tendency which has driven all the merchants out of the city and into the suburbs, had already begun, and Mr. and Mrs. Henry Sharpe and their family removed to Hampstead in the spring of 1841. Their pleasant home, in the most beautiful of all the London suburbs, speedily became a favourite resort of all the brothers. Samuel Sharpe records the spending of the first Christmas with them in their new home, on the eve of Sutton's fatal illness. Of Mr. Henry Sharpe's public and philanthropic work at Hampstead, of his residence there for more than thirty years, during which all his leisure was devoted to the education and improvement of the young working men of the town, of the affectionate esteem in which he was held by all classes, and especially by the poor, who all knew him as a constant benefactor and friend, more must be said in a later chapter.

The third and last of the brothers to settle in a home of his own was William, the youngest but one. He had been established in business as a solicitor in 1826* and in 1835 he and his brother-in-law Mr. Field had joined Mr. Edgar Taylor and Mr. Turner at 41 Bedford Row. Mr. Taylor died in 1839 and Mr. Turner soon afterwards, when the firm became that of Messrs. Sharpe and Field, and is now that of the well-known Parliamentary agents and solicitors, Sharpe, Parkers, Pritchard and Sharpe. William Sharpe had taken an active part in the registration of voters in the City, and after the great triumph in 1835 when four Liberals

* Chap. II. p. 34 and Chap. III. p. 40.

headed the poll, the assembled citizens cordially recognized by their cheers his share in the work. The business had flourished. Mr. Field had singular force, courage and capacity, as well as a remarkable power of attracting and influencing those with whom he came in contact, while Mr. William Sharpe had the quiet patience, the power of sympathy, the willingness to deal with small details and to see to matters of finance and routine, which are essential to the success of such a business. Of the esteem in which he was held by his clients, many pleasant proofs might be given. At the time of his marriage in 1841 he was giving much time to the Anti-Corn Law movement, working with Mr. C. Villiers who was a personal friend.

During all these earlier years he lived with his sister, and he speaks in one of his letters of "the happy home where—through her ability, her intellectual and kindly attractions," he had seen " so much intellectual and sensible society drawn together, and where every thing and every person had a tendency to raise one or to make one desire to raise oneself." His sister speaks of him in equally warm terms. In a letter to Mrs. Samuel Sharpe after telling her of "the delight it gives me that William has at length fixed upon a wife," and describing the lady of his choice, Miss Lucy Reid, and her family in terms of the warmest appreciation she adds, " I feel it will be a great addition to my happiness to be connected with them, though I know not how I am to part with William who has been so much to me. But it has long been the first wish of my heart to see him happily married, and therefore when regret rises in my mind, I think of that and am content." He had left his sister's home before his marriage and taken a house in Woburn Square. Hither he had brought his wife and here their first three children were born. They moved to 1 Highbury Terrace in 1845, close to their elder brother and his family, who had gone from Canonbury to 32 Highbury Place five years before.

The youngest brother, Daniel, was never married. His tastes were scientific, and though he was as diligent as his elder brothers in his attention to business, he found time for the very successful prosecution of the study of Geology. As this chapter has opened with an account of the eldest of these brothers, it may be well to close it by carrying forward to its completion the life of the youngest. There is a melancholy parallelism between them. In the address delivered at the anniversary meeting of the Geological Society of London on the 20th of February, 1857, Colonel J. E. Portlock said a few words about the death of Dr. Buckland and then added—

The great philosopher whose labours we have endeavoured however feebly to notice lived to complete his task and enjoy all the honours which were so justly his due ; but we must now turn to another, who, taking up the subject of Geology at a more advanced stage of its history, was apparently destined to carry it much nearer towards ultimate perfection, when a fatal accident removed him from amongst us, only a short time after the unanimous vote of the Geological Society had placed him at its head as President. The gloom which was thus suddenly cast over us will never be forgotten, as every one had anticipated a most glorious scientific career for Daniel Sharpe.

He had joined the Geological Society in 1827, and

his first active work in the advancement of science was the bringing up from Somersetshire in 1828 of a slab of stone, at which he worked for some months, revealing the skeleton of an Ichthyosaurus, a description of which he published.   In 1835 he went to Portugal on business, remaining there till 1838, and in 1839 and 1840 he read papers to the Geological Society on the geological structure of the neighbourhood of Lisbon.   In an appendix on the great earthquake of 1795 he pointed out the curious fact that the shock operated on the tertiary strata only, the line of quiescence being the boundary between the secondary and tertiary rocks.   He next made an investigation into the geology of the south of Westmoreland, which he described in a paper of which Colonel Portlock speaks as bearing striking testimony to the great ability of its author.   In 1842 and 1843 he inquired into the age of the Bala limestone, and in the next year made important observations on the geology of North Wales.   In 1848 he examined the district of Oporto, and discovered slates which contain several most distinct Silurian fossils.   This was followed up two years later by a paper completing his labours with respect to Portugal.   In 1854 he read a paper on the Structure of Mont Blanc, and in 1855 made what his successor in the Chair describes as "a bold attempt to determine by the supposed marks left by the sea on the sides of the Alps, the age of the last elevation of that mighty mountain chain."   On the subject of Cleavage "the two papers of Mr. Sharpe must always be reckoned," says Colonel Portlock, "among his most striking contributions to science."   Of some of his other writings the description may best be given in Colonel Portlock's own words :—

Mr. Sharpe's palæontological papers are of considerable interest and value. For a genus of Gasteropodous shells abundant in Portugal he proposed (1849) the name of *Tylostoma* considering it distinct from *Globichoncha, Natica,* and *Phasianella.* The genus *Nerinæa* he enriched with six new species ; dividing it into four subgenera—*Nerinæa* 65 species, *Nerinella* 10, *Trochalia* 6, *Ptygmatis* 12, besides eight species which he thinks ought to be placed in other genera ; so that this genus of fossil Gasteropods is alone supposed to exhibit at least 93 species ;—one of the many examples of the extraordinary multiplication of species in those early ages . . . . Twelve species were found in Portugal, six of which had previously been described as cretaceous species, so that Mr. Sharpe concluded that the *Nerinæ* in Portugal or the South of Europe are cretaceous fossils whilst in the North they are oolitic.

Sir Charles Lyell having submitted ·to Mr. Sharpe for examination the fossils he had collected in North America, the result was a very able analytical paper (1848) on the Mollusca of the collection, being so far an estimate of the labours of the United States Geologists. . . . . One remark of Mr. Sharpe's requires especial notice, as being proof—and he gave many—of that philosophic spirit which so strongly characterized him. " It would be interesting," he says, " to trace out the first appearance of each species in many countries, and to see whether it is found in one at an earlier period than in another country, and thus learn of what region it was originally native" —an inquiry which were it possible to trace out also the extent of variation to which species may have been subject from gradual alteration of place and circumstances, would assuredly be one of the most interesting the geological naturalist could follow out.

Every member of the Society is aware of the zeal and industry with which Mr. Sharpe applied himself to the investigation of fossils, whether collected by himself and to be used in illustrating his own papers, or collected by others and merely submitted to him for examination in aid of labours not his own. In conjunction with Messrs. Bunbury, Salter and Ruper

Jones he described the fossils collected by Senor Carlos Ribiero from the Carboniferous and Silurian rocks of Portugal. . . . . Passing by some minor papers, one of which, however, on the sand and gravels of Faringdon, is highly interesting, and all of which have their peculiar value, I must pause for a moment to record the labour and the scrupulous precision with which Mr. Sharpe fulfilled the task which he had undertaken for the Palæontographical Society of describing the Mollusca of the Chalk of England. Part 3 of this description containing a portion of the Cephalopoda, has been published since his lamented death, and has just been placed in my hands. It contains the description of 25 Ammonites, 11 Turrilites and 8 species of the curious body called Aptychus which Mr. Sharpe endeavours with great ability to allocate to their respective species of Ammonites.

Colonel Portlock then proceeds to discuss at great length the paper on the structure of the Alps—and concludes this portion of his address by saying "I have thus endeavoured to do justice, though imperfectly, to the labours of Daniel Sharpe, and I will only add that his quiet humour, his manly straightforward assertion of truth, and his well-known liberality and benevolence endeared him to us as a friend, whilst his shrewd discernment, his accurate observation, and his extensive knowledge made us admire him as a philosopher and geologist."

A similar testimony was borne by Lord Wrottesley, who after enumerating to the members of the Royal Society Daniel Sharpe's numerous contributions to science concludes with these words—

Such is a brief outline of some of the scientific labours of Daniel Sharpe, a man whose mind alike powerful, active and well cultivated urged him successfully to grasp and make his own a wider range of subjects than many geologists dare to attempt. Neither should it be forgotten that all the while he was unceasingly engaged in mercantile pursuits, and it was only during brief intervals of leisure, when more imperative labours were over, that he accomplished what many would consider sufficient work for their lives. And it is not in Geology alone that he is known and appreciated; philologists and ethnologists equally esteemed him. With marvellous versatility of talent he grappled with the ancient Lycian inscriptions, brought home by Fellows, Forbes and Spratt, and revealed the secrets of an unknown tongue written in an unknown character. In debate he was clear, keen, severely critical and at times sarcastic, occasionally alarming to an opponent unaccustomed to his style; but those who knew him best were well aware that an unvarying fund of kindly good-humour lay beneath, and that if he hit his adversary hard, no man more than himself rejoiced in a harder blow in return. His private life was full of unostentatious benevolence. In conversation with his familiars he was intelligent, lively, and quick in perception, and his attached friends of the Geological Club, of which he lately was President by virtue of his office as head of the Society, will long mourn his loss, and miss the quaint humour and quiet laugh that so often helped to animate their board. Mr. Sharpe was a Fellow of the Linnæan, Zoological, and Geological Societies. In 1853 he became Treasurer of the Geological Society, and on the retirement of Mr. Hamilton was elected its President in 1856. In 1850 he was elected a Fellow of the Royal Society. On the 20th of last May, while riding near Norwood, he was thrown from his horse, and sustained a fracture of the skull. In a few days he was so far recovered as to be able to recognize the relations that were admitted to his chamber, and his numerous friends rejoiced in the prospect of speedy restoration, but a sudden relapse succeeded, and he died on the 31st of May, sorrowed for by all who knew his worth.

# CHAPTER VIII.

## THE ACTIVITIES OF MIDDLE AGE.

THE year 1844 was a critical one in the history of the Unitarian body in England and Ireland. The long story of the struggle for religious freedom contains no more interesting or important chapter than that which begins with the decision of the Hewley case in 1842, and ends with the passing of the Dissenters' Chapels Bill in 1844. The Toleration Act of 1689 was an incomplete measure. John Locke, who had been working for it for some years, expressed his dissatisfaction with it when it appeared, and immediately wrote his First Letter on Toleration, publishing it anonymously in Latin.* The Act excluded from its operation the two most ancient forms of the Christian faith. The Roman Catholics on the one hand and the Anti-Trinitarian Dissenters on the other, were omitted from the contemptuous tolerance flung to Protestant Nonconformists who were willing to submit to a test of orthodoxy. The eighth section, which required subscription to the doctrines of the Church, would alone have excluded those who have always made non-subscription to articles and creeds a chief feature of their

* Lord King's Life of Locke, v. 1, pp. 291, 327.

organization and fellowship. But this was not enough to satisfy the Trinitarian zeal of the time, and the seventeenth section especially excluded from the benefits of the Act all who in preaching and writing denied the doctrine of the Trinity. A further Act, passed in 1697, made the denial of the Trinity blasphemy. Happily the administration of the Toleration Act was much more liberal than the Act itself; and all through the eighteenth century the ministers and congregations of the old English Presbyterians were able to continue faithful to their principle of non-subscription. They refused to make a profession of Trinitarian belief a condition either of membership of their Churches or of the occupancy of their pulpits. But Trinitarianism has always needed these paper bulwarks. It rests upon them. It perishes without them. The waves of free discussion speedily undermine its sandy basis. Most of the congregations which have been left open to theological change have undergone change. They have become first Arian and then Unitarian, and the progress has been so gradual and so natural that it has taken place, as the Kingdom of Heaven is to come, "without observation." The fathers were orthodox in a moderate sense, the sons, sitting in the old pews and keeping up the old congregational institutions, became Arian, and the grandsons, still occupying their fathers' places, became Unitarian.

Notwithstanding this natural and, in the absence of limiting creeds, inevitable transition, Unitarian opinions continued to be technically illegal all through the eighteenth century. Unitarians had

nevertheless gained such general respect for their
learning, their high character, and the eminent
literary, scientific and social position of many of
their ministers and laymen, that nobody thought of
enforcing the penal laws against their congregations,
though those laws had been occasionally enforced
against individuals.  Mr. Emlyn, for example, had
been tried in Dublin in 1703, Whiston had been
deprived of his professorship at Cambridge in
1710, and Mr. Evanson had been prosecuted for
heresy in 1773.  Later in the century Dr. Priestley
had been persecuted in Birmingham, but it was
rather as a sympathiser with political freedom
abroad than as a heretic at home, and his chapel,
called the New Meeting, which was destroyed by
the Church and King mob in 1791, was rebuilt by
a Parliamentary grant of £2,000 and a private subscription of another £1,000 in 1802.  In 1813 Mr.
William Smith, the eminent Unitarian who represented Norwich in the House of Commons, got an
Act passed repealing the Act of 1697 which made
Unitarianism blasphemy, and the eighth and seventeenth clauses of the Toleration Act.    Unitarian
teaching was thus made legal and the benefits of the
Toleration Act were extended to Unitarian worship.
In 1817 a dispute arose respecting the occupancy of
the pulpit of a chapel at Wolverhampton.   This
chapel had been Unitarian for many years.   It had
schools which Unitarians had built, and the majority
of its Trustees and supporters were Unitarians.
But an orthodox minority contended that they had
a right to the chapel and its endowments, because,
at the time it was founded, the preaching of Unitarian

doctrines was illegal. Lord Eldon decided that this contention was correct, and that all trusts for religious purposes must be regarded as being in favour of religious opinions the preaching of which was lawful at the time when the trust was made. It followed from this decision that every building erected and every endowment created before 1813, even though, like Essex Street Chapel, it had been expressly built for Unitarian purposes, was to be held in law to have been Trinitarian. The case was carried to a higher court, and remained in abeyance till 1835, when Lord Eldon's view was confirmed. It was finally decided in Lord Eldon's sense after the judgment of the House of Lords in the case of Lady Hewley's charities in 1842.

The Hewley case was much the same in principle as that of the Wolverhampton chapel. " In the Lady Hewley case it was held by the Judges and ruled by the Lords that without any inquiry into the fact and even in direct contradiction of the known fact, the law would assume that no endowment could possibly have been intended in favour of a form of worship which the law did not tolerate at the time of the endowment, and that this original defect was not cured by any subsequent legalisation of the same form of worship."* It followed from this authoritative exposition of the law, that the clauses in the Toleration Act which were directed against Anti-Trinitarian opinions had a kind of posthumous effect. Their full force had only been discovered after they were repealed. The legislature

* Introduction to "Parliamentary Debates on the Dissenters' Chapels Bill."

had expressly intended to legalise the preaching and worship of Unitarians, in passing, without a division, Mr. William Smith's Act in 1813 ; but it was now found that though their worship had been legalised, their buildings and endowments might be taken away from them.   The Unitarians at once formed a Committee, and put their case before the Government. The hardship of the position was recognized and relief promised.   A Bill was introduced by the Lord Chancellor in the House of Lords and into the House of Commons by the Attorney-General. It had the cordial support of the leaders on both sides in both Houses.   All the Law Lords were in its favour, and Lord Brougham, Lord Cottenham and Lord Campbell spoke in the debates.   The only division taken in the Lords was on the third reading which was carried by 44 against 9.

In the House of Commons the Bill was opposed at every stage.   The Congregational Union and the Wesleyan Conference petitioned against it.   An anti-Unitarian agitation was got up.   "There is a cry against Unitarians through this country," said Mr. R. L. Shiel in an eloquent speech in favour of the Bill.   "At one time you did not pursue a Unitarian when you had a Papist for your game, but now the sport is capital if a Socinian is to be hunted down."   The prospects of litigation for the confiscation of the property of Unitarians to orthodox purposes, proved too tempting for Divines, and statesmen had to step in and teach them morals.   Mr. Shiel described it as "litigation in which controversy and chicane are combined—in which the mysteries of Calvinism are rendered

darker by the mystifications of jurisprudence, and
in which the enthusiasm of orthodox solicitors is
associated with the rapacity of orthodox Divines."
Sir Robert Peel, then Prime Minister, told the House
of Commons that he and his colleagues entertained
so strong a belief of the justice of the principles on
which the Bill was founded, that they were prepared
to make every other consideration subordinate to
the fulfilment of the duty of supporting it. Lord
John Russell said, "I must say I was never
more convinced that a Bill was necessary for the
purpose of doing justice to a class of our fellow-
subjects." Mr. Gladstone wound up a long and
powerful speech by saying, "Our religious belief
should guide us in this as in other acts. But I
contend that the best use you can make of your
religious belief is to apply it to the decisive perfor-
mance of a great and important act—an act which
whether the consequences to arise from it may be
convenient or inconvenient (and I believe the balance
will be found to be greatly on the side of convenience, but that is the second question, not the
first, now before us) I hope I have in some measure
proved to be founded on the permanent principles
of truth and justice." Mr. Macaulay spoke in the
same sense, and the second reading of the Bill,
which had the cordial support of the late Lord
Harrowby, then Lord Sandon, was carried by 309
against 119. On the third reading the votes were
203 for, to 83 against. On its return to the Lords
as amended in the Commons there was another
great debate, but on the Lord Chancellor's motion
"that this Bill do now pass" the votes were 202

against 41. By these great majorities did the two Houses of Parliament withstand and rebuke an agitation which originated in theological intolerance and was sustained by a complete public ignorance of the facts of the case.

In Samuel Sharpe's Diary he records in April 1844 the signing of a petition in favour of the Bill "as fifth in descent of a race of attenders at public worship" at Newington Green Chapel. They were,—

1. Samuel Harris, an East India Merchant, who probably was one of the Founders.

2. Daniel Radford who married his daughter Mary. He left £100 to it by will.

3. Thomas Rogers who married his (Daniel Radford's) daughter Mary, in whose time the Copyhold was bought and my uncle Samuel made first Trustee.

4. My mother,* who attended there till her marriage.

5. Myself, who joined the Congregation in about 1830.

6. My children, three of whom teach in the Sunday School.

This petition, shewing, as it does, the direct descent of existing worshippers in this Chapel from its original founders, is an illustration of the hereditary character of many of these Congregations. Scores of such petitions were presented to both Houses of Parliament in favour of the measure. Samuel Sharpe puts on record his regret that though he took much interest in the Bill, he was little able to help its promoters, because of his forced attention to business.

* Chap. I, p. 15. She was daughter of the Thomas Rogers named just before.

He found time however to promote petitions and attend meetings, and in July 1844 we find him moving a resolution at a congratulatory meeting of the General Committee of the Presbyterian Union, declaring the especial gratification they felt " to witness the support given by several distinguished members of the Episcopal bench to an application of the principles of religious liberty, more immediately in favour of men whose opinions they necessarily view with peculiar disapprobation." The Bishops who supported the measure were Maltby of Durham, Stanley of Norwich, Musgrave of Hereford, Thirlwall of St. Davids, and Pepys of Worcester.

The Unitarians justly regarded the passing of the Bill as a new triumph of the principle of religious freedom, and determined to celebrate it in a practical way. Mr. Sharpe could not agree with them in the form they gave the memorial. Speaking of the Bill he says :—

When it was passed my friends, the promoters, built University Hall, Gordon Square, as a memorial. I declined to join them because they made the educational part of the scheme secondary to the board and lodging. From the after results I was never sorry that I held aloof.

University Hall, Gordon Square, was intended to be a place of residence for Unitarians and others who were receiving their education at University College. Some years later when Manchester New College was removed to London, its library was established and its classes were held in the building. The passing of the University Tests Act, opening Oxford and Cambridge to those who cannot conscientiously sign the thirty-nine articles, rendered such a Hall of Residence no longer needful. Most of those to whom it might have been useful had the sectarianism of the Universities been kept up, now go to the old seats of learning. The building has therefore been handed over to Manchester New College as a place of residence for its students.

Samuel Sharpe's literary activity during these years is best described in his own words :—

In 1844, I received a letter from Mr. Birch of the British Museum, inviting me to join a new Syro-Egyptian Society, to which I unwillingly though immediately gave my consent. I had no great love for Societies, or faith in their usefulness. I wished each student to rely more upon his own energies. I thought that many even were rather hindered than helped in their studies by them, and often lost their self-reliance while waiting for the encouragement and help of their fellows. I had long left off attending the meetings of the Geological Society of which I had been a member above twenty years. I had also dropped the meetings of the Numismatic Society, which I had more lately joined, and which was more in agreement with my present antiquarian pursuits. I had resolved to join no more societies as they took me away from a happy home and broke in upon my studies. I made, however, a prophetic reserve in favour of an Egyptian Society which I thought would one day or other be proposed by somebody, and accordingly, when it was proposed I felt that my own attention to Egyptian studies was too well known to allow me to decline joining. I found that the society was not altogether in good hands. The best men refused to join it, and Mr. Birch himself withdrew from it. I have, however, continued to attend its meetings and with not a little profit. I met many Egyptian travellers there, and heard what was being done by discoverers on the banks of the Nile ; and I learned yet more by endeavouring from time to time to explain to the Society my own views on hieroglyphics and chronology. We began a series of Egyptian inscriptions, but it did not go beyond six plates. I preferred publishing such inscriptions at my own expense, to being encumbered by the help of the Society and its Secretary. We also printed two small volumes of Original Papers, to each of which I was a contributor ; but I did not feel proud of the volumes, and our poverty and discretion together checked further publications. I was enabled however by this Society to improve or to gain the acquaintance of several valuable scholars and travellers, more particularly of Dr. Lee and my excellent friend Mr. Bonomi.

The friendship thus formed lasted till the end of Mr. Bonomi's life. This Egyptian traveller, artist, and sculptor was one of the gentlest and most genial of men. He was a little older than Samuel Sharpe, having been born in 1796 ; but his manner and his looks were youthful, and his merry laugh, his love of fun, his quaint stories from the Talmud, his Italian proverbs, and his artistic knowledge and enthusiasm, made the family regard him with more than common affection. He had studied sculpture, had taken a course of anatomy under Sir Charles Bell, and had gained the silver medal of the Royal Academy for perspective. He went to Rome to study art in 1822, and from thence to Syria and Egypt. In Egypt he spent fifteen years, and was the first to point out the monument which according to Herodotus was set up by Sesostris on the Syrian coast to commemorate his victories. Much benefit to both came from the intimate and prolonged friendship of the travelled and untravelled Egyptian scholars. Samuel Sharpe regarded his friend as an almost unique example of the union of uncommon attainments with unusual modesty. His visits were looked forward to with enthusiasm and looked back upon with delight. Mr. Bonomi was equally welcomed by young and old. He would go and stay in the house, setting the young people to some artistic work, such as making casts of hands, or giving them lessons in perspective by a series of charming drawings, and leaving the house rich with his own masterly and rapidly executed pencil-sketches. At other times he would plan with their father some new paper on Egypt or Nineveh. He wrote on " Nineveh and its Palaces " before Sir Henry Layard went to the mound at Nimroud, and in a Volume of Photographs entitled "Egypt, Nubia and Ethiopia" he sketched the wood engravings while Samuel Sharpe wrote the Notes. The account of the sarcophagus of Oimenepthah they published together.

This close association in literary work grew up in after years out of the friendship now begun. At present other matters occupied the author of the " History of Egypt." His Egyptian studies were continued through the whole of the years covered by the last two Chapters ; but they did not at present lead to any new work. The only publication of the year 1844 was the second edition of his New Testament of which his own account is all that need be given.

It was now four years since I had printed my translation of the New Testament, and as I had spared no pains to find out its faults and correct them, I was impatient to print again. I made no change in my plan, which was to

keep to the Authorised Version and to aim at antiquarian
exactness rather than what might be more pleasing to an
idle ear.   I sold off what was left of the first edition to a
dealer in remainders and printed the second edition in the
summer of 1844.   To a careful writer a second edition is
a great comfort; it enables him to correct his faults of
hastiness.   I thought my translation was now worthy of
notice.   I therefore printed a thousand copies and published them at the cost price.

The autumn of 1844 was however not favourable
to his attention either to public matters or to private
studies. The times were difficult for men of business,
and the banking firm of Rogers, Olding, Sharpe and
Boycott, had their own peculiar anxiety. One
Monday morning in November 1844, when the
acting partners went down to business at the
usual hour, they were confronted with what at
the first glance must have looked like a threat of
ruin. When the great iron safe, in which all the
valuables of the Bank were kept, was opened, it
was found to be empty. When it was closed on
Saturday night it had contained more than £40,000
in bank notes, over £1,000 in gold, and £5,000 in
Bills of Exchange. The safe had been opened some
time in the course of Sunday with one of its own
keys, the whole of the money and bills taken out
and the iron door closed again. The iron safe was in
an inner office and was meant never to be left un-
guarded. One of the partners lived on the premises,
and one of the clerks was always supposed to be in
the bank, day and night. On Sunday the 24th of
November the day clerk asked permission to go out
for a few hours, and as one of his employers was on

the premises the leave was given. It was thought that, during his absence, the robbery was effected by some persons who had been helped and warned by a dishonest servant.

The thieves were prevented from profiting by their immense booty, by the admirable promptitude with which the matter was followed up. It was a race between the owners of the notes and the robbers, which should be first in reaching foreign banks. The thieves had the start; but so promptly were the numbers and dates of the stolen notes communicated to home and continental bankers, that the thieves were unable to make use of them. Their promptitude was shown in the fact that a single note, which in the haste had been omitted from the list, was instantly cashed at the Bank of England before the firm had discovered the omission. Two months after the robbery the Bank of England repaid to Messrs. Rogers & Co. the value of the stolen paper, £40,710, upon the usual guarantee of indemnity in case the notes should ever be presented for payment. In the end the actual loss was small, but until the notes had been recovered and cancelled at the Bank of England a constant source of anxiety remained. A reward of £3,000 was first offered. This failing, it was reduced to £2,500; and at the end of about two years, just after notice had been given that, on a day named, it would be further reduced to £2,000, the notes were got back and the £2,500 was paid.

This anxious time was not without its alleviations. Friends and neighbours at home and in the City flocked in with offers of money. Samuel Sharpe was much touched with the kindness and confidence thus manifested, but he declined the proferred help, as only adding to the responsibility put on him by the disaster.   Mr. Rogers put down his carriage, and the household at Highbury Place sent away a servant and dropped all needless expenses. These had been very few indeed, for Samuel Sharpe had always brought up his family to consider that habits of economy were as good as wealth.   Friends had often told him that he lived far too quietly and inexpensively for a London banker.   But he had quite other thoughts on the subject and knew his own circumstances best.   He was carrying on a good business, with the help of partners, for a rich uncle.   He had brought in no capital of his own and only possessed what he was able to lay by from year to year.   No man in his senses could fail to think of the time when the rich uncle would die, and his capital be withdrawn from the business, to be divided between his nephews and nieces.   For this inevitable event the nephew had always prepared by adding to his share of the capital, and each incoming partner did the same.   As it happened, Mr. Rogers lived on to the unusual age of ninety-three, so that long before his death the partners were well prepared to go on by themselves.

There is no reference to this robbery in the Diary. In his autobiographical sketch he merely says that his studies were sadly interrupted, because for many months the cares of the day were so severe as to leave his mind very little at leisure in the evening. But he was not idle.   His literary work went on, and 1845 brought a crisis of some interest in

the history of his authorship.  Of this period he
writes :—

I endeavoured to drive away less pleasant thoughts by
attention to my three histories.  The first I entirely re-
wrote.  It had been an antiquarian inquiry ; I now cast it
into the same form as the second and third and added to
it the materials which seven years of study had enabled
me to collect.  I paid still further attention to neatness
and correctness in writing, always reading my sentences
aloud to my wife and daughters to try how far they were
easy to be understood.  I ventured more than I had done
before to add an opinion on the events as they occur, and
thereby to give a more moral and personal tone to the
whole.  Such is the variety of subjects contained in a
volume of history that in writing about Egypt I was able
to give utterance to every opinion that I held in religion,
politics or literature, and as I read the whole of it aloud
to my children, I was agreeably kept in remembrance of
what ought to be a writer's aim, to make his readers better
as well as wiser.  At this time of difficulty in business I
did not feel rich enough to indulge myself as before in
the expensive amusement of printing ; what I had hitherto
published had not brought me back one half of the outlay.
But fortunately Mr. Moxon, the publisher, began to think
well of my books, and he proposed that I should unite
the three into one complete History of Egypt, and he
offered to publish it on joint account.  This offer I gladly
accepted.  I needed no delay.  While always adding to
my book and endeavouring to improve it, I had always
kept the Manuscript in a state ready for the printer.  In
the beginning of 1846 I therefore published a second
edition of my three histories in one volume, under the
title of " The History of Egypt from the Earliest Times
till the conquest by the Arabs A.D. 640."

Though  this  work  was  a  reproduction  of  three

previous works and was therefore a second edition, it was practically a new book. It was more popular in form and treatment. It had been made more readable in every respect, and it speedily attained some success and distinction. It gained for its author that general and popular recognition which had not been given to his earlier writings, or to the same work in its previous shape. The former works had been for students, this was for the public. They had attracted the attention of Egyptian scholars; this received general notice. It did not take the popular view of Egyptian chronology. It differed as to the length of the earlier periods of the Egyptian history from all the other authorities, from Lepsius and Bunsen, from Wilkinson and Birch. It took the strictly independent view which characterised its author in all his works. It was favourably noticed in the *Edinburgh Review*, then under the able editorship of Mr. Empson. In those days the great Quarterlies were the arbiters of the literary fate of authors. Their notice was fame, their approving nod was supposed to confer immortality. The *Edinburgh* article was written by Mr. Donne and gave Mr. Sharpe great satisfaction. It did not deal with the disputed questions of Egyptian antiquity, but almost confined itself to the parts of his history which deal with Alexandrian life and literature. It contained a cordial recognition of his special merits as a historian, and of the established position he had gained by the publication of the "History of Egypt." There is a further sign of the estimation in which Samuel Sharpe was now held among literary men in an entry in Crabb

Robinson's Diary dated on the day after Christmas Day, 1846.

Yesterday passed very agreeably. My breakfast went off very well, though the omelette which my niece advised me to have was a failure. I had a *partie quarrée*. To meet Donaldson, I had Sir Charles Fellows, the traveller, and Samuel Sharpe the historian of Egypt. Fellows and I modestly retreated and left the field to the two scholars.

The literary work of the next few years grew out of the increased recognition of his large knowledge of Egyptian history and his mode of dealing with the questions suggested by the chronology and antiquities. It may best be described in his own words:

Among other travellers my Egyptian writings introduced me to Mr. Bartlett who had then lately returned from Jerusalem and Petra, and in the autumn of 1848 when he printed his "Forty Days in the Desert" he accepted from me a short chapter on "The Land of Goshen and the Jews' March out of Egypt." I had before written on this geographical subject in the *Christian Reformer* and then in my History of Egypt. This paper therefore in Mr. Bartlett's book contained my views, as corrected a second time, respecting the changes in the head of the Red Sea, and on the place where the Israelites crossed. It gained some attention, particularly in the *Athenæum* where Professor Airy under the signature of A.B.G. and Miss Fanny Corbeaux wrote in its favour. In the following years I gave to Mr. Bartlett for his "Nile Boat" a sketch of Egyptian History, and for his "Overland Route" an account of the Shipwreck of the Apostle Paul, and the Historian Josephus, who, I argued, sailed from Cesaraea to Italy in the same ship. For his "Jerusalem Revisited" I gave him a paper on the Plan of the Temple at Jerusalem.

While busy on the History of Ancient Egypt I also compiled a map of the country. This I did by making a tracing from the French survey identifying the ruins which are marked therein, and then adding the other towns and the *Nomes* from Ptolemy's Geography and the Itinerary of Antoninus. This map I offered to Mr. Wyld for publication, but he declined it saying there was no sale for ancient maps. Mr. Bonomi, however, lithographed it and published it on his own account and I believe was tolerably successful in selling it. To lessen the expense to him my daughters coloured the whole edition. I had the pleasure of seeing two copies, stretched and varnished hanging up in the private rooms of the British Museum. That part of the map which embraces the route of the Israelites from the Nile to the Red Sea had before been copied by Mr. Hughes, the engraver for Mr. Bartlett's "Forty Days in the Desert." Mr. Hughes was a good Geographer and he thoroughly approved of my plan for the Land of Goshen. He was much employed in engraving maps for school atlases and religious publications, and for these he always copied it and soon made it well-known.

Encouraged by the success of the map, Mr. Bonomi then undertook to lithograph and publish the hieroglyphical names of the Egyptian Kings, which I had arranged in the order of their succession. To this list I added the map of Egypt, the plan of Thebes, the site of ancient Memphis, the plan of ancient Alexandria, and a few pages of letterpress. It was published in 1849 under the title of "The Chronology and Geography of Ancient Egypt." We afterwards added to it a page of alphabet by which the King's names could be read. In this also my daughters coloured the maps and Mr. Bonomi was successful in selling copies enough to repay himself the cost of the publication and for his own trouble as lithographer.

In the same year, 1849, Samuel Sharpe gave to

the Philological Society the Greek "Fragments of
Orations in Accusation and Defence of Demos-
thenes respecting the money of Harpalus," with a
translation. These fragments had been traced by
Mr. A. C. Harris of Alexandria from a papyrus in
his possession. They were afterwards reprinted by
Mr. Churchill Babington and yet later the remainder
of the fragments were published.

# CHAPTER IX.

## INTERCOURSE WITH SAMUEL ROGERS, MISS AIKIN, AND OTHERS.

PERHAPS the most interesting records which a man can leave behind him are those which detail his intercourse with eminent persons whom he has met. Nothing makes a biography so popular as such gossip, but it presupposes in the subject of the biography a gossiping spirit. A man who can sit down at night and place on record the stories he has heard, the repartees he has enjoyed, the conversations in which he has taken part, must possess an overweening sense of his own importance, or a love of work for which no other satisfaction is found, or a fondness for dwelling on the past, for the indulgence of which he is willing to undertake constant toil. Such a man is likely to become a mere social Autolycus, a snapper-up of unconsidered trifles of talk. Society would become impossible if such note-takers as the late Bishop Wilberforce were general, and their note-books were given to the world. There is no temptation to the biographer of Samuel Sharpe to make indiscreet revelations. Though many distinguished scholars and travellers constantly found their way to Highbury Place, and though at the houses of

Mr. and Miss Rogers, of his own brothers, and of such friends as Crabb Robinson, he often met eminent and interesting persons, he has not left much on record concerning them. Some of the entries which relate to Mr. Rogers's breakfast parties have already been given. There are a few others in the Diary of later years, some of which tell stories which are already familiar to the public, but which are worth reproducing.

Here are glimpses of a man whom the present generation has almost forgotten, but who was well-known in literary society during the last fifteen years of the previous century and the first forty years of this :—

August 25, 1843.—I called on Mr. Maltby at the London Institution and walked for two hours with him. He has lost the use of one eye, but is as cheerful and full of conversation as ever, quoting books of note and talking about men of note.

1847. December 7.—After examining references in the London Institution, I called on Mr. Maltby. He was so blind that he had to ask who I was. He showed me a letter from Sydney Smith thanking a friend for a pheasant. "Barn-door fowls," he says, are "good enough for Dissenters, but for a real clergyman, a thirty-nine articled clerk, the true thing is a pheasant." Mr. Maltby told me of his being steward to the Revolution dinner in 1792, when he restrained the rashness of the toasts.

Mr. Maltby had been for many years one of Samuel Sharpe's fastest friends, to whom he had looked up as a young man looks up to an elder. Mr. Maltby had been the early friend and schoolfellow of Mr. Rogers. Maltby and Rogers when young men had so great an admiration for Dr. Johnson that they proposed calling on him. They went together to the great man's door, and one of them had his hand on the knocker when their courage failed them and they turned away. Mr. Maltby had retired from active duty in 1834, but continued to live at the London Institution till his death, in his ninetieth year, in 1854. His manner in his old age was quiet and reserved, and in his visits to the house of his friend he loved to sit in the arm-chair with his eyes shaded from the light, and to be appealed to by a younger generation. His reading had been very extensive, and his recollection of what he had read was singularly vivid and fresh. If a question arose as to the actual terms of a quotation, or where it was to be found, everybody said, " Ask Mr. Maltby." He had succeeded Porson in 1809 as Librarian to the London Institution, and Samuel Sharpe had seen much of him there in the early days when he was frequently a reader in its library. The friendship of Mr. Maltby for the young student's relations led to a friendship with the student himself, which lasted till the close of Mr. Maltby's life.

The next entries record recollections of Samuel Sharpe's visits to Rogers, and the first of them contains one more illustration of the goodness of heart of a man of whom Carlyle spoke with the prejudice born of his own inability to appreciate social qualities, and with the ignorance of mere superficial observation :—

February 8, 1844.—My uncle Sam complained that Dr. Howley, the Archbishop, had used him very unhandsomely. The Archbishop had consulted him about filling up a vacancy in the Museum. My uncle had recommended Cary, but had also mentioned Cary having twice lost the use of his faculties through domestic affliction. The Archbishop weakly told this to Cary as his reason for appointing Panizzi. On this Cary quarrelled with him; but my uncle had the satisfaction of getting him a pension of £200 a year from Lord Melbourne, the week before the Whigs went out of office (in 1841). Peel would certainly have given it if not done before. This Melbourne knew.

July 4.—I spoke to my uncle Sam of Campbell's funeral yesterday in Poet's Corner, and of his not being there. He said, "I did not attend your uncle Henry's nor your brother Sutton's, and so, of course, I did not go to Campbell's. Besides, I did not want to be elbowed by Lords who never did anything for him when alive. Remember, Sam, you are my executor, I am to be buried in Hornsey Churchyard. Let no consideration whatever induce you to bury me in that place (Westminster Abbey). Those men attended to honour themselves, not to honour Campbell, but to catch some reflected glory from him. I have explained that sentiment in one of my notes when speaking of Kings and Cardinals following Petrarch to the grave."

October 20.—My uncle again spoke of the folly of burying Campbell in Westminster Abbey, and praised Pope for refusing to be buried there. He thought the sentiment of seeing the poet's tomb in the Village Churchyard so much more valuable than seeing it among a crowd of vain candidates for fame in Poet's Corner.

This idea seems to have possessed Mr. Rogers, and he was determined to press it upon his nephew and executor. Two years after the above entry in the Diary is another in the same sense. In the next year there is nothing till almost the close :—

1847. December 7.—In the evening Mr. Crabb Robinson came. He had been reviewing "Happy Ignorance," which he thought not to be by Archbishop Whateley. We called together on Mr. Madge, who thought it was. Mr. Madge thought the new "History of the Hebrew Monarchy" was by Mr. Newman. He thought it dull. "Happy Ignorance" concedes to the Unitarians all they ask. Dr. ——— of Manchester has just left £50,000 to University College.

December 12.—Breakfasted in St. James's Place. Mr. Spedding thinks in an impartial life Bacon will stand much better than in Macaulay's review.

My uncle spoke of the aristocracy with contempt, and quoted his father's saying—"Never go near them, Sam." He had not followed this advice, but acknowledged its wisdom.

The nephew, however, acted on this principle, and believed in its wisdom. No man was more anxious for the society of men of learning and genius. Travellers, writers, artists, antiquarians, biblical students, men of science, politicians, preachers; all who had any personal characteristics which made them worth knowing were always welcome at High-bury Place. But for men whose only distinction is a title, as for people whose social position is decided, not by any qualities of their own, but solely by the part of London in which they live, he had the scorn which every self-respecting person feels. Even for friends who drifted off westward to be in the fashion he had but little toleration. Like all men whose names become honourably known, he had opportunities of meeting many well-known persons, but he embraced only those which brought him into pleasant intercourse with men who had something more than "but the guinea's stamp," as Burns calls it, of rank or fortune. The next note in the Diary illustrates this choice :—

1847.   December 22.—Breakfasted at St. James's Place ; Mr. Dyce, Mitford, Harness, Spedding, Gould, Dr. Henderson.   Harness was against Dr. Hampden, everybody else seemed against the Bishops.   Mr. Dyce was alarmed at the news of some more going to be published from Gray's note-books.   He said his scholarship was much over-rated.   Nothing can equal the pleasure of these conversations.   Dyce, Mitford (nephew of the historian), and Spedding are simple, unaffected  men, learned, full of conversation and literature.   Dyce and Mitford are very little of clergymen.   Harness more so.

Samuel Sharpe himself contributed much to these conversations.   Crabb Robinson records one of these breakfasts about this time:—

Oct. 9, 1848.—I went out early and breakfasted with Rogers ; a small and agreeable party, only Samuel Sharpe, Harness and sister, and Lord Glenelg.   Samuel Sharpe said but little, but what he said was very good.   The recent conviction of Smith O'Brien was a matter of doubt, but most thought an execution necessary, though Samuel Sharpe thought it would lead to murders of landlords.

The following recollections of the same conversation by Mr. Sharpe and Mr. H. Crabb Robinson show a conflict of evidence :—

28th.—S. R. quoted Horne Tooke telling his brother, "You rise by your gravity, and I sink by my levity."   He (or Sydney Smith) said in his illness his thoughts had been wandering between the nine Articles and the thirty-nine Muses, and he did not know which was which.

N

There is a similar record in Crabb Robinson's Diary:—

Aug. 28, 1849.—Breakfasted with Rogers. A small, agreeable party. Luttrell, Dyce, Samuel Sharpe, and Moxon, all in good humour. To-day or about this time Rogers told us that Sydney Smith said to his eldest brother, "Brother, you and I are exceptions to the law of nature ; you have risen by your gravity, I have sunk by my levity."

There is no doubt that Crabb Robinson is wrong and Sharpe is right. Rogers tells the story himself in his "Recollections" of Horne Tooke. Crabb Robinson's is the common version, but Thomas Moore attributes the saying, on the authority of Mr. Shiel, to an Irish Barrister, Keller, in addressing a judge. Keller was Moore's godfather. Mr. William Sharpe, in a note to Rogers's "Recollections," points out that Rogers's record must have been earlier in date than Moore's.

The following notes of conversations at the Tuesday breakfasts are interesting, as supplementing those in Mr. Dyce's volume of Rogers's "Table Talk," and in a few cases giving a somewhat different version of a familiar story.

30th.—S. R. quoted Horne Tooke saying that the Reformation had rejected Purgatory and kept Hell. Mr. Donaldson praised Müller's books which he was translating. S. R. praised D'Aubigné's "Reformation" as a sober, well-written book. Donaldson, on the other hand, did not like its Genevan religious views, and praised Ranke as more impartial.

The following epigram on two persons now forgotten caused much amusement when it was written. Miss Seward and William Hayley were contem-

porary poets, much admired at the close of the
last century and the first years of this. When
Rogers published his first poem he was much
gratified by Hayley's praise. Rogers remarked
about Hayley in later years that he was formerly
over-rated, but was latterly under-valued.

Miss Seward: Ode didactic, epic, sonnet,
　　　　　Mr. Hayley, you're divine ;
Mr. Hayley : Madam, take my word upon it,
　　　　　You, yourself, are all the Nine.

Mr. Jesse reminded my uncle of Theodore Hook and
—— —— dining with him some time ago. Hook, giving
an account of it, said Mr. Rogers had emptied his wine-
cellar into his bookseller. Mr. Rogers said he could give
—— ——'s epitaph in two words—"Drunk or sober,
always a gentleman."

Mr. Luttrell mentioned an Irishman who, when reproached
for being a Pluralist, said, " If you don't take care you may
find me a Duellist."

Mr. Mitford said his uncle had been urged to write the
" History of Greece" by Gibbon whom he knew in the
Hampshire Militia. Mr. Donaldson gave us the new
inscription proposed at the dinner-table at Trinity College,
Cambridge, for the snuff-box, as suitable to the place and
the purpose, " Quicunque vult," the first words of the
Athanasian creed.

When Rothschild, returning thanks from the hustings
last autumn, said he was the choice of the people, a voice
cried out from the back of the hall, " So was Barabbas."

4th July.—Lord Brougham told S. R. that Macaulay
would fail in narrative (his History is coming out at Christmas). Milman thought he might easily change his style to
that, but would be unable to cease to be an advocate—
" he has taken a fee and holds a brief from his convictions."

S. R., though a worshipper of Gray, disapproved altogether of his fundamental rule, that the language of poetry should be a little antiquated. The language of the heart is the language of the nursery. Milman thought people could remember more lines of Gray than of Pope, though Pope's matter was more quotable.

"Duty" is spoiled into duties. A gentleman pays his "devoirs" to a lady. A clergyman does the duties of his church. A soldier is "on duty" in the solemn sense.

William Spencer took "Anacreon" Moore to Lady Jersey's. She presently said, "Get the little man to give us some of his noise." This was the way in which a lady of title asked a man of letters to sing his own songs.

S. R. had known most of the good talkers of his day, but no one so quick and clever as Mr. Luttrell, except, perhaps, Horne Tooke. Jekyll's conversation was rich in humour, but Luttrell's and Tooke's were of a higher class.

Pope, "Moral Essays," iii., 203–218.* Roscoe curiously mistakes the meaning of these lines, and blames Pope for an attack upon a man who dispenses his wealth in the service of his country. But surely the character is

* What slaughtered hecatombs, what floods of wine
Fill the capacious 'Squire and deep Divine !
Yet no mean motive this profusion draws,
His oxen perish in his country's cause ;
'Tis George and Liberty that crowns the cup,
And Zeal for that great House which eats him up.
The woods recede around the naked seat,
The sylvans groan—no matter—for the Fleet :
Next goes his Wool—to clothe our valiant bands,
Last, for his Country's love, he sells his Lands.
To town he comes, completes the nation's hope,
And heads the bold Train-bands, and burns a Pope.
And shall not Britain now reward his toils;
Britain, that pays her Patriots with her spoils?
In vain at Court the Bankrupt pleads his cause,
His thankless Country leaves him to her Laws.

that of a pretended patriot, of Whig politics, who wastes his property, sells his timber and then his lands, ruined by electioneering expenses and county dinners. Then being refused a pension by his country is left to the bankruptcy laws.

S. R., when visiting Winchester on a tour before he was one-and-twenty, went to the college and took with him to the inn Edward Maltby, a boy with whose family he was intimate. This boy was afterwards Bishop of Durham, and used to say that he never ate such excellent duck and peas as on that evening.

1848. October 20.—Nobody was at my uncle's breakfast to-day but Mr. Harness. He told us several interesting anecdotes.

Horne Tooke, when going to Paris, took a letter of introduction to D'Alembert as one of the chief of their men of letters. Before delivering it he thought it necessary to get rather a handsome suit of clothes in the French fashion. He was received politely. D'Alembert asked him if he had seen the last new comedy, if he had visited Madame ——, if he had seen certain sights, and so forth. Horne Tooke made his visit short, thinking he was treated coldly. David Hume, who was present, followed him, and apologized for D'Alembert. " He seems to have mistaken your character ; he does not know that you are a man of letters ; perhaps he was misled by your dress."*

When Campbell was writing his " Lives of the Chancellors " Rogers gave him in writing Erskine's own account of his being engaged in the Greenwich Hospital case. But Campbell made no use of it, except to borrow one point from it, and returned it saying that the family said it was not true.

Campbell used to treat his father-in-law Scarlett with marked rudeness when they were both at the Bar. Scarlett could hardly retaliate or defend himself against the man on whom depended the happiness of his daughter.

* See " Recollections by Samuel Rogers," pp. 147, 148.

S. R. was staying at Lord Bathurst's when news was brought in the evening that the Princess Charlotte was confined; that the child was dead, but the Princess herself was doing well. At four o'clock in the morning there was a stir in the house. An express had arrived to tell Lord Bathurst that the Princess was dead. He got up immediately to carry the news to the Regent, her father. He went to town and called up the Duke of York at St. James's Palace, and took him with him. When they got to the Regent's they roused Colonel Bloomfield, told him their errand, and begged him to inform the Regent of his daughter's death. He positively refused. " Tell it yourselves," said he. " Let him know then that we want to speak to him," said the Duke of York and Lord Bathurst. This Bloomfield did, and they were shown up. The Duke of York made Lord Bathurst go into the room first. They found the Regent sitting up in bed, and told him they had sad news for him. He said he had heard it, the child was dead. They then let him understand that his daughter was dead. He was, of course, much upset; but three hours afterwards he was consulting with those about him as to the ceremony of the funeral.

October 23.—Breakfasted with my uncle. A lady said to Foote, " I am afraid you don't go to church, Mr. Foote." " No, Madam, I do not," replied Foote ; " not that I think there is any harm in it ! "

Hoppner, looking round on the pictures and vases at 22, St. James's Place, said, " What an enviable man this is, and d—— him, he is not married." Hoppner's domestic life was not happy.

The dramatists, said S. R., are the best novelists. Monk Lewis told me that he took his " Bravo of Venice," which is so striking in its effects, from a German Drama.

As Lord Byron and S. R. were stepping across the street from a house at which there had been an assembly to their carriage a link-boy called out, " This way, my lord." He perhaps knew neither. Rogers remarked to Byron, "Every-body knows you." Byron answered bitterly, "It is because I am deformed." His temper was soured by his lameness.

S. R. was in Italy with my aunt when Bonaparte returned from Elba. They came home hastily through Germany. They had been introduced to Murat. S. R. went to Italy a second time after printing the first part of "Italy." It was published in his absence without his name. He then visited some spots described in the poem which he had not visited before. The poem did not sell well; he was dissatisfied with it, and destroyed part of the impression.

On the death of Lord Spencer, when Lord Althorp removed to the Upper House, the Cabinet proposed to Lord John Russell to become Chancellor of the Exchequer. He answered that figures and finance had not been his study, but if his colleagues thought it best he would under-take it—he would undertake any post in which they thought his services were needed or would be useful. Hobhouse, meeting Sydney Smith in the street, mentioned these words of Lord John. So when Sydney Smith had occasion to attack Lord John in his letters to Archdeacon Sinclair, he spoke of his presumption. "He would venture on any-thing; he would not shrink from cutting off a leg or taking command of the Channel Fleet."

S. R. used to spend some weeks at Broadstairs every autumn, and usually slept at Rochester on his way down. He then stopped at Canterbury, and while there always stepped into the Cathedral to hear the service chanted in that venerable building. One year he was recognized as he sat in the Cathedral by the clergyman in authority, who, to show his respect to the Poet, sent a verger to him to ask him which chant he would like to have performed. This marked civility was repeated every year as he passed through Canterbury. He was, of course, gratified by the attention, but his pleasure in the music was sadly lessened.

He had been willing to fancy that the band of clergymen
were celebrating the service for their own devotion and for
the glory of God, but he found that their thoughts were
really engaged on amusing himself.

These short recollections of the conversation at
Rogers's Tuesday breakfasts may be supplemented
by two other entries which come in at a somewhat
later time.  Speaking of his uncle in his autobiographical sketch he says :—

As his infirmities increased the circle of visitors lessened,
and after a time it was limited to those few whose good
sense and good feeling enabled them to make allowance
for an old man's deafness and occasional forgetfulness.
Mr. Mitford, the editor of Gray's works, in some doggrel
lines addressed to him when removing to Brighton for the
winter, thus describes the reduced list of Tuesday morning
visitors :—

> Happy the man, and happy he alone,
> Who passed the winter months at Brighthelmstone.
>    He who secure within can say,
> I've 'scaped from all my London friends away.
> From Robinson the loud and Dyce the gay,
> And Henderson, who gives the best Tokay,
> And Mitford, ever prosing about Gray,
> And Sharpe, who rules o'er Egypt like a Dey.
> Now my friends do your worst, for I have lived to-day.*

"The epithets are not all happy," said Mr. Dyce

* The lines are parodied from one of Dryden's Imitations
of Horace, the 29th Ode of the 3rd Book, which begins
Tyrrhena regum progenies.  Rogers says that Fox was fond
of quoting Dryden's lines, which he preferred to the original
of Horace.

when the lines were read, and in his case at least the word gay was used satirically. Like Crabb Robinson, he was a great diner-out, but he was a man of much refinement and culture, the translator of Athenæus, and editor of Shakespeare. His friends called him "Alexander the Great," as he domineered over the lesser lights of criticism. He was of a tall, handsome figure, but had a weary and lethargic manner, and stood bending as though to come down to the level of ordinary men. For many years he wore an ugly brown wig, but after an illness came forth with a magnificent head of his own white hair, a most striking transformation. Mr. Henderson had written a learned book on Ancient Wines. To Crabb Robinson the epithet loud was not quite appropriate. This genial, popular, and ever welcome person was more voluble than noisy, persistent rather than loud. He was short and thick, with a fine intelligent countenance and a bluff hearty manner, and looked the picture of health and self-content. He began to talk as soon as the door was opened, would talk all the way upstairs, would keep on without stopping through his whole visit and till on his departure he was out of earshot in the street. He was proud of his own conversational powers; but his goodness of heart, his wide knowledge of the world, his recollections of his friends Goethe and Wordsworth, and his large reading, made him a most welcome visitor, and an immense favourite with all who knew him.

Mr. Rogers was very tender and gentle in his old age. Wishing the children of his nephews " Good-

night " he would say to them, " Speak kindly of me
when I am gone." He was fond of repeating Mrs.
Barbauld's beautiful lines beginning "Life, we've
been long together," and especially their exquisite
ending. He used to speak of having repeated them
to Wordsworth, who had never heard them before.
Wordsworth was much struck with them. He
walked up and down the room repeating them to
himself, and then exclaimed, " I do not often envy
other people their good things, but I should like to
have written those lines."* When the news was
brought to Rogers of his sister's death he exclaimed, " What a great blessing, I wish I could
die too." He was then ninety-two, his sister
was a year or two younger. They were spending
the winter together in his house at Brighton, and
she died there in January 1855. They had both
been confined to their chairs by similar accidents—
the breaking of the thigh-bone in the hip-joint. In
December, 1855, the wish that he could die too was
granted, and he passed quietly away in his ninety-
third year, leaving his nephews Samuel and William
Sharpe his executors, and committing to their charge
large numbers of journals and letters, very few of
which have yet seen the light of day.

---

* The lines are:—
    Life, we've been long together,
  Through pleasant and through cloudy weather;
    'Tis hard to part when friends are dear,
    Perhaps 'twill cost a sigh, a tear;
    Then steal away, give little warning,
      Choose thine own time :
  Say not " Good-night," but in some happier clime
    Bid me " Good-morning."

Samuel Sharpe records his uncle's death in his autobiographical sketch :—

In 1855 my uncle Samuel Rogers died, leaving his property to be divided among his nephews and nieces, and appointing my brother William and myself his executors. His valuable collection of pictures and other works of art was sold by auction. The sale attracted great attention from his known good taste as a collector, and the pictures in particular brought great prices. He left his copyrights to me, which I looked upon less as a piece of property than as a duty that I should take care that his poems were reprinted as often as possible. His aim had been to obtain for them a circulation, and he valued the illustrations in the first place as a step to that end. They had sold so largely during his lifetime—helped, no doubt, by his social position and personal influence, that shortly after his death Moxon and Co. sold off by auction what they had printed, and refused to continue to print them ; and it was not till ten years later the demand again revived for them. Very soon after Mr. Rogers's death, indeed, sooner than was quite becoming, Mr. Alexander Dyce published a volume of his conversation under the title of " Recollections of the Table-talk of Samuel Rogers." It was not a judicious book, nor, indeed, well-written. It by no means did justice to Mr. Rogers's conversation. Moreover, it had many mistakes about persons, and gave offence to many. Some of the members of our family felt very sore at it, and went so far as to tell Mr. Dyce so. But I well knew that in taking notes of Mr. Rogers's conversation he was acting with Mr. Rogers's full knowledge and approval, and, moreover, that Mr. Dyce had a sincere regard and respect for him ; that the book was well meant, and that its faults were wholly unintentional. And amid the storm of blame that rose against him I made him very happy by telling him so.

In 1859 my brother William published a volume of

Notes which Mr. Rogers had left behind him ready for the printer.* Soon afterwards I published a biography of Mr. Rogers, as a preface to the volume of his poems. It was of a very few pages, relating to little beyond those particulars of his family and youth which could not be generally known. I made use of all the biographical passages in his poems, but gave no account of that part of his life in which he was well known to the literary and artistic public. Mr. Rogers had been dead four years, and that short time had cooled all curiosity about him. My memoir gained no notice, while four years before, Mr. Dyce's recollections of him had been wholly sold on the day of publication.

In his Diary about the same time Samuel Sharpe writes :—

The following sentences may hereafter be added to my "Life of Samuel Rogers," at present it might give pain to Dr. Beattie :—" In 1844 Campbell died, and was buried in Westminster Abbey, when the Prime Minister and five noblemen acted as pall-bearers. But Mr. Rogers did not think this any honour to the poet, who had never asked for notice from these men who now consented to appear as his friends. Mr. Rogers did not follow among the mourners, and gave particular directions that no such doubtful honour should be asked for for himself. He praised Pope's refusal to be buried there, and whenever the subject was mentioned Mr. Rogers added, ' Remember, Sam, I am not to be buried in Westminster Abbey.' "

It may not be inappropriate at this point to record some notes of conversations which took place a few

---

* " Recollections," by Samuel Rogers. Longman & Co. It contained Mr. Rogers's own recollections of Fox, Burke, Grattan, Porson, Horne Tooke, Talleyrand, Erskine, Walter Scott, Lord Grenville, and the Duke of Wellington.

years later between Samuel Sharpe and Miss Lucy
Aikin. They were written down by his daughters,
and contain some points of literary and social
interest. Miss Aikin was in her old age. She had
vivid recollections of her earlier life, and looked back
with especial pleasure to her childhood. She said
one day to Samuel Sharpe: " From ten to seventeen
I lived in Broad Street Buildings, and there was
always a great deal going on in the house. I was
brought very forward and saw plenty of good
society. Then when other girls come out, as it is
called, I went in, for we removed to Stoke Newington. Oh! wretched Stoke Newington. It nearly
broke my heart." She lived twenty-three years,
from the age of seventeen to that of forty, at
Stoke Newington; from whence she removed to
Hampstead, where she spent the bright evening of
her days, and where she died in 1864 at the age
of eighty-three. At this latter period of her life it
was the custom of her friend Samuel Sharpe to go
over to her house rather frequently for evening tea.
She was full of recollections of people she had met,
and told the stories she had heard from her father Dr.
Aikin and her aunt Mrs. Barbauld with great zest and
vivacity. She remembered Godwin calling on her aunt
when she was a child. She left the room, but Mrs. Barbauld went after her, and told her Godwin was a remarkable man, and that she ought to listen to his
talk. Many years later she met him at a party. He
was very much bowed down with age and trouble,
but she introduced herself to him and he recognized
her in a moment. She was very impatient of his
daughter, Mary Wolstonecraft Godwin, who, she

said, had gained the reputation of being a wit by saying everything, proper and improper, that came into her head. She had seen Charles James Fox. " There was a great charm about him," she said. " When he looked down he was only a large heavy man with a fat face and projecting eyebrows, but when he looked up and you met his dark eyes it was like the opening of the heavens."    .

Another of Miss Aikin's stories was of John Howard. When Howard was living at Church Street, Stoke Newington, Dr. Price was chaplain to Mr. Streatfield. Howard married the landlady in whose house he lodged, and during the three years she lived he stayed on at Stoke Newington. It was at the house of Miss Aikin's grandfather, Mr. Jennings, that he used to meet her father, Dr. Aikin. Howard had been brought up in a strange way, without the education that befitted his station. When he wrote his work on Prisons he needed some one to look over the proofs for him, and he found the aid he wanted in a very intelligent printer at Warrington, who used to print for the Academy, and who printed Mrs. Barbauld's works. When Howard set out upon that last journey abroad from which he never came back, Dr. Aikin went to him and took much trouble in arranging his papers and helping him to start. "He was very kind to all children," said Miss Aikin ; "when he was out on this visit abroad he sent home a straw box of foreign make as a present for me, which I have kept and always look at, thinking of him."

She remarked of Rogers to his nephew, " You say your uncle's conversation was not witty. It is well he does not hear you. He really was a wit. But his brother Henry said the cleverest things, and so easily and naturally. Your uncle Sam used to say, 'Henry says better things than any of us, and thinks nothing of them.'" She talked of Scott. She enjoyed the Lay most because it was new. Scott had read Ritson's "Ancient Ballads," and the Lay was the result. " How much we admired it when it came out," she exclaimed, " I wish anything half so interesting would appear now." The Lay was most admired because it came first. But she thought "Marmion" the best; the "Lady of the Lake" was pretty, but not so good as the earlier poems.

She told a characteristic anecdote of Wedgwood, for whom she had the warmest admiration. It was said with truth that he had spent a thousand pounds in experiments for the making of his vase, in deciding whether the white figures were to be fastened on or to be made by cutting away the white substance down to the blue. In his earlier days he had a white swelling on his knee. The doctors told him that he must have the leg amputated or lie on a sofa and rest it for a year or two. " I lie on a sofa for one or two years," he exclaimed; " impossible ! " " The leg was taken off, and he stumped about for the rest of his days—that was the man," said Miss Aikin, with enthusiasm. She was fond of telling the story of a new curate who once called on her some time after he came into the parish. With characteristic taste and tact the youth began to remonstrate with Miss Aikin for her Unitarian opinions, and excused himself by saying, " Consider, Madam, that I am responsible for your soul." She drew herself up and answered, " Sir, you are the first person who ever told me that there was any one responsible for my soul except myself." As she said this she sailed across the room, rang the bell, and told the servant to bring the gentleman's horse to the door at once. She had the old-fashioned objection to Dickens's novels, that he sought for virtue and refinement in the kennel. But it does not seem to have occurred to her that he has taught all the world to look for both virtue and refinement in very humble life, and to find it too.

## CHAPTER X.

### "LABOUR PHYSICS PAIN."

THE anxiety which the great robbery at the banking house had caused to Samuel Sharpe had a
serious effect upon his health, and he allowed himself too little recreation to preserve full physical vigour.
In the autumn of 1845 he suffered from a weakening
attack to which he paid no proper attention and
which greatly reduced his strength. His fear, at
this time, was of paralysis, such as had carried off
his brother, Sutton, and such as he actually died of
in his old age seven-and-thirty years later. His
brother Henry took him to an eminent physician
who assured him that he was only suffering from
nervous depression and great general weakness. He
had been adopting his usual remedy of starvation,
the doctor recommended feeding up and prescribed
stimulants and tonics and a month's rest. But a few
days at Brighton with his old friend Mr. Janson
were all the holiday he could be induced to take.
Nothing seemed less likely, at this period, as at many
other times, than that he should outlive all his
brothers and be capable of hard work at eighty.

This want of vigorous health joined to the absorbing nature of his business anxieties in the gloomy

period which followed the repeal of the Corn Laws, caused a cessation of literary production, though not of studious activity, during the next few years. The pause extended from the publication of the second edition of the " History of Egypt " in 1846, to the issue of the "Chronology and Geography of Egypt" in 1849 and the translation of the "Fragments of Hyperides " in the "Philosophical Transactions " in that year ; and again from the date of these publications to the issue of his " Historic Notes on the Bible " and the " Egyptian Guide Book to the Crystal Palace " in 1854. The work of these years was that of preparation for years to come. The Vocabulary of Hieroglyphics was rewritten, and made twice as large as the published volume, but it was not published. Meanwhile work on the New Testament was making progress. It was now four years since the issue of the second edition ; and in the meantime a number of fresh emendations had gradually accumulated. These were printed in 1849 on a flyleaf of four pages, entitled " Further Corrections," and were intended to be stitched into the volume at the end of the Preface. " This," he writes, " I may almost call a third edition of my New Testament." But the chief labour of these years was given to the improvement of his " History of Egypt." He was always collecting new materials for this purpose ; and in 1851 he printed a third edition, considerably enlarged and improved. It was in two volumes octavo and in bulk was about one quarter larger than the second edition. A good deal of it had been re-written, many new passages were added, and it was in his opinion a much better book. He now dedicated the work to his eldest sister, acknowledging, as he was always glad to do, that he owed to her his education and his love of learning.

There are records in the Diary about this time which show that the sagacity which has been already noted in the exercise of his judgment on some political questions, was equally shrewd in its application to monetary problems. In October 1850 he wrote a paragraph in the Money Article of the *Morning Chronicle*, calling attention to the imminent danger of depreciation of the currency by the gold which was then just beginning to pour in from the newly-discovered Californian mines. "Nobody," he says in his Diary, "has yet pointed it out." A day or two later the *Manchester Guardian* threw ridicule on the apprehension, but he followed up the subject by two more articles in the same autumn. A few years later the question became one of general interest. In 1859, eight years after Samuel Sharpe had anonymously called attention to the subject, M. Michel Chevalier published his book "On the Probable Fall in the Value of Gold," which was translated into English by Mr. Cobden. The great increase in the use of gold more than counteracted the effects of its augmented production ; but Mr. Sharpe never changed his opinion as to the altered value of the metal. He expected the depreciation of the currency to show itself earlier than it did, and regarded its effect in making everything dear as simply a matter of time. At present a reaction has set in, and the appreciation of the currency has lowered the price of commodities, just as the earlier fall in the value of gold raised prices. But there were no signs of this change either in 1850 or 1859.

Other notes in the Diary are worth reproducing.

1848. Oct. 10. Dr. —— ——, who has just reviewed my " Egypt " in the *Dublin University Magazine*, made so many unsuccessful offers of marriage, that when at Trinity College he used to be called the Solicitor-General. Once hearing that a young lady and her mother had taken two places in the coach to the north, he went and took the two other places for himself, that he might introduce himself to them. They changed their hour and the Doctor travelled the journey alone.

Oct. 19. I met at Mr. James Yates's at Highgate Mr. Roberts, the President of Liberia ; half a negro, who gave an interesting account of that black colony. Quite a gentleman, quiet in his manners, spoke slowly and very good English.

1849, March 5. Walked into the City with Cockerell, the Architect, who pointed out the spots in Fleet Street and Ludgate Hill from which he thought St. Paul's was best seen. Praised the view as the finest in any city in the world. He should not be on speaking terms with anybody who wished to pull down the houses to lay the church more open. Wren built the spire in Ludgate Hill himself as a foil.

Aug. 21. Dr. Price's uncle succeeded Dr. Watts as chaplain in Lady Abney's family. He told Mr. Maltby that Dr. Watts, before his death, changed his opinion respecting the Trinity. He had probably become Arian.

Porson was not pleased with his reception in the London Institution, although he was treated handsomely. He said their conduct was mean beyond even mercantile meanness.

Benjamin Travers, the eminent surgeon of Bruton Street, took a very pretty place at Garston, near Watford,

and wrote a poem on the beauties of his new retirement.
Sydney Smith, on reading it wrote at the end—

> Garston, thou art all a cheat,
> Take me back to Bruton Street.

So Travers soon found it ; he parted with Garston House
and returned to his successful practice.

1850, September 3. I certainly felt mortified on reading the articles on the Ptolemies in Dr. Smith's " Dictionary
of Classical Biography." They were all written by E. H.
Bunbury with the help of my " History of Egypt," and without any acknowledgment, though he even borrowed the
volume from my brother Dan for the purpose.

There are a couple of glimpses of Samuel Sharpe
at this time in Crabb Robinson's Life.   On the 18th
January, 1851, he enters in his Diary—

> Yesterday, I had at breakfast Dr. Donaldson, Dr. Boott
> [an American], Sharpe, the Egyptian, and Edwin Field.   The
> morning went off exceedingly well.

Nine months later, Crabb Robinson says in a letter
to his friend Paynter—

> This fine weather is marvellous.   Talking the other day to
> Sam Sharpe, on the complaints of the landowners now, he
> made me a wise answer.   " We all have it in our turn.   A
> few years ago an Act of Parliament took away one-half of our
> income by legalizing Joint-Stock Banks.   There was no use
> making a fuss about it.   We submitted then, the squires must
> submit now.   In the end everybody is the better.   Individuals
> must suffer when the public gain."   Sharpe is by no means
> an optimist, and on the papal question he is a great deal
> worse than you.

This common-sense mode of regarding inevitable
social changes was characteristic of him.   The nine
months which intervened between these two refer-

ences to him by Crabb Robinson were, however, not likely to have left much room for optimism. There was the saddest possible contrast between the public gaiety of those times and the private sorrow which came with the bright summer days. To the nation at large the year was one of the greatest hope and promise. The first half of the nineteenth century lay behind, with its wars, its political agitations, its social calamities and its unrest. Trade had recovered from the panic of a few years before, the nightmare of the Irish famine had passed away, and the formidable movement of the Irish Confederates under Mr. Smith O'Brien, which had ended amid the laughter of the world in Widow Cormack's cabbage garden at Ballingarry, had been succeeded by a time of apparent content and peace. The repeal of the Corn Laws had brought plenty and prosperity at home, and after the revolutionary outbreaks of 1848 and 1849, Europe seemed settling down into lasting quiet and peace. The first year of the second half of the century found all England in a sanguine mood. The Crystal Palace was rising in Hyde Park, and the Great Exhibition it was to contain was to be opened on the first of May as a festival of universal brotherhood. As the year advanced the very heavens seemed propitious to the hopes of men. A cycle of fine seasons had begun, and bright summer sunshine, with a good harvest following it, reconciled the farmers to the loss of Protection. The nation passed through a short period of social and political optimism. Old experience laid aside its prophetic strain, and all England agreed for a while to indulge the daydreams of high-spirited and generous youth. There were not a few who really believed that the federation of the nations was at hand, and that the time had come when there should be war no more.

Samuel Sharpe was too little·of an optimist at any time to be led away by glowing expectations, and he did not regard the opening of the Great Exhibition as the beginning of a new era of peace and goodwill. But interest in public affairs was eclipsed during the summer by a great private sorrow. In the last days of May his wife was taken with an illness which seemed at first comparatively slight. She made too little of it herself; and it became serious with alarming suddenness. In less than a week it ended fatally. Her husband writes in his Diary, probably some time after the event—

At a quarter past ten at night, Tuesday, June 3, 1851, my dear wife Sarah breathed her last. The three eldest children were with me in constant attendance at the time. She had been ill five days. They had been helpful nurses. I bid them bear their grief without crying, for they had done their duty· God's will be done.

This great and terrible loss weighed heavily on his spirits. It was the first breach in the charmed circle of home. It was the loss of a companionship which had been his support and satisfaction through more than thirty years. They had been married nearly four and twenty years ; but they had known one another from childhood, had sympathized with each other in all the pursuits of early life, and their attachment as cousins had gradually grown into the deeper affection which led to their marriage and made their married life content and happy. There had been complete agreement between them on all matters of domestic management. The husband's love of home, his desire to live far within their means and his dislike of show, were all fully shared by his wife. She had the warmest admiration for his literary labours, and fully and heartily participated in the pleasures and disappointments of the man of letters. The loss of such a companion makes the world desolate. Her husband had now to go into a new life, to begin the world again, as it were, without the tender help which had been the solace of his earlier years. Happily there had grown up meanwhile other home affections which, in time, filled the empty place. There was complete sympathy with him on the part of his children, whom he had inspired with his own love of art and literature, and who had had, with their mother, some part and lot in his literary labours. The cloud passed, as all such clouds do, and meanwhile he found, as of old, consolation and refreshment in his studies. The work of the next two or three years is summed up in the following short paragraphs of his autobiography :—

In 1852 I began a second series of Egyptian Inscriptions. The former plates were lithographed by my own hands, but now my daughters worked for me. We proceeded with this new work slowly but steadily, as we were able to obtain materials from Mr. Birch, Mr. Bonomi, the British Museum and other sources, and we hope to carry it forward till it shall contain a hundred and twenty plates, the number of the former series.

Three years later the volume was published. It

was the largest collection of hieroglyphics that had ever been issued, and though the sale was small, it was of much use to himself and to others. He puts on record his opinion that the smallness of the sale for such works ought to be no discouragement to their production, "as it is only by such drawings that the student can make any progress in his knowledge of hieroglyphics." Simultaneously with the leisurely progress of this work, he says—

I turned more in earnest to my papers on the several books of the Old and New Testaments. Some of them had been already published in the *Christian Reformer*, the " History of Assyria " had been printed in Mr. Bonomi's "Nineveh," the " History of Edom " I had read before the Syro-Egyptian Society ; and in 1852 and 1853 working slowly and without much zeal I completed the whole. During these two years also I delivered several lectures, for which I had gained ample experience first at the literary discussions at the Islington Institution, and afterwards at the meetings of the Syro-Egyptian Society. The Lectures on Egypt and the Bible at University Hall were very well attended, and helped to bring about other courses of popular lectures in that building. My lectures on the same subjects in the rooms of the Unitarian Association were only to a small class.

The Lectures at the rooms of the Unitarian Association were delivered in connection with the London District Unitarian Society. This Society had been formed in 1850 to spread Unitarian Christianity in London. It aimed at doing this by two methods, each of which had Samuel Sharpe's hearty sympathy and support. One of the methods was that of giving lectures on biblical and doctrinal

subjects in halls and school-rooms ; the other was
that of opening places of worship which, however
humble at first, might form the nucleus around
which self-supporting congregations would afterwards grow.   The courses of lectures came first,
and Samuel Sharpe was greatly interested in promoting them.   They were given in different parts
of London, and several of the existing congregations
owe their establishment or revival to this early
effort, which he justly regarded as one of the signs
of the awakening of religious earnestness and zeal
in the Liberal section of the Christian Church.

His own lectures were delivered from notes written
on a single sheet of paper.   The notes consisted of
nothing more than the heads of the address, and a
glance at each in turn was all he needed.   He was
so full of the subject, and had his information so
completely in hand, that lecturing in this mode presented no difficulty to him.   His style was entirely
conversational.   He attempted nothing but the
impartation of knowledge.   In speaking of the
lectures to his friends, he would point to his
diagrams and illustrations and say "These are my
eloquence."   The illustrations and diagrams were
drawn by the members of his family, and together
with his clear explanations made the lectures very
interesting and instructive to all who cared for the
question in hand.   As in his writings, so in his
Lectures, simplicity and clearness were all he aimed
at.   His object was to give information, not to pro-
vide amusement ; to create interest in the subject,
not to call attention to himself.

A good deal of interest was excited at this time

by the proposal to remove the Crystal Palace from Hyde Park and to re-erect it, as a permanent pleasure house of art on the slope of Sydenham Hill. Mr. James Yates urged members of the Antiquarian and Archæological Societies to take shares in the undertaking and to support him in the effort to give it an educational character by reproductions of ancient architecture and art. The idea was carried out in the Fine Art Department, in the Assyrian, Egyptian, Greek, Roman, Byzantine and Alhambra Courts. Mr. Owen Jones was placed in charge of the whole Fine Art Department, and Mr. Bonomi was engaged under him in the modelling of the Egyptian Court. The scale of the models was necessarily small, but they gave an opportunity, for the first time, of realizing some of the effects of Egyptian art. Mr. Sharpe and his family were frequent visitors to the works in progress on Sydenham Hill; and some pleasant hours were spent in watching the workers. "It was very pleasant," says his eldest daughter, "to get in among the scaffoldings and planks on Sydenham Hill in those days, to thread your way in between the heavy waggons full of iron-work and blocks of granite and to see Mr. Owen Jones and Mr. Bonomi, with their white holland pinafores on, working merrily with trowel and brush upon the stucco columns, and to hear them talking Italian all the while with the foreign workmen who had been sent over to bring and put up the casts."

Samuel Sharpe's share in this work was to put dates to these copies of the Egyptian bas-reliefs and monuments; and to write in the picture writing of Hieroglyphics the long sentence that runs as a frieze around the ceiling of the Court. This sentence which reads from left to right and occupies the whole length of the façade, literally translated is as follows :—" In the seventeenth year of the reign of Her Majesty, the ruler of the waves, the royal daughter, Victoria, lady most gracious, the chief architects, sculptors and painters erected this palace and gardens, with a thousand columns, a thousand decorations, a thousand statues of chiefs and ladies, a thousand trees, a thousand flowers, a thousand birds and beasts, a thousand fountains, and a thousand vases. The architects, and painters and sculptors built this palace as a book for the instruction of the men and women of all countries, regions and districts. May it be prosperous."

When the building was finished he was asked to write the "Historical Sketch of the Egyptian Buildings and Sculpture" in the Guide Book to the Egyptian Court. The work was issued under the title of "The Egyptian Court, described by Owen Jones and Samuel Sharpe." Mr. Owen Jones's half was accompanied by footnotes contributed by Mr. Bonomi. The "Historical Sketch" is a short summary of Egyptian history, in which each portion of the Egyptian Court is described in its relation to that history. Each figure and monument is thus fitted in to its historical place. He speaks of the work as "an agreeable little task, as enabling me to put before the public in cheap form my views of Chronology." He refused to accept any remuneration for it, in order that he "might have the pleasure of contributing something to an undertaking which promises to improve the taste of the nation in architecture and sculpture."

In the same year he was elected as one of the Trustees of Dr. Williams's Library. This old Nonconformist foundation is now housed in a very large and handsome building in Grafton Street East, nearly opposite University College Hospital. The Library, the support of which is one of the smaller objects of the Trust, to which only about a tenth of its yearly income can be devoted, is now in excellent condition. Dr. Williams's own books, which formed the nucleus of the Library, included a great number of valuable historical works in various languages, besides a very large collection of English divinity. To these have been added year by year important historical and theological books; and a large number of persons, students and others, make use of them. In 1853, when Samuel Sharpe became one of its Trustees, the Library was still in its old building in Redcross Street, City, which was soon afterwards required by the Metropolitan Railway. It was removed from thence to a temporary abode in Queen Square, Bloomsbury, and eventually the freehold building in Grafton Street was erected for it out of the proceeds of the sale of the Redcross Street house. Writing of his election as a Trustee, Samuel Sharpe says—

I accepted the office because I thought I could be useful there. The Library had been sadly neglected, though the estates, schools, and scholarships of the Trust had been very carefully attended to. However, my co-trustees were quite willing to allow and assist my reforms. I got closets full of books entered in the catalogue, many volumes of

tracts bound, the Baxter and Wilson manuscripts bound,
and an appendix to the catalogue printed.   In order to
make the Library more useful I circulated cards of admission, had the fire kept alight in the Reading Room during
the winter months, and a brass plate put upon the door.
By these means we brought more readers into the room
than the Librarian had ever before known.   I also proposed
some alterations in the examinations for scholarships, in
order to make them more Biblical.   I know of no institution to which my attention could be more usefully turned.

The reforming zeal thus brought into an old, and
at that time, so far as the Library was concerned, a
decaying institution, necessarily created some disturbance.   The Librarian, like the Last Minstrel, was
infirm and old, and the Trustees were unwilling to
hold him to the bond in which his duties were
defined.   He admitted his neglect, and as it was
practically condoned, Mr. Sharpe in 1857 retired
from the Trusteeship.   But his action was not
without large results.   On the death of the old
Librarian, the Rev. Thomas Hunter was appointed,
and he has brought to the duties of his important
post a zeal and energy which have resulted in making
the Library more generally useful than it has ever
been at any period of its history.   Mr. Hunter has
been very successful in making the Library known to
students and ministers of the so-called orthodox
Dissenters.   Its removal to the capacious building
in Grafton Street has given further opportunity for
development, while Dr. Williams's Trustees have
been authorized to expend a somewhat larger portion of their funds in the purchase of books and in
its general support.   The Library has been further

increased by handsome donations of books, the latest
of which is the large library of philosophical works
collected by the late Mr. George Henry Lewes, and
presented by his son; Mr. Charles Lewes. The new
era on which the Library has thus entered may fairly
be said to have been begun by the reforms introduced by Mr. Sharpe, during the four years in which
he remained one of its Trustees.

The autobiographical sketch hitherto quoted
was written in the year 1854. It is dated in
September, and is addressed to his children. Its
opening and concluding paragraphs curiously illus-
trate his state of mind respecting his own work at
this period of his life. There is nothing unusual in
the feeling he expresses. At fifty-five most men
become conscious of some slackening in their physical energy. The bound and glow of youth are gone,
the restorative power of sleep becomes somewhat
less, the sense of an inexhaustible fund of energy
which characterizes a strong man's physical prime
has passed away, and he is very likely to misunder-
stand the change. The first sense of unaccustomed
weakness comes upon him with a chill, and from the
illusion that he is still young he passes to the illusion
that he is old, and that his natural strength is
abating. He soon finds that his intellectual power
is as great as ever, that it is only his physical
strength which has diminished, and he goes on his
way once more with only the slight consciousness
that whereas for half his life he bounded up the hill,
now he is quietly walking down. Samuel Sharpe
had just come to this dividing line, and nearly half
his busy and useful life of literary labour still lay

before him, when he wrote the first and last paragraphs of a sketch which he evidently regarded as a
final summary of his labours.   It begins :—

I am now fifty-five years of age, and have lost much of
that power of working which I once enjoyed, and which
has been a great source of happiness to me through life.
I still look forward to having the pleasure from time to
time of correcting and reprinting some of my works, but
I can hope to do nothing now that requires much study.

The concluding paragraph is in exactly the same
tone :—

While these pages are being written I am passing through
the press my "Historic Notes on the Books of the Old
and New Testaments."   This has been lying by finished
for some time.   It ought, indeed, to be all rewritten, not
for me to reconsider any opinions there expressed, which
were formed carefully and after full study, but that the
arguments might be stated more clearly, and the whole
made more readable.   But my powers of working are so
far lessened that I doubted whether I should be able to
make it what it ought to be.   I therefore print it as it is,
and hope that it may be useful.   My wish for it, as for my
New Testament and History is, that it may root out
mistaken opinions about the Bible, without hurt to religion,
and that it may help to disarm scoffers by teaching those
who value the Bible to throw overboard those mistaken
opinions about it which cannot be defended by sound
criticism.

This last sentence expressed the motive which
animated him in all his Biblical works.   The feeling
grew upon him as years advanced, and towards the
end of his life his chief anxiety seemed to be to
save the Bible from the undue depreciation with

which it was threatened. To Unitarian ministers, and to the ministers and students of other churches with whom he came in contact, he was accustomed to say that one of the great duties of the pulpit in these times is to rescue the Bible from neglect. Idolatry has produced iconoclasm, and after half a dozen generations have worshipped the Bible, treated it as an infallible oracle, spoken of it as the Word of God, the present generation seems inclined to rush to the opposite extreme, and to throw it away as an idol that has been broken. These methods of treatment rest on ignorance of its history, misreading of its contents, and misconception of its claims. As an ancient religious literature, as the record of the noblest line of religious tradition and development, as the purest and simplest expression of the religious faculty, leading up to the perfect manifestation of our religious nature in Jesus Christ, this collection of writings will always have supreme interest and importance. The Bible has had no more diligent student than Samuel Sharpe, and his sense of its infinite superiority to all other "Scriptures" was always increasing. It alone, he was accustomed to say, had brought into the world a new motive for virtue in teaching men to act from the love of God, and in appealing to that disinterestedness which is the motive power of all enthusiasm, and of all that is highest and best in man. Men are only to be raised by lifting them out of themselves, and of this lifting power the Bible is full. The great thing which needs to be done for it in this generation is, therefore, he believed, to make it understood, to humanize it, to show its relation to the circumstances amongst

P

which it was produced, and to teach a wise estimate
of its value and its claims.

This was the object of the "Historic Notes."
They exactly corresponded to their title. The book
was a small volume into which a large amount of
learning and shrewd criticism was condensed. It contained the matured opinions of its author as to the
age of the several parts of the Bible, and it described
each book, nearly in the order in which it stands in
the Authorized Version. The book is of interest as
being a kind of first edition of a different work
which he himself valued much more than this earlier
production. The attempt to treat the books of the
Bible in a straightforward order gradually appeared
to him to be impossible and misleading. Years of
study convinced him that, to handle the Biblical
writings with any sort of chronological exactness, it
would be necessary not merely to divide the several
books with greater minuteness, but to invert the order
of many portions of chapters and even of verses,
and to intermingle one book with another; in fact,
entirely to rearrange the whole, setting piece by piece
anew, in a skeleton or framework of history which he
must draw up. This idea he accordingly carried out
in the "History of the Hebrew Nation and Literature," which was written and published many years
later. This is the work referred to in the last paragraph of the first autobiographical sketch, which has
just been quoted. It was the rewriting of the
"Historic Notes" "that the arguments might be
stated more clearly and the whole made more readable" which he there says ought to be done, but
which he doubts whether he shall ever have the

strength to do. Nearly fifteen years after this
doubt was expressed he sat down, then within a few
days of seventy years old, to continue the account
of his life. He completed this second part of his
autobiography in 1870, and in 1879 added to it
a short further sketch which will come in at its
appropriate place. It is only needful to note here
that it was not the least useful, industrious, or pro-
lific period of his whole life, which still lay before
him at the moment when, closing the first part of
his autobiography in 1854, he thought his work was
almost done.

The result of his Biblical studies was to produce
in his own mind, and in the minds of many others, a
strong wish for an authoritative revision of the
Authorized Version of the Old and New Testaments. He gives his own account of the origin of
Mr. James Heywood's motion on this subject in the
House of Commons:—

> In the beginning of 1855 I met Mr. James Heywood,
> the member for Lancashire, at Edwin Field's, at Hamp-
> stead. I had never been in his company before. After
> talking to him about his motions for the reform of the
> Universities, I added a wish that he would move in the
> House for an Address to the Queen in favour of a new
> translation of the Bible. He seemed not to have thought
> of the subject before.

The motion was made, and Mr. Heywood's speech
in making it was duly reported, and the subject was
discussed in the daily papers. This was probably
the first time that subjects of Biblical study had
been thus introduced into the leading articles of the
morning journals. The silence upon such topics

which was then broken has never been renewed. From time to time the press has continued to treat them down to the present day. Mr. Heywood's motion awakened a permanent interest in the question of Revision, and early in the next year Samuel Sharpe drew up a petition in its favour from "the congregation assembling for worship at the Meeting House at Newington Green," which was signed by Dr. Cromwell as Minister, by Samuel Sharpe as Trustee, by Mr. Andrew Pritchard as Treasurer, and by other persons. It was the first petition with this prayer which was ever presented to Parliament. It set forth :—

That your Petitioners have been again and again informed by Divines and scholars upon whose judgment they can rely, that the Authorized Version of the Holy Bible is not so free from faults as the translation of such a book ought to be. That from the improved knowledge of the ancient languages, and the discovery of many better manuscripts of the Holy Bible, a version might be made which should far more faithfully represent the original.

That your Petitioners are aware that many new translations into English have been made of parts of the Bible, some by members of the Church of England and some by Dissenters, and some of these translations your Petitioners often read in private. But your Petitioners, though Dissenters, hesitate to make use of these unauthorized versions in their public worship, and are interested in endowed schools and charities in which it would be illegal to use such unauthorized versions.

The petition was not the only contribution he made to the discussion of this subject. A third edition of his translation of the New Testament was published in the same year, and a little volume of " Critical Notes on the Authorized Version of the New Testament," in which the texts, in which his translation differed from that of the Authorized Version, were set forth with the reasons for the corrections made.   In the very able speech with which Mr. Heywood introduced his motion for an Address to the Queen for a revised version, he prominently referred to this volume, and made good use of it. Its author further printed a small tract for popular circulation, giving reasons for the demand of a new translation, and actively assisted in the promotion of lectures on the subject.

The establishment of the Unitarian Home Missionary Board at Manchester in 1854 excited a good deal of controversy in the Unitarian body.   It was, in many respects, a new development of missionary zeal.   The old educational institution, at which nearly all the leading ministers of the body had been trained, had always been faithful to the fundamental principle of non-subscription to creeds and of neutrality in theological controversy.   It was then, and it continues to be, the only theological seminary in this country which leaves its students and professors unpledged as to theological conclusions.   It is founded for "Free teaching and Free learning in Theology," and it has been careful, before all things, to preserve its freedom.   It has kept up, moreover, a very high standard of scholarship among the ministers of the group of congregations which accept its principle and yield it pecuniary support.   Manchester New College, as it was called on its establishment at Manchester in 1786, was the direct successor of the Warrington Academy.   It had been removed to York in the earliest years of the present century, but had returned to Manchester in

1840, and was finally brought to London in 1853. The new Home Missionary Board differed from it in being distinctively Unitarian, in aiming at producing a less learned and more popular class of missionary ministers, and in giving facilities for men of a somewhat different social grade to enter the Unitarian ministry. Its opponents consequently regarded it as a rival of the older institution, and as likely to lower the status and change the character of the body to which it belonged. The anticipated evils have not followed. Room has been found for both colleges, and ample work for each. Samuel Sharpe speaks of it as established "for the education of young men as preachers to the poor," and adds—

I did not at once join it, as it had the appearance of being set up in rivalry to Manchester New College, then removed to London. But I thoroughly approved of its aim, that of carrying Unitarianism to the poor; and as soon as all thoughts of rivalry had blown over, I became a subscriber to it, and supported it heartily. By the establishment of that institution, and of the *Unitarian Herald* newspaper, Dr. Beard has done more for the spread of Unitarianism in England than perhaps any man living.

This hearty support of the Home Missionary Board was continued to the end of his life, and he felt great satisfaction in its increasing usefulness. For Dr. Beard, its founder and Principal, he entertained great admiration and esteem. The two men had much in common. They had the same love of Biblical study, the same marvellous capacity for hard work, the same unresting energy, and the same zeal for the Unitarian views which they held in common. Dr. Beard was not only a hardworking student, but a man of great practical sagacity and knowledge of affairs. He was one of those energetic men who take the lead of others by never sparing themselves. Deficient in imagination, and without much of that poetic instinct, that power of spiritual insight, which makes men's hearts burn within them as they listen, and transforms the preacher into the prophet, he was nevertheless a great leader and organizer and teacher, and has left a very considerable mark on the history of Liberal religious thought in the North of England. The establishment of the *Unitarian Herald* was carried out by the energetic co-operation of the Rev. Brooke Herford and the Rev. John Wright.

# CHAPTER XI.

## RETIREMENT FROM BUSINESS AND USE OF MONEY AND LEISURE.

THE life of Samuel Rogers, written as a preface to his Works, had been published in 1859; and in the same year a fourth edition of the "History of Egypt" was issued, illustrated with woodcuts. The publisher undertook this edition on his own account, and produced two very handsome volumes. The woodcuts had been prepared at Highbury, having been drawn for the most part by the author's eldest daughter. They were intended to be explanatory and illustrative rather than merely ornamental; they added much to the value and interest of the work, and have been reproduced in later editions. Meanwhile Dr. H. Jolowicz, of Königsberg, had published at Leipsic a German translation based upon the third edition. The work was annotated by some German scholars, who expressed opinions on the chronology with which its author did not agree. But he cordially admitted the few mistakes they pointed out, and incorporated their corrections in the next edition of the book, with an acknowledgment in the preface that he had done so. The German edition was in

two volumes. Its translator, Dr. Jolowicz, was a
Jewish scholar, to whom Samuel Sharpe had been
introduced by Crabb Robinson.

Samuel Sharpe was circulating at this time a quarto
volume of forty-nine lithographed pages, with seven
of explanatory letterpress, entitled " Alexandrian
Chronology from the Building of the City till its
Conquest by the Arabs, A.D. 640." The compilation is a work with which he says he had taken a
good deal of pains. It represents an immense
amount of patient labour and inquiry, setting as it
does, in parallel columns, the years before and after
Christ, and the years according to other methods of
reckoning,—the Olympiads, the era of Menophres, of
Nabonassar, the year of Rome, of Alexander's death,
of the Selucidae, afterwards of Augustus, of Antioch,
and of the new Sothic period. The tables were
lithographed by his eldest daughter. The volume
was published in 1857, rather for gratuitous distribution than for sale. It was given away to all who
valued it ; copies were sent to every college in the
Universities, as well as to Libraries in Paris, Berlin,
Copenhagen, Rome, Madrid, Turin, Göttingen and
other places abroad. Its author regarded it as
" having quite established the system of regnal years
in Egypt, both before and after the introduction of
the Julian leap year."

Another thin quarto was published in 1858, under
the title of " The Triple Mummy Case of Aroeri-ao,
an Egyptian Priest, in Dr. Lee's Museum at Hartwell
House, Buckinghamshire." It consists of twenty-
five pages of Letterpress by Samuel Sharpe, and
eight large plates drawn by Mr. Bonomi, and was

published for the Syro-Egyptian Society of London. The cases, with the mummy they held, had been sent to England by Mr. Salt, the British Consul-General in Egypt. They were bought by Mr. Pettigrew, who afterwards sold them to Dr. Lee. The mummy, which was wrapped as usual in linen bandages, was unrolled by Mr. Pettigrew, before a large audience, in the lecture room of the Royal Institution on the 30th of May, 1836. One of the pictures on the outer case represents the blue vault of heaven, in the shape of the goddess Neith bending over and touching the ground with her arms. Under this vault is the deceased priest, with the two bodies into which death divides him. His earthly body is red, and is falling, his heavenly or spiritual body is blue and stands erect, raising its hands to heaven. This is a pictorial representation of the idea expressed many centuries later by St. Paul, " There is a natural body and there is a spiritual body (1 Cor. xv. 44). It contrasts with the older representations in which the spirit returns to the mummy in the form of a bird. That was the more ancient Egyptian view and made the resurrection of the body needful to future existence. This picture belongs, therefore, to a more culti-vated class, or a more enlightened time. "In the opinion of this artist," writes Samuel Sharpe, "the resurrection of the earthly body would seem un-necessary." So early, therefore, had the deep spiritual insight of the Egyptian priests superseded the mate-rialistic doctrine still taught in the Apostles Creed. In all the relics of the ancient world there is nothing more beautiful than this pictured teaching of the revelation which awaits us all, when the immortal rises from the death of the mortal, and finds the heaven which broods over it no longer cold and empty, but warmed and filled with the presence and the life of the encompassing God.

While this beautiful volume was going through the press, its author had turned his attention from this remote antiquity to the questions of the day, and published in the Bankers' Magazine an article on Decimal Coinage, in which he took the view that our present system is more convenient for retail trade than the decimal system, and that the value of the penny could not be changed without much inconvenience and injustice to the humbler classes.

Meanwhile, the work of amending and correcting his translation of the New Testament was never arrested. He turned to it from time to time as opportunity arose, and, indeed, from this time forth, that and the Revision of the Old Testament may be said to have been the chief interest and occupation of his life. A fourth edition, lower in price, and of 2,000 copies was issued in 1859. He records with satisfaction that his translation "was all this time gaining some little notice, and this edition was very much praised by the orthodox reviews." He adds with equal satisfaction, "Bagster, the publisher of Bibles, had called the third edition a soul-destroying book, but it was gaining approval for its impartiality." He had offered copies of it to the authorities of the orthodox colleges at Cheshunt and St. John's Wood, but the gift had been declined. The fact is the better worth recording, because fifteen or twenty years later the same book met with ready acceptance from the same persons,

who seemed to have learned in the interval that
there is nothing irreverent or dangerous in the
attempt to present the writings of apostles and
evangelists in the English language, with as near an
approach to the original as impartial scholarship
can give.

Another effort to promote Biblical studies is recorded by himself.

I had for some years past been giving prizes to the students
at the Carmarthen College,* and the Home Missionary
Board at Manchester for knowledge of Biblical History,
Geography and Antiquities. To Carmarthen, at the request
of the Examiners, I every year sent a list of questions.
To the money prizes at the Home Missionary Board, I
usually added copies of my " History of Egypt." I had
offered prizes on the same subjects to the students of
Manchester New College, but after some correspondence
they were declined by the Secretary and Principal. They
asked me to change the subjects of my offered prizes, but
that I refused to do. I had always kept the students of
Manchester New College and the Home Missionary Board
supplied with copies of my New Testament and I sometimes sent a stock to Carmarthen College.

In the next year he severed his connection with
the old chapel at Newington Green, which he had
regularly attended for eight-and-twenty years, and
joined the small body of Unitarians who were then

* Carmarthen College is an old Presbyterian foundation in
which Unitarian and Orthodox meet together on equal terms.
The Theological Professor is Orthodox, but its Principal, who
is also Professor of Hebrew, Greek, and the New Testament,
is Dr. Vance Smith, the learned and accomplished representative of the Unitarians on the Revision Committee.

meeting in a hired room in Islington. The old chapel in Carter Lane had been sold, and with the proceeds the present Unity Church and schoolroom in Upper Street, Islington, were being built. Samuel Sharpe disliked Gothic for Unitarian Chapels. He once met Gibson, the sculptor, at Mr. Bonomi's, when the artist held forth in the most amusing though in the most dogmatic fashion, giving nobody else room to slip in a word. He talked of his coloured statues, of his lady pupils, and among other things of architecture. "The Gothic architecture," said Gibson, " came *from* the barbarians and is fit *for* the barbarians ; and of one thing I am quite certain, if there is an architecture in heaven it will be the Greek architecture." With Gibson's objection to Gothic our author at least thoroughly sympathized. He thought it to be inconsistent with the simplicity of the Unitarian worship. He regularly attended the Islington services, and had the greatest respect for and sympathy with the minister, the Rev. Henry Ierson. But when the congregation moved into their Gothic church, and the minister put on his gown, and the prayers became liturgical, he and his family went down to Stamford Street for simpler worship.

The last few years had been a very trying period. His second son, Albert, had long been in precarious health. For some years consumptive symptoms had been present, and latterly the disease had been fully manifested, and he had spent each winter at Hastings. Beyond attending a little at the office of his uncle Henry in the City, Albert Sharpe had never been strong enough to do much in the way of business. Had he recovered he would have joined his brother in the Bank, but he became gradually worse, and died at Christmas, 1857. Three years and a half later his eldest brother Frederick, whose health had never been robust, was carried off by a sudden attack of the same disease. The loss of both his sons at the early ages of nineteen and twenty-six made an important change in their father's life. He had retired from business before Frederick's death, and himself records why the resolution was come to and how it was carried out.

During these latter years I had been far from well, and I felt the anxiety of business too much for me. As I became more important in the firm my hours of attendance had lessened, but my cares had increased. I was not able, with comfort, to take any long holiday; and in 1861, at Lady-Day, I finally quitted the Banking House in Clement's Lane, Lombard Street, at which I had attended regularly for more than forty-five years. I left behind my late partners, including my son Frederick and also Mr. John Warren. But the consequence was very unfortunate. My son died within the year; Mr. John Warren shortly retired to join another partnership; and the survivors sold the business to an insolvent Joint Stock Company called the British Bank. This soon stopped payment, and so came to an end a Banking House which had been a credit to everybody connected with it for exactly one hundred years.

Here there has to be recorded one of the most striking resolutions to which any successful man of business ever came. He had lived far within his income, and had brought up all his children in the habits of economy which he had chosen for himself.

He had often told them that they would thank him more for their inexpensive tastes than for any fortune he might leave them. They were, however, amply provided for, the motive for saving was removed, and there was no reason why the whole of his yearly income should not be spent. But how spent, was the question. Most men would have resolved to spend it in a larger house, in more company, in travel, perhaps in public life. They would have allowed themselves more pleasures, more indulgences, more personal and family enjoyment of their ample means. But Samuel Sharpe did nothing of this kind ; and the choice he made, which cannot be better described than in his own simple words, gives him at once a very high rank among the benefactors of his time. Writing of it in 1879, the year in which he reached fourscore, he says :—

I entered business, the youngest in the firm, with a very small capital. I saw at once that by the death of partners responsibility would always be growing upon me, and that it was my duty to live economically and to prepare for it by laying by money. When sixty years old my health failed, and I went out of business. Elder relations had left me money, and when I withdrew my capital and invested it I found myself possessed of ———— a-year, with the habit of spending one-third of it, or less. My children were dropping around me, and I did not wish to change my quiet habits. I saw the folly and even the wickedness of accumulating without a rational motive, and I seriously turned over in my mind how to spend money usefully. Besides ordinary charities, the three lines then open to me were, to print and give away my books, which were of a class very little saleable ; to help University College which I saw was moving the education of the nation ; and, thirdly, to help the unpopular cause of Unitarianism.*

I began giving small sums freely to Unitarian appeals for help to chapels, meaning to set an example which I hoped might be followed, of giving £10 or £20 in place of the former £5; and £100 or £50 in place of the former £20. This example, I am glad to see, has often been followed.

My translation of the Bible and "History of the Hebrew Nation" cost nearly £200 a-year to give every Dissenting student for the ministry whose college would accept such gifts.

In thus giving away money my daughters nobly encouraged me, and were quite content with our quiet inexpensive way of living.

Those are the simple terms in which this munificent friend of unsectarian education and rational religion records the benefactions of twenty years. That he looked back with deep satisfaction on this use of his money may be taken for granted. But he made no boast of his charities. Very few of the supporters of University College know how greatly that institution is indebted to him. Many pleasing acknowledgments of this indebtedness have, however, been made from time to time, and one of the class rooms is called by his name. In addition to his actual gifts, he assisted many boys to get their education at University College School ; and the private help he gave to many other persons and families in procuring educational advantages for them, which were far beyond their own means, ex-

* Up to the year 1879 he had given University College about £1,000 a-year ; £20,000 in all.

tended over a large area and reached a considerable sum every year.

This great development of a liberality in gifts of money which had always distinguished him, was simultaneous with a considerable increase in his service of Unitarian Christianity. In this, too, it is best to describe his motive in his own words.

Being now at leisure, I gave more attention to the attempt which was always being made by some of us to spread Unitarian opinions ; to this indeed many of my literary doings had been very much directed. I often attended and spoke at the quarterly meetings of the London District Society, and occasionally lectured on Biblical subjects such as the mistranslations in the authorized New Testament, and the age of the several parts of the Pentateuch. I also wrote more in the Unitarian periodical papers, and occasionally invited to my house the students of Manchester New College. I felt that the spread of our unpopular opinions was a great and good cause, and as I was independent of the world's frowns or smiles, I could not do anything more useful than give my countenance to that course of action. Since the Dissenters' Chapels Bill had passed in 1844, the popular prejudices on the subject had been very much lessened, and the path was more open for the spread of theological truth. The chief hindrance now was that such an attempt was not genteel.

Among the efforts thus undertaken was that of establishing a Unitarian Chapel at Hastings. The family had, unfortunately, much to do with that pleasant watering place. Albert had spent several winters there with some of his sisters for companions, and soon after his death, his youngest sister, Eleanor, showed symptoms of the same fatal disease. She, too, had to be sent to Hastings for the winter ; and though she was usually accompanied by her eldest sister, all the other members of the family, the father among them, were frequent visitors.  They were not accustomed to neglect public worship, but highly ·appreciated its value for instruction, consolation and inward renewal, yet as earnest believers in Unitarian Christianity they were unable to join with profit in Trinitarian services.  If Jesus Christ is not God, he is not a proper object of worship.  If the doctrine of the Atonement is a superstitious dream of the middle ages, teaching which is permeated with it is more shocking than it is edifying ; and prayers which assume it and are based upon it can have no meaning to those who disbelieve and reject it. Hence the necessity for special Unitarian services, and hence the justification of the separate existence of the Unitarian body.  With this feeling, Miss Emily Sharpe endeavoured to establish a Unitarian congregation at Hastings.  A few resident Unitarians assembled in a room and one of them read a service to the rest.  After a few years they engaged a minister jointly with the old congregation at Battle ; and in 1868 they were able to build a chapel, with the help of subscriptions from others.  The chapel is a permanent memorial of the visits of the family from Highbury Place to this warm and sheltered and beautiful portion of the Sussex coast.

It is difficult to give any vivid impression of the vast and varied activity by which Samuel Sharpe filled up the void which the giving up of his work in the City would otherwise have left.  No man who has spent five-and-forty years in active city work can wisely leave it off, while his powers are still substantially unimpaired, unless he has some resource in public work or private study. Men who have no such interests to occupy their minds and fill up their leisure, are very likely to lose their faculties, to break down in health, or to creep back in some way or other to their old haunts and their accustomed work. Samuel Sharpe had plenty of interests, and he turned with new zest to them all. The first few years after he retired from business were almost the busiest, and in a literary sense they were the most productive of his life. Perhaps it was in the varied character of his pursuits that he found the secret of that freshness of mind, which, in addition to the promptitude and decision which business gives, he brought with him out of his forty-five years of banking, and carried with him through his remaining twenty years of studious leisure. One looks with wonder at a man who, having in the intervals of business not only mastered the hieroglyphics of Egypt and written the history of that mysterious land, but completed his knowledge of Greek and retranslated the New Testament, could betake himself at the age of sixty-three to the study of Hebrew and the revision of the English version of the Old Testament. Yet this is how Mr. Sharpe became a Translator of the Bible.

His eldest daughter says of this change :—" None but those who lived with him during his more than twenty years of Egyptian study could understand how naturally and insensibly these researches were leading him to a close grammatical study of the old Hebrew writings. The Jews of primitive times migrated out of Egypt under Moses, therefore it was amongst the earliest laws of the Jews that traces of Egyptian civilization and opinions must be sought for. Again, the Jews during the whole time of their monarchy were alternately trading with Egypt and quarrelling with Egypt, therefore in the Books of Kings and of Chronicles, and through the Prophets, here and there, might an historian of Egypt expect to collect many scattered particulars. Further, the Hebrew Scriptures were first translated into a Gentile language in Egypt, the Apocryphal Books were chiefly written in Egypt, and the Gnostic opinions that were to overcloud Christianity almost as soon as it appeared, were but a Jewish graft upon the Egyptian superstitions. Therefore, whether the student is busy upon the more ancient or upon the later and Christian periods of Egyptian history, it is to the pages of the Bible that he turns for explanations and for additions to his meagre materials, and in doing this he is met at every turn by the need of an amended translation. Nor was it any use to wait patiently for a New Translation. The theologian and the man of poetical mind might best re-translate the doctrinal parts and the grand poetry of the Bible. But no one but the antiquarian could correct the translation of those geographical and historical chapters which he needed most in his work of compilation. Therefore there was nothing for it but to re-translate the Bible himself. He hesitated and delayed for several years, saying that it was too great a task, but that he should certainly undertake it as soon as he grew younger. But finding that this did not come to pass, he began."

His own account of it is in the simple style, without the least particle of self-consciousness or boasting, in which his resolutions on the spending of his income are recorded. Speaking of the years from 1861 to 1864 he says :—

During these years I had rather neglected hieroglyphics, and turned to the study of Hebrew. I had forty years before learned the alphabet, and very little more than enough to enable me to look for a word in the dictionary, but now I turned to it in earnest, and began to translate the Bible. I added to a copy of the Authorized Version a large margin on which I made the corrections I proposed. By the time I had got to the end, I, of course found that many of the corrections were wrong and had to be altered. When that was done and this copy thus spoilt, I got a second copy with similar margins, and translated the whole a second time. When I reached the end, this also had to be again corrected, but not so much but that it was in a state to send it to the printer. From this, in 1865, I published my " Hebrew Scriptures Translated." It met with some success. My New Testament had been dispersed over the land by sale or gifts to the number of 8,000 copies, and had thus prepared the way for the Old Testament. It was, however, published at a price below what it cost. The low price at which the Bible Society sells the Authorized Version makes it necessary that another version should not be charged much higher. Indeed, the only chance of mending the world in theology is by addressing the arguments to those that are not rich. The wealthy and well-educated are more shut up from such knowledge by the bonds of fashion than the poor are by their ignorance.

The statement that he had "rather neglected hieroglyphics" must be taken quite in the qualified form in which it stands. He had published in 1861 another edition of his Hieroglyphical Vocabulary. It was entitled "Hieroglyphics, being an attempt to explain their Nature, Origin and Meaning." In three or four important characters he differed from most of the students of hieroglyphics, and though they had the ear of the world, he desired to put his own views on permanent record because he had adopted them deliberately and after full inquiry, and had full confidence in them. In the next year, 1862, he published "Egyptian Antiquities in the British Museum Described." In this work he mentioned all the objects to which he thought he could put a date. It contained numerous woodcuts drawn by Mr. Bonomi upon the wood, and by his daughter Emily. This volume was the more interesting because it exhibited very clearly his differences from the orthodox interpreters of the Egyptian monuments. He says:—

I did not adopt either the names or the dates placed upon the objects by Mr. Birch, the keeper. This probably checked its sale. At any rate it did not gain his countenance. But my aim was to correct opinions which I thought mistaken. I was as much a Dissenter in Egyptian studies as in Theology.

His dissent in Egyptian studies was, however, like that in Theology, entirely based on differences of interpretation. Just as he kept the Scriptures, but read in them other meanings than those which the Scribes and Pharisees of ecclesiastical tradition have forced upon them, so he kept the sculptured scriptures of Egypt, but disagreed with the accepted

interpretation of them. Hence in 1862 he had
communicated to the *Parthenon*, a literary and
scientific journal edited by Mr. C. W. Goodwin, the
writer of the Essay on the Mosaic Cosmogony in the
Essays and Reviews, a series of letters combating the
views of Sir George Cornewall Lewis, who had proclaimed his entire scepticism as to the whole of the
supposed Egyptian history. Sir George Lewis went
so far as to say that there was no sufficient ground
for placing any of the buildings in the Nile valley
earlier than the building of Solomon's Temple,
1012 B.C. In these letters, which are signed with his
initials, Samuel Sharpe gives up to what he calls
Sir George Lewis's "just ridicule," the chronology of
Lepsius and Bunsen, and speaks of "the wild views
of Bunsen's 'Egypt's Place in Universal History;'"
but at the same time declares that "Sir George
Lewis's scepticism would lead us further from the
truth than the fanciful theories which he aims to
overthrow." It may be worth while to quote from
the last of these letters a passage which while it
replies to Sir George Lewis on the one hand, indicates on the other exactly in what his latest and
ripest views on Egyptian chronology differed from
those of "the long chronologists" who are still in
fashion.

Every great building and almost every part of a building
bears the sculptured name of the king who made it, and often
tells us his parentage and something of his pedigree. By the
help of these inscriptions we are able to put into a series the
names of above thirty Theban Kings. We are enabled to say
with the utmost certainty that above half that number reigned
in unbroken succession ; and that the Kings who built the
Pyramids lived yet earlier.

The reigns of these, the half of the Theban Kings, must
have occupied more than four hundred years, and the reigns of
the whole at least six hundred years, and we are enabled to say
with equal certainty that they all reigned in succession before
King Shishank who fought against Rehoboam, the son of Solomon. Shishank, after his conquest of Judea, and after he had
made himself master of Upper Egypt recorded that conquest
on the walls of the Theban temples, or the temples raised by
the Theban Kings already spoken of who had already passed
away. After the time of Shishank, who is mentioned by the
Hebrew writers, an interval of two-hundred-and-fifty years
brings us to the Kings Sevek or So and Tirhaka, who are
again mentioned in the Bible. And even if the Egyptian
records be distrusted, by which we fill up these years of civil
disturbance and struggles among the cities of the Delta for
the mastery of all Egypt, yet it is impossible that to those
years can be assigned the reigns of the great Theban Kings
or of the Kings who built the Pyramids. Even an examination of the monuments in our British Museum, where we have
records of most of the reigns, is almost enough to prove that
they reach back for a period of thirty reigns before the time
of Solomon. Our earliest monuments cannot be so modern as
the year B.C. 1600. The record on the rock near Beyrout
proves the march of the Egyptian army through that country
under Rameses II., which cannot have taken place after the
time of the Judges, as it would otherwise have been noticed by
the Hebrew writers.

These few considerations alone, if properly looked into,
absolutely prove that Thebes had risen and fallen from its
high estate before the time of Solomon. For this we need not
rely upon Manetho, nor upon any reading of hieroglyphics
beyond that most simple and certain portion—namely the
reading of the Kings' names. We rely upon the Kings' names
and the monumental evidence alone. It is true that Bunsen
and Lepsius and other most respectable authorities, who may
be called the long chronologists, lengthen out the period of
history, thus proved by the monumental evidence, by about
fifteen hundred years. They insert a period of two hundred
years between the time of Solomon and the reigns of the great
Kings of Thebes. They insert a second period of five hundred years in the middle of the reigns of the Theban Kings,

when they suppose that Egypt was governed by the Phœnician shepherds. They insert a third period of eight hundred years between the reigns of the earliest Theban Kings and those Kings of Memphis who built the Pyramids. For these three long periods they have no monumental evidence. They rely upon the figures and periods of time mentioned by Manetho. This lengthened chronology I by no means undertake to defend from the remarks of Sir G. Lewis; and in conclusion have only to add that though I think he has undervalued the results of the last half-century's Egyptian studies, yet he has done good service to the cause of science by warning us against taking guesses for certainties and early traditions for history.

The Egyptian lore was turned to the support of his Theological Dissent in the way he thus describes :—

In my " History of Egypt " I had been necessarily led to show the Egyptian origin of many of the corruptions of Christianity. But the subject was rather lost in the two large volumes, and in 1863 I published much of the same matter in a smaller form, under the title of " Egyptian Mythology and Egyptian Christianity " with their influence on the opinions of modern Christians. To this I added the woodcuts which had been made for my other books. In this, as in my History, I had the direct aim of undermining orthodoxy; but I did it only by the statement of facts. I never hinted disapproval, but, when necessary, stated it openly. As this gave no direct offence, my views were never opposed or answered; the orthodox took the wiser course of leaving them to neglect, which was too much their fate. But as I chose to speak in favour of what I thought the truth, I had no reason to complain. I had only to be patient and to persevere.

Another publication, one of the most complete and exquisitely finished in which he was engaged, was undertaken, in conjunction with Mr. Bonomi, in this same period of partial neglect of hieroglyphics.

Mr. Bonomi, who was then the Keeper of Sir John Soane's Museum in Lincoln's Inn Fields, had been occupied for more than a year in copying and lithographing the hieroglyphics on the alabaster sarcophagus disentombed by Belzoni at the Biban el Molook or Valley of Kings Tombs in 1815.

There are still men living who remember the exhibition which Belzoni gave of his Egyptian treasures, to the London public, during all that winter. He had fitted up a room of the shape and size of the rock tomb he had unburied in the hills of Thebes, and after painting its inner walls in imitation of the gorgeous interior of that sepulchre, he placed the royal ornaments and relics he had brought to England, in almost the actual position in which he had discovered them. The exhibition was visited by all the scholars and the curious of the nation. Sir John Soane, the Architect, bought the sarcophagus from Belzoni, and set it up in his house in Lincoln's Inn Fields, where he left it after his death, together with his statues, pictures, vases and library of architecture to the care of trustees who should keep it open as a public museum. Mr. Bonomi had known his countryman Belzoni in early years. He had seen this clever adventurer perform as an acrobat before admiring audiences. Mr. Bonomi, like Belzoni, had searched the Egyptian temples and tombs, when he was living amongst them for ten years, employed as an artist by Messrs. Burton and Salt. Therefore, when late in life Mr. Bonomi came to be elected curator of Sir John Soane's Museum, it was a congenial task to him to copy and to lithograph the hieroglyphics upon this richly carved sarcophagus, and he did the work with the minutest care. The pictures thus most carefully copied form a series of nineteen folio plates. They were published under the title of "the Alabaster Sarcophagus of Oimenepthah I., King of Egypt;" and are accompanied by five-and-forty pages of descriptive letter-press by Samuel Sharpe. An appendix sets forth his reasons for differing from the received Egyptian chronology.

Samuel Sharpe was conscious all this time that the enthusiasm which characterized all his work was turning from its old Egyptian field to that of Biblical translation and research. This was the chief interest and absorbing occupation of his latter years. Egypt and its antiquities were never altogether neglected, but they became less and less, and Palestine and the Hebrew history and literature became more. His Egyptian researches became subservient to his Bible studies, and proved of immense value in throwing light on Biblical problems. There are no signs of the occupation of his busy pen with anything Egyptian for the next half-dozen years. In 1866, however, he showed his continued interest in the subject by a very handsome and costly present to the British Museum. This was an Egyptian statue of a son of Rameses II., in hard gritstone, standing and very nearly perfect. "I had had," he says, "ample opportunities of judging its worth. The Trustees had refused to purchase it, and I thought myself fortunate in being of use to the national collection in a matter for which my studies had qualified me." The statue cost him about five hundred pounds, and he considered it well worth the money.

# CHAPTER XII.

## TEN YEARS OF THEOLOGICAL PROGRESS.

THE ten years from 1860 to 1870 were a period of much excitement and very definite progress in theological matters in England. A decade which began with the agitation evoked by the mild heresies of the " Essays and Reviews," and which ended with the proposal of the Southern Convocation for a revised translation of the Scriptures, was necessarily one in which every friend of free inquiry in theology had much to interest and encourage him. The " Essays and Reviews " were published in 1860. There was nothing in the book with which every Unitarian had not been long familiar. There was little in it which did not at once commend itself to the common-sense and the natural religious feeling of the great bulk of educated laymen in the Established Church. A sense of astonishment rose in the minds of the vast majority of those who read the book at the anger and excitement it aroused in clerical circles. The Essayists themselves were probably the most surprised of all, and the prosecutions and persecutions which followed did not find some of them at all worthy to be leaders in the new reformation which they dimly foreshadowed.

It is needless to say that the" Essays and Reviews "
were read with complete sympathy by the heretical
scholar at Highbury.   He gladly joined in the subscription raised by Mr. Thomas Scott, of Ramsgate,
for the defence of the Rev. H. B. Wilson in the prosecution to which he was subjected.   Similar help
was offered to Dr. Rowland Williams.   Dr. Temple
needed no such aid.   He seemed inclined at first to
take an active part in the liberal theological movement of the time ; but he was made a Bishop in
1869, and has been careful ever since to let his
Churchmanship and orthodoxy appear.   He was
thus lost to theological liberalism, drowned, as people
said, in the See of Exeter.   Mr. C. W. Goodwin,
author of the Essay on " the Mosaic Cosmogony,"
had become acquainted with Samuel Sharpe through
a common interest in Egyptian studies.   As a layman he had not the same reason for shyness towards
Unitarians which affects the clergy.   He was a frequent visitor at Highbury Place, and when Samuel
Sharpe and his brother-in-law Mr. Edwin Field
established a course of Biblical Lectures at University Hall, Mr. Goodwin consented to be one of the
Lecturers, together with Dr. Martineau, the Rev. J. J.
Tayler, Professor Marks, Samuel Sharpe himself, and
others.   One day Mr. Goodwin went up to Highbury
to carry a piece of real news.   It was rumoured that
a Bishop was coming out among the heretics ; and
it was thought that the publication of his book would
cause a greater commotion than even the " Essays
and Reviews."   There was a little disappointment in
the public mind when it proved that the courageous
prelate was only a Colonial Bishop, though the agi-

tation caused by the publication of the first part of Bishop Colenso's work on the Pentateuch and the Book of Joshua quite justified the anticipations respecting it. This conscientious and courageous book raised a still greater storm than the Essays, and, unlike some of the Essayists, the high-minded and enlightened Bishop refused to trim his sails to the ecclesiastical weather. His faithfulness to his convictions gained for him the respect of all who can appreciate heroism, whether they agree with his opinions or not. That respect, and the knowledge that he has done much to advance the true knowledge of the Jewish histories, have hitherto been Bishop Colenso's only reward. He is one of the noble band of men, some of whom are born as the salt of the earth in every age, who are willing to suffer for what they believe to be the truth.

Writing in 1869 of the Bishop and his work, Samuel Sharpe, under the date of 1864, says :—

I became acquainted with Bishop Colenso first by meeting him one evening in company, and then by spending two days with him at Dr. Lee's house at Hartwell. I was very much impressed with his frank honesty of purpose, and was glad to be of use to him, or rather to the cause of Biblical criticism, by lecturing sometimes on the Pentateuch and by writing against his opponents. A number of Bishops had last year agreed, on the proposal of the Speaker, to issue a Commentary on the Bible, which should have their joint approval, and set at rest all doubts that Dr. Colenso had raised. I have several times called the attention of the public through the newspapers to this promise, but even now, in 1869, it has not yet made its appearance. The Bishops promised an impossibility ; namely, that they would get scholars to write such opinions on the subject as the divines should declare orthodox.

The Speaker, afterwards Lord Ossington, did not live to see the work he had suggested carried very far. Samuel Sharpe, however, saw the greater part of it published, and the fulfilment of his anticipation in its uselessness and failure. In Bishop Colenso's later visits to England he gladly renewed the acquaintance pleasantly begun at Dr. Lee's hospitable house at Hartwell. An occasional correspondence took place between them, extending over several years. The Bishop's letters, some of which are of considerable length, contain very careful and detailed arguments in support of some of his own critical conclusions which his correspondent at Highbury was unwilling to accept. Mr. Sharpe held, contrary to the views of Graf, Kuenen, Reuss, Kalisch, and the Bishop of Natal, that the ceremonial laws in Leviticus and Numbers were in all probability written in the century and a half before the end of the reign of Hezekiah. Many of his arguments in favour of this view were based on the historical veracity of the two Books of Chronicles, which Bishop Colenso regards as utterly untrustworthy, except where the Chronicler has copied from the Books of Samuel and Kings, and in a few other particulars. There are many other smaller points of divergence, but these are the chief; and the Bishop's letters deal with the various points with that minute care which characterizes all his criticisms, and with an earnest desire, as expressed in his own words, "that we who labour in this field should come to agreement as soon as possible and as far as possible, and should avow our agreement, since union gives strength in this domain also, and want of harmony between critics on minor points is used as a specious argument by the ignorant and indifferent, to depreciate all the results of modern criticism." There is no reason to believe that this controversial correspondence led to any considerable modification of divergent views on either side. The letters, however, confirmed the friendly feelings of the two students towards each other, and left behind a strengthened and heightened estimate of the laborious earnestness, the complete sincerity, and the admirable courage and consistency of the enlightened Bishop.

Being asked by the Hibbert Trustees in 1863 to examine their students in the Greek of the New Testament, and the Bible generally, in place of his friend Mr. James Yates, Samuel Sharpe accepted the duty because, as he says, it enabled him "to press these subjects, the latter in particular, upon the students, and through them, on their tutors in Manchester New College." He was afterwards invited to become a trustee of the Hibbert Fund, but declined to do so in the belief that he could do more good as an Examiner. It was unfortunate that he did not join the Trust. Some years later he sympathized strongly with many Unitarians who greatly regretted the use made by the Trustees of the large funds which had been entrusted to them for Anti-Trinitarian purposes. The examinations were undertaken as serious work, and he continued them, with much satisfaction, for eight years.

This year there is a glimpse of holiday occupations :—

While spending a few weeks this summer at St. Albans to be near Mr. Bonomi, I made what I thought an interesting discovery of the limits of the British town of the Cassii, which Julius Cæsar fought against and took. I sent an account of this to *Notes and Queries*, and two years afterwards to the Archæological Society.

This paper was read to the Archæological Society by Mr. James Yates, F.R.S.  It says:—

I was led to the inquiry by coming upon the "Beech Bottom," a very remarkable ditch, about a mile long, which may be compared to a deep railway cutting, with earth thrown up on both sides, though chiefly southwards, or towards the town of St. Albans. Its depth may vary from twenty to thirty feet. Its banks are covered with woods. It is so obviously an ancient military work that I was naturally led to search for traces of its continuation, and the conclusion I came to was that the fortified area was about two miles and a quarter long and a mile and three-quarters broad, enclosing the town of St. Albans. Its breadth is measured on the high road from London to Dunstable, and its length, at right angles to that road by a line from the river, through the Abbey Church, towards the town of Sandridge. Cæsar, in his "Commentaries on the Gallic War," describes the city of Cassivelaunus as fortified by woods and marshes, and then holding a large number of men and cattle that had come there as a place of safety. And to explain what a British town was to his Roman readers, who might expect to hear of buildings or at least of dwellings of some kind, he observes that when the Britons have fortified, with bank and ditch, woods which were otherwise nearly impassable, so that they might take refuge there from an incursion of their enemies, they called the place a town. He adds that the town of Cassivelaunus was in this manner excellently fortified, both by nature and art ; and that when he took the place he found there a large number of cattle. Cæsar does not give a name to the town, but it was probably called Verulam, the name given by the Romans to their fortified camp in the neighbourhood. The name of the tribe the Cassii, and that of their leader Cassivelaunus may yet be traced in Cassiobury, the name of the hundred in which St. Albans stands. . . .

Except at the "Beech Bottom" already described, the British ditch has been very much filled up and its space reclaimed for the purposes of agriculture, and the yearly ploughing has given it an appearance of a natural depression in the ground. But here and there we find traces of art sufficiently clear to enable us to follow the line of work on the map. From the west end of "Beech Bottom," it meets the river Ver, opposite to St. Michael's Church ; this is its north-west limit. Its south-eastern side begins at Sopwell Mills, on the same river, passing by Camp House. It then turns to the north, crosses the Hatfield Road, and joins the northern end of "Beech Bottom" at the Sandridge road.

He concludes that we have in the Beech Bottom the oldest work of the hand of man in these islands ; the only one that can be shown to have been made before Cæsar landed on our shores.

These antiquarian researches naturally had great charm for the historian of Egypt. A few years before this holiday discovery he had followed with much care the attempt of his friend Mr. Arthur Taylor to fix the site and limits of Roman London at its earliest date. He arrived with Mr. Taylor at the conclusion that it was much smaller than it is usually described to be, a narrow ellipse, according to the fashion of a Roman camp. East and west it reached from St. Dunstan's to Walbrook, while north and south it was included in the space between Fenchurch Street and Thames Street.

It was through his able and energetic brother-in-law Mr. Edwin Field that Samuel Sharpe was led to take a strong interest in the working of University College. In the leisure of his later years he had become able to devote some of his time to this valuable institution. He began by planning with Mr. Atkinson, the secretary, and with some of the professors of the College, a few courses of evening lectures open to the public at very moderate fees. This experiment would, of course, need money to carry it through, as the Lecturers could not expect much remuneration from their pupils. A donation towards this scheme was the first of Mr. Sharpe's gifts to the College. These gifts resulted in his election on the Council of the College in 1866. "I gained their notice," he says, in recording the election, "by a donation towards the establishment of evening classes. I was put on the Committee of Management, and rarely absented myself from their meetings, and I gave a second sum of money towards enlarging the building. This had become necessary from the increase of the number of students ; and a portion of the south wing was soon afterwards built." The second sum of money thus modestly spoken of was a gift of £6,000. The question of ways and means was under discussion, and there seemed to be no chance of carrying out the necessary improvement, when Mr. Sharpe quietly said, to the surprise of all his colleagues, that he would give that amount. The new school buildings were at once erected by means of this splendid gift. At a later period he gave £5,000 towards the extension of the college buildings. To the Fund for retired Professors he contributed £3,500 ; and one of the pleasures of his later years was the carrying out of a proposal to catalogue the library, which he did at a cost of £1,000. The glazing of the cloisters was also done at his expense; and for some years he paid the fees at the school of a considerable number of boys.

His election to the Council of University College made him a witness of one of the most painful controversies which have taken place in connection with that institution. The retirement in June, 1866, of Dr. Hoppus, an Independent minister, who had held the chair of Mental Philosophy and Logic from the foundation of the College, rendered necessary the appointment of a successor by the Council. The Senate of Professors reported that the Rev. James Martineau was the most eligible candidate. The Council, however, rejected him by the casting-vote of the chairman, Lord Belper; and Mr. Croom Robertson, whom the Senate, on a second reference by the Council, had reported as exceedingly well qualified next to Dr. Martineau, was appointed in his stead. The whole story of the controversy and its results is told by Mrs. De Morgan in her admirable and interesting life of her husband.* Dr. Martineau was rejected because he was an eminent Unitarian, and Professor De Morgan resigned his Professorship because the College had thus ignored and contradicted its fundamental principle of absolute neutrality in matters of theological belief. Professor De Morgan, in his letter to the chairman of the Council, resigning his Professorship, told the whole story of this intrigue when he said that in the rejection of Dr. Martineau there were two cross currents. There was an objection to his psychology as well as to his religion; "the first,"

* Memoir of Augustus De Morgan. By his wife Sophia Elizabeth De Morgan : pages 336 to 361.

said Mr. De Morgan, "is too far from atheism to please the philosopher, the second too far removed from orthodoxy to please the priest." It was the philosopher who was most to blame. The Unitarians on the Council could easily have elected Dr. Martineau, but some of them were forced into a position of neutrality by the charge, which was industriously spread abroad by those who were on the side of Mr. Grote, that Mr. De Morgan and the Unitarians were working to bring in their own candidate. Samuel Sharpe's brief account in his diary of the voting on the occasion of Dr. Martineau's rejection is of historic interest :—

When the Senate of University College were considering the merits of the candidates for the Professorship of Mental Philosophy and Logic, they determined that no one could be mentioned as at all equal to the Rev. James Martineau. Dr. Hoppus, the retiring Professor, agreed with this opinion. Professor Seeley, however, proposed to add to the Senate's recommendation the proviso, " if his being a Unitarian Minister is not thought a disqualification." Professor De Morgan objected to this, and these words were not added. He was simply recommended to the Council as the fittest candidate.

At the meeting of the Council Mr. George Grote proposed a resolution, that any minister of religion was unsuitable for the Professorship ; but this was rejected as *ex post facto* and unjust.

At the election, however, Mr. Martineau was rejected.

There voted for him :—
Sir F. Goldsmid, Jew.
Dr. Hodgson, Scotch Presbyterian.
W. Fowler, Quaker.
Myself, S. S., Unitarian.

Against him :—

　Mr. George Grote, Broad Church.

　Sir E. Ryan, Broad Church.

　Mr. James, Q.C., Colenso's barrister, Broad Church.

　Mr. Charles, Colenso's barrister, Broad Church.

　Lord Belper, chairman, had been a Unitarian.

Did not vote :—

　Mr. Busk, Unitarian.

　Mr. R. Fowler, Quaker.

Absent :—

　Mr. Edwin Field, Unitarian.

　Mr. Edward Enfield, Unitarian.

　Mr. H. Crabb Robinson, Unitarian.

On the morning after the election Samuel Sharpe went to Hampstead to call on Dr. Martineau's colleague, the Rev. John James Tayler. Dr. Martineau had gone to Scotland for his usual summer holiday among the hills and the heather, but Mr. Tayler had remained behind to await the issue. So many members of the Council were away from home, that Samuel Sharpe found himself the only member present at the election who could carry the details of the transaction to Dr. Martineau's friends. He had, of course, to tell Mr. Tayler not only of the vote, but of the discussion which led up to it, and of the strong view Mr. Grote took against Dr. Martineau, both because he was a Unitarian, and because he was a minister. He told the story with so much sympathy for Dr. Martineau—from whom he differed, as he did also from Mr. Tayler, as to the use of the word Unitarian to describe their free, spiritual theology,—that Mr. Tayler exclaimed with warmth, "Almost thou persuadest me to be a Unitarian."

When the College re-opened in the autumn, Mr. Sharpe went to hear the opening address of the new Professor, Mr. Croom Robertson, to whom, of course, he had no personal antagonism, or objection. He had no sympathy with the school of Mr. Alexander Bain, to which Mr. Croom Robertson was known to belong, and decidedly leaned to Dr. Martineau's philosophical views. But it was not this leaning which had influenced him. His advocacy of the claims of the most eminent member of the Unitarian body to this important chair, was entirely due to his sense of the immense superiority of Dr. Martineau's qualifications over those of all other candidates. He had in view only the interests of the College. Like Professor De Morgan, he was anxious that it should remain faithful to its fundamental principle of religious neutrality; he had also the further desire that the ablest and most eminent men who could be got should be encouraged to join its Professorate. Mr. Grote, on the other hand, wished his own views to be represented in the teaching of the chair.

Samuel Sharpe, and the three members of the Council who voted with him, differed from Dr. Martineau in very many respects. Though the comprehensive name of Unitarian included both the eminent Principal of Manchester New College and the author of the History of Egypt, they were far asunder in their mode of reaching kindred conclusions, and in the form in which they held them. Samuel Sharpe may be spoken of as a Biblical Unitarian. His intensely practical mind, and his business training, joined with his great though rational reverence for the Bible, made him long for definite views expressed in Scripture language. But no Unitarian could be prouder than he was of Dr. Martineau's genius, nor more delighted with his splendid vindication of the spiritual philosophy against the materialism of Bain, and the apparent materialism of Dr. Tyndall and other men of science. He read Miss Cobbe's striking essay on Intuitive Morals with full sympathy, and listened with pleasure to the talk of his friend, Mr. R. W. Mackay, in his enthusiastic exposition and defence of the transcendental philosophy. He could not ascend with Mackay into the higher heaven of Kantian speculation; but looked up at it with some wonder from below. He admired Channing's writings for the elevation of tone which pervades them, the transcendental glow which shines through them, the presence in every page of that kindling power of disinterested love and faith, the absence of which and the presence in its place of the utilitarian philosophy made some of the older Unitarians so clear and cold.

The study of the Hebrew Scriptures now began more and more to absorb his time. It fell in with, and was in some degree a continuation of, his Egyptian studies. The two lines of inquiry greatly helped each other. The ancient monuments threw light on many obscure passages in the prophets and historians of the Old Testament, and it is one characteristic both of his translation and of his illustrative comments that the Egyptologist comes in to the aid of the Biblical critic. In 1866 he published a small volume entitled "Texts from the Holy Bible explained by the help of the Ancient Monuments." This was a very striking and interesting contribution to a better popular knowledge of what the writers meant. It was illustrated with a large number of woodcuts, chiefly drawn by Mr. Bonomi, with some assistance from Miss Emily Sharpe. It is a little book of permanent value and interest ; from the side-lights it throws upon expressions which were familiar enough when they were written, but which have been made difficult to understand by the changed conditions under which they have now to be read.

The repeated readings of the Hebrew Bible which were rendered needful by his efforts as a translator led to another work. To go through the Old Testament carefully, making use of the Concordance in order to weigh the exact value of every word, usually took about twelve months. He was thus occupied through the whole of 1867 ; and in 1868 he published a small volume of 72 pages on the Chronology of the reigns of the Hebrew Kings and the texts that supported his arrangement. It contained also a chronology of Christ's Ministry, in which he fixes the date and hour of the Crucifixion as Thursday, April the 14th, at noon, the day of the Preparation of the Passover. In the next year he published " The History of the Hebrew Nation and its Literature." He described this work as being his former " Historic Notes" treated in an inverse order ; by taking each separate portion of the Hebrew Scriptures in the order of its age and putting it into its place in history, instead of attempting to explain the books one by one as they stand in the Bible, as he does in the " Historic Notes." He had read with some admiration Mr. Francis Newman's " History of the

Hebrew Monarchy," and had in some degree made that work the model of his own. In the Preface to the first edition of this book his view of the Bible is clearly expressed :—

The History of the Hebrew Nation must be carefully studied if we would understand the Bible. The Hebrew writings are the well-spring of our religious thoughts, they furnish the key to the Christian Scriptures, and they are the Ark which during so many centuries has held safe from the attacks of Paganism, that great religious truth that the Almighty Creator of the world is One, simple and undivided. But these writings have come down to our time in a very confused condition ; that part of the Bible called the Old Testament contains writings, some of which must be dated in every one of the eleven centuries before the Christian Era. Not only are they put together with very little regard to date, but the writers in many instances did not scruple to weave their new matter into the old fabric. Writings which have been handed down in manuscript, at the mercy of every scribe who made a new copy, were naturally altered from time to time both by receiving additions and by suffering curtailment, and again by having two pieces joined into one or one piece cut in two. It is easy to show cases of all these alterations. Thus the Book of the Law, of which the earliest part may have belonged to David's or Solomon's reign, received additions long after the fall of the monarchy. The Books of Ezra and Nehemiah seem both to have been curtailed of matter that they once contained. The Prophecies of David cannot have been the work of fewer than six authors living at as many different times ; nor can the short Book of Zechariah be otherwise than made up of writings that belong to three different centuries. The Psalms belong to every century from David's reign to that of Antiochus Epiphanes. Such being the confused state in which the Hebrew Scriptures have reached us, no commentary on them can be so valuable as the attempt to ascertain the date of each part.

The great value of the Hebrew books arises from the firm belief of the writers in one God as the Creator and Governor of the world, and from the readiness with which they acknowledge His will as the cause of everything that befalls the nation.

Their misfortunes are treated as God's punishment for their sins; their blessings as His reward for obedience to His laws. So strong was their trust in God's guidance that they thought not only conscience but reason also spoke His direct commands. The prophet whose zeal in the cause of justice and religion raised him to become a teacher of his countrymen, claimed to have a message from Jehovah, and the priest who gave answer to the questions that were brought before him, whether of moral duty or of civil justice, spoke in the name of Jehovah. It is this strong religious feeling which gives to the Hebrew books their value.

This book went through several editions, growing in size and completeness with each issue. The first edition, in 1869, was a small volume of 232 pages; the fourth edition, issued by Messrs. Williams and Norgate in 1882, is a handsome octavo of 455 pages. This posthumous edition contains the many additions and corrections he had left behind ready for the printer. The Hebrew Chronology is added to this volume as an appendix; and the book in the form in which it is thus posthumously published contains the ripe results of the Biblical studies of its author's whole life. The publication of the first edition occurred soon after his New Testament began to attract general notice, and he remarks that his venturing to translate the New Testament was at first frowned upon, and that it was only after the translation had been five-and-twenty years before the public that it began to be looked upon with favour. He anticipates the same fate for the "History of the Hebrew Nation."

His New Testament got gradually into notice and favour as public interest in the question of revision increased. He found out by an accident that it had been published at too high a price, and thus the result of what the publisher thought the failure of the fourth edition was a very widely extended sale. Under the date of 1862 he writes :—

In this year the publishers of my New Testament, .finding the sale of the fourth edition very unsatisfactory, sold off a large remainder of 1,500 copies to the bookstalls at a few pence a copy. This was no loss to them, and to me it was in every way satisfactory. The purchasers bound it, and sold it at a shilling a copy, and the sale soon rose to one hundred and fifty per month. Then for the first time I learned at what price the public wished for the book. The publisher even had to buy back a hundred copies for his own trade. Upon this I made arrangements with another publisher, Mr. J. R. Smith, that he should print a fifth edition of 5,000 copies, to be sold at eighteenpence a copy. This he did at the end of this year, and the sale continued at a hundred a month for some little time. It then declined a little, making an average during these years (1862 to 1869) of about six hundred a year. This brought it into some notice. The orthodox religious reviews pronounced it thoroughly impartial, and the best translation extant. One or two Calvinistic papers alone found fault with it. Upon that my Unitarian friends took courage and began to recommend it. Its sale, however, remains confined to the more humble ranks of society ; and it is quite clear that if I had put notes, and thus made it a more expensive book, it would not have gained the notice even of those who now ask for the notes.

The sale of this translation of the New Testament, and of the new version of the Old Testament, which proceeded side by side with it, showed a growing feeling in the public mind of dissatisfaction with the Authorized Version, and of desire to know more accurately what prophets and historians and psalmists under the older religion, and apostles and evangelists of Christian times, had actually written. The "Critical Notes on the Authorized Version," of which a second edition was issued in 1866, contributed to this result. This book, as has been already said, consisted of a collection of passages in which the Greek of the New Testament has been incorrectly translated, each passage being gramatically explained and carefully amended. The volume could not be said to have done its work until King James's translation should be set aside, and it was kept in print. Samuel Sharpe also now printed a four-page tract called "Controversial Texts Corrected," containing more than a dozen of what he thought to be the most important mistakes in the Authorized Version. This tract was several times reprinted for distribution, and was found useful in the controversy. It seemed like a happy sequel to these efforts when, in May, 1870, the Southern Convocation resolved that a revised translation of the Scriptures should be undertaken, and two Companies of Revisers were formed for the purpose. The Convocation, in a spirit of liberality which deserves the most cordial recognition, not only nominated a body of its own members to undertake the work of revision, but left them, in the words of the resolution, "at liberty to invite the co-operation of any eminent for scholarship, to whatever nation or religious body they may belong." The resolution passed in this liberal and comprehensive spirit was carried out with equal impartiality. Samuel Sharpe was one of four scholars of the Unitarian body to whom a message was sent asking them to choose among themselves, or to advise application to, some scholar of their own opinions who might sit in the Company of the New Testament revisers. He declined the honour for himself. He felt that had he been young enough to do the work required, he had an over-whelming reason for keeping aloof, as he was still busy in correcting and superintending the issue of successive editions of his own translation. He could not, moreover, be sanguine enough to hope that the Revision thus undertaken would be complete enough to satisfy him, or would not be injured by com-promises between divergent views. He cordially recommended Dr. Vance Smith as the Unitarian member of the Revision Committee, and his appoint-ment gave Mr. Sharpe, as it did all Unitarians, very great satisfaction.

In recording the resolution passed by Convoca-tion calling the Revision Companies into existence, Samuel Sharpe notes that his own translation of the New Testament had by this time "gained full notice and unwilling approval ; " and he had reasons for thinking that its wide circulation had some influ-ence in moving the Southern Convocation to make their remarkable proposal. One of the Bishops, in urging Convocation to take up the work, had said, "If you do not do it, the Dissenters will." One Dissenter had, in fact, already done it. In 1869 he had begun to stereotype a sixth edition, and each successive issue contained fresh emendations, and was brought up to the latest results of his studies and investigations. About 9,500 copies of the first five editions had been printed, and at the end of 1868 only a hundred copies still remained in the hands of the publisher. His new edition in 1869 consisted of 1,000 copies, and it was followed by 1,500 more in 1870. This made 12,000. In 1874 the thirteenth thousand was printed, and in 1881 the fourteenth thousand. This was independent of the edition, which was the eighth, contained in the beautiful stereotyped Holy Bible published by Messrs. Williams and Norgate at the close of 1880.

The "History of the Hebrew Nation" was also selling steadily at this time, and a translation into German was issued by Dr. Jolowicz. The German translator shortened the book, and made many changes in it, which modified its views, and thus gave its author much displeasure. A second edition of "Texts from the Bible Explained" was also asked for, and issued by Mr. Russell Smith with the usual additions and emendations of the author. So far as printing and publishing was concerned this was the busiest period of his life. "In 1870," he says, "I printed more than I had ever done before; first the 'Decree of Canopus,' 250 copies; next the 1,500 more copies of the New Testament; then a fifth edition of the 'History of Egypt' with the plates, stereotyped; and lastly, I began to print the second edition of the 'Hebrew Scriptures Translated,' with the corrections which I had prepared." This was the work of part of the first and great part of the second year of his eighth decade, for he was seventy-one in March, 1870.

His eldest daughter draws the following picture of his interests and activities during these years :—

"Those were exciting days when the nation was beginning to pay attention to matters that had so long been the subject of my father's quiet study. Through these years of lessening bodily activity his friends could see only an increasing activity and versatility of mind. So fertile was he in new thoughts in these years that rarely would a morning rise that he did not come out of his bed-room to the eight o'clock breakfast piping hot with some paragraph that must be inserted into one of his books, some letter that must be written, some article for the Unitarian papers that had been planned in bed, .some hard point of translation he had been ruminating upon, and that he must at the moment consult Lexicon and grammar upon—something, in short, of whatever nature it might be, that he must absolutely settle his mind upon and put down upon paper before he could sit down to the table and put a mouthful into his mouth. And to this as to his other meals, breakfast, dinner, or tea, he usually came with a sheet of paper in his hand, being the words he had been busied upon when called to the meal, and these he would read aloud to his family upon the spur of the moment. It was in this way that without pre-arrangement the greater part of his works were read aloud at home, and nearly all his bright sparkling articles on religious politics, which in early days were printed in the *Inquirer*, and in later years in the *Christian Life*, were read over, talked over, laughed over, and sometimes added to and re-written before they were sent to the papers."

The translation of the "Decree of Canopus" was

his next work. Three years before this time the
Germans had dug up in Egypt a tablet with a
bi-lingual inscription, Hieroglyphics and Greek.
It is a Decree issued by the priests of Egypt, in
the reign of Ptolemy Euergetes, B.C. 238, similar in
many respects to the Rosetta Stone in the British
Museum, but some forty years more ancient.
Samuel Sharpe no sooner got hold of the German
publication of this new tablet, than he perceived the
immense help it might give to the student of
Hieroglyphics. He therefore lithographed the plates
from the German work, and set himself to translate
the Decree into English ; and he printed it "with
an examination of the hieroglyphical characters."
In this work, which was published in 1869, he once
more showed his large differences from Dr. Lepsius
and other hieroglyphical scholars ; but was content
with simply owning the fact and not entering into
controversy about it. The enlarged knowledge of
hieroglyphical characters gained from the study of
the "Decree of Canopus" enabled him to translate
the Rosetta Stone more correctly than he had
hitherto done, and in 1871 he lithographed and published the inscriptions on the Rosetta Stone in a
thin volume by itself, Hieroglyphics and Greek,
with a translation, an explanation of the hieroglyphics, and a list of kings' names.

The history of these two publications may illus-
trate the modest and simple-minded way in which
Samuel Sharpe through his whole life accustomed
himself to revise his old opinions and his old doings ;
amending them, setting right his mistakes, and
enlarging his views at every opportunity afforded

S

to him. It is not every author who can bring himself to do this. In his preface to the translation of the Rosetta Stone he alludes to the expression of a fellow-student—" But we do not want to go to school again." He also speaks of some of the earlier attempts to read the Hieroglyphics, as—

ingenious but unproved guesses, many of which may now be brought to the test of the greater certainty which can be gained from the " Decree of Canopus." This re-examination of received opinion, this going to school again, is, however, a troublesome task, which some minds do not readily submit to. Hence the cold reception of the " Decree of Canopus," and the unfavourable opinion expressed of the Author's publication in some Reviews. One critic says: " We have got beyond all that." Another calls the Author's publication "a mischievous work," as unsettling the received and " orthodox " opinions. A third thinks that what we learn from the " Decree of Canopus," and its Greek translation, should be judged by the results which ingenuity may have derived from the untranslated inscriptions, and would thus try to decypher the *ignotum per ignotius.*

During the whole of the period since he had left business he had taken a lively interest in the affairs of the Unitarian body, and had spent much time and money in promoting the interests of Unitarian Christianity. He had printed tracts, delivered lectures, encouraged the building of chapels, and promoted all the missionary efforts which a period of religious revival called forth. He and his family had joined the congregation of which the Rev. Robert Spears was then the energetic minister, in Stamford Street, Blackfriars Road.

He did this, passing by Unity Church, Islington, on his way, from preference for a plain service over an ornate one, and for the old Presbyterian form over a liturgy. Some years before this he had assisted Mr. Spears in the establishment of a new kind of missionary agency in London called the London Lay Preachers' Union. He thought that the difficulty of supporting small congregations might be met by educated laymen undertaking to conduct religious services and to cultivate the habit of speaking on religious subjects.

As to the surroundings of the service, he held very distinct and strongly formed opinions. His dislike of Gothic buildings as places for Protestant worship has already been mentioned. He preferred four plain walls to "long-drawn aisles and fretted vault," clear glass and ample illumination to "storied windows richly dight, casting a dim, religious light;" and a minister in plain coat to any imitation of gowned teacher or robed priest. He was anxious that the forms and ceremonies of worship should not be misleading to the worshipper. He was keenly awake to the powerful sway which music and architecture exert over all our minds, and he believed that he had seen in many examples around him, in what direction a florid service draws individuals and congregations. Hence, he was strongly opposed to every kind of ritualism, disliked liturgical services and musical responses, and preferred the Puritan hymn to the more ancient chant. But even on these points he thought more of substance than of form, and for the sake of preaching with which he was in sympathy, consented to put up

with a liturgical service and with musical responses
in the Free Christian Church, in Clarence Road,
Kentish Town, at which place he became a regular
attendant during the last years of his life. His
objection to ornate services—which in this case he
consented to waive, but did not in any way modify—
was based on the grounds that the love of beauty
is not religion, and that too much ministering to
the sense may keep us from feeling the spirit of
worship. For the same reasons he was strongly
opposed to the introduction into the pulpit of anything that was not directly connected with practical
religion or with theological discussion. Philosophy,
criticism, science, politics, were everywhere in place to
him except in a sermon ; were always of interest and
importance, except in the hour set apart for prayer
and praise and thoughts of God. "I want religion,
and not science or speculation," he was accustomed
to say with respect to the services of Sunday. And
by religion he meant everything that relates us to
the Unseen, and that brings into operation the disinterested motives inspired by the Love of God.
As Christ is the Christian ideal, the object of Christian teaching should be to make the people feel
his life of spiritual motives to be the pattern of
their own.

With all this desire to promote the simplicity and
spirituality of religious services, he united a very
lively interest in the propagandism of Unitarian
views at home and abroad. There might often be
seen in his library or dining-room a great bill
announcing some course of Unitarian Lectures, the
expense of which had been paid by him. The

Transylvanian students at Manchester New College were invited to his house, and the translation of his Unitarian tracts into Italian and Welsh gave him as much satisfaction as the translation of his Egyptological works into German. A large placard containing an outline of Unitarian Christianity, printed in Italian by Signor Bracciforti, for posting in the streets of Florence, long had a place of honour on his walls. Similar placards posted in London by the Rev. Robert Spears had similar support and approval. If an enterprising Unitarian minister saw an opening for sowing a little seed of Liberal thought in some town which was given over to orthodoxy, he had only to write to Mr. Sharpe and show a clear case, and the money for the enterprise was pretty sure to be sent in the course of a post or two. Every appeal for help to build or enlarge a Unitarian chapel was usually submitted to him in the first place. His help in such cases was liberal, but by no means indiscriminate. No money of his went for mere ornament and vanity, he exacted a pledge that it should be for use alone. He had the plans before him, and took the trouble to investigate them. If the building was a Gothic one, he would make it a condition of his help that the pulpit should be placed in the middle and not on one side, and that there should be no altar. If a congregation wished to spend money in stained glass, or carvings, or other ornament, they did not even ask for help from Highbury. If, being Unitarians, they were too timid to call themselves so, they rarely got much countenance from Mr. Sharpe. He preferred, moreover, to give large aid to small congregations, rather than to

assist those who could help themselves. The principle which ran all through his life was that of
befriending the poor rather than cultivating the
society of the rich ; and it was carried consistently
into the munificent distribution of his money in the
help of Unitarian ministers and congregations. He
never made a gift without clearly ascertaining that
it would be well bestowed.

It was not always needful that direct application
should be made to him for help. He sometimes went
out of his way to give aid to movements which had
enlisted his sympathy. One example of this liberality
is worth notice, as indicating not only the breadth of
his sympathy with the poor, but his political and
social leanings. When the movement of the agricultural labourers first began to attract attention in
1872, Mr. Arthur Clayden, who had become a member
of a Consultative Committee, formed to assist the
National Agricultural Labourers' Union, and who
afterwards wrote a history of the agitation under the
title of "The Revolt of the Field," made an appeal in
a letter to the *Nonconformist* for pecuniary help. In
a day or two he received a letter from Mr. Sharpe, to
whom he was personally a stranger, asking where he
could send some pecuniary gift. The result was that
Mr. Arch got a cheque for fifty pounds. This is only
one instance among many of quiet and unnoticed
help being given, not because he was personally
applied to, but from his own desire to help a suffering
person or a struggling cause. Many a poor minister
has been gladdened by such unsolicited gifts from
this generous friend.

When he had just attained his seventieth year he

was asked to become President of the British and Foreign Unitarian Association. He says in his autobiographical notes, that he accepted the office very unwillingly; "but to have refused," he adds, "would have looked like affected humility. I had for many years given all such countenance and encouragement as I could to missionary efforts for the spread of Unitarianism; and at this time the tide seemed turning a little in our favour. At least the sect had ceased to lessen, and since 1864 the number of Unitarian ministers had increased." The duties of this office occupied a good deal of his attention between Whitsuntide 1869 and Whitsuntide 1870. The Rev. Robert Brook Aspland was then Honorary Secretary of the Association, with the Rev. Robert Spears as Assistant Secretary; and the head-quarters of the Association were in a small narrow room over Mr. Whitfield's shop at 178, Strand. It was a year of much excitement in ecclesiastical politics. The Bill for the Disestablishment of the Irish Church was before Parliament, and received the cordial support of the Association and its President. He approved of this tardy act of justice, however, for somewhat different reasons from those which moved some of his Unitarian friends; as he was an opponent of the principle of State Churches, was alive to the immense injury they inflict on religion and the obstacles they offer to the progress of opinion in religious matters, and looked forward to the time as not very far distant when, in England and Scotland as well as in Ireland, the last stone of the venerable edifice of religious inequality and theological favouritism should be thrown down to the ground.

The visit to England of the founder of the Brahmo Somaj, the Baboo Keshub Chunder Sen, took place before the year of his presidency of the Unitarian Association closed. A meeting was held at the Hanover Square rooms to welcome the Indian reformer, over which as President of the Unitarian Association it was his duty to preside. The variety of religious bodies represented on the platform gave him the liveliest satisfaction. Lord Lawrence, who had returned from his successful administration of the Indian Government little more than a year before, Dean Stanley, Dr. Martineau, Dr. Mullens the eminent Congregationalist, besides representatives of the Wesleyans and the Baptists, united in paying respect to the distinguished representative of the cause of Indian reformation. Dr. Marks was also present, and his admirable speech was greatly welcomed and praised. The assembly was something more than a union of Christians among themselves ; it was a union in which they shook hands with those who, like the Jewish doctor on the one hand and the Indian reformer on the other, are beyond the bounds of Christianity.

# CHAPTER XIII.

## THE FAMILY STORY DRAWS TO ITS END.

THE family history which has been narrated in this volume draws to its close as the eighth decade of the century advances. It is not often that a biographer has to look back over a complete domestic history, and to tell the story of one whole generation of a family from its beginning to its end. Very rarely indeed does the story of the children of one father stretch out, as this does, over a hundred years. Catharine Sharpe, the eldest sister, was born on the 2nd May, 1782, and Samuel Sharpe, the last surviving brother died on July 28th, 1881. The hundredth year is thus touched, and a few more months would have completed the century covered by the two lives of this brother and sister. All the rest of the family group fell by the way. There is nothing more striking than to watch the movement of a family, as in this biography, through its history of a hundred years. The six younger children, who were left to the care of their elder sister in the sixth year of the first decade of the present century, entered on the second and third decades as an unbroken group, and thence onwards one fell off with every decennial period, till only one was left to look over as it were into the ninth decade, touch the hundredth year of the family life, and then follow all the rest along the predestined and inevitable way. Mary Sharpe, then Mrs. Edwin Field, died in 1831 ; Sutton, the eldest brother, was taken in 1843 ; the youngest, Daniel, followed him in 1856, surviving the eldest sister, Catharine, by three years ; in 1870, seven months before the completion of the seventh decade William Sharpe had died ; in the eighth decade, the death of his last surviving brother Henry in 1873 had left Samuel Sharpe alone.

The success of Catharine Sharpe's early effort to preserve in the young group committed to her care the sense of family life is another marked feature in the story. The brothers never lost sight of one another. There was no scattering except by death ; and they were much to one another to the last. Her training, and the excellent social influences with which their youth had been surrounded, had as their result the uniform though varied success of all the brothers. There were striking differences between them ; but each left behind him a large circle of attached and admiring friends, and each deserved and received the recognition due to valuable public service.

The last mention of William Sharpe in the preceding chapters was of his careful editing, as one of the executors of his uncle Samuel Rogers, of the interesting and valuable volume of Rogers's " Recollections." He had been in practice as a solicitor from 1826 ; and during the forty-four years over which his practice extended he made a very large number of personal and professional friends. He was distinguished for the warm personal sympathy which he carried into professional relations. Many private testimonies to this sympathy were given after his death by men who said that his careful attention to their affairs, his cautious advice, and his habit of thoroughness, had saved them from ruin. His patience in the mastering of minute and difficult details brought him the complete confidence of more than one generation of successful pleaders at the bar. Many of them have said that they always felt safe when the case was in William Sharpe's hands. He had given much attention to the Bankruptcy laws, and on one occasion was consulted by the Lord Chancellor as to a Bill which was next day to be introduced into Parliament. He sat over the Bill during a good part of the night, and hurried off early the next morning to make prompt report that the scheme was impracticable. "You are quite right," said the Lord Chancellor with a characteristic shrug and smile; "the Bill won't work, but it must pass, for we have promised the places." The Bill was passed, and, as he expected, it did not work. But the places had been given, and when, very shortly afterwards, a change was made, the placemen were compensated. The very last legal papers that came into his hands in 1870 were from Lord Hatherley and Lord Cairns, asking for further revision and review of some matters connected with the Judicature Act, which he had assisted in preparing.

This may be described as amateur work, undertaken from purely public motives. A good deal of such work comes into the hands of any successful lawyer who has public spirit enough to do it; and who commands the complete confidence of the profession. There is no higher testimony to a man than this professional confidence and esteem. Lawyers are the most severe critics of each other; and where they give trust and admiration to members of their own profession, the public outside may be always quite sure that it is fully deserved. In William Sharpe's case there was no cultivation of the arts of popularity. He did not desire to go into public life. His chief literary work was the editing of the " Recollections " of his uncle Rogers ; and the preface and notes which he attached to this work give striking evidence of the care and thoroughness with which he did everything he undertook. This may be said to have been his characteristic. His business life was spent in the steady, careful, and successful practice of his profession, in the service of his clients, and in promotion of the interests of the profession itself. As a member of the Council of the Incorporated Law Society, and at one time its President, he did the whole body valuable and important service. In the words of their resolution, passed after his death, " He was always ready to deal promptly and judiciously with matters connected with the profession, and as the head of a large agency office, and possessing great practical knowledge, combined with a high sense of professional honour, his loss will long be felt by his professional brethren."

His life at home had all been lived in the house to which he had removed in 1844 ; where most of his children had been born, and where he died. He had a full share with all of his brothers and his two sisters in the good taste and love of art which were hereditary in the family. He, as well as his sister Mary, inherited his father's artistic gift, and much of his happy leisure was spent in its cultivation. There is no more delightful form of recreation for a busy man, and they are greatly to be envied who can turn to it—whether in the form of pencil drawing, painting, sculpture, or music—in the intervals of work. It has already been said that his great natural talent as a draughtsman had, in early days, suggested his adoption of another profession from that which he eventually followed, and it was perhaps fortunate that this delightful gift, could, all his life, be used for recreation. He was apt, in his conscientious anxiety to do the best for his clients, sometimes to carry their cases home with him ; to their advantage doubtless, and to nobody's discomfort but his own. Like his brothers Samuel and Henry, he was essentially a domestic man, a lover of home, and beloved at home. He died, after an illness of some months, on the 20th of May, 1870, in the sixty-sixth year of his age.

There is yet another form of public service which this glance back over a family history reveals. Not one of these successful men lived to himself. They were all disciples of the Gospel of Public Duty. It has often been asked why so small a body as the Unitarians should have had in it so many eminent names, should hold so large a space in the Nonconformist representation in Parliament, and should be what Mr. Trevelyan calls "the most over-represented sect in the Kingdom." Mr. Trevelyan indirectly suggests an answer to the question in his Life of Macaulay, by saying that "men are not willing to attend the religious worship of people who believe less than themselves, or to vote at elections for people who believe more than themselves."* This is only a partial explanation. Another reason is derived from the absence in the minds of most Unitarians of any sense of the ecclesiastical and pietistic distinction between secular and religious duties. Their view of life and of their relation to the world and its work differs from that of the ecclesiastic on the one hand, or of the evangelical on the other. They are not narrowed into Churchmen, nor drilled into Dissenters. A Unitarian is a Man of the World, and sees no trail of the serpent over it all. He is not afraid to enjoy life; and he thinks it his duty to help others to enjoy it also. Everything that makes the world a little brighter for other people, brings out their intelligence, developes their taste, sharpens their intellectual faculties, improves their morals, and makes them honest men, is, in his view, part of God's service. The Unitarian religion comes out in fact far less in what the populace regard as being religious than in being public-spirited. The public spirit rests on a basis of religious duty, the love of God comes out in the love and service of man.

All this was illustrated in the lives of these brothers. Perhaps it was most exhibited in the one who of them all came least before the public, and lived his active, cultivated, and useful life quite out of the public eye. Henry Sharpe continued in busi-

* " Life and Letters of Lord Macaulay," vi. p. 289.

ness to the end of his life, and. devoted a great
part of his leisure to the teaching and improvement of the young shopmen, and many of the
working men of Hampstead. He had classes of
them at his house, where he read with them,
encouraged them to learn and superintended their
studies. For many years one or two of these
young men, who had no other leisure for such work,
went to his house before breakfast, and received
lessons from him in French or Latin. For years also
he went one morning in the week to teach Latin to
a few of the top boys in Harp Alley School. Their
exercises were constantly arriving by post, and were
carefully corrected and returned. Many pupils were
thus taught by means of correspondence. This love
of communicating knowledge was its own reward.
The young men thus taught looked up to him with
the liveliest admiration and gratitude, regarded him
as a friend and benefactor, asked his advice, consulted
him on all their affairs, and were always sure of wise
counsel and sympathetic action. They went their
several ways, to all parts of the world, but never
forgot their generous friend at home. Letters came
from America and the colonies, expressive of their
gratitude, and he was always made to feel that in
their confidence and esteem, and even more in the
great advantages they had gained from his instruction, he had a rich reward for his self-denying efforts
on their behalf.

He did this work not merely out of a great love
for teaching and great capacity for it, but from a simple
desire to do good. He was a great reader of the

classics and of the best literature, and often read
aloud to his children in the evening.  They could
not feel that they were neglected in the beneficent
efforts to instruct others, for he gave them continuous
help in their studies and was interested in directing
their reading.  In conjunction with Mr. Evans and
the Rev. Richard King (then curate of the parish
church), he established in 1844 the Hampstead
Reading Rooms, which were for many years the only
institution of the kind in the town.  He spent a
good deal of time at these rooms in evening classes,
and in the general management, which soon fell into
his hands.  The first drinking fountain within the
Metropolitan district was set up at his expense in
1859, and he soon followed it by two more.  The
first seats on Haverstock Hill and some of those
on Hampstead Heath were also placed where they
are, at his cost and on his design, and he was one
of the most active promoters of the movement
by which Hampstead Heath was saved from the
encroachments of the builders and dedicated to
the public use for ever.  He shrank from any
public recognition of the great services he had
thus rendered the people of Hampstead, but after
his death a handsome memorial tablet, with a life-
sized medallion portrait, was erected by subscription in the Parish Church.  This was done by
his old pupils, some sixty of whom, at home and
in the colonies, joined in asking the sanction of his
family to this public expression of their gratitude.
The inscription sums up in simple and touching
words the story of his life :--

## HENRY SHARPE,

### MERCHANT,

BORN, AUGUST 21ST, 1802; DIED, APRIL 27TH, 1873.

THIS MONUMENT IS RAISED
BY THOSE WHO DERIVED BENEFIT IN THEIR YOUTH
FROM HIS DISINTERESTED EFFORTS FOR THEIR INSTRUCTION
AND IMPROVEMENT, AND WHO, THOUGH SCATTERED THROUGH THE
WORLD, GRATEFULLY UNITE TO PERPETUATE THE MEMORY
OF A LIFE DEVOTED TO THE GOOD OF OTHERS.

*" None of us liveth to himself."*

The sole survivor of the orphan family of 1806 might now fairly regard himself as having reached old age. The world had thought him an old man for many years, for he was old in manner and in appearance except for the vivacity of his conversation and the fire of his bright grey eyes. He had become bald, as some of his brothers did, in comparatively early life; and the fine dome of his head was fringed with grey hair. He was always taken for ten years older than his real age, and as he had never thought it likely that he should live to be old, he had none of that sudden awakening to the fact that he was an old man which some men describe as so disagreeable a revelation. He had thought himself old at fifty-five, and so the world had thought him; and at seventy-five he probably felt but little older, and was not then taken to be older. Advancing years brought no change in his habits, except a little more admission of the necessity for rest. He was generally to be

T

found at work sitting at the table in his capacious drawing-room with his back to the fire, and with his translation of the Scriptures or any other work he was busy upon, before him, and books of reference within easy reach.  He turned from his work as a welcome visitor came in, looked up with a smile and some words of greeting, and often plunged at once into talk about some point in which he had been engaged, or about the political news, or the comments upon it in the morning paper (the *Daily News*), or whatever subject he and his visitor had in common.  Everybody was struck by his eagerness, which showed that the age was only in the outer part of him and had not penetrated within.

In the summer he usually spent much time in the garden behind his house.  There was a favourite seat on the south side, where he and his friends sat to talk, and where many questions of politics, theology, archæology, and lighter subjects, were discussed. Near the seat were two picturesque stumps of old apple trees which had been cut to serve as stands for a telescope.  As the stumps grew shaky he compared them to the Established Churches of England and Ireland, and many a humorous speculation was indulged in as to whether the old stumps or the institutions after which they had been named, would last the longest.  By an odd coincidence the stump named after the Irish Church toppled over just at the time when the Irish Church Act was passed and the Established Church of Ireland was removed.  Many sage prophesyings were made over the condition of the sister institution in England ; but, alas ! the stump tumbled over too soon to suit history, and he did not live to see that establishment of justice and equality between all sects and all opinions in England which is still somewhere in the future. The consolation of those whose hopes in this matter are disappointed is that the longer the realization is delayed, the fuller, the more satisfactory and the more complete will the removal of all symbols of religious favouritism be.

There was much to give satisfaction to a veteran in the ranks of political and religious reform in all these declining years. If he looked with pain and disapproval on some of the newer developments of rationalistic teaching, he had, at the same time, the satisfaction of seeing that there was a steady growth of rational religious opinion in the orthodox churches. He watched with the deepest interest, and pointed out to his friends, all the signs of the decay of the old orthodoxy and of the spread of a juster estimate of the Bible, and of happier views of the position and destiny of mankind. His long study of the Bible and his profound admiration for its moral teaching produced in his mind a different feeling towards it from that which characterises the rationalistic movement generally. He was as distinct and definite in his principles of conduct as in any of his intellectual opinions. His right and wrong he would describe to be the right and wrong of the Bible. In conversation he often pointed out how the Bible rule of conduct differs from that of every other ethical system, in that it allows of no waiting to argue, but bids us submit our actions to the Divine verdict as spoken in conscience, leaving to the judg-

ment only the secondary task of finding the means
of carrying out the imperative command. He was
accustomed to say that many of the difficulties which
are made respecting the Bible arise out of forgetfulness of the Biblical test of a moral act, the approval
or condemnation of conscience. He believed that
those who spoke of the Hebrew Psalms as fierce and
revengeful, and found the early books of Judges and
Genesis to teach cruelty and immorality, were bringing to these books a foreign scale of right and wrong
with which the Bible had nothing at all to do. He
used to say that though many vicious and wicked
actions are recorded in the Bible, it would be difficult
to point out one passage in which a writer recommends
or even sanctions the doing of anything that conscience forbids, except, perhaps, in the single case of
the words of Elijah to Naaman the Syrian, where
the prophet seems to excuse and allow the going of
that officer with his master to bend in worship in the
temple of Rimmon.

In this simple rule for distinguishing between right
and wrong in conduct, he maintained that the Bible
stood alone and apart from the teaching of any other
system, ancient or modern. In this rule he believed,
by this rule he lived himself, and under it he brought
up his family. The habit of mind thus produced is
the key to many a silent and otherwise unexplained
withdrawal from committees of management, trustee-
ships, societies, and individuals with whom he had
attempted to work. It explains some of his political
views. He thought, not only that the current
morality of so-called Christian civilization is lower
than it ought to be, but that the reason why the

standard is so low is, that honourable men are too often willing to do that which is expedient rather than that which is just. He felt keenly pained when his associates and friends of the Liberal school appeared to him to be guided by what he called the Pagan rule of conduct, instead of doing simply what their sense of honour and justice told them to be right. Hence he differed from his political and theological co-workers on many questions. He showed his difference however with perfect good humour. He used for example to say of his friend Dr. Lee, of Hartwell, who belonged to the Peace Society, but was not opposed to the Crimean War, "He is in favour of universal brotherhood, after we have taken Sebastopol." This stern consistency, as in the eminent example of Mr. Bright with respect to that war, sometimes alienates a man from his party, but generally results, as in Mr. Bright's case, in the world eventually coming round to his opinion. On many points in which Samuel Sharpe was sometimes thought crochetty, he proved to be right, both in the internal politics (as we may call them) of the Unitarian body, and in general politics. It was always possible to learn from him what view of any question would be taken by a mind which looked at it from the solid ground of fixed and definite political principle ; and one valued and influential friend, who nevertheless frequently disagreed with him, gave expression to the feeling produced by his resolute consistency by saying in jest, that he came to Highbury Place to set his watch.

During all this period the house at Highbury was the centre of a very delightful society.. It was the very place from which all narrow minded people on the one hand, and the mere creatures of fashion on the other hand, were sure to keep away. Mr. Henry Crabb Robinson, and the Rev. Alexander Dyce have already been spoken of as among the constant visitors at Rogers's Tuesday breakfasts at St. James's Place ; but they were also frequently at his nephew's house at Highbury. The Rev. George Skinner, of Cambridge, who had married a distant cousin, was also an occasional visitor, bringing with him the latest talk of the University. He was reader at King's College, and his exquisite voice and impressive manner, made his reading perfect. He was a great classic, but he was also an immense reader of English literature, and seemed to remember all that he read. He described it to be his custom to go every day to the University Library, where all the new books published each week are to be found together on a certain table, and to glance through them all. He used to say, " I never read reviews, I review for myself." No more pleasant visitor, nor more genial talker, nor more courteous guest, ever came to the well-known house at Highbury Place than the Rev. George Skinner.

The Rev. Thomas Madge had been for many years one of the nearest neighbours. For some time he had lived next door, and the intercourse between the well-known Unitarian writer and the foremost of Unitarian preachers had been exceedingly intimate. Mr. Madge had retired from the pulpit of Essex Street Chapel in 1860, after occupying it for thirty-four years, as the worthy successor of Lindsey, Disney, and Belsham. During those years the congregation was fully worthy of the chapel which was regarded as the headquarters of the Unitarian body. It included more persons of high social standing and great intellectual distinction than any other Nonconformist congregation in London. Mr. Madge was thirteen years older than Samuel Sharpe, and the younger man had always looked up to the elder with the respect due to his eminence as the chief pastor of the Unitarian body in London, and its most popular preacher. For the ten years of his bright and happy old age, after his retirement from public work, Mr. Madge kept up his lively interest in all matters of theology and politics, and was a remarkable example of the possibility of keeping the ravages of Time to the outer part. Cowley must have had just such an old age in view when he wrote in the sixth stanza of his ode to Hobbes—

> Nor can the snow, which now cold age does shed
>    Upon thy reverend head,
> Quench or allay the noble fires within ;
>    But all which thou hast been,
> And all that youth can be, thou 'rt yet,
>    So fully still dost thou
> Enjoy the manhood and the bloom of wit,
>    And all the natural heat, but not the fever too.
>
> .   .   .   .   .   .
>
> To things immortal Time can do no wrong,
> And that which never is to die, for ever must be young.

Mr. Madge died on the 29th of August, 1870, at the age of eighty-three. In the previous year two younger men had passed away, the Rev. John James Tayler, Principal of Manchester New College, and the Rev. Robert Brook Aspland, Secretary of the British and Foreign Unitarian Association ; the first at the age of seventy-two, the second at the age of sixty-five. It seemed to be a time of great losses to Liberal Dissent, for Mr. Tayler, the scholar who charmed everybody who knew him by his gentle charity, was a striking example of that union of boldness with reverence, and of new views with old faiths, which is the great need of the time ; and Mr. Aspland, the skilful reconciler of divergent tendencies, whose organizing power had done his sect long and valuable service, was in the fulness of his popularity and usefulness. When Mr. Madge had followed them, the old order seemed changing indeed, and giving place to new. Samuel Sharpe's brother-in-law, Mr. Edwin Field, died in the next year, 1871, and all these losses made him feel like one who had outlived many of his friends, though younger men came to fill the places of the dead.

Among the visitors at Highbury at this and an earlier time was Mr. N. E. S. A. Hamilton, of the Manuscript Department in the British Museum, "Alphabet" Hamilton as he reported himself to be familiarly nicknamed by his friends. Mr. Hamilton published a volume contending for the modern character of many of the emendations of Shakespeare made by Mr. Collier's "Old Corrector ;" and giving fac-similes of what he regards as modern pencil lines underneath the corrections which were supposed to have been done by Shakespeare's own hand, or by the hand of one of his contemporaries.

Another welcome visitor was Mr. J. R. Robinson, Manager of the *Daily News.* His large literary connection, and wide acquaintance with men and things, made a talk with him especially valuable to

a man who, like Samuel Sharpe, kept up a very
lively interest in all the political, social, and literary
movements of his time, yet lived apart from the
actual hum and shock of men.  Mr. Robinson enjoyed the racy criticisms of his host on persons and
events, and Samuel Sharpe in his turn, was interested
by the merry and genial talk of an admirable story-
teller.

Dr. Samuel Birch, of the Antiquities in the Museum,
was an occasional visitor, and Sharpe often met him at
the Museum.  Dr. Birch never found that the wide differences between his views and those of the Egyptian
scholar at Highbury made their intercourse less pleasant.  He was always ready to enjoy a joke against
himself, and took the genial banter of his host with the
kindest good humour.  His opponents said of him
that if a quaint pattern on the window-curtain were
presented to him as hieroglyphics, he would read them
straight off.  He bore with perfect complacency Mr.
Sharpe's occasional criticims on the arrangements of
the Museum, and to the demand for more names, and
fuller information and explanations to be affixed to the
objects, for the sake of the unlearned, would gaily
reply, "Write to the papers." Mr. George Smith, of the
British Museum, came to talk of subjects he and the
author of the History of Egypt had in common, and
often surprised the translator of the Bible by his
intimate knowledge of the Jewish writings.  His
modesty, it might almost be called timidity, was as
striking as the fulness of his information, while his
enthusiasm for antiquarian and critical research was
a point of warmest sympathy between him and the
veteran student whom he came to consult.  His

early death was nowhere more lamented than in the household at Highbury.

Many other students and lovers of antiquity naturally gravitated towards Highbury, such as Mr. R. W. Mackay, author of "The Progress of the Intellect," whose transparent simple minded-ness gave uncommon charm to his conversation, and who was equally at home in discussing Kant, in talking over the writings of the Apostle Paul, or in descanting on Plato ; Mr. Poynter, who desired to talk over Egypt in preparation for his splendid pictures of its antiquities ; Mr. Edward Falkener, who had travelled in Greece, had brought home masterly sketches, and published a book on Greek Antiquities, illustrated with photographs, in days when photographs were more rare than they are now ; and, chief of all, most welcome of all, Mr. Bonomi, of whom much has been already said.   On the last page but one of his friend's diary, his death in March, 1878, is thus recorded :—

This month I lost my excellent friend Joseph Bonomi ; with whom I had been acquainted above forty years, and intimate the larger part of that time ; a most cheerful, amiable man, generous of his time and faculties, a most careful observer in his own path of Egyptian Antiquities. Few people ever brought more life and cheerfulness into the house.

A good deal of life and cheerfulness came also with Mr. W. Watkiss Lloyd ; the genial and accomplished author of "The Age of Pericles" and other learned works.  His conversation, not only on the topics which two scholars have in common, but on public affairs and on current literature, was full of interest for the family at Highbury. Mr. Lloyd, in a letter to the writer of this biography gives his own very valuable and interesting account of this intercourse.

When I first knew Mr. Sharpe, I regarded myself as a young man cordially accepted as an acquaintance by one much older, and though as years went on the relative difference of age became less and less considerable, I continued to the last to regard him with the same feelings which had made me habitually refer to him at my own home as Father Sharpe.  I was never so fortunate as to have more than one other friend—and he too now has gone—with whom I sympathized so entirely on the leading interests of our life, and with whom I was so anxious to keep myself in sympathy.  His learning, his unremitting industry, his concentration of his energies on what he believed to be the most useful employment of them, were worthy of all admiration. But the very central principle of his life, and what was I believe the secret of the charm of his society, and of the influence that he exercised, was his veneration for truthfulness—for sincerity.  It was delightful to interchange thoughts with one who was ready to listen to any opinion that was entertained frankly, and to respond with entire explicitness and frankness on his own part.  Subjects which could not be comfortably mooted elsewhere as to theology or politics, from experience that after a second sentence delicate ground was approached, and courtesy warned one off, could always be ventured upon in his house.  He had an innate repugnance to the compromises and equivocations by which so many play fast and loose with their consciences, and never was taken in by the sophistications that help so many to slip comfortably into honours and preferments, by public professions inconsistent with their better knowledge.  After the painful task of keeping one's countenance and holding one's tongue among people calling themselves educated and even liberal, but as politic in their expressions and tolerance of expression as a college of augurs, an evening at Highbury was like a breath of healthy air.  An occasional thought of what was Mr. Sharpe's standard of truthfulness might always have sufficed to brace a faltering moral tone.

The years thus filled with happy friendships and charming intercourse with appreciative friends, brought their losses.   He had survived his brothers and sisters, and he was to survive all his own children but two. For many years the family at Highbury had consisted of the father and three daughters, but in 1877 his daughter Mary, the youngest of the three, began to show signs of the fatal disease which had carried off her two brothers and a younger sister.   She died in 1878, and her death cast a shadow over her father's declining years.

# CHAPTER XIV.

## THE CLOSING YEARS.

It is inevitable that with the most active of men the burden of increasing years should bring some relaxation of productive energy. But the story of an industrious life, which is the main substance of this volume, has no long pause of rest or idleness before its close. The river does not lose itself in dead marshes before it joins the ocean, but in this case, at least, pours itself clear and strong into the tideless sea. There were eleven years between the Whitsuntide at which Samuel Sharpe gave up the chair of the Unitarian Association to his successor, Mr. C. J. Thomas, and that Whitsuntide in which the feeling that his work was done proved at last to be prophetic. The years as they came brought new interests and new labours, and the old man who was advancing in his eighth decade was as ready to meet them as he had been thirty years before. He was as fresh and clear and vigorous in mind, and almost as strong in body as he had been in the earlier time. If there was any change in him, it was that he grew busier as he grew older. As an old man he was as much alive to the things about him as he had been in his youth, and was more ready to take up new work than he had been in middle age.

His most constant occupation in these latter years was his translation of the Hebrew Scriptures. The second edition of this translation was published in 1871 ; and a large portion of it was circulated gratuitously. He found that it was very acceptable to professors and students in many Dissenting Colleges in which Hebrew was carefully studied. Students of Hebrew found it valuable as being more literal than the authorized version, and their appreciation of it encouraged him to further work in its improvement. This improvement was always going on. Between 1871 and 1876 the whole Hebrew Bible was carefully and critically gone through a fourth time, and a third edition was issued in that year. In this edition a number of dates and proper names were introduced between brackets, by way of explaining allusions in the text. Taken altogether, they added only a couple of pages to the bulk of the volume, but, sprinkled about as they are, they do much to explain obscure passages. "Such few words," he says with great truth, "introduced into the text, but with a clear mark to show that they are the editor's own, are often better than a lengthy footnote." Meanwhile he had published in 1874 a small and very useful volume, entitled "Short Notes to accompany a Revised Translation of the Hebrew Scriptures." These Notes are intended to elucidate the history, they are geographical and antiquarian, and are explanatory of difficulties and contradictions. They are adapted, of course, to his new translation, and in some places explain a thought which is not to be found in the Authorized Version. They constitute in fact a kind of translator's commentary, making the meaning clearer that it can be made without insertions in the text. They are such notes as Rogers and Byron, and other writers of those days, attached to their poems, in order that their readers might clearly understand descriptions of places and allusions to persons and events. It is impossible to read any ancient writings with intelligence and profit without such explanations; and probably no greater mischief has been done to the Bible than its universal circulation without such elucidatory Notes. The unlearned reader cannot know to whom or to what the ancient writer is alluding, and it is surely the duty of the translator to inform him. A passage which seems meaningless or mysterious, is brightened into the most perfect clearness, by a single line which puts the modern reader in possession of facts which were in the minds of writer and readers at the time, and are consequently only vaguely alluded to and not told at length. The greatest service which can be done to the Bible is to make it understood by those who read it now, as it was understood by those who read the various books when they were written.

Another occupation of these years was the patient putting together of an historical puzzle, in the study and attempted translation of the Sinaitic Inscriptions. These mysterious sentences have given to the small barren plain on the route from Egypt to Mount Serbal the name of Wady Mocatteb, or Sculptured Valley. The writings are cut in uncouth characters on the face of the rocks or the sandstone boulders. Various opinions have been formed as to the language and the meaning of these inscriptions. Professor Beer regards them as the work of Nabatæans, inhabitants of the district in the fourth century of our era ; the Rev. Charles Forster in his "Sinai Photographed," supposes them to have been cut by the Israelites on their desert journey to the Land of Promise, and that they celebrate the miraculous cleaving of the Red Sea. The late unfortunate Professor Palmer, on the other hand, thought they had nothing to do with the children of Israel, but were the work of traders and carriers, and were of little worth. Quoting these conflicting opinions in his preface, Samuel Sharpe points out that not one of these writers has satisfied the conditions required. "We cannot trust Professor Beer's transcripts without the translations, nor Mr. Forster's translations without transcripts. Professor Palmer's work has neither transcripts nor translations. The decipherer should produce first an alphabet or table of characters, and then to some extent a language, and lastly a probable meaning to each sentence." Samuel Sharpe endeavours to produce this alphabet, which he regards as Hebrew, and reads the inscriptions as lamentations and prayers over the ruined and desolate condition of Jerusalem. The title of the book is "Hebrew Inscriptions, from the Valleys between Egypt and Mount Sinai, in their original characters, with translations and an Alphabet." The first part, published in 1875, consists of the inscriptions copied by Mr. G. F. Grey, and printed in 1832 ; the second part, published in 1876, is chiefly devoted to the inscriptions edited by Dr. Lepsius for the Prussian Government in 1860.

The next work, which had been going on at the same time with these, was a volume, entitled "The

Journeys and Epistles of the Apostle Paul." It is a
little book of about a hundred pages, with a preface
in which the principle on which the author has pró-
ceeded is set forth and vindicated. It is in no sense
a commentary on the Epistles, but an attempt to
form a consistent sketch of the Apostle's life, out of
the scattered biographical details in the Epistles,
and to harmonize those details with the statements
in the Acts of the Apostles. The author believes that
the apparent contradictions which Baur and others
have pointed out may be almost wholly removed,
and a better understanding of the Epistles arrived
at, by correcting a few mistranslated passages, and
then placing the Epistles in a better order. He
regards Conybeare and Howson's " Life and Epistles
of St. Paul " as failing to remove the difficulties and
disagreements which keener critics have discovered.
Baur's " Paul," on the other hand, accepts the usual
arrangement and translation, and very successfully
points out how the writings hopelessly contradict
each other throughout. Baur's criticism of the
Epistles is, however, mainly based on the religious
and philosophical opinions expressed in them ; and
Sharpe thinks he would have stood on firmer ground
if he had relied more on their biographical contents,
in which they are very rich, and had considered the
Apostle's opinions after he had settled the order
of his writings. This is Sharpe's own method.
He takes the statements of Luke in the Acts of the
Apostles as a clue to the numerous biographical
notices scattered through Paul's Epistles. By following this clue the maze falls into order ; and we
are enabled, he thinks, to show the Life and Writings

U

of the Apostle to the Gentiles as a complete and harmonious whole, in which every part supports the other parts. The biographical notices are so numerous, and yet all fit together so satisfactorily, that his arrangement, he says, proves itself to be correct. In his view, and in the view of those who are able to follow his ingenious arguments, no place is left for doubt as to the genuineness of any of the Epistles, nor of the trustworthiness of those parts of the Acts which relate to Paul, nor as to the order in which the Epistles are to be placed.

Another small but laborious work which arose out of his translation of the Bible was a short Hebrew Grammar without points. This was written in 1876, and published in the next year by Messrs. Bagster. He says of it :—

This led to my reading the Hebrew Bible a sixth time with a special regard to all grammatical peculiarities, in order to enlarge my grammar, and make it useful to more advanced students. I felt strongly on the subject of the Hebrew points, that they were useless to myself as a translator, and troublesome to the learner ; and, moreover, that they were misleading for the study of the Hebrew mind, as standing between us and the original writers. This sixth reading of the Hebrew naturally led to further corrections in the margin of my third edition in preparation for a fourth.

While this further emendation of the Translation was proceeding, the Book of Isaiah was published as a separate volume, with a chronological arrange- ment and ample notes. His aim was to explain the book historically, hence its several parts were chronologically arranged in the order of the events

to which they relate, which, he says, is not the same
as the order in which they were written. Nearly all
the next year—1878—was given to other work.
The last records in his diary bear the date of March,
1878, and are exceedingly characteristic of him.
The first of these contains one of those confessions
of incapacity for further work which are found in his
diary in earlier years. The Bible and Hebrew
Grammar were ready for a new edition. The History of Egypt had been stereotyped, and the sixth
edition, which he justly regarded as the final shape
the book had taken after the emendations of more
than half a life-time, had been issued in 1876. So
he writes in 1878 :—

I thought it too late to enter upon any new work, or any
new line of hard study. I therefore turned, for the first
time in my life, to the reading of new publications as an
employment. As Lucy Aikin said, "I am reduced to
Mudie books."

> I who was once as great as Cæsar,
> Am now reduced to Nebuchadnezzar.

I began with Lecky's History of England, a cold dispas-
sionate book, showing no enthusiasm for what is good,
scarcely touching the more noble characters of the time,
while busy with the meanness and selfishness of the statesmen. A sad contrast to Green's History of the English
People.

Yet there were, as we shall see, a couple of tasks
which may be regarded, not only as new work, but
one of them at least as a new line of hard study.
He had, indeed, two years before, taken to some
work which, if not new, was at any rate a reversion

to labour which he had undertaken and dropped as distasteful three-and-forty years before. He had then assisted in the establishment of the *Inquirer ;* he now did the same for the *Christian Life.* The very last record in his Diary, dated March 1878, is the expression of his resolution to keep up the work of sending Mr. Spears about a column a week ; and the statement of his opinion that "his paper is doing good service in keeping alive Unitarian zeal, and indeed religious warmth among Unitarians, as opposed to the fashionable indifference which leads to countenancing insincerity."

He undertook this writing entirely from sympathy with, and respect for, the Rev. Robert Spears. Mr. Spears came to London from the North, and to the Unitarian ministry from the Methodist body, and he brought with him northern energy and Methodist zeal. As Assistant Secretary to the British and Foreign Unitarian Association under the Rev. R. Brook Aspland, and as Secretary after Mr. Aspland's sudden death, Mr. Spears had shown an energy and an organizing power which had quickened all the pulses of the machine. After he resigned the secretaryship he started a weekly paper called the *Christian Life*, to be, as he regarded it, the organ of those Unitarians who lay especial stress on their Christian beliefs. Samuel Sharpe did not agree with all the views advocated by Mr. Spears and his friends ; but he had a hearty admiration for that energetic, earnest, and devoted minister. The friendship with Mr. Spears was one of the warmest personal attachments he formed in his old age. He believed that Mr. Spears had had a good deal to do with the new warmth of religious feeling and the fresh zeal for their opinions which Unitarians have exhibited in recent years. Most of the articles contributed by Samuel Sharpe to the *Christian Life* were either against agnosticism in Unitarian pulpits, or against indifference among the congregations, and their prevailing motive was to urge the bringing out of the positive and the Christian aspects of Unitarianism, both in the teachings of its ministers and in the life and conduct of its adherents. He contributed also reviews, Biblical criticism, explanations of difficult passages, and other matters of theological and antiquarian interest. He continued writing these articles till he could write no longer.

In the month in which he entered his eightieth year the boys of University College School gave him a present in the shape of a volume containing the photographs of all the six hundred boys then in the school, with their masters. It was a very well designed recognition of his unparalleled services to the school.

Another presentation which was made in the next year was, if possible, even more gratifying, as it was a recognition of the general appreciation in which his character and work were held all over the country. On his eightieth birthday, the 8th of March, 1879, he received a call from two of his friends, the Rev. Robert Spears and Mr. S. Seaward Tayler, and found that they had come as the bearers of an address, signed by two hundred and seventy-nine persons in all parts of the country, congratulating him on the completion of his eightieth year, and expressing their admiration for his long and useful life, and thei high appreciation of his labours. In presenting it Mr. Spears and Mr. Tayler informed him that only a few days had been given to the preparation and signing of the address, and that the number of signatures might easily have been increased indefinitely. The address, with the names of those who signed it, is printed as an appendix to this volume. When the presentation of the address was announced in the papers he received a number of letters from persons who had not had an opportunity of signing it, but who desired to join in the expression of regard and esteem.

His eightieth year brought no incapacity for work and no indisposition to it. In 1879 he printed the Book of Genesis, Chapters i. to xxxii.; and xx. to xxx. 10, in Hebrew without points. The Hebrew text is printed after the style of modern books, in paragraphs, with full modern punctuation, and with a large letter at the beginning of every sentence and of every proper name. The prefixes, moreover, are cut off and stand as independent words.

Another little book of the same year, 1879, which also arose directly out of the careful study of the Bible, was, "An Inquiry into the Age of the Moabite Stone." This celebrated relic of antiquity is written in Phenician characters in the Hebrew language, and many scholars, Dr. Ginsburg among them, regard it as genuine. It purports to have been written by Mesha, King of Moab, who lived in the reigns of Omri, Ahab, and Jehoram, Kings of Northern Israel. Its date is therefore fixed at about 850 B.C. Its language is almost that of the Bible, and, "if the name of Jehovah," says Mr. Sharpe,

" were substituted for that of Chemosh, it would read like a chapter of the Book of Kings." This similarity suggests imitation, and when he finds that it is inconsistent in some of its statements with the historical facts stated in the Hebrew history, and that some of its words have forms which only came into use in later days, he concludes that the inscription is, probably, the forgery of some prefect of Moab in the third century of our era. His very interesting argument is summed up in the concluding sentences :—

We have thus found a time when our Inscription may perhaps have been written. It was after Dibon had become the capital of Moab ; after the causeway and bridge had been made across the Arnon valley ; and after the basaltic blocks had been carried as far northward as Dibon ; and when the sovereign who appointed the prefect of Moab was a Syrian. Our aim has been to show that there was a time, many centuries after the reign of Mesha, with which the characters, the language, the subject matter of our Inscription, and even the motives of the writer, would all agree ; and thus, to answer the question very naturally asked by those who defend this Inscription's genuineness, " If it was not written in Mesha's reign, when, and for what purpose, could it have been written ? " The date which we propose for it is about A.D. 260, when Odenathus was ruler of Syria and the East, as the friend of Aurelian and Gallienus ; and the purpose of it was, we suppose, to argue that the province of Moab included the land of Reuben.

This was the work of his eightieth and eighty-first years. In his eighty-second year we come to his last separate publication—" The Epistle of Barnabas from the Sinaitic Manuscript of the Bible, with a Translation by Samuel Sharpe." The epistle had claimed his notice in the study of Paul's journeyings, " first because the two apostles had at one time lived in close friendship, and it in part explains why at a later time Paul's feelings towards Barnabas were changed, and, secondly, because it offers the earliest example of the Gnosticism which was creeping into the Christian Churches, very much to the trouble of Paul." He had found no English translation of it that he thought satisfactory. Hence he translates it himself, and discusses its character and claims in an introduction of seven-and-twenty pages. This introduction is dated July 21, 1880 ; and the Preface, the 11th of September. He was then far advanced in his eighty-second year.

He was still working at his Bible, and towards the close of 1880, he had the great satisfaction of seeing it complete in one handsome, stereotyped volume— "The Holy Bible, Translated by Samuel Sharpe. Being a Revision of the Authorized English Version." He had dated the Preface on his eighty-first birthday, the eighth of March, 1880. But the production of such a volume occupied much time, and the title page consequently bears the date of 1881. He regarded the completed work with great satisfaction. When he saw it, in his finished form, he exclaimed, "Now my work is done." So he said to all his friends as he showed them the volume. The same date, 1881, is on the title page of the Revised Version of the New Testament; which was issued on the 17th of May. He welcomed it with satisfaction, rejoicing greatly that he had lived to see it. But he did not live to criticise it in detail.

In the Preface to his Bible he gives some account of his object in undertaking the work, and of the chief features which distinguish his translation from others. He says that he has not confined his care to passages of theological importance, but has desired to throw light on ancient manners and customs, upon geography and upon antiquities. Of the changes in the text he says, laying down a true canon of revision, " he has seldom ventured upon any great change of words, except where his own judgment was supported by scholars who have gone before him in Biblical studies." He has given a more detailed account of his method of work in a memorandum written in 1878. The method has, however, been fully described already ; but it may be well to reproduce a description of some of the results at which he arrived.

The improvements in the Translation are most marked in antiquarian matters, in manners and customs, in geography, natural history, and also in political history, by removing vague generalities, and allowing the writers to point clearly to persons living in their own time.

The courts of the Temple are much explained, when compared with the known form of the ground, by showing in 2 Chron. iv. 9, that the court of the priests was a raised terrace. The form and situation of the altar are explained by showing in Ezek. xliii. 13, that it had a trench round it, of which traces yet remain in the rock under the mosque of Omar.

Much light is thrown on some passages by merely tabulating them, as the genealogies at the beginning of 1 Chron., the stations where the Israelites rested in Numb. xxxiii., and Solomon's officers in 1 Kings iv.

By keeping in use the Babylonian titles, Pasha or captain, and Sagin or lieutenant, we are able to show from Ezra ii. 6, that a Jew had been appointed to the office of Pasha of Moab by Nebuchadnezzar ; and from Isaiah xli. 25, that the Jews, who accepted the office of Sagin under the Babylonians, were hated by their countrymen, and from Ezra and Nehemiah that they were not so hated under the milder government of the Persians. By correcting Dan. ix. 25, "while there is an anointed ruler shall be seven weeks," we learn how long Zerubbabel was Pasha of Judea.

By writing literally Sons of Adam and Sons of Men, we show that some Hebrew writers called the Israelites alone Sons of Adam, while the rest of mankind, as in the Talmud, are Sons of Men.

The natural history of the Bible is made interesting by the usual names of animals, such as the Crocodile, the River-horse, the Buffalo, the Stork, the Ostrich, the Tsaltsal Fly of Abyssinia, Isaiah xviii. 1, the Parrot, not peacock, 1 Kings x. 22, the Panther and the Horned Serpent, Isaiah xxx. 6, where also the African lion is distinguished from the lion of Asia, which was better known to the Israelites. In plants we have the Ebony, 1 Kings x. 12, the Sweet Cane and the Paper-reed, Isaiah xxxv. 7, and the Water Lotus under which the river-horse hides himself, Job xl. 21. In the mineral kingdom we have the Iron-stone, out of which the mineral oil flows, Deut. xxxii. 13, and the Mixed Metal or Alloy, not tin, Isaiah i. 25.

The parts of Ezra, Daniel, and Jeremiah, that are in Chaldee are marked by stars in the margin. The Italics mark quotations, as in the Book Nehemiah from Ezra.

Many passages are made clear by a name placed within square brackets. Thus the Servant of Jehovah in Isaiah lii. 13, is said to be Zerubbabel; he who is to leave a meat offering and a drink offering behind him, in Joel ii. 14, is Tiglath Pilezer; the Saviours hoped for in Obadiah 21 are the Persians; she who is to rejoice in Lam. iv. 21, is Zion, as is she who is to shout aloud over the Philistines in Ps. lx. 8; the Anointed One in Ps. ii. 2 is Solomon, in Hab. iii. 13 he is Josiah, in Ps. lxxxix. 38 he is Jehoiachin, in Ps. lxxxv. 9 he is Zerubbabel, as also in Dan. ix. 25; but in Dan. ix. 26 he is king Aristobulus. The King in

Isaiah viii. 21 is Hoshea; as time runs on, in Jerem. xiii.
18 he is Jehoiakim; yet later, in Ezek. vii. 27 he is
Jehoiachin.   The Prince in Ezek. vii. 27 is Zedekiah; in
Ezek. xliv. 3 and xlv. 7 he is Zerubbabel.   The Cruel
Lord in Isaiah xix. 4 is Antiochus Epiphanes; and the
Saviour, in verse 20, who is to deliver the Egyptians by
merely rebuking him is the Roman Ambassador, Caius
Popilius.   Some of these passages are prophetical, and the
name here given may be doubtful; but most of the
passages are simply historical, and the addition of the name
is quite necessary to enable an ordinary reader to understand who is being spoken of.

In geography the route of the Israelites out of Egypt
and the identification of Hahiroth with the ruins of Heroo-
polis, of Rameses with the ruins of Heliopolis, are established by the help of the Roman roads in the *Itinerarium
Antonini*, a work intermediate between our modern survey
of the country and the Book of Exodus.   That mount
Sepher, *written*, in Gen. x. 30, the Shepher of Numb. xxxiii.
23, is mount Serbal, is proved by the writing yet remaining
on it, and by the map which shows how correctly the Arabs
are described as dwelling between Mesha, near the south-
east corner of the Red Sea, and Serbal in Sinai.

Having in this way prepared my Translation of the
Hebrew Scriptures for a fourth edition, I then added to
the New Testament on the same plan a few words of com-
ment, here and there, placed within square brackets.   These
are a few dates, references in the Epistles to the Acts,
showing an agreement between the two, where it had
been very unfairly, as I thought, denied by some German
critics; also the names of the Roman emperors in the
Revelation.   In this way the Old and the New Testament
were made alike with a view to printing them together in
one volume.

The volume, as has been already stated, was issued
in the spring of 1881, completing, as he thought, the

work of his life. There had already been ample recognition of his labours. Not only had Biblical students and scholars found their way to Highbury from time to time, but he had considerable correspondence on the Revision question. Some time before the publication of the Revised Version of the New Testament, he had printed a short note calling the attention of the Members of the Revision Committee to one or two points which he thought to be important. This drew him into a very interesting correspondence with two or three of the Revisers who paid the venerable scholar the compliment of giving their own views of the passages in question.

The Bishop of Winchester writes a couple of letters in November, 1879, stating in some detail the reasons why he had strenuously resisted on the Old Testament Revision Committee the changing of the words "The Lord" into "Jehovah." Mr. W. Aldis Wright also expresses his individual opinion that the word Jehovah is not the one to use, and his doubt whether Jahveh would find favour. The Dean of Rochester discusses the meaning of some Greek words in the New Testament in which he differed from Mr. Sharpe; and expresses his dissent from his views with respect to the "Epistle of Barnabas." The late Professor E. H. Palmer writes (in December, 1876) to thank him for his work on the Sinaitic Inscriptions, and to say that he intends to publish all his inscriptions, as an appendix to the Ordnance Survey Reports, when he can find time, but that for the last year or two he has been compelled to put it aside for other, and to him, more interesting work. Of the long correspondence with the Bishop of Natal some account has already been given. There are many letters from Professor D. W. Marks, discussing with the most careful minuteness of detail obscure points of Hebrew scholarship. Dr. Marks disagreed with his correspondent on the vexed question of the points. He was nevertheless the valued friend to whom Samuel Sharpe had applied many times during his years of Hebrew study and translation for help in difficulties, and who never failed him. His great knowledge of the Talmud and of other Rabbinical writings was always placed ungrudgingly at the service of the diligent translator at Highbury. It is worthy of remark that both the Bishop of Natal and Professor Marks approve of many of his readings of the Sinaitic Inscriptions, though the latter considers that some of them are more ingenious than true, and is at variance with Mr. Sharpe with respect to the date at which the inscriptions were written. The Rev. H. R. Reynolds, the learned Principal of Cheshunt College, also discusses in letters in 1879, 1880, and 1881, some points of scholarship, and expresses his sense of the great ingenuity of many of the suggestions in the "Journeys and Epistles of the Apostle Paul." He admits that the view taken of the closing chapter of the Romans (the separation from it of verses 1—20, containing the greetings to friends, and the finding a place for them elsewhere),* does remove many diffi-

---

* These verses are separated from the Epistle for the reason that " When the Apostle reached Rome as a prisoner he found no friends there. These intimate friends belonged not to Rome, but to some place where he had already passed some months, as, for example, Ephesus." They are consequently regarded as

culties, and points out that it has been accepted by
Canon Farrar. Dr. Reynolds had sent to Mr. Sharpe
his own "Life of John the Baptist," and no letters
were more valued, for their shrewd criticism and wise
suggestions than those from Cheshunt.

The very last public matter in which he showed a
lively interest, was the issue of the Revised Version
of the New Testament. He had been waiting for it
with some anxiety, and had ordered a copy from the
bookseller some time beforehand. The bookseller
was an hour or two late in delivering it, and one of
his nieces had the satisfaction of bringing him the
first copy. He sat down at once to look up the passages in which he was most interested, and when
later in the day other friends came with their copies,
he had already referred to the chief points. He
found that the passages to which he had called
attention in his own tract, "Controversial Texts Corrected," had all been rendered in the new translation
as he desired they should be, except one, and that
had the true version in the margin. He at once sent
off a post-card to his friend, Mr. Spears, of the
*Christian Life*, saying, "It is all right ; give the book
a favourable review." His increasing weakness, however, allowed him to do no more than this. He was
never able to compare the new version with his own,

"Fragments to Ephesus," and he thinks they "were written
from the neighbourhood of Cenchreæ during the journey to
Greece (Acts xx. 3), as they were sent by Phebe of Cenchreæ ;
and they were written to a city where Aquilas and Priscilla were
living, and where he had gained many friends during a long
stay." See "The Journeys and Epistles of the Apostle Paul,"
Preface, pp. xi. and xiii.

though, had he done so, he would have seen in how many instances his own improvements have been adopted, and in how many others he had kept the old familiar expression when the Revisers have needlessly changed the word without changing the sense.

In the spring of 1881 he began to show signs of the paralysis which was to end his life in the summer. It came so gently that no one noticed its beginning, but he used to say : " I began this on the first of April." What he then began was to make odd mistakes in spelling, and afterwards in the choice of words. " Think what I am come to," he would say laughingly to his family ; " I can't spell Bible." He saw from the first that this was the beginning of the end, and said so to all his friends, but he made no trouble of it, taking it in the happiest and most gentle spirit ; and when, later on, he had to be helped with a word and the helpers could not hit upon the one he wanted, he would make a smiling gesture, as much as to say, " It is of no use." When the Revised Version of the New Testament was issued in the middle of May these signs of failing health had become more serious. They were not very important at first, and he kept on with his usual work, refusing to see a doctor. But the power of choosing words grew rapidly less and less as the summer advanced, and speedily became an almost total inability to find language to express his ideas, which were still clear. He understood all that was said to him, and tried to answer, but failed, and gave it up with a smile. Yet, even when the faculty of expression was almost gone, it was evident that he clearly understood what he

meant to say, and on a point on which his view of
the meaning of a Greek phrase had been disputed,
and words altogether failed him to explain, he took
down the grammar, put his finger on the passage,
and smilingly indicated that what he wished to say
was expressed there.

These closing months were brightened by his
patience and genial submission. He enjoyed the
visits of friends who came to see him, and understood and appreciated their conversation, though
he was unable to reply. As paralysis gradually
came on, it became difficult to get him up and
down stairs, though he had continued to come down
into the dining room till within a few days of his
death. He liked to sit in his armchair upon the
garden steps, with the calm countenance of the
great bust of Melpomene before him, and with the
Hebrew text he had written on the garden wall
behind him: "Hear, O Israel, the Lord our God
is one Lord." The lingering was not long. A few
weeks of increasing infirmity, then a couple of days
of confinement to his bedroom, and after that the
end. It was gentle and quiet, as the consummation
of such a life ought to be—a death by natural decay
—a coming to his grave, according to the old promise, in a full age, like a shock of corn coming in
in its season. He had been eighty-two on the 8th
of March, and died on Thursday, the 28th of July,
having thus lived for four months and twenty days
of his eighty-third year.

The funeral took place on the 3rd of August, at
Abney Park Cemetery. It was conducted by the
Rev. Robert Spears, who·spoke a few appreciative

words in the cemetery chapel, and the Rev. Henry
Ierson made a short address at the grave, pointing
out that sincerity, simplicity, and devotion to truth
had been the chief features of Samuel Sharpe's
character.  He was buried in the family vault,
where his wife and his sister Catherine had been
placed, and where three of his children lay.  There
was a large gathering of friends, representing all
the various interests—social, political, antiquarian,
and theological—which had occupied his busy life.
There were no needless regrets.  All present felt that
it was a completed life of which they were witnessing
the closing scene.

# APPENDIX.

*The following is the text of the Address referred to in pages 293 and 294.*

To Samuel Sharpe, Esq., of 32, Highbury Place, London, on his Eightieth Birthday, March 8th, 1879.

DEAR MR. SHARPE,—

We beg you to accept our congratulations and our best wishes on your having attained the venerable age of eighty years.

We are persuaded that the causes which, in the order of Divine Providence, give to the world an increasing proportion of persons of mature age and experience, tend to promote public wisdom and virtue and the happiness of our race. But it is not merely at the fact of your lengthened years that we express to you this day our pleasure, for we well remember that your life has been filled with deeds of a kind which the wisest and best men of all ages and of all countries have never failed to esteem and honour.

It must be to yourself, as it has been and will continue to be to many, a gratifying recollection that your pen has been engaged for nearly half a century in the production of learned and valuable works, bearing especially upon the great subjects of Biblical study, on which your researches have thrown considerable light ; and that during this period you have also manifested the greatest interest in the education of the young, and have shown in many practical ways your deep sense of the importance of a well trained Christian ministry. We gratefully remember that the range of your munificence through a long life, has not been confined to schools and colleges, nor even to churches of your own persuasion, which have so largely benefited by it, but has been extended to whatever you thought would promote knowledge, virtue and true religion amongst mankind.

We are glad to believe that an unspotted life of homely beauty, of great industry, of loyalty to truth, of Christian simplicity and godly sincerity, like your own, that has paid court to nothing but what you believed would increase learning and wisdom among all classes,—whom you have ever regarded as God's children, and therefore brothers and sisters,—will always be remembered as a bright and encouraging example, and will animate others to use their powers and means for the public good.

May it be the will of our Heavenly Father that you may continue with us for many years, and may all your remaining days be peace.

John W. Aikin, King's Lynn.
Thomas Ainsworth, The Flosh.
L. M. Aspland, London.
Owen Aves, Mansfield.
Henry Austin, Cirencester.
William Andrews, Bristol.
Alfred P. Allen, King's Lynn.
Henry S. Bicknell, London.
George Buckton, Leeds.
Henry P. Buckler, Tenterden.
William Blake, South Petherton.
Charles T. Bowring, Liverpool.
Thomas Bowring, Maidstone.
Addley Bourne, London.
W. J. Beale, London.
Jacob Boys, Brighton.
John Birks, Taunton.

William Binns, Birkenhead.
William Butcher, Bristol.
William Birks, Wolverhampton.
James Black, Stockport.
Charles F. Biss, Gloucester.
Arthur Bromily, Bolton.
John A. Briggs, St. Leonards.
Thomas B. W. Briggs, Folkestone.
William Barnard, Sawbridgeworth.
William B. Carpenter, London.
William H. Channing, London.
Arthur Chamberlain, Birmingham.
Russell L. Carpenter, Bridport.
P. W. Clayden, London.
Thomas Chatfeild Clarke, London.
Frederick Collier, London.
Joseph Clephan, Gateshead.

John A. Crozier, Newry.
J. Estlin Carpenter, London.
Charles Clarke, Birmingham.
Charles C. Coe, Bolton.
G. S. Coxwell, Southampton.
George Carter, London.
Samuel Charlesworth, Sheffield.
John J. Clephan, Stockton-on-Tees.
John Crossman, Maidenhead.
John C. Conway, London.
Edward Cowell, Canterbury.
Andrew Chalmers, Cambridge.
Edwin Clephan, Leicester.
James Drummond, London.
Robert B. Drummond, Edinburgh.
J. Withers Dowson, Norwich.
H. Enfield Dowson, Gee Cross.
Thomas R. Dobson, Brighton.
Thomas Dunkerley, London.
Thomas Davis, Allt-y-placa.
G. R. Dalby, Preston.
Edward Enfield, London.
Frank Evers, Stourbridge.
Charles Ellis, Maidstone.
William Earl, Edgbaston.
John Every, Lewes.
Joseph T. Ellerbeck, Liverpool.
William Elliot, Sunderland.
J. Barker Ellis, Newcastle-on-Tyne.
Henry Fordham, Royston.
T. W. Freckelton, London.
John Fox, Newark.
George Fox, Park Lane.
A. J. C. Fabritius, Dulwich.
Thomas Furber, Cheltenham.
W. Fallows, Middlesbrough.
William Gaskell, Manchester.
Charles S. Grundy, Manchester.
Thomas F. Gibson, Tunbridge Wells.
John Gordon, Kenilworth.
Alex. Gordon, Belfast.
John Grundy, Bury.
John Green, Edgbaston.

Charles Green, Northwich.
T. M. Greenhow, Leeds.
Edward Grundy, King's Lynn.
D. A. Gibbs, London.
J. Joseph George, Aberdare.
William P. Greenway, Dudley.
Edward R. Grant, Maidstone.
John Glover, Newcastle-on-Tyne.
Benjamin Glover, Huddersfield.
Orlando E. Heys, Stockport.
John Page Hopps, Leicester.
Edward S. Howse, Bowdon.
Edward Higginson, Swansea.
James Hopgood, London.
James Heywood, London.
Abel Heywood, Manchester.
Joseph C. Haslam, Bolton.
Williams Hollins, Mansfield.
Thomas Hincks, Clevedon.
J. Panton Ham, London.
John J. Hart, London.
Alexander Hutcheson, Glasgow
John Hobson, Sheffield.
Thomas Hunter, London.
Michael Hunter, Sheffield.
Richard Harwood, Salford.
Henry Hawkes, Portsmouth.
Benjamin Heape, Prestwich.
Charles Howe, London.
James Harwood, Manchester.
Jesse Hind, Nottingham.
E. C. Harding, Manchester.
Saunders A. Harris, Plymouth.
Henry Ierson, London.
Henry Jeffery, London.
Walter D. Jeremy, London.
Christopher James, Bristol.
Charles H. James, Merthyr Tydvil.
R. Crompton Jones, Sevenoaks.
T. Fielding Johnson, Leicester.
Thomas Jolly, Bath.
Rees C. Jones, Lampeter.
Courtney Kenny, Cambridge.
Andrew L. Knox, Glasgow.

William Kempson, Leicester.
Richard Kinder, London.
Timothy Kenrick, Edgbaston.
William Lawrence, London.
James Clarke Lawrence, London.
James Lupton, Leeds.
Henry Long, Knutsford.
John B. Lloyd, Knutsford.
I. S. Lister, London.
Bernard Lewis, London.
George D. Longstaff, Wandsworth.
H. Lunn, Loughborough.
George Lawford, London.
Henry·Leigh, Swinton.
George Lucas, Darlington.
Chas. D. Leech, Bury St. Edmunds.
Benjamin Lansdown, Trowbridge.
E. W. Lloyd, Aberdare.
James Martineau, London.
David Martineau, London.
Jerom Murch, Bath.
Thomas L. Marshall, London.
C. J. McAlester, Holywood.
R. E. B. Maclellan, Rochester.
J. R. Mott, Birmingham.
J. R. McKee, London.
Charles Moore, Bath.
John Ellis Mace, Tenterden.
D. Maginnis, Stourbridge.
J. Towle Marriott, Manchester.
E. J. Morton, Halifax.
J. K. Montgomery, Chester.
Robert McAlmont, Belfast.
Alexander Mackie, Burnley.
Henry McKean, Oldbury.
II. J. Marcus, Heaton Norris.
F. McCammon, Banbridge.
John Marten, London.
M. P. Manfield, Northampton.
H. J. Morton, Scarborough.
J. E. Manning, Swansea.
Alexander Macdougall, Braintree.
David Matts, Ballymoney.

Frederick Nettlefold, London.
Edward M. Needham, Belper.
Herbert New, Evesham.
Samuel C. Nelson, Downpatrick.
David Gordon, Downpatrick.
Robert Nicholson, Bowdon.
John Orr, Comber.
A. Follet Osler, Edgbaston.
W. J. Odgers, Bath.
J. Edwin Odgers, Liverpool.
John Owen, Whitby.
J. Scott Porter, Belfast.
Andrew Pritchard, London.
William P. Price, Gloucester.
Alfred Paget, Leicester.
Robert N. Phillips, London.
Joseph T. Preston, London.
James Philp, London.
Thomas H. Pargeter, Stourbridge.
Edward Plimpton, London.
C. F. Pearson, London.
William A. Pope, Chelmsford.
Thomas Prime, Birmingham.
Charles T. Poynting, Manchester.
Jesse Pilcher, Manchester.
Robert Pinnock, Newport, I. W.
Alfred Payne, Newcastle-on-Tyne.
William Rathbone, Liverpool.
Thomas Rix, Stratford.
Harry Rawson, Manchester.
John Robberds, Cheltenham.
C. W. Robberds, Bath.
James Russell, Birmingham.
J. R. Robinson, Kensington.
John H. Rowland, Neath.
Henry Riley, Leicester.
James Robson, Stockton-on-Tees.
George Ruck, Maidstone.
W. Wynn Robinson, Gainsborough.
William Robinson, Crewkerne.
Stephen Robinson, Stockport.
Mark M. Lambert, Newcastle-on-Tyne.
Thomas Cooper, Framlingham.

Henry W. Crosskey, Birmingham.
S. Alfred Steinthal, Manchester.
William Spiller, London.
G. Vance Smith, Carmarthen.
Thomas Sadler, London.
William Shaen, London.
Hugh Stannus, London.
Henry Solly, Croydon.
Benjamin Stych, Edgbaston.
James C. Street, Belfast.
B. K. Spencer, Southampton.
Edgar Smallfield, London.
Thomas H. M. Scott, Dunmurry.
William A. Snaith, Darlington.
Edward Swaine, York.
William Croke Squier, Manchester.
Richard Shaen, Royston.
O. A. Shrubsole, Reading.
J. Hunton Smith, Carmarthen.
John G. Slater, Manchester.
William Shakespeare, Ilkeston.
Robert Spears, London.
John H. Thom, Liverpool.
John Troup, London.
Charles F. Tagart, Lewes.
Francis Taylor, Diss.
Christopher Thomas, Bristol.
James Taplin, Kingswood, Birmingham.
Stephen S. Taylor, London.
Frank Taylor, Bolton.
William Titford, London.
Ephraim Turland, Ainsworth.
Samuel Thornton, Birmingham.
John Tribe, Rochester.
N. M. Tayler, London.
Lindsey Taplin, Todmorden.

William Thomas, Llandyssul.
David Thompson, Dromore.
Thomas Taylor, Taunton.
Thomas Thomas, Llandyssul.
George Robert Twinn, Birmingham.
Thomas Timmins, Southsea.
John Taylor, Bolton.
Charles B. Upton, London.
William Unicum, Cranbrook.
Walter Venning, London.
N. H. Vertue, Teddington.
Edward Whitfield, Ilminster.
Charles Wicksteed, London.
Philip H. Wicksteed, London.
John Wright, Bath.
George Withall, Beaconsfield.
James Wrigley, Windermere.
J. T. Whitehead, London.
I. M. Wade, London.
Henry Williamson, Dundee.
Thomas Waterfield, Brighton.
W. Whitelegge, Cork.
E. Cox Walker, York.
Charles H. Wellbeloved, York.
S. Fletcher Williams, Liverpool.
Charles Woollen, Sheffield.
Joseph Wright, Nottingham.
Jeffery Worthington, London.
W. Carey Walters, Whitchurch.
Thomas Jessop, Sheffield.
Edwin Ellis, Shalford.
E. Horton, London.
H. Weston Eve, London.
Talfourd Ely, London.
Alex. B. W. Kennedy, London.
Henry Morley, London.

*[The following is a list of the principal works of Samuel Sharpe which were in print at the time of his death, with the edition which had been reached.]*

The Holy Bible translated, being a revision of the Authorized English Version.

The Book of Isaiah, arranged chronologically in a revised translation and with historical notes.

Short Notes to accompany a revised translation of the Hebrew Scriptures.

The New Testament, translated from Griesbach's Text. Thirteenth thousand.

Critical Notes on the Authorized English Version of the New Testament. Second Edition.

The History of the Hebrew Nation and its Literature. Third Edition.

Text from the Holy Bible explained by the help of the Ancient Monuments. Second Edition.

The History of Egypt from the Earliest Times till the Conquest by the Arabs in A.D. 640. Sixth Edition.

Alexandrian Chronology.

Egyptian Inscriptions from the British Museum and other Sources. 216 Plates in folio.

Egyptian Hieroglyphics ; being an Attempt to explain their Nature, Origin, and Meaning. With a Vocabulary.

Egyptian Antiquities in the British Museum described.

Egyptian Mythology and Egyptian Christianity ; with their Influence on the Opinions of Modern Christendom.

The Decree of Canopus in Hieroglyphics and Greek.

The Rosetta Stone in Hieroglyphics and Greek.

Hebrew Inscriptions from the Valleys between Egypt and Mount Sinai in their original characters, with translations and an alphabet. Parts I. and II.

The Chronology of the Bible.

A Short Hebrew Grammar without points.

The Book Genesis I.-XVIII. and XX.-XXV. 10, without points, and with prefixes and suffixes detached.

The Journeys and Epistles of the Apostle Paul. Third Edition.

An Inquiry into the Age of the Moabite Stone.

The Epistle of Barnabas from the Sinaitic Manuscript of the Bible. With a Translation.

# INDEX.